"PURE TALENT. IF YOU HAVE NOT READ A BOOK BY JESSICA BIRD, YOU ARE MISSING OUT."
—Huntress Book Reviews

PRAISE FOR THE NOVELS
OF J. R. WARD
WRITING AS JESSICA BIRD

Leaping Hearts

"Readers who . . . are fans of Nora Roberts . . . will savor every well-written page." —*Booklist*

"This romantic drama has it all . . . an emotionally enthralling read." —*Romantic Times*

"A fascinating book from beginning to end." —The Best Reviews

An Irresistible Bachelor

"Mystery, intrigue, power, passion, and a love story too beautiful for words." —The Best Reviews

"Irresistible . . . a well-written, engaging, and intelligent love story." —*The Romance Reader*

"[An] emotion-filled romance." —*Booklist*

continued . . .

An Unforgettable Lady

By J. R. Ward

The Black Dagger Brotherhood Series
Dark Lover
Lover Eternal
Lover Awakened
Lover Revealed
Lover Unbound
Lover Enshrined
The Black Dagger Brotherhood: An Insider's Guide
Lover Avenged
Lover Mine
Lover Unleashed
Lover Reborn

Novels of the Fallen Angels
Covet
Crave
Envy

Writing as Jessica Bird
Heart of Gold
Leaping Hearts
An Unforgettable Lady
An Irresistible Bachelor

HEART OF GOLD

J. R. WARD

Writing as Jessica Bird

A SIGNET BOOK

SIGNET
Published by New American Library, a division of
Penguin Group (USA) Inc., 375 Hudson Street,
New York, New York 10014, USA
Penguin Group (Canada), 90 Eglinton Avenue East, Suite 700, Toronto,
Ontario M4P 2Y3, Canada (a division of Pearson Penguin Canada Inc.)
Penguin Books Ltd., 80 Strand, London WC2R 0RL, England
Penguin Ireland, 25 St. Stephen's Green, Dublin 2,
Ireland (a division of Penguin Books Ltd.)
Penguin Group (Australia), 250 Camberwell Road, Camberwell, Victoria 3124,
Australia (a division of Pearson Australia Group Pty. Ltd.)
Penguin Books India Pvt. Ltd., 11 Community Centre, Panchsheel Park,
New Delhi - 110 017, India
Penguin Group (NZ), 67 Apollo Drive, Rosedale, Auckland 0632,
New Zealand (a division of Pearson New Zealand Ltd.)
Penguin Books (South Africa) (Pty.) Ltd., 24 Sturdee Avenue,
Rosebank, Johannesburg 2196, South Africa

Penguin Books Ltd., Registered Offices:
80 Strand, London WC2R 0RL, England

Published by Signet, an imprint of New American Library, a division of Penguin
Group (USA) Inc. Previously published in an Ivy Books edition. Publisher by
arrangement with the author.

First Signet Printing, August 2012
10 9 8 7 6 5 4 3 2 1

To the Ladies of the BIDMC, with highest regard.
With thanks to J. Mark Waxman, Esq., for his legal
direction,
and
Richard M. Strum,
Director, Interpretation and Education,
Fort Ticonderoga, for all his aid and counsel.

Dear Reader:

Heart of Gold is my second published book, and as I think back on it now, I remember making a conscious choice to "go with what you know" when I wrote it.

It was a good call. The thing is, writing is like all other endeavors—a little bit of God-given talent and an interest will get you started. But man, there's a long way to go between that and when you actually know what the heck you're doing. When I started drafting this manuscript, I'd only been professionally edited once, and I was still seat-of-the-pants'ing it (now I'm totally into outlines—for good reason!) Naturally, I felt lost, and decided to create my own safety net by heeding the advice I had heard from so many. . . . I went with what I knew: a flashy businessman as the hardhearted hero, a heroine who loves the past, and the Adirondack Mountains.

The hero, Nick Farrell, is an alpha male all the way around, even though, unlike the Black Dagger Brotherhood vampires, he doesn't wear leathers or carry guns and knives. (No tattoos, either.) He's the financier type of warrior, and believe me, they can be every bit as brutal as MMA fighters when they get in the boardroom. Also, pin-striped suits can be extremely sexy, if the right pair of shoulders is filling them out! Looking back on it now, I can see how Nick is the start of my fixation on over-the-top dominant males. His life paradigm is totally different from that of the Brothers, but as with them, he's a real powerhouse who's, nonetheless, never opened himself to anyone—until he's crossed with his perfect match.

On that note, Carter Wessex, the archaeologist heroine, comes directly out of the Indiana Jones in me. Growing up, I was always that kid watching *Raiders of the Lost Ark* over and over again, wishing that I could be out in the jungles or the desert with a whip on my hip and a pith helmet on my head. When she showed up (as all my characters tend to do—they kind of just walk into my mind, pick a spot and hang out until I write them,) I was all excited because I thought the idea of her going off and looking for buried treasure was AWESOME!

Annnnnd then I did some research into what archae- ologists actually do. My romanticized vision of that pro- fessional and scholarly endeavor was not at all based in reality—in fact, it proved to be far more methodical, dis- ciplined and, well, less dramatic than I had pictured. The good news was, though, that archaeologists really do hunt for treasures of all kinds, and they do unearth the past—and, yes, sometimes they actually do strike gold, as it were. The bonus was, that once I had a more accurate vision of what Carter did, she became so much less car- toony and more believable—and better right as Nick's partner because both of them brought such focus and excellence to their work.

Which brings us to the setting: the lovely Adirondack Mountains of upstate New York. Following the theme of "go with what you know," I have to say that the Adiron- dacks are so much a part of me that they are my home no matter where I'm living. I spent all my summers as a kid up there, and I've just started going again on a regu- lar basis now. At the time when I was drafting *Heart of Gold,* however, I was working around the clock, and it just wasn't possible for me to spend good chunks of July and August there. Solution? Write about them. In a lot of ways, as I was putting Nick and Carter on the page, I was taking a mini-vacation, the images and scenes of the lake and the mountains transporting me to where I wanted to be. Also, what a great place to fall in love in the summer! I know for some a sandy white beach is the epitome of the romantic scene, but I'll take a fragrant pine bough over a palm tree any day.

A word on the plotting of the story. At this point in my early career, I was still trying to "think" up books. I was very conscious of the conventions of romance nov- els, and determined to stick with them—I wanted to write something that followed the predictable patterns and colored within the lines because I thought that playing it safe was going to keep me with a job. This is not to say I'm not proud of this book, or that I think it's lacking—I love Carter and Nick together, and I'm really happy with their story. But I was about three-quarters of the way through the first draft when the side plot of Nick's nephew really started to take off. I wrote a great scene of this boy and a young girl running away from their parents through the woods—it heightened the tension, keyed up the drama, really changed the feel of the book . . . and I had to take it out.

In retrospect, that tangent was my first foray into what I do a lot in my Brotherhood and Angels books. Opening the points of view (POVs) up to other people and their experiences adds a lot to stories, in my opinion—because it's more like real life. Nobody lives in a vacuum—we're surrounded by folks going through things similar to or opposite to our own dramas and happiness—and I believe part of the way we assess things is in contrast or comparison with what others go through. For books, and storytelling, I think well-done subplotting gives a texturing that makes everything feel deeper and more realistic.

That being said, the danger with multilayering is that you run the risk of losing, or burying, the main story under so much stuff that the reader doesn't know who they're supposed to be focused on, or, just as bad, the narrative collapses under its own weight. It takes a really accurate, critical eye to tell the difference between additive and obstruction (believe me, I know, because I've made some mistakes in this area), and back then, I really didn't have a clue what I was doing. I had a sense that the running-away bit was a great scene, but because of the way the rest of the book was flowing, ultimately it was an out-in-left-field kind of thing. In the coming years, however, I would get into, and stay in, the habit of doing multiple POVs and story lines—balancing them, for the most part, in an appropriate way. (You know, come to think of it, it's been really fun to look at my first couple of books and see the directions I was going in—even though I had no clue where I was traveling, as it were.)

I truly hope you enjoy Nick and Carter as much as I did, and do. They're a great couple, and they deserve all the happily-ever-after they get—plus this book has one of my favorite ending scenes that I've EVER written! Just look for the eighteen-wheeler at the end, s'all I'm sayin'.

Happy Reading!

J. R. Ward
December 2011

1

"I AM not a gold digger."

Carter Wessex cradled the phone against her ear while emptying a duffel bag onto the floor of her laundry room. The clothes that came out were covered in dirt, moss, and some other things that looked like they were moving.

"I never said you were." Her oldest friend's voice was soothing, and Carter recognized the tone. It was the same one that had gotten her into trouble when they were teenage girls.

"Yeah, well, I'm also not a masochist," she countered, trying to ward off the attraction she felt toward the opportunity. "The guy who owns Farrell Mountain is a real piece of work. He's thrown more of my colleagues off that pile of dirt than a starting pitcher."

Laughter came over the line. "C.C., I hate sports analogies, and that one barely works."

Carter decided to fight harder, hoping her plan for taking the summer off wouldn't be ruined by a proposition she couldn't turn down. "Well, from what I've heard, Nick Farrell takes misanthropy to a new level, and he's got a particular distaste for archaeologists. Do you know who he is? The corporate raider whose name was splashed all over the papers because he double-crossed some guy in a business deal?"

"I know the story and his reputation."

"So why are you doing this to me?" The words came out in a groan.

"Because it's about time someone solved this mystery. The story's been left hanging since 1775."

"It's a fairy tale, Woody."

"Woody" was more commonly known as Grace Woodward-Hall. The two had first met at a picturesque New England prep school where they'd spent four years specializing in winning field hockey games and smuggling packs of wine coolers into their dorm. They'd been popular thanks to both.

As adults, they had a personal and a professional relationship. Carter's specialty as a historian and an archaeologist was the colonial period. Grace's family ran the Hall Foundation, one of the nation's largest sources of grants for the discovery and preservation of American history. Carter had received Hall funding for a number of her digs.

"You've read that Brit's journal, right?" Grace's Upper East Side background marked her words with perfect intonation, but Carter knew the truth. For all her prim and ladylike exterior, Grace had a raucous sense of humor and an affection for trouble, both of which had cemented their relationship.

"Farnsworth's diary? Of course I've read it. All colonial historians have a copy. It comes with the bizarre predilection for musket balls and minutemen."

Carter glanced down and saw a spider crawling out from under a pair of khakis. She wasn't prepared to kill the thing but didn't want it as a housemate, either. Reaching over the washing machine, she picked up a coffee can full of nails, dumped it out on top of the dryer, and covered the arachnid.

"So you've got to wonder what happened," Grace prompted.

"I know what happened. An American hero was slaughtered, a fortune in gold disappeared, and the Indian guide was fingered as responsible. End of story."

"I find it hard to believe," Grace said dryly, "that you aren't struck by all the holes in that narration. Someone needs to go up on Farrell Mountain and find out what happened to the Winship party."

"Well, it doesn't have to be me." Carter started loading shirts and socks into the washer, careful not to tip over the can. "What they really need is a paranormal investigator to put to rest all that haunting nonsense. Red Hawk's ghost guarding the gold? Give me a break."

"Look, specters aside, this really is the perfect project for you. In your period, up in the wilderness, a prime piece of history ready for the picking."

"I just got home from a dig," Carter moaned. "I've got twelve pounds of dirt under my fingernails, I'm in desperate need of sleep, and I have it on good authority there are black flies the size of bats in the Adirondacks this time of year."

She knew because they were alive and well in the Green Mountains of Vermont, too. Glancing through a screened window, she saw a cheery June day beckoning on the other side but she wasn't fooled. She'd been chewed on by them in her garden that very morning.

"Aren't you curious about what happened to the gold?"

"Like I am about the Easter Bunny. You show me some proof that an upright rabbit carrying a basket of chicken eggs exists and maybe I'll believe there's a treasure up in those mountains."

"Come on, that gold couldn't have disappeared into thin air. And what happened to the remains of the men who were killed?"

Carter leaned a hip against the washing machine. "The Americans should never have transported that kind of fortune while they had a captured British madman on their hands. They were bound to get ambushed. The only surprise was that Red Hawk was the one who turned on them. If one of the aggressors didn't take the gold, someone else probably found it and had the good sense to keep his mouth shut. As for the bodies, they could be anywhere. You know how big the Adirondack Park is? It would be like winning the lottery to find them."

She peered over her shoulder into the washer. Hitting that mess with water was going to create some kind of mud bath but there was room to stuff in a little more. She bent down to pick up another pair of khakis.

"Did I mention we have bones?" Grace drawled. "From a site that's identical to the one Farnsworth described in the journal."

Carter snapped upright. "Bones? What kind of bones? Where were they found?"

Grace's satisfaction came through loud and clear over the phone. "Conrad Lyst found them up on Farrell Mountain."

At the sound of the man's name, Carter's jaw clenched. "That rat. That nasty . . ."

She allowed herself a couple of truly raunchy but descriptive adjectives. And followed them up with a doozy of a noun.

"You finished now?" her friend asked with amusement.

"Hardly. It's a wonder that man can find his butt in his own pants. And if by some miracle he did, his next move would be to sell it to the highest bidder."

"Professional rivalries aside—"

"That bulldozer is no professional. He's a looter and a thief."

"I can't argue with either of those, but he did find a femur and part of an arm. We examined them here in Boston and they're from the period."

"That doesn't mean they're from—"

"They were found with a crucifix."

Carter forgot all about the laundry. "Any markings?"

"Winship, 1773. We haven't analyzed it fully yet but it looks legit."

The Reverend Jonathan Winship had been the one in charge of the colonists escorting the general. He was one of the men who had been killed up in the mountains.

Carter's heart started pounding in her chest.

"So, you want to talk about an Easter egg hunt?" Grace inquired smoothly.

A half hour later they'd ironed out a grant and, though the laundry remained dry in the washer, the spider had been carefully released back into the wild. After pacing around the house for most of the time they talked, Carter ended up in her kitchen, sitting at her breakfast table in the sunshine.

"I still don't understand why Lyst presented you with the cross," she said. "That's not his style. The more people who know about a find, the harder it is for him to sell it on the black market."

"He says he wants a grant. We won't give him one, of course. If he did dig, he'd just pocket anything of monetary value and mistreat the rest so it couldn't be studied."

Carter let out a snort of derision. "Someone needs to take that man's shovel away, and I could tell them right where to stick it. The real mystery is how the hell Lyst got permission to dig on that mountain."

"He didn't. He trespassed and, as you know, Farrell's idea of a welcome wagon doesn't exactly include zucchini bread and lemonade. Lyst claims some rabid woodsman chased him off with a gun, almost killing him in the process."

"Too bad the guy didn't get the job done."

"Well, it got Lyst's attention, which may be the reason he came to the foundation. He probably figures a Hall grant will give him credibility when he tries again."

"He'd go back?"

"You know Lyst. What he lacks in scruples, he more than makes up for in follow-through. That's why you need to go talk to Farrell right now. I know where his summer house is on Lake Sagamore and you can't live more than an hour away from it. I've heard he's usually there on the weekends this time of year. Just drive over this Saturday and ask for permission to dig."

"What makes you think the response I get will be any better?"

"You're going to ask first. And you have better legs than Lyst does. Anyway, doesn't your father run in the same business circles as Farrell—"

"Stop right there." Carter stiffened as anger rushed like acid up into her throat.

Grace was instantly contrite. "I'm sorry, C.C. I didn't mean to . . . ."

The use of the old nickname reminded Carter of the long history she had with her friend. She took a deep breath, trying to let go of the rage that came up anytime William Wessex was mentioned. It took her a moment before she could respond.

"If I go, I won't be using my *father* as pull." The word was intoned like a curse.

"Of course not. I shouldn't have brought it up at all."

When they got off the phone, Carter went out onto her back porch. Up ahead, mountains rose steeply, brushing the bright blue sky with their evergreen shoulders. She'd bought the land and the broken-down barn that came with it for the magnificent view. It had taken her two years to convert the decaying building into livable space but, now that it was finished, she wasn't sure whether she liked her home or the scenery better. It was a shame she didn't spend more time enjoying them.

Arching her neck, she let the sun fall on her cheeks and forehead. All around, the leaves of poplar trees were twinkling in the breeze and she could hear the distant *chika-brd-brd-brd* of a red-winged blackbird. If she listened hard enough, she even caught the sound of the stream that was on the far edge of her property.

She slowed her breathing down, trying to draw the calm surroundings into her body.

How much longer would it take before she could stop flinching at the mention of her father's name? Before she could let go of the past?

It was two years and counting, so far.

She turned away from the natural splendor and went upstairs. What had previously been the barn's hayloft was now her office and her bedroom. The long, rectangular space was her favorite in the house — an unbroken expanse she'd paneled in pine and opened up at either end with picture windows.

Her desks, computers, slide projectors, and research library dominated the room. Against the long walls, she'd installed bookcases that were crammed with scholarly works, some of which she'd written. It was a collection of the resources she used most, and what she didn't have at her fingertip she could easily get at the University of Vermont in nearby Burlington. She'd been an assistant professor of archaeology there for close to three years and had an office on campus.

As much as she liked her students, she preferred doing her own scholarship at home. She'd spent a lot of late nights deep in thought in her pine-scented sanctuary, time forgotten as she tried to make sense of the clues history left behind.

In the midst of her all-nighters, when she got too tired to keep her eyes open, she would go to sleep on a small bed that was pushed into a corner, an afterthought concession to her body's need for rest. Other personal effects were also footnotes. Hidden in an alcove, she had a closet full of khakis, a dresser full of T-shirts and sweaters, and a little bathroom that had a shower stall and sink, but no tub. There were no curtains on the windows and no rugs on the pine floor.

For Carter, the loft reflected her life's priorities. Work was first. Her personal life, a distant second.

Walking past her desk with a grim expression, she went to the dresser and pulled open a drawer. Inside, she fished around the T-shirts until she found the black leather box she was looking for.

Damn him to hell, she thought, opening it.

Cosseted in a satin bed was a weighty Colombian emerald, dangling from a chain of diamonds. It was a ridiculous gift, one more of her father's attempts to buy back her love. The box had arrived the week before, via Federal Express, on the eve of her twenty-eighth birthday.

And now Carter was stuck trying to unload her father's present. Again.

He always sent her jewelry. For her twenty-seventh birthday, it had been a dauntingly large pair of diamond and pearl earrings. She'd auctioned those off and given the money to the local hospital. For her twenty-sixth, it had been a ring sporting a ruby the size of a marble. She'd sold that one to a jeweler, and the proceeds had helped the local elementary school set up a computer lab.

And now this emerald.

Maybe the town needed a new ambulance. Or two.

The gifts were awful on her birthdays, but Christmas was worse. Her father sent her watches. Each year. They were always expensive and gold, sometimes with diamonds on the face, sometimes with other precious gems. She'd taken to donating the money they brought to the local women's shelter.

Fingering the emerald and watching light get trapped in its glorious facets, Carter wondered where her father thought she'd wear such a necklace. When she'd left his house that last time, she'd walked away from the lifestyle she'd grown up with and he knew it. In one day, the day her mother died, she went from being a social register sweetheart to an outcast of her own choosing. The self-inflicted exile meant that gala parties were part of her past, just like her father was, and she woke up every morning grateful for their absence.

Carter ran a finger over the diamond chain, watching it sparkle.

In her current life, she was more likely to need a pup tent than a palatial suite of rooms, a can of bug spray instead of hair spray, a compass around her neck, not an emerald. She relished her simple life. She was free to explore her passion for history and she had a career where her contributions were respected. She truly liked her life.

Most of the time.

On occasion, when things got quiet and her mind wandered, she did feel alone. She had few friends. As for family, she was an only child and her closest cousin, A.J., lived far away and had her own busy life in the equestrian world. Now she even had a husband.

Carter wondered whether her own future would ever include a partner.

The immediate answer was no. She worked every waking minute so there was no time to date, although, if she was honest, she didn't think more free time would solve the problem. She knew everyone at the university and there was no one who really struck a chord inside of her. Besides, the ghost of her family's tragedy trailed her wherever she went. With her father's betrayal always with her, she was reminded constantly of how she couldn't trust men.

Not exactly fertile ground to meet Mr. Right.

Carter shut the box and crammed it back into her drawer. She had better things to do with her time than focus on things she couldn't change.

For someone who pursued the past as a profession, Carter was determined not to dwell on her own. She lived in the present and tried not to think about everything she'd walked away from. She was successful at it, too, except when the gifts arrived on her doorstep. Twice a year, she was forced to confront the shadows of her past, and she hated the disruption, resenting the hell out of her father's dogged persistence. She wished he'd stop pretending they had anything other than a biological link between them and was tempted to tell him to stop sending her things.

Except she couldn't bear the thought of speaking to him.

Carter paused in the middle of her room, surveying the books and the slides, her papers and her project logs. She reminded herself that she was on her own. She was free.

And whatever price she paid for not living a lie, it was worth it.

She headed to her desk, intent on calling her frequent collaborator, Buddy Swift, and telling him they had another job. Another dig gig, as he'd say. The two had partnered on many projects, and his wife, Jo-Jo, and daughter, Ellie, frequently joined them on the excursions. The Swifts, who lived in Cambridge, Massachusetts, were the closest thing to family Carter had nearby and the reason she didn't eat TV dinners alone on holidays.

She didn't make it to the phone. She got derailed when she caught sight of her reflection in the bathroom mirror. The woman staring back at her had long, glossy black hair, ice-blue eyes, and fair skin that was showing a faint sunburn.

Carter glared at herself. Since the horrible day of her mother's death, every time she looked in a mirror, she saw her father staring back at her. They had the same coloring, same bone structure, identical teeth, for Chrissakes.

On a daily basis, Carter could forget about how the man's selfishness and infidelity had destroyed their family. She could pretend she was an orphan in the world, untethered to the events that still woke her up at night in a cold sweat. Except for when the dreaded FedEx man came twice a year, she was mostly able to get past it all.

But mirrors remained a constant problem, even in her own house. She hadn't wanted any under her roof, but the contractors had installed them in the bathrooms before she could express the preference.

As she turned away, she wondered how much it would cost to rip the things off the walls.

Nick Farrell slowly lowered the legal document he'd been reviewing. He was beyond frustrated. Full-blown irritated was more like it. "Cort, we've been through this before."

But Cortland Farrell Greene, his sixteen-year-old nephew and adopted son, was determined to fight. The kid leaned forward and planted his hands on Nick's desk, exuding angry heat. The fact that the kid's hair had been teased so it stood straight up in spikes seemed fitting. "*We* haven't been through anything. *You* may have decided something but there was no *we* involved."

Nick took a deep breath. When that didn't help, he tried taking another. "I'm not going to let you go on a six-week, cross-country driving trip with the Canton brothers. They're in college—"

"Which means they're responsible."

"Doing Jaegermeister shots until someone passes out on one of their father's lawn sculptures is not being responsible."

Nick's level stare was met head-on. "It only happened once! And that doesn't mean they're bad guys."

"How about the time they decided to express themselves feloniously by stealing a car?"

His nephew looked away.

"Getting in touch with one's inner burglar isn't a virtue," Nick said dryly. "It's a crime."

Cort straightened and folded his arms over his chest. He looked as if he was searching for another attack approach.

Nick waited and wasn't surprised when his nephew's eyes snapped back to his.

"You think you can lay down any rule just because my mother . . ." But the kid couldn't finish. He stumbled into silence, leaving the past dangling between them.

"Because your mother put me in charge of your welfare?"

"Because I was willed to you like a piece of property. She stiffed us both if you ask me."

Nick raked a hand through his dark hair. "Don't say that."

"Why not? It's true. You got stuck with me like I got stuck with you."

"I'm not stuck with you. You're family, which means come hell or high water, we're in this together."

"Oh, come on!" Cort threw a hostile gesture at the desk. "Those papers are your family. You're into your companies and your deals. The only time we talk is when you're telling me I can't do something. We only spend time together when you're taking me to some doctor. Why don't we just bag this whole happy family thing? It's not like you need my trust fund. It's couch change to you. You could send me away—"

"I don't shirk my responsibilities."

"Maybe you should try it sometime."

Nick started massaging his temples, feeling as if the skin across his forehead had been pulled tight.

When Cort had first come to live with him five years ago, after his parents were killed in a plane crash, it had been eerie being around the boy. He looked so much like the sister Nick had loved. He had Melina's flashing eyes and keen intelligence, and seeing the boy's face had been an exercise in torment and regret. It was a vivid reminder that Nick had never taken enough time to let his sister know how much she meant to him. He'd vowed the same thing wasn't going to happen with her son but things were not working out as well as he'd hoped.

There had been grieving in the beginning on both sides, something Nick had no idea how to get over himself much less help the boy through. After the pain had become less acute, the daily grind of running a multitude of companies and investments worked against them. Nick's far-flung business interests kept him on his jet and in his boardroom a lot of the time. Trying to balance the demands of his work and Cort's needs was a drain like nothing Nick had ever experienced before.

He was also flying blind when it came to parenting. His own mother and father had been dead for years and the people he dealt with were versed in the S&P 500 and the Dow, not in what to do when you had a ten-year-old bawling his eyes out because he'd lost his mom and dad.

Nick had tried to research his way out of their estrangement. He'd read books, called psychiatrists, even gone to a therapist. He was desperate for some kind of index or graph that would show how to manage the parent and child relationship but he never found one. There was no quantitative chart to tell someone when to be strong, when to let go. When to let a child learn on his own and when he needed protection.

The kid's illness was another complication. The limitations juvenile diabetes placed on Cort's activities were at the root of many of their disagreements. Lately, the fighting seemed incessant but Nick was determined to not give up trying to reach out. Aside from taking the responsibility his sister had given him seriously, he viewed Cort as his one chance to be a father. Nick doubted he'd ever marry. Women had a habit of seeing a bottomless wallet when they looked at him and he wasn't inclined to make some socialite's dream of the high life come true.

He focused on his nephew. He didn't know what to do with the kid but couldn't imagine his life without him. "I'm sorry. I just can't let you go."

Cort didn't miss a beat. "Then I want to spend the summer hiking in the Appalachians."

Swallowing a curse, Nick did his best to not let his frustration explode. "You know I can't let you do that either."

"Why?" Cort's voice got louder.

"You know why."

"I'm not an invalid!"

"It's too much for you."

The kid started shaking with rage. "How will I know if I don't try? How will I know what I can do if you keep me locked up? I'm going to go batshit if I get stuck here for three months!"

Nick decided to let the curse slide. He had to pick his battles. "You're not going to go insane and you know you shouldn't be taking those kinds of chances."

"You never let me do anything! You get to travel around the world—"

"This is not up for negotiation," Nick cut him off grimly.

"But the doctor said—"

"No."

Cort glared at him and rubbed his hair, breaking

down some of the spikes. When Nick just stared back, the kid eventually gave in with a resentment that was palpable.

"Fine, have it your way," he muttered. "I'll just stay up here alone and rot all summer while everyone else gets to have a life."

"You won't be alone."

"I won't?" There was a wealth of suspicion in Cort's voice.

"I've decided to work from up here this summer, instead of the city."

Nick smiled wryly at the kid's expression. It was priceless, like someone had dropped a frying pan on his foot. "But you can't. You've got businesses and—"

"Ever hear of videoconferencing and fax machines? It's amazing what technology can bring to a person's life."

"This is going to suck!"

"Your life's intolerable if you're here alone and it's intolerable if you're not?"

"I'd rather be alone than with you!"

Cort bolted from the room, slamming the door so hard its mahogany panels wobbled.

Nick shook his head, feeling ancient. He had done end runs on some of the most ruthless men on Wall Street, had dreamed up financial transactions that revolutionized mergers and acquisitions practice, had been an advisor to presidents, for God's sakes.

But ten minutes in an enclosed space with Cort and he felt like he didn't know his ass from his elbow.

He rose from his leather chair and went to the bank of windows that overlooked the lake. He could feel a migraine coming on, his back was stiff from flying in from Japan the night before, and he had the nagging sense he'd forgotten something important. Trying to ward off six hours of pain and nausea from the headache, he put a couple of pills under his tongue and rubbed the back of his neck while they dissolved.

A soft knock sounded behind him.

"Come in," he said, without turning.

Immediately, Nick knew who'd entered his study. He could smell her perfume, an expensive French concoction he hated. It was sickly sweet and clung to the insides of his nostrils, egging on the migraine.

Pivoting around, Nick watched as Candace Hanson, his girlfriend of six months, walked across the study. She had a placid smile pinned on her lovely face, and her shoulder-length blond hair was styled in a breezy, I'm-at-the-lake kind of look. The white linen shorts and polo shirt she was wearing were perfect for a tennis game they would never see, and her athletic shoes were sparkling fresh, right out of the box.

Flawless as always, he thought, feeling nothing as he looked at her.

Their relationship was strictly a social convenience, with little intimacy other than sex. It was just what he wanted, all he had time for, and, up until recently, she'd played by the rules. She'd never pushed him for more, had always been available when he wanted her, and was good at playing hostess at his parties. There was trouble on the horizon, however. The *m*-word had crept into her vocabulary, and that meant her days were numbered.

Candace sat down in the chair opposite his desk, crossing her legs modestly and folding her hands together on her knee.

Nick groaned. Whenever she took a seat, he knew it was going to be more than a five-minute review of the social calendar.

"I want to reassure you," she said in her prim way, "that everything is all set for tomorrow evening."

This pronouncement was followed by a wide smile that didn't add life to her eyes. Even though her teeth glimmered a cheerful white and her lips were arranged with the appropriate lift in the corners, there was something vacant in the arrangement of features. In fact, there was something fundamentally expressionless about her face. At first this had intrigued him, making him wonder what was behind the mask. But, as he'd gotten to know her better, he'd begun to suspect that her best assets were the exterior ones.

"What about tomorrow night?" He crossed his arms over his chest.

"Our party, darling," she murmured. "For the opera house."

Nick blinked. The migraine was really gearing up now, poking holes in his vision until Candace was lost in the sea of black spots.

"We have fifty coming for dinner," she prompted gently.

So that was what he was forgetting.

The phone rang on his desk.

Annoyed, he wondered whether there was anyone else who wanted to chime in and thought they'd better do it quick. In another ten minutes, he was going to be out of commission.

"Excuse me," he said, knowing she would wait.

Nick picked up the phone and when he heard who was calling, he put it against his shoulder and turned back toward Candace. "We'll talk more later."

She stood up and smiled serenely. "That would be lovely, but don't worry. Everything's taken care of."

"I'll bet it is."

The door closed behind her with barely a sound.

She was a ghost, he thought. Someone who just floated through life, not really touching anything or anyone.

"Mr. Farrell?" the voice on the line repeated.

"I'm here," he clipped, trying to see his watch. Moving it into the part of his vision that was still working, he decided he was down to about five minutes before the pain would hammer him flat.

"Mr. Wessex is now on the line."

"Nick, how are you?" the man said.

"Fine," he replied, falling into his chair. "But I'm a little busy."

He was going to have to start throwing up soon.

"I understand completely." Wessex's voice had the polished resonance of money, power, and the man's blue-blood lineage. "I'm just calling to check in on our little transaction."

"Our little transaction" was the business deal Nick had been poring over when the latest squall with Cort had blown into the room. The negotiation involved close to a billion dollars *and* was a joint assault against an enemy Nick was determined to crush.

"Tell you what," he said, his mouth growing dry as the pain arrived. "We're having a get-together tomorrow night. Why don't you come up? You can fly into Albany, take a limo from there. We've invited a good number, but you and I can find a quiet corner and cover the issues then."

"That's a lovely invitation. Tell me, when are you and that beautiful Candace going to tie the knot?"

Nick had two words come to mind. Snowball and hell.

"Are you free tomorrow?" he asked, dodging the bullet.

"Unfortunately, no. I'm going to spend the rest of this month in South America, and I need to get everything settled here in the city before I go. My lawyers will know where I am at all times, of course, but I'm assuming we won't be ready to stage the ambush until I get back."

Nick started breaking out in a cold sweat.

"I think that's right," he mumbled, out of time. "Have a safe trip."

Somehow, he managed to hang up the phone and limp over to his couch, dragging a wastepaper basket with him. Lying flat on his back, he put his forearm over his eyes to block out all the sunlight in the room.

Why couldn't his ancestors have built their summer retreat in a cave?

The pain was white-hot, shooting through his head like fire, pulsing with the beat of his heart. Images swirled in his mind, hallucinations from the headache and the medication. He was trying to make sense of the collage when someone lifted his arm and put an ice pack on his forehead.

"Gertie," he groaned. "How come you always know?"

The older woman laughed quietly and he heard her going around and shutting all the drapes. "I just do."

When she came back to him, Nick opened his eyes a crack, seeing the coarse, wrinkled, and beautiful face of the woman who'd raised him. Gertie McNutt had been with the Farrells all her life, as had her mother before her and her grandmother before that. There'd been members of her family working on the Farrell land as long as there had been Farrells owning it.

She reached down and stroked his hair.

"I hate this," he said, his deep voice uncharacteristically thin in the still air.

"I know, *chou-chou*," Gertie murmured. "But it'll be over soon."

"Yeah, but it's getting from here to there that's going to hurt."

She stayed a while longer and then left him to the darkness and the agony. There was nothing more she could offer him in the way of relief. The tempest was his, and only his, to endure.

Good thing he was tough, Nick thought as another wave of pain crashed over him.

His stomach lurched and he rolled over, grabbing blindly for the wastepaper basket. The last thing he did before he passed out was throw up the lunch Gertie had made for him.

2

THE NEXT day, Carter took the ferry across Lake Champlain to New York State. She was first going to visit a colleague's excavation on the grounds of Fort Sagamore and then she was going to talk Nick Farrell into letting her dig holes in his mountain. After spending a couple of hours on the fort's grounds, she followed Grace's directions and headed a few miles south until she saw two stone pillars at the side of the road. Pulling her Jeep in between them, she went up a gravel drive marked by an alley of chestnut trees.

When the mansion was revealed in all its glory, her breath caught. Perched on a bluff, the estate was framed by the lake and the towering peak of Farrell Mountain. She wasn't sure what was most impressive—the house, the shimmering water, or the looming presence of the mountain.

She pulled over and slid out of the driver's seat, intent on taking a look around. The gravel drive she'd come in on formed a circle in front of the mansion and had an offshoot that headed over to what she imagined was the service entrance.

Farrell's vacation home was a sublime example of the Federal style, a white palace with black shutters that had a gracious, formal facade. The center torso of the place was balanced by two wings, which meant a small army could probably sleep under its roof. As she lost count of the windows and porches, she imagined that a person would be able to hear the sound of water lapping against the shore and catch the whisper of a summer breeze in every room.

Turning toward the lake, she smiled at the sight of a six-sided gazebo, an invitation to spend a lazy afternoon reading if she'd ever seen one. It was also painted white but had a red asphalt roof and intricate, curvaceous details around its eaves. Down farther, there was a matching gingerbread boathouse at the water's edge and, just off the dock, she saw a sailboat bobbing on soft waves. Over to the left was a tennis court tucked against the woods and a croquet set was marking the side lawn, just waiting for a game.

Summer camp for the wealthy, she thought wryly. You get reserve cellar Burgundy instead of bug juice at dinner and everyone has their own bathroom.

Turning back to the house, she noticed a wildflower meadow behind it filled with Queen Anne's lace, goldenrod, and long grass. The two-acre expanse stretched back to a forest of pines, birches, and poplars that carpeted the foot of the mountain.

Carter guessed the field would probably be filled with fireflies at night. Just like hers was.

Suddenly, the peacefulness of the place was shattered. With a roaring noise and sprinkle of gravel, a van came down the drive and almost mowed her down.

In the split second before she leapt out of the way, she saw the name of a caterer she remembered from her society days in New York City. As she choked on dust, she wondered what it was doing upstate and watched as it joined others that were huddled around the service entrance of the house. In contrast to the rest of the estate, which exuded serenity, people were frantically running around, carrying heavy loads. She was surprised she hadn't noticed the commotion sooner.

All the activity galvanized her, and she marched over to the mansion, leaping up glossy black stairs to the front door. There, she was confronted by a brass knocker the size of a football. She lifted the lion's head and let it fall. The resulting sound was like thunder and she winced.

Noise like that could wake the dead. It made her wonder if Farrell had a butler like Lurch to answer it.

While waiting, she inspected two white, ceramic dogs that were parked on either side of the doorway. Their amber eyes were fixed ahead on some distant, timeless fascination, and they were in perfect condition, just like the rest of the estate. Antiques—she guessed they had been bought new by one of Farrell's ancestors.

Hearing something approach from above, Carter glanced up just as a magnificent red-tailed hawk swept down out of the blue sky and landed on one of the tree limbs just over her head. The bird reordered its wings with a minimum of fuss and looked down at her, as if it were waiting for her to go into the house.

How odd, she thought, feeling a chill.

Carter was debating whether to tackle the lion's head again when the door opened. Lurch wasn't on the other side but he might have been an improvement over what answered the door.

She'd seen more welcoming expressions in a dark alley.

The blond woman staring back at Carter was a patrician beauty queen. Standing at the threshold of the mansion, she was exhibiting the kind of elegant inhospitality that only the very privileged could pull off.

Carter knew the type.

"I'm here to see Mr. Farrell." Her voice was deep and full of command and the woman on the other side looked surprised.

"I beg your pardon?"

It was interesting how the right tone of voice could turn even polite words into an insult, Carter reflected.

"Mr. Farrell," she repeated slowly. "I'm here to see him."

Disapproving eyes passed over her, from her hair, which was pulled back into a ponytail, to her bare arms, to her formfitting shorts and her tattered running shoes. When the blue chips swung upward again, they were even more frosty.

"I can't imagine he is expecting *you*."

As if the man would no sooner be waiting on a truck-load of manure.

"If you could just let him—"

"I'm glad you're finally here," came another voice. An older woman appeared, wiping her hands on a gingham apron. Her hair was white and pulled back with combs, her face lined and tanned. Although she was addressing Carter, her eyes were focused elsewhere, beyond the doorway. Curious, Carter turned and saw the red-tailed hawk leap from its perch, its great wings punching the air as it flew away.

As the chill went through her again, Carter mulled over the legends of Red Hawk's visits to the mountain. Trying to shake a feeling of premonition, she turned back.

"I thought I told you to have the waitresses come to the back door," the blonde was saying with haughty authority.

"Yes, you did."

The reply was an offhand remark and with it, Carter knew exactly who was in charge. It sure as hell wasn't the woman who'd opened the door.

"If you'd move your car?" the older woman asked Carter politely. "Meet me around back at the service entrance."

Carter nodded. When they met up again amidst the busy but well-ordered rush in the kitchen, the woman introduced herself.

"I'm Gertie McNutt. I run this place."

"Carter Wessex." They shook hands briskly.

"Dinner will be served at seven thirty but you'll need to pass hors d'oeuvres from six on. We have uniforms here. What size are you?"

Carter frowned in confusion. "I'm not here to wait-ress. I'm here to see Mr. Farrell."

The brown eyes staring at her narrowed suspiciously. "About?"

"I'm an archaeologist and I—"

The woman started shaking her head. "He doesn't like archaeologists much."

"So I've heard. I just want to ask him if I can dig up on the mount—"

"He doesn't like people digging up there."

Carter took a deep breath. "Heard that, too. But if I could just ask him—"

"He doesn't like being asked."

She couldn't help rolling her eyes in frustration. "Does the guy like anything? Or is he really as bad-humored as his reputation suggests?"

Flushing, Carter clamped her mouth shut. Great, she thought. She'd just managed to insult Farrell to his staff while trying to get in to see the man without an appointment.

"Sorry about that crack," she muttered.

There was a pause as she was subjected to a frank appraisal. While she waited to be summarily tossed off the property, she wondered whether cops were going to be involved.

Instead, the woman smiled. "Tell you what. I'll give you twenty minutes to see for yourself if he's that awful. If you're crazy enough to want to give it a try, you might as well get the full experience. Besides, the way he'll throw you out will be a heck of a lot more interesting and inventive than anything I could do to you."

Carter gave the woman a frozen smile, feeling like she'd volunteered for torture. "Thanks."

Swallowing unexpected fear, she followed the woman through the house, taking in the spacious rooms. Every one was filled with antiques and an air of elegant leisure, with freshly cut flowers adding to the sophistication and grace. When they came to a stout mahogany door, the other woman paused before knocking.

"Do yourself a favor. Make it short and sweet. He likes things that way."

She knocked, and when a muffled reply was heard, the housekeeper opened the door and they walked into an old-world study.

Nick Farrell looked up from an ornate desk and Carter's feet stopped working.

The man's eyes were the most unusual color, a gray so pale that the irises were almost invisible, and being looked over by them was like getting hit by a blowtorch. He seemed to absorb every nuance of her appearance—her expression, the space she took up. He was, she realized, powerfully intelligent, immutably domineering, and, surprisingly, the hardness emanating from him only added to his allure. It made her wonder if there was any softness in him at all, and she imagined that women had driven themselves crazy trying to find it.

With a shiver of awareness passing through her body, she knew his face must have launched a thousand women's fantasies. He had high cheekbones, a chiseled jawline and a strong, straight nose. His hair was thick and dark, brushed off his forehead, and his skin was tanned. The lips caught and held her attention. The lower one was fuller and she wondered, in a flash of insanity, what it would be like to kiss him.

Her heart began to pound and, as if he'd caught the scent of her thoughts, she saw speculation flare in his expression. Abruptly, she was assessed as a woman. As those eyes narrowed and lingered on her legs, a flush bloomed deep inside of her.

Before she allowed herself to speculate on what he thought of her, she told herself not to bother. The man was a heartbreak waiting to happen. Not for her, of course. But she pitied whoever fell for someone like him.

"This woman is here to see you," Gertie announced.

One dark eyebrow rose sardonically. "I don't recall asking to meet with any teenage girls."

His deep voice wrapped around the words, creating cynical shadows in the syllables. Carter was distracted by the sound and then realized he'd just insulted her.

Recovering quickly, she replied with a tart clip, "I

can't speak to your schedule, but I've been out of my teens for a decade, thank you very much."

The eyebrow took flight again. Her tone had been every bit as commanding as his had been, and it occurred to her that he wasn't used to being addressed in such a way. Their eyes clashed as the housekeeper left.

She took a steadying breath. "I think we should start over. Mr. Farrell, I'm—"

The door burst open and bounced off the bookcase with a slap, causing her to jerk in surprise. A teenage boy brushed past her, as if she were just another piece of furniture in the room.

Even though she'd jumped at the interruption, Nick Farrell's expression never varied. The only change had been where his eyes were directed. The man was more self-contained than a tank.

"You can't let her do this!" the kid exclaimed, putting both hands on the desk and pushing out his chin. He was dressed all in black, his hair styled so it stood straight up off his scalp. She wondered how he got it to stay vertical like that.

"And what has she done?" Farrell's voice was calm, but she noticed there was a subtle tension in his body.

Maybe he wasn't above human emotions after all.

"She says I have to wear a damned tuxedo if I'm going to eat tonight. I live here. She doesn't. Who the hell—"

"That's enough with the swearing and the theatrics." The tension in Farrell came out in the muscles of his neck, tightening them into thick cords.

"I'm not wearing a tux and I'm not going to the dinner party."

There was such defiance and anger in the kid's face that Carter realized, like so many arguments between parents and children, the explosion wasn't just about the topic at hand.

"I'll speak with her."

The kid snorted. "Like that does any good. Why do you put up with her? It's not like you're going to marry—"

"You can keep your thoughts concerning my relationship to yourself."

"'Keep it to yourself,'" the kid aped. "I keep *everything* to myself."

"If that were true, I wouldn't need my doors rehung from all the slamming," Farrell returned dryly.

The kid turned on his heel and noticed Carter for the first time. His eyes widened with surprise.

They looked just like Farrell's, she thought.

"Hi." His voice changed as a lot of the hostility was lost.

"Hello."

He glanced back at Farrell. "Who's she?"

"I was about to find out when you came barreling in." The two looked at Carter expectantly.

"Carter Wessex," she supplied.

"Are you staying for dinner?" the kid asked.

"No. I'm here to see him." She nodded across the desk.

"Will you stay for dinner?"

"I thought you weren't going to the party," Farrell interjected.

The kid looked stumped, caught between rebellion and an unexpected urge to assimilate. "If she's coming, I'll throw the tux on."

"I'm not coming."

"Then I'm not wearing one." The kid turned to Farrell. "And you're going to talk to Blondzilla."

Farrell shot a laconic look over at Carter. "You free for dinner?"

She glanced back and forth between them, waiting for him to take the invitation back. He didn't.

Her eyes widened. "I'm hardly dressed appropriately if tuxedos are involved."

"I think you look fine just as you are," the kid remarked bashfully.

Farrell's lips tightened as she blushed.

"Thanks for the invitation, especially if you're serious. But I—"

"He's always serious," the kid muttered resentfully.

Farrell crossed his arms over his chest. "That's not true. I laughed twice last year. Now, why don't you leave us so I can find out what this woman wants from me?"

"Dismissed like a damn dog—" the kid began grousing as he walked away.

"Watch the language."

"One speaks it, not sees it."

"I'll use it correctly if you do."

"You first," the kid said as he shut the door, hard.

As the sound bounced around the room, Carter felt Farrell's undivided attention come back to her.

"So what do you want?" he demanded.

"I'm an archaeologist and I—"

"No." His eyes left her and he started rifling through papers as if she'd left the room.

Carter bristled. "Excuse me?"

"The answer is no."

"But I haven't asked for anything yet."

"The operant word being *yet*. Letting you chatter on before you get to the asking would only be a waste of our time." His voice was clipped and cold.

She was stunned into silence and, for a moment, all she could do was watch his eyes trace over words on some document.

"You know, you don't have to be so rude. And you could look at me while we're talking."

An arrogant brow arched though he didn't look up. "I always knew Miss Manners came with a shovel. I just assumed it was for slinging drivel, not digging up other people's property."

"And it's hard for me to believe someone living in a place like this has the social skills of a cow."

Gray eyes popped up to hers. She saw that the speculation had returned.

"Fine." He put the papers down and leaned back in his chair. "Is this better? Tell you what. I'll even go one further and remember to say *please* when I ask you to leave."

As his eyes bored into her, Carter was willing to bet the guy was more than a match for Blondzilla.

"So," he said briskly, "will you *please* leave?"

"You can't just toss me out before I have a chance—"

"I can't? I've got a deed in the safe that says this is my land and I don't think there's any law that mandates the cheerful tolerance of trespassers."

"Lucky for you," she shot back. "I don't think you could pull off cheerful to save your soul."

Crossing his arms over his powerful chest, he looked her over once more. "How old are you?"

"Twenty-eight."

"Try eighteen." He glanced at her clothes. "You look like you could be a babysitter. Or even need one."

"It's hard to look mature in cutoffs and a T-shirt," she said indignantly.

"You pulled that getup out of a closet, not me."

"I had to go to an associate's dig before I came here."

"Hopefully not as an image consultant."

"I'm not here to talk about my clothes." She glared at him defensively.

"You seem determined to talk about something. Since I'm not going to discuss your digging up my land, I figure clothes are a natural launching pad for inane conversation. Considering you're a woman."

She took a deep breath, trying like hell not to lose her temper.

"Look, I know Conrad Lyst found a cross that could be Reverend—"

"Perhaps I need to be more clear. I'm not discussing anybody digging on my land. Your questionable taste in sportswear is still on the table, however."

"I didn't wear this for you!"

"Obviously. Although I must say it made quite an impression on the teenager who just left. But then, he's mistaking you for a contemporary."

Carter felt like she was getting picked clean by a vulture and had to fight the urge to yell back at him again.

Doing her best to regard him calmly, she forced herself to keep her voice down.

"Mr. Farrell, all I'm asking is for you to hear me out."

"Call me Nick and forget the speech. It won't improve your bargaining position any more than those shorts do."

"Are you always this nasty?"

"As a rule, yes. But sometimes I'm worse."

She rolled her eyes. "No wonder you have to get doors rehung."

"It's good for the local economy."

"How generous of you."

"I think so."

There was a long silence. She had the feeling she was amusing him, and that pissed her off as much as when he'd been verbally attacking her.

"I'm a professional, Mr. Farrell, not an itinerant ditch digger. You may be sitting on the answer to one of the great puzzles of the Revolutionary era. No one really knows what happened to the Winship party and the gold they were carrying. You owe it to posterity—"

"To let you come in and rescue the solution from my land?" His brow furrowed deeply. "I've got news for you. I don't think it needs rescuing. As far as I'm concerned, the past is best left buried and posterity these days is far more interested in Ozzy Osbourne's family life. They couldn't care less about minutemen and redcoats."

"That's a pretty narrow view."

"I'm a narrow kind of man."

"I can tell."

He chuckled. "So Miss Manners is also a behaviorist?"

"No, it's the flashing ROYAL PAIN IN THE ASS sign over your desk."

There was a long pause, and then Nick Farrell tilted back his head and laughed. It was a rich, rolling sound. When he focused on her again, he was smiling, and the grin lit up his austere face, pulling an unlikely dimple out of one cheek.

Somehow, now that she'd made him laugh, she wasn't quite so angry at him.

"Do you have any idea how many people come at me each spring asking to tear into Farrell Mountain?"

"No, but I don't care."

"You don't?"

"When you go after some company, do you worry about what all the other little raiders are doing?"

His grin disappeared. "Been doing some research on my history?"

"You're pretty well-known."

He shrugged but clearly wasn't happy with her remark. "What would you do if I decided to let that Lyst guy have a go at it?"

"I'd say good luck and good riddance to both of you." It sounded like a straight answer but she knew the anger behind her voice gave her away.

"Something tells me," he said, getting to his feet, "you wouldn't be quite that phlegmatic."

She gave him a disparaging look.

"I'm wrong?"

"You think I'm underage because of my shorts. In my opinion, that doesn't give you a whole lot of clout in the judgment department."

Farrell came around the edge of his desk and approached her, stopping only when he was a foot away. Carter's throat went dry. He was taller than her by at least a head and that was saying something, considering she was five-nine. As the full force of him hit her, she had to stop herself from stepping backward.

Across a desk, he was insulting and intimidating. Up close, she found him totally compelling.

Not exactly an improvement, she thought, running her tongue over her lips.

That was a mistake. Like a predator, he watched the movement, eyes sharpening on her mouth. The way he was looking at her made her body swell with something she was determined to think of as anxiety, even if it felt more like hunger. She thought about turning around and walking out. Running away, actually.

"What is it you really want?" he drawled.

"I don't understand." Carter's words were mumbled, coming out fast and tense. He couldn't possibly be insinuating that she had come for him. Right?

"Everyone has a hidden agenda. What else are you after?" His eyes traveled down her body and then came back to her face.

She shook her head, trying to clear it. "I just want to dig."

Abruptly, almost angrily, he broke eye contact with her and returned to the papers on his desk. His voice was offhand when he addressed her again.

"I think you should put your learner's permit to good use and drive yourself back to wherever you came from. You aren't going to get what you want here, either in the dirt or from me. However much I wish I could be . . . accommodating. I like women, not schoolgirls."

Carter's mouth dropped open.

"Are you suggesting . . ." She couldn't even finish the sentence.

"Shut the door behind you," he commanded before adding, *"Please."*

Her breath came out in a hiss. "You insufferable, egocentric—"

"There you go with the compliments, making me blush," he murmured, flipping a page.

"I hope you rot in hell."

"See you there," he said cheerfully.

On the way out, Carter slammed the door as hard as she could.

As the clap of wood reverberated through the room like a gunshot, Nick winced and put the documents down. His head was still tender from the migraine, and he massaged his temples, waiting for the sting to wear off.

That was one hell of a beautiful woman, he thought.

Those crystal blue eyes so alive with defiance. That expressive face showing him every emotion she was feeling. Her mouth, with its full lips and its pink tongue.

Heat flared in his body again.

It was a damn good thing she'd left. Reeling in his impulses had been more difficult every time that tongue of hers had come out for a lick. Moves like that had been performed for him countless times before but, because they were calculated, he'd never been tantalized. The trouble with the archaeologist was that he got the sense she didn't know how enticing she was.

Which couldn't be possible.

Beautiful women were always willing to leverage their assets. He didn't fault them for it. He'd made a fortune doing the same thing, only his bait was dollar bills, not the promise of sexual thrills, and his acquisitions were companies, not marriage licenses. Futile as it inevitably was for the other party, he always enjoyed bartering with women over what they wanted from him in return for their time and attention.

And that one in the cutoffs could have been a real contender. Aside from her beauty, she had a keen intelligence and a heavy dose of wit, and she wasn't afraid of giving as good as she got. In his life, no one dared to spar with him. People either wanted something or owed him money, neither of which was breeding ground for resistance, even of the playful variety.

She'd been captivating when she was angry, he thought. A flush on those cheekbones, her breath coming in drumbeats, her mouth open, agape at his rudeness. She'd lit up like a Christmas tree. Delightful. Utterly delightful.

He looked at the door, as if he could see her through it.

Carter Wessex.

Could she be related to Wessex? he wondered suddenly.

Wouldn't that be interesting.

Nick tried to recall what he knew about William Wessex's family life. The man had been married but something had happened to the wife. Something tragic. Had there been a daughter? Wessex never showed up anywhere with one, never mentioned one, but Carter's coloring was startlingly similar to his and she had the same kind of arresting good looks.

Nick picked up the phone and dialed his office in New York. It was answered on the first ring.

"Fredericka Ulrich," his chief of staff said brusquely. Aside from having a brilliant head for business, the woman was a walking encyclopedia. She knew everything about everyone who was anyone, and what she didn't know, she could find out.

"Freddie, does William Wessex have a daughter?"

"I think so," she mused. "But I know who to call. Wait by the phone."

This was Freddie at her best, Nick thought. He was still smiling when his line rang moments later.

"Late twenties. Estranged. Really estranged," she told him.

"Name?"

"Carter. Lives somewhere in Vermont. Archaeologist. One of the best in the country even though she's relatively young."

"Does Wessex care about the split?"

"Tremendously. He's frantic about it. Been a couple years or so, since the mother died. Apparently the daughter won't see him or even talk to him."

"Ms. Wessex showed up here today."

"Not surprising considering that hill behind your house. You going to let her dig?"

"I said no."

"And now you're wondering what it might be worth to William Wessex if he had a shot at making nice with his little girl?"

Freddie was also a terrific strategist.

Nick smiled grimly. "You know I like to make sure my business partners are in debt to me. Financially or otherwise."

"What's the downside?"

"Apart from the two of them turning my peaceful retreat into a war zone if things don't work out?" He pondered a moment. "If she digs up my damn mountain and finds the remains of any of those slaughtered men, I'm going to have even more two-bit tourists with shovels hunting for gold. Hell, look at the commotion that guy Lyst stirred up by claiming to find a cross and talking to the local paper. The phone hasn't stopped ringing and Ivan tossed three more trespassers off my property this morning. I come up here to relax, not run a park service."

"And if she finds the gold?"

"There isn't any."

"How do you know?"

"I just do. Hell, maybe I should leave well enough alone."

"But if father and daughter reconcile, Wessex will owe you for life," Freddie reasoned. "He could prove even more useful than he's been."

Nick mulled over his options. "And maybe if she digs around a little, we can finally put all this silliness to rest. I'm tired of guarding an empty safe."

After hanging up the phone, he went to a window and looked out toward the lake. As he watched the sunlight reflect off the waves, he noticed something out of the corner of his eye. It was a large red-tailed hawk sitting in a tree, watching him through the glass.

He thought of the woman who had just left his home.

And found himself looking forward to seeing her again.

3

CARTER WAS making a beeline for the front door, muttering under her breath, when the teenager leapt out in front of her.

"Hi! I'm Cort!"

She pulled up short to keep from running into him. "Er—pleased to meet you."

In contrast to when he'd been around his father, the kid was smiling widely. "Are you sure you're not staying for dinner?"

"I'm sorry but I have to go."

And she was never coming back. The world was safe only if she and Nick Farrell didn't get into another enclosed space together.

Cort's face fell and she noticed again how much he and Farrell looked alike. The major deviation was their wardrobes. Whereas his father had been wearing linen pants, handmade loafers, and a monogrammed button-down, the kid had on ratty shorts and a T-shirt that read, SPAM: THE OTHER PINK MEAT. She decided not to inquire what the first kind was.

Still, they were obviously related. The younger Farrell was lanky, but he was clearly going to fill out to the elder's size. And the bones of the teenager's face, which had not yet hardened into the planes and angles she could see in his future, held the promise of Farrell's stunning looks.

"I think I better get going," Carter said in a rush.

Cort followed her out the front door, his hands and feet flopping around as he walked. She imagined he'd grow out of that, too, and move as Farrell did. Like an elegant prowler.

"So where are you going?" he asked.

"Home."

"Where's home?"

Carter looked around and remembered she'd left the Jeep by the service entrance. "Burlington."

"Where's your car?"

"In back." They started around the mansion.

"What do you drive?"

"A Jeep."

"The army kind or the SUV?"

"SUV."

"The army kind is cooler. What color is it?"

"White." She had to laugh. "You always ask so many questions?"

"Pretty much. When are you coming back?"

"I'm not."

His expression darkened. "Because of him, right?"

Trying to seem casual, she shrugged. "I don't really have a reason to—"

"You wanted to dig, didn't you?"

"How did you know?"

"I looked in your car."

"So why did you ask me what kind I drove?" She shot him a dry look and the kid flushed. At least he had the grace to be sheepish, she thought with a grin.

"I wasn't sure it was yours. Anyway, most people don't show up with surveying equipment and four different kinds of shovels if they aren't interested in setting up shop on the mountain." Cort sent a baleful look toward the house. "He always does that. He always turns people away."

"I'm sure your father has his reasons—"

Cort grabbed her arm.

"He is *not* my father." Anger clouded his eyes, and she was surprised at the depth of the animosity.

"I'm sorry," she said gently. "I assumed because you look alike —"

"He's my uncle. And I don't look like him." The words were short and emphatic.

They started walking again, more slowly.

"I really am sorry," she told him. "I've always hated it when people tell me I look like my father. I should have known better."

Cort was silent until they stopped in front of her car. Abruptly, he smiled. "If you do look like him, your dad must be real handsome."

"He is." Now it was her turn to grow quiet. She covered up her awkwardness by getting out her keys.

"I don't know why," the teenager said with frustration, "but my uncle hates anyone digging up on the mountain. You should have seen what happened when that other guy was here. Ivan was ready to shoot him, and Uncle Nick was going to let it happen. I was there. I saw the whole thing. Hey, you want to see where the guy was digging?"

Carter had her car keys ready, even had her hand on the door. She wanted to say no. She really wanted to say no.

"Okay."

With a wide grin, Cort led her behind some barns and a garage, through the meadow and over to the edge of the forest. In between a white birch stand and some honeysuckle bushes, there was a break in the undergrowth. No more than a foot wide, the path cut through the brush and guided them into the cool refuge under the trees. Ferns, lady slippers, and bright green elf grass grew beside the thin trail and, as they walked along, the sounds of moving creatures mixed with the cracks of snapping twigs under their feet. The forest's perfume was a blend of good earth and growing things, an ancient scent full of life.

The ground began to rise and boulders appeared, casualties of the glacier that had carved out the lake and then receded thousands of years before. At a steady clip, they climbed the mountain, and Carter noted that the grass and ferns disappeared and the deciduous trees changed to heartier hemlocks and pines.

A half hour later, they came to a clearing close to the top of the mountain and Carter gasped at the view below. Cradled between twin mountain ranges, the lake was a shimmering valley of water that stretched out in both directions as far as the eye could see. Over to the left, on a peninsula that jutted out into the lake, she could see the magnificent stone walls and buildings of Fort Sagamore.

One of the oldest military fortresses in the United States, it was a national treasure and a popular site for tourists and scholars. After the stronghold had been built by the French in the early 1700s, it had changed hands a number of times and was eventually captured by the Americans in the Revolutionary War. This final, successful coup had been led by Nathaniel Walker, a man who figured prominently in the mystery of the missing gold and lost men.

As she took in the vista, Carter let out a low whistle.

What she was looking at mirrored a description General Farnsworth, the Brit who had been escorted by the colonialists, had scribed in his journal. He'd detailed a clearing exactly like the one she was now standing in, including the landscape down to his fort and the flat-topped mountain across the lake. It had been, he'd noted, close to where the slaughter occurred.

Her heart rate shot up.

"Some kind of pretty, isn't it?" Cort asked. "The guy was digging back here."

They walked a couple hundred yards farther up the mountain until they were confronted with an uneven circle of huge boulders. The bulky sentries guarded an inner sanctum that was about a square acre in size. Carter was astounded as she stepped inside.

This was it, she thought. This had to be where the slaughter occurred.

She began to pace over the coarse grass and the pine needles, trying to imagine what secrets might be hidden in the earth. Farnsworth had described the spot where the party had set up camp as a Stonehenge in the Adirondacks. With handy access to a nearby stream and the boulders offering protection from the wind and potential enemies, it was the perfect place for a party of weary travelers to rest their heads.

Carter caught sight of a bottle and went over to pick it up. Aside from the empty Bud Light, there was other evidence of modern visitations. The fire pit in the middle, created by a cloister of stones, had relatively fresh ashes in it. More significantly, she saw ragged gashes dug carelessly here and there in the ground all over the place.

It was typical Lyst, she thought. Raping and pillaging his way through the site.

Carter bent down and plied the earth with her hand, letting the dirt fall through her fingers.

Damn you, Farrell.

She stayed on her haunches a moment longer, wishing for a chance she wasn't going to get.

"Well, thanks for bringing me up here," she said as she got to her feet.

Cort beamed. "If you want, I can show you a place no one knows about."

"Where—"

"What are you doing there, boy?" Out of nowhere, a man appeared in the circle. He was small, built like a bulldog, and had dark eyes crowned by a disapproving brow. More significantly, he had a shotgun cradled in his arms and the look of someone itching to use it.

"Hi, Ivan," Cort mumbled.

"You know you're not s'posed to bring anyone up here." The man moved with the quiet grace of an expert woodsman, his footsteps silent over the ground.

"I know."

"So what're you doing up here?"

"He was just showing me the view," Carter said, hoping to deflect the criticism.

The man looked at her and shifted the gun up to his shoulder. Closer to firing position.

"And I think I've seen enough," she added quickly.

"So do I," came his dark answer.

The march back down the mountain was grim. The woodsman followed behind them like a prison guard, and Carter was thinking it had been a mistake to go up to the site. Farrell wasn't going to change his mind and all she'd done was torture herself with impossibilities.

As well as volunteer for a brush with death.

When they cleared the forest, Carter thanked Cort and got in her car. As she drove off, she saw in her rearview mirror that the woodsman was watching her go.

It was obvious who almost shot Lyst, she thought.

Heading to the ferry that would take her home, she burned with frustration. It was a hell of an opportunity, and she wished her meeting with Farrell hadn't gone so badly. But how could she have expected anything different? Her reception had been no better than others of her ilk had gotten and at least she hadn't faced down the business end of that shotgun.

The side view had been more than enough to get her attention.

When she got home, she called Grace with the disappointing news.

"It's a no-go," Carter said while going out to the back porch. She looked over her meadow as the sun set. "I guess my negotiating skills aren't what they used to be."

Although she seemed to have acrimonious arguing down pat, she reflected, remembering the sparks that had flown in Farrell's study.

"Well, maybe it's for the best. Lyst's cross is a fake," Grace muttered. "We gave it a thorough examination this morning. It's no older than the chicken salad I had for lunch at the club."

"Somehow that doesn't surprise me. Still, I feel like there's something up there."

"Is that optimism I hear?" her friend teased. "From the woman who announced that finding anything on that mountain would be like winning the lottery?"

"Grace, I saw the site. It's amazing, just as Farnsworth described it."

Her friend laughed with admiration. "How'd you pull that off?"

"I had a tour guide."

"Farrell?"

"Not bloody likely. His nephew sneaked me up." Carter paused. "I'm telling you, there's something at that site. I could feel it in the dirt."

Grace sighed. "Too bad Farrell's so difficult."

"'Difficult' is too nice a word for that man."

Their conversation drifted in other directions, but when Carter hung up later, Farrell Mountain was all she could think about. When the phone rang again, she figured it was Grace calling back, still on the fence over whether or not to buy a painting she loved.

Carter picked up with a laugh. "Look, I told you to accept your fate. If you're going to buy the Thomas Cole, you need to belly up to the fact that you're a Hudson River School junkie. Just because everyone else is buying modern, doesn't mean you have to."

"Thanks for the advice but I collect Old Masters." Nick Farrell's deep voice burned in her ear. "Even the turn of the nineteenth century's too new for my taste."

"How did you get this number?" Carter blurted, jerking to attention.

"James Earl Jones said I could be connected for an extra charge but I dialed it myself."

"What do you want?"

In the background, she could hear voices and the clinking of crystal.

"I've been thinking about our conversation," he drawled.

His arrogance made her prickle. "Funny, I've been trying to forget it."

"I understand you went up the mountain."

She hesitated. "Don't blame Cort."

"Tell me again why you want to dig."

Frustration swelled in her chest.

"What for? You've already turned me down. And you should know that Lyst's find wasn't legit. That cross was a fake."

"I know."

"So why are you calling me? If you don't want anyone on that mountain—" Carter paused. "How did you know it wasn't authentic?"

"Because I have the real one."

She fell silent as his words sank in.

"And I'm rethinking my earlier decision. How would you like to come back tomorrow and take a look at my little slice of history?"

She stayed quiet while ambition warred with her instinct for self-preservation. "I don't trust you."

He laughed. "That's smart, but I have something you want, don't I? Shall we say noon?"

Even though his lure was bordering on irresistible, she shook her head. "I don't think so."

"Don't tell me you're busy."

"What am I coming for? So you can dangle an artifact in front of my face and turn me down again? As you so aptly put it, that would be a waste of our time."

"Aren't you just a little curious about my cross?"

Curious didn't go far enough. Try desperate, she thought ruefully. Still, she'd be damned if she was going to present herself as some kind of amusement for him again.

"Farrell, I don't believe in conversions, at least not with people like you. There's no way in hell I'm driving back into New York State again just so you can shut me down. I did that earlier today. I don't need to reprise the rejection or put additional miles on my car."

"Fine, I'll come to you. We don't need to be near the damn thing to discuss your coming to work on my mountain."

Carter hesitated, wondering what kind of game he was playing.

The feel of the dirt in her hands came back and temptation rose. It would be the chance of a lifetime to get to do a real study of that site, to find out what had happened. But she had to wonder if he was setting her up somehow. Why would a man who had turned away so many, including herself earlier that very day, suddenly call up and ask her to come dig? It just didn't make sense.

"Farrell, if you're toying with me, I'm going to have a lot to say about it."

"It couldn't be anything I haven't heard before."

"Don't knock innovation," she muttered.

There was a long pause.

"So do we have a date?"

Reluctantly, feeling as if she'd tripped and was falling into thin air, she gave him directions to her house.

"I'll see you at noon," he said and hung up.

How appropriate for a standoff, she thought.

The next morning, she couldn't settle down to accomplish anything. She had a paper she wanted to finish and she should have gone into her office at UVM, but she did neither. Instead, she ended up in her garden, weeding as if possessed. Surrounded by blooming irises and lilacs, hands deep in topsoil, she lost track of time, and when she heard a car approach, she looked up in surprise. A black Porsche was coming up her driveway. The man behind the wheel looked as though the car had been made with him in mind.

Carter got to her feet, pushed her hair out of her face and tried to brush the grass off her bare knees. Mud was caked on her shorts and her T-shirt and she flicked some of it off.

Not much of an improvement from yesterday's outfit, she noted. At least the other pair of cutoffs had been clean.

She watched with trepidation as Nicholas Farrell unfolded his long legs from the car and got out with a stretch. She was surprised to see he was wearing a dark suit and wished she didn't notice how the pale blue shirt under the jacket emphasized his tan. He looked her way and smiled but she couldn't see his eyes through his sunglasses.

With an economical movement, he bent down and picked up something from the front seat. As he strode across her small lawn, a black leather briefcase in one of his hands, he exuded masculine power.

Unlike myself, she thought; I'm just exuding the need to take a shower.

"You like dirt, don't you?" he said in a husky voice when he was standing in front of her.

She caught a whiff of cologne, something sophisticated and fitting for a man like him. Expensive but elemental.

Dammit, did she have to like the way he smelled?

She could feel him looking at her, even through the sunglasses, and was disturbed by the way her body flared in response. Resenting the reaction, because it was strong and unconscious, she couldn't prevent the sharpness in her voice. "Let's get down to business."

She started to turn away and walk toward her house, but he didn't move.

"You've got a beautiful garden."

Carter wheeled around impatiently and he flashed her a smile that took her breath away. The sun was high overhead and the angle of the light emphasized the hard lines of his face and highlighted that stupid dimple.

Was he flirting with her?

She shot him a prim look. "I'd like to see the cross now, if you don't mind."

"Don't I get a grand tour first?" He nodded at her house.

"There's nothing to see."

"That's a matter of opinion."

Carter blew a piece of hair out of her face with frustration. Things were not going well. Farrell seemed to have the upper hand even though he was on her turf. Her plan had been to take a look at the cross, figure out whether he was serious about the offer to dig, and then shoot him down the road. All of this was supposed to be accomplished without her losing her temper or doing something really dense. Like becoming attracted to him.

Unfortunately, the reality of him standing in front of her was more of a challenge than she'd bargained for. As far as she was concerned, the sooner he packed off in his ridiculously overpriced car, the better. She hadn't been in his company for long at all and already she was feeling distracted and woozy.

Maybe it was just heatstroke, she thought hopefully.

"Look, Mr. Farrell—"

"Nick."

"Mr. Farrell—"

His smile got bigger. "Are you always this stubborn?"

"Yes."

"Good."

Carter cocked her head and stared at him. "You are so odd."

"That's kind. Considering what you were tempted to say, I'm sure."

She huffed at him. "Just trying to be polite. Not that I'm returning the favor."

"I did say *please* once or twice yesterday."

"When you were kicking me out."

"Asking you to leave," he amended smoothly, seeming to eat up her antagonism.

With a casual movement, he took off his glasses. His true intent was no clearer now that she could see his eyes but she was intimidated by how closely he was looking at her. She was tempted to ask him to put them back on.

"Most women like to show off their nests," he pointed out in a voice that was just on the polite side of condescension.

She planted her hands on her hips. "Birds have nests,

Mr. Farrell. People live in houses. And I'm not most women."

"At least we can agree on that," he countered softly, some of his smile lost. "If nothing more."

Warning bells started to go off in Carter's head. It wasn't that his expression had changed. His riveting face was still all sardonic amusement. His eyes still gave away nothing of his inner thoughts. But there was a thread of something different in that tone of his, some subtle shift that made the tiny hairs on her arms prickle with an alarming delight. It was as if he had stroked his hand across her skin.

With a wave of heat, her body let her know it wanted in on his promise of pleasure. Desperately.

Dammit, she thought.

When she remained silent, he shrugged. "Well, if there's going to be no tour, we might as well get down to business."

With a stiff nod, she led him into the house. She watched how he took it all in, his eyes traveling over her things with the same disturbing focus he'd trained on her.

When she got to the foot of the stairs, he said laconically, "You don't have to change on my account. I'm already used to today's getup."

Her eyes shot sparks at him. "I wouldn't change my clothes for you even if you were offended."

"Especially if I were offended, right?" A slow smile spread over his face, pulling the dimple back into place.

She wished like hell he would go back to being argumentative. His arrogance got on her nerves but that smile could prove deadly.

"My study's up there," she said with a frown.

"Of course it is."

Carter marched up the stairs, preferring to let that one go. When they got to the second floor, she regretted having her workplace and her bedroom in one space. Both were revealed before him, a road map into her intimate world. She felt naked and didn't like the idea of having a memory of Nick Farrell being in the same room where she slept.

Clothing herself in determination, Carter approached her desk. "Let's see what you think you have."

"Think I have?"

"Fakes are well-known in my business," she said briskly, flipping on a gooseneck lamp.

"Then you and I have something in common, after all."

Carter held her tongue, anxious to get through the meeting.

Despite her impatience, or maybe because of it, he loitered with the briefcase in his hand, taking his time to look over the desk and her books, the view and the bare floorboards. His eyes lingered on her small twin bed with its simple white comforter and its lonely pillow. By the time he finally fixed his gaze on her, she was ready to jump out of her skin.

"You live here by yourself?"

"What business is it of yours?" Carter began drumming her fingers on the desk. When his eyes skirted over to the sound, she forced herself to sit still.

"Just curious."

"Get used to the feeling."

"Tough talk from a gardener." But he put the briefcase on her desk, released its two brass locks, and opened the lid. She noted absently that the inside of the case, which was done in red silk, was as beautifully finished as the outside.

Farrell took out a cloth bundle and gently unwrapped it on her desk.

Carter's breath left her in a reverent gasp. Lying in the cloth was a simple wooden cross, made from two pieces of hardwood with a square-headed nail in the center. Blackened with age and ragged on the ends, it was four inches long and three inches wide and had a metal circle at the top through which a piece of cloth could be threaded.

Pulling over her lamp, Carter sat down and put on an

elaborate set of magnifying glasses. Before she touched the cross, she slid on some cloth gloves to keep the oils from her skin off the wood. Carefully, she turned the piece over in her hands, noting its sturdy construction.

Just like the faith it symbolized, she thought.

On the back, cutting through the wood grains like trails through history, she saw the engraving *Rev. J. Winship*.

"You look very fierce," he said softly. "Although your hands are gentle."

Carter stiffened but kept her mouth shut, hoping he'd go back to staring at her things.

"You don't like being watched, do you?"

"I don't know anyone who does," she clipped. "Or why you're bothering to."

"Those glasses make you look like a scientist. That smudge of dirt on your nose makes you human. It's an interesting combination."

She couldn't help it. Still examining the cross, she started rubbing her nose.

"A little more to the left," he directed. "But I like it where it is."

Carter rubbed even more vigorously and heard him laugh.

"Where did you find this?" She looked up from the artifact.

"In the circle of rocks."

"Was there anything else with it?"

He shook his head. "We've found a lot of arrowheads up there but nothing else like this."

"So all that digging at the site wasn't just Lyst's?"

"You mean those holes? No, they're all his handiwork. I was sixteen when I found this." Nick looked down at the cross. "That was a long time ago."

Carter tried to imagine him as a boy, digging in the dirt. "Do you know if anyone else has excavated up there? Any professionals?"

"Members of the family have hit the mountain with shovels over the generations but no one with formal training's ever been up there. We try to keep the experts and the amateurs away."

"You've taken good care of this. It's well preserved."

"That's more luck than stewardship. Right after I found it, I was afraid it would get taken away from me so I kept it under my bed. In college and business school, it lived in my bookcase. Lately, it's been marking time in my safe."

Carter could see how attached he was to the piece by the way his eyes caught on the aged wood and held. He seemed nostalgic and it made him more approachable. Unexpectedly, she found herself warming to him.

Clearing her throat, she said, "It looks like the real thing to me."

He smiled with approval. "So it seems like we have something to discuss."

Carter shut off the light and glanced up at him. "And that is?"

Because he was so tall, she had to arch her neck to see him, making her feel like she was at a disadvantage. She got to her feet.

"Are you still interested in doing a little digging?"

She shrugged. "Maybe. But what's with your sudden change of heart?"

"I did a little research."

"On the value of history?"

"On you."

She swallowed through a tight throat. "And what did you find out?"

"You're at the top of your field." Farrell began to stroll around the room, the heels of his shoes landing sharply on the floorboards. She could see how commanding he would be in a boardroom. "Specializing in early American history, you're on track to become one of the youngest full professors at UVM. Part of that's because you graduated from prep school at the ripe young age of sixteen and doubled up on your classes at college. Mostly it's because you're widely respected as an archaeologist and a historian and are known for being painstakingly meticulous both in your fieldwork and your scholarship. You lecture around the country, a part of your job which is complicated for you."

He leaned over to look at some of her books.

"Oh, really?"

"You hate to fly."

Carter was surprised he knew about her phobia.

He straightened and resumed walking, heading for her bed. She was struck by an urge to shoo him away from it.

"You're tough to get ahold of and prefer to work alone. When you do collaborate, it's with a Harvard guy, Branson Swift. Most recently, you were in charge of excavating a four-block section of Manhattan before a new underground subway platform was constructed. That was this spring, and, come autumn, you should be ready to start presenting on those finds."

He bent down to her bedside table and picked up the mystery novel she'd been reading. "Kinsey Millhone. I like Grafton, too."

When she remained silent, he put the book back and faced her. "You're a workaholic. I venture most of your relationships are based on your profession and you like it that way. I'd also bet you haven't taken a vacation in years, if ever. And you obviously live here alone, which I have to believe is by choice. Considering your looks."

A warm glow spread through Carter's body. She beat it back with determination.

"That's all pretty accurate factually," she said tautly. "Although I'm not going to comment on your conclusions. Are you a private eye as well as a corporate raider?"

"We prefer the term 'takeover engineer,'" he tossed back. That slow half smile crept across his face again.

Carter began to feel fuzzy in the head. Flustered, she broke their eye contact and walked over to the window farthest away from him.

She took a deep breath, wrapping her arms around her body. "So I'm supposed to believe you've asked around, read my curriculum vitae, and suddenly decided the sum of my virtues is sufficient to justify changing your mind? I don't get it."

"Perhaps conversions happen," he murmured, "even in people like me."

"I'll believe that when I see it."

"Maybe you just need to get to know me better. I could have a heart of gold under this gruff exterior."

"That would be fool's gold, no doubt."

He laughed, a low, husky sound.

Carter turned to face him. "Why me?"

"Because I believe you when you say it's not about the gold. You're known for being an academic, not a gold digger."

She had to hide a smile at his choice of words. "Well, at least you got that part right. Would you be prepared to put any artifacts I find on permanent loan to the museum of my choice?"

"Of course."

"And what if I find the gold?"

"You won't."

"Don't think I can?"

"I don't think it's there to be found. Chances are whoever slaughtered the Winship party took it along with their scalps."

"So you think Red Hawk ran off with it after he killed them?"

"You tell me. You're the expert." Nick's eyes were steady on hers. She began to think he was serious about changing his mind.

"My team and I are going to have to camp out by the site."

"Team?"

"I'll have at least one other person digging with me. Maybe a third."

"The talented Branson Swift?"

"Yes."

Farrell inclined his head. "Fine. You can all stay at the house."

"Out in the woods is more convenient," she said quickly. And safer than sleeping under Farrell's roof, even with the mountain lions and rattlesnakes.

"You're prepared to turn down all the comforts of home for a tent and sleeping bag? Should I take this personally?"

"Buddy and I set up a good camp."

Farrell's face grew pensive. "So you and Swift like to get cozy on these digs—is that it?"

"What do you mean?"

"Nothing. Just humor me and consider it an open invitation. We can get some cold nights, even in June. When will you start?"

"Day after tomorrow?"

Nick nodded and went over to her desk where he started rolling the cross up in its cloth. "I'm going to expect regular reports from you."

"Of course. Buddy—er, Dr. Swift and I will be happy to present—"

Those gray eyes flashed over to her. "I want them from you."

"But he and I always—"

"I don't care what you always do. I don't want a lot of people chatting my ear off. You're the project leader. I want to hear from you." There was no arguing with the tone in his voice.

Carter frowned. "Okay. Whenever you're at the lake, I'll fill you in."

"I'll be there the whole time." He laughed as her jaw slacked open. "Why does everyone greet the prospect of me being up here for the summer with the same expression of horror?"

"You'll be there the whole time?"

"Until Labor Day. Is that a problem?"

She pulled herself together. "Of course not. I'm just surprised you'd be away from your businesses so much."

"I am my business. People come to me, not the other way around."

Carter had to imagine that was true.

"If you'd like, you can leave the cross here so I can study it in greater depth," she offered as he resumed wrapping up the artifact.

"This stays with me." Nick returned it to the briefcase, thumbing the locks back in place. "But you can always come and look at it."

He picked up the case from the desk and extended a hand toward her. She made no move in his direction.

"Aren't we going to shake on our agreement?" he prompted. "Surely a woman who is willing to sleep in the great outdoors doesn't fear anything as civilized as a handshake?"

Carter approached slowly and slipped her palm into his. His fingers enveloped her hand, his skin warm and smooth against hers. Immediately, a shock went through her and her eyes shot up to his. She watched as his expression changed from one of sardonic teasing to something altogether serious. When she went to pull her hand back, he held on for a moment before letting her go.

"I'll see you in forty-eight hours." His voice was very deep, his eyes hooded and burning under dark lashes.

As they left the room, Carter hurried down the stairs despite the fact that her legs felt shaky. She was desperate for fresh air because, through some shift in the laws of science, he'd made the wide-open space of the loft seem cramped and suffocating. He was, she thought, larger than life.

It took several deep breaths before she was ready to face him again.

"So long, Carter Wessex," he said when she met his eyes. With an enigmatic grin, he slid his sunglasses back on, went to his car, and shot off down her driveway.

Oh, God, she thought. The man was going to be at the lake the entire time she was there.

Distance was going to be critical, she decided. She was going to stay on top of that mountain, do her job with lightning-fast efficiency, and avoid the man like he was contagious.

That was just the way it would have to be.

Setting her shoulders, she went back upstairs and left word for Grace that the dig was a go. Then she called the Swift household. By the time she put the phone down, Buddy and his daughter were prepared to meet her at Farrell's house by the end of the week. Jo-Jo, Buddy's better half, would be staying in Cambridge for the summer to finish her current book.

Carter smiled as she thought about her friend and colleague. She'd met Buddy on the historical lecture circuit and they'd bonded immediately. He was an expert on early North American military conflict and an excellent archaeologist. Theirs had always been a relationship based on respect and friendship, and she liked his wife tremendously. Jo-Jo, who was a professor of chemistry, understood the closeness between the two historians and was happy to have Carter in their lives.

The Swifts, who had been married for almost twenty years, seemed like an unusual pair. With a crop of wiry red hair on his head, Buddy was built like a string bean and had boundless energy, whereas Jo-Jo was a petite, quietly intense woman. Their daughter, Louella, who refused to answer to anything but Ellie, was halfway between the extremes of her parents. She had her father's height and her mother's formidable intelligence, and could be by turns gregarious and focused. They were a wonderful family and a lot of fun to work with.

Snapping out of her reverie, she got up from her desk with purpose. There was packing to do, she had to go to her university office and get some of her tools, and she needed to think about provisions.

Carter was about to go downstairs when she turned and looked back at her room. Everything was the same as it had been when she'd woken up that morning. Her clothes were still in the drawers and hanging in the closet; her papers were filed next to her desk; her books were where she had left them.

But somehow, it was all different. It was as if everything in the room had been moved one inch in another direction.

Carter thought of Nick Farrell standing by her desk, his wide shoulders taking up so much space, those pale eyes watching her. Her memory of him was so clear, it was as if a hologram of him remained after he'd left.

Why the vividness?

She wasn't sure, but she didn't want to dwell on that.

And why did she feel so exposed with him in her study?

Of the answers that came to mind, one bothered her most.

In the year since she'd moved into the farmhouse, he was the first man she'd invited into her home.

Carter groaned.

Why did she have to pick him? Why couldn't it have been someone more run-of-the-mill? An exterminator. A plumber.

An extraterrestrial, for Chrissakes.

4

On Tuesday, Carter pulled up in front of the Farrell mansion feeling conflicted. She'd spent the previous two nights staring into the darkness and seeing Nick Farrell's face. The lack of sleep and a curious, aching frustration were both making her cranky.

It wasn't the usual way she kicked off a dig. Most of the time, she'd be so excited to get started she could barely stand it.

Stepping from the Jeep, Carter wondered whether she had to check in with someone before she headed up the trail. She was anxious to establish camp and knew from experience that lugging her supplies and equipment was going to take most of the day. Doing a meet-and-greet with the Farrell household would only slow her down.

Liar.

She knew the real reason she was so eager to get going, and it didn't have anything to do with tents or shovels. She had a strong desire to avoid Nick Farrell. Their two previous encounters had established a disturbing trend. Each time, he got further under her skin, and her unwanted attraction to him seemed to be getting stronger. One more meeting and she could end up doing something really ludicrous. Like kissing the man.

Just then, Cort leapt out of the front door. Even though his jagged black hair was standing at stiff attention, he was wearing a fresh pair of khaki shorts and a white polo shirt. The look was a cross between postmodern Goth and the British Sloane Ranger set. His smile was all-American track star.

The kid was going to be a lady-killer just like his uncle, she decided, waving at him.

"I saw you drive up and told Uncle Nick you're here. He's on the phone, as usual, and is gonna be for a while. Hey, you need some help with all that?"

Carter laughed as she opened the rear. "Does a drowning man need a life jacket?"

"You know what you want?"

"A gondola?"

"I'll be right back."

With a practiced hand, she began unloading, stacking duffel bags and crates on top of one another. As the pile grew beside the car, it looked more overwhelming than it had when it was still packed inside.

Minutes later, she heard a roar and saw Cort racing over on a four-wheeler.

"That's the most beautiful thing I've ever seen," she exclaimed, seeing the task become exponentially more manageable and the chances of not tangling with the elder Farrell improve. Hopefully, they could get her stuff out of the man's front yard before he ended his call.

"There's an access road that hooks into the back trail," Cort explained. "I can get pretty close to the site and carry the stuff the rest of the way."

"You are heaven-sent!"

As Carter turned back to the car, she caught a glowing smile on the teenager's face. It was sweet of him to be so helpful, she thought.

Using bungee cords, they secured a load on the back rack of the four-wheeler and Cort ran it up the mountain, dropped it off, and returned. In just over an hour, the car was empty and Carter was further along than she'd expected to be by the middle of the day. Nick hadn't shown his face either and she felt as though a small victory was in reach when the last load was anchored on the machine. Quickly, she changed into hiking boots, twisted her hair into a ball, and tugged a baseball hat over it. Then she strapped on a full pack that weighed sixty pounds.

"That's real heavy," Cort commented with awe. "Shouldn't we take it up on the four-wheeler?"

"I'm fine. Hauling this on a separate trip would be a waste of gas."

"Are you sure I can't—"

The kitchen's screen door clapped shut and both of them turned to see Nick come out of the mansion. Carter smothered a curse. She'd been so close.

"That's quite a load you've been moving," he drawled.

She watched as a laconic smile lifted his lips and had to tell herself not to look away quickly. He was even more attractive than she remembered, unfortunately. Dressed in tennis whites with a bag of rackets slung over his shoulder, he looked tan and virile. His arms were imposingly strong and so were the muscles in his legs. She was a little surprised at how athletic he seemed to be.

She wondered what he looked like in swimming trunks and then wanted to kick herself.

To her chagrin, Nick didn't stop until he was standing two feet from her. She tried to inch away but found the Jeep's rear bumper pressed up against the backs of her legs. With him so close, she could smell that tangy aftershave, and she noticed he was freshly shaved.

"Do you always bring this much stuff?" he asked with a teasing light in his eye. "Looks like enough for an army. You planning on invading Canada in your spare time?"

She fought the urge to smile back at him. "It's my standard gear and supplies, and there'll be more when the rest of my team arrive."

"More? Hard to imagine."

"I'm very thorough."

"Or a consummate overpacker."

Cort came to her defense with a defiant tone. "She's a professional. She needs these things."

Nick checked his watch, growing grave when he

looked at his nephew. "Are you heading up the mountain again?"

"She needs me."

"Then I think you better go inside first."

"But I—"

An arched eyebrow cut the kid off. Something serious passed between the two.

"Meet you up there?" Cort finally grumbled to her.

After she nodded, he ran into the house and Nick let out a frustrated breath. "I swear that kid would fight with me over which way is up."

Carter wasn't sure she wanted a response from her. He appeared preoccupied with private thoughts, but then he looked over at her and she felt compelled to respond.

"He's at a difficult age," she offered gingerly, unsure of what his reaction would be to any comment she made. "Is he any better with his parents?"

"No." Pain flared in Nick's eyes only to be covered quickly with a cool mask. Catching a glimpse of the emotion, Carter stared at him curiously. She was trying to figure out a way to ask him more about Cort but then the kid reappeared.

Striding across the lawn with his head set at a high angle, he ignored his uncle. "I'll run up the last load if you're sure you'd rather walk with the pack."

"Thanks. I'll be fine on the trail."

"See you there."

When Carter turned back to Nick, his face was totally unreadable and, as interested as she was, she didn't pursue the conversation about his nephew.

"You won't see me for the next few days," she said. "I'll be setting up camp, doing some surveying, and staking out the site. After my team arrives, and we've done some real work, I'll come back down to report."

His expression lost its tension and he smiled at her. "On the contrary, I think we'll be seeing plenty of each other."

"Oh no, we won't." Carter shook her head vigorously. "I'm not going to waste time coming down the mountain just to tell you where I pitched my tent and what I'm having for dinner."

His dimple got bigger. "You forget, I know my way up the trail very well. I also have a vast curiosity about the eating habits of archaeologists. No telling how many times I'll feel compelled to come up for a visit."

"I don't think that's a good idea."

"Why?"

She racked her brain for a response that wouldn't reveal anything. "I'm a professional and my work isn't a spectator sport."

"I'll be the judge of that." His eyes passed over the backpack. "By the way, are you still insisting on sleeping in the woods? We have plenty of space down here, not to mention running water."

Nick laughed at her shake of the head.

"If I didn't know better," he murmured, "I'd say you want to avoid me."

His eyes became hooded and a speculative, stunning light seeped out from under the lids.

Dragging herself from the sensual pull, she said quickly, "I'm used to working without interference."

"Anyone ever tell you you're too independent?"

"All the time." She turned to go.

"I'll see you later today."

"Do whatever you want," she muttered.

"All the time, Carter Wessex. I do that always."

When Carter reached the clearing that faced the lake, she was glad she'd made the climb. The effort of hoofing it up the mountain with a heavy weight strapped on her back had released some of her frustrations. She leaned against a rock and took a moment to catch her breath. Getting pushed to the physical limit had a way of prioritizing things. She'd been so distracted by the necessity of drawing air into her lungs, she'd almost forgotten about him.

As she scanned the lake, taking in its gleaming reflection of the sky and sun, she was surprised to find herself once more on Farrell's mountain. She'd been so sure, as she'd pulled away from the mansion days ago, that her first visit was going to be her last.

With a final, deep inhale, she headed through the trees to search for Cort and found him halfway between the big view and the circle of rocks. He was coming from the opposite direction, duffel bags hanging off him like he was a bellman's trolley. By the size of the mound that was already on the ground, she could tell he'd made a lot of trips from wherever the four-wheeler had been parked.

"I'm almost finished." He dropped his load. "I think this'll be the best place for you to camp. There's a stream down to the right and you're close to the site, but I can move these anywhere you like."

Carter inspected the flat stretch of ground nestled in a protected glen of pines.

"You picked the perfect place."

Cort's eyes lit up with pride. "I'll be right back."

While the sounds of him walking through the woods diminished, Carter peeled off her pack and surveyed the area. She was eager to get at the dig site, but she knew she'd appreciate having an established camp when night fell. By the time Cort came back with the last bundles, she'd set up her tent and was gathering rocks to make a secure fire pit. Even though she'd brought a butane-fueled hot plate and a portable grill, the fire would be a welcome balm against cool evenings.

Together, she and Cort strung up two dark green tarps, one to serve as the mess tent and the other to cover the office area. Under each, they erected folding tables and chairs and then consolidated the food hampers and her equipment appropriately. The rest of the afternoon was spent unpacking and getting things ready for the digging to start. As they worked, Cort was fascinated by the variety of shovels, brushes, and lablike vials she'd brought up to the mountain.

"What's the coolest thing you've ever found?" he asked, inspecting a wooden-handled trowel.

Carter looked up from the printer she was attaching to a portable generator.

"I don't really have a favorite. Everything is amazing to me. Sometimes I just sit with a find in my hands, trying to imagine what life was like for a minuteman in the colonial army or his wife and family. It's all just so astounding."

"Yeah, sure. But what about gold statues and rubies and—"

"You mean the Indiana Jones stuff?"

Cort nodded with enthusiasm.

"I hate to crush your burgeoning interest in the field, but that's the movies. Real archaeology is about painstaking, methodical work and slow, steady progress. It's a lot of hard labor, and sometimes you come up with nothing." She grinned as his expression grew less fervent. "Don't look so disappointed. We also don't have poison darts being shot at us and to my knowledge no one's face has ever melted when they've taken the lid off something they've dug up."

"So you haven't uncovered any tombs or secret catacombs?"

"Nope. And I don't own any bullwhips or sharplooking fedoras either. But I love what I do."

"I guess that's cool." He glanced over her shoulder as she started unpacking journals and books. "What's all this for?"

"Daily logs for recording each digger's work and forms for describing any finds. Some reference materials, mapping paper to sketch out the site. We've also got the requisite cross-referencing papers to document the relationship between and among the finds. Here's a copy of Farnsworth's journal."

Cort took it and flipped through the pages, not reading them.

She held up another book, regarding it curiously. "And this is a Fodor's guide to Budapest, although how it got in here I have no idea."

"I didn't think there'd be so much stuff that looks like homework," he muttered.

"We don't call the office tent Papercut Central because it's a barrel of laughs."

Cort grinned. "So who else is on your team?"

"Buddy Swift and his daughter, Ellie. I'll bet you two will get along. She's your age."

Cort frowned. "How old is she?"

"Fifteen."

"She's younger than I am. I'm sixteen." There was a stern note to his voice.

"Oh, sorry." Carter hid her smile. "They're coming on Saturday. And even with the age difference, I think you'll like Ellie. She's funny and very smart."

He shrugged offhandedly. "Yeah, sure. Hey, are you going to be okay up here all alone until then?"

"Absolutely. I'm used to camping by myself."

"But there are dangerous things in these woods and it's almost a week. Maybe you should stay at our house." He looked worried for her, his brows drawn in arches over his eyes.

"I'll be fine."

"Maybe I should stay up here with you."

Carter was about to answer cavalierly when she caught the expression on his face. It was full of hopeful warmth.

Uh-oh, she thought, as she began to see his attentiveness in a different light.

She smiled at him gently. "That's very kind of you but I'm looking forward to some time by myself."

"Oh. But I could come up during the day, though. You'll need help before your team gets here, right?"

"I'm sure you have other things to do." She rolled up an empty duffel and crammed it into a vacant crate.

"I would have other stuff, if I was allowed to have a life," he grumbled. "I wanted to go cross-country or hiking this summer but my uncle gets his kicks out of torturing me."

"Well, it's not going to be fun and games up here. I'm going to be working nonstop."

"That's okay. I just want to be with—up here."

Carter fell silent, unsure what to do as she glanced in his direction. The kid's eyes were showing the aching vulnerability that came with young crushes, and she felt at a loss. She hoped that whatever he had for her was merely the amorous equivalent of a twenty-four-hour virus. An intense case of infatuation that he'd get over quickly. She didn't want him to get hurt.

"Is it that you don't want me here?" His voice wavered.

"It's not that, but—"

"Great! I'll come every morning. Early."

Carter shook her head ruefully and decided it was too bad they didn't have some kind of over-the-counter that could clear up puppy love. A decongestant for fantasies.

"All right," she said. "But I'm going to put you to work. And don't come before eight. I'm really ugly until I've had my coffee."

"I'll bet that's not true." The words were blurted out as his eyes skipped away from her.

"Cort," she began softly. She wasn't sure where she was going to go with it but she needed to set some boundaries.

"What?" he asked with an optimistic tone.

The sound of snapping twigs turned their heads and they both stiffened as Nick came out of the woods. He was wearing hiking boots and shorts and had a maroon sweatshirt tied around his waist. Carter looked away from him quickly and concentrated instead on Cort. As the kid's eyes turned resentful, she decided the intrusion was like stepping out of quicksand and into the path of a stampede. Not an improvement, just a change in perils.

"I've been waiting anxiously for that tent-staking report," Nick said smoothly to Carter.

She felt her skin flush.

"I think I should stay up here with her," Cort interjected with force. "At least until the others come."

Nick's eyebrow arched.

"She needs someone to protect her."

His uncle laughed. "Based on my limited experience with Ms. Wessex, somehow I doubt that."

"She shouldn't be alone."

"Then she should come down to the house. You, however, are not going to stay up here with her."

"Why not?"

As anger and frustration flared between the two, Nick looked up to the sky. "Let's not do this."

"Tell me why!"

"Carter, is there anything you need that you don't have?" Nick asked pointedly.

"I want you to tell me why!" the kid shouted.

"Cort, I'm not going to do this now."

"Don't brush me off."

"I'm not brushing you off."

"The hell you aren't. Why don't you say what you're really thinking."

Nick took a deep breath and wrenched a hand through his hair.

"Fine. I'm thinking that we should change the subject. It's getting late and we should go down for dinner."

"You are such a liar! I'm not going anywhere until you—"

"That's enough," Nick said darkly. "You're excused."

"I'm not a child."

"You're acting like one."

"I am not!"

"Throwing a temper tantrum isn't adult behavior. And if Ms. Wessex needs anyone to protect her, it wouldn't be a sixteen-year-old who behaves like a toddler, would it?"

Carter gasped as Cort flushed and ran away.

Nick cursed under his breath.

"What did you do that for?" she demanded angrily.

He didn't respond.

"I asked you a question. Why were you so mean to him?"

"You think that was mean?"

"No, you're a real self-esteem builder." Her voice was sarcastic. "That kid busted his ass up and down this mountain for me. I accomplished more in an afternoon with his help than I could have alone in two days and you just took a hunk out of him."

"This doesn't involve you."

Carter stared at him. "I'm beginning to think you're not only rude. You're malevolent."

Nick pegged her with a look she was sure had made others think about life in the hereafter. His voice was piercing as he spoke.

"I am responsible not only for that child's amusements and petty whims. I'm responsible for his life. Do you understand the difference or are you such an adolescent yourself you can't make the distinction? There's a hell of a discrepancy between what a teenager wants and what he needs."

Carter met him head-on, leaning forward on the balls of her feet. "I may be on the sunny side of thirty but I know no kid wants or needs to be embarrassed like that in front of anybody. Even if you didn't want him to stay up here, you could have let him down more easily."

"There is no easy letdown with him," Nick growled. "He's a fighter and he doesn't stop until he pushes me to the limit."

"Then you should try harder. You're the grown-up."

They were squared off, head to head, as light began to fade from the sky.

Nick gritted out, "Let me remind you that you're here to dig in the dirt. Keep your theories to musket balls and stay the hell away from my family. I don't need someone else to argue with around here."

"Then you better stay off this mountain. Or get a personality transplant."

They glared at each other in acrimonious silence until she sighed angrily and looked away from him.

"This may have been a big mistake," Carter muttered, brushing some hair out of her eye.

"Not if you do your job and stop playing social worker."

"I think you should go."

His eyebrows arched. "Are you dismissing me?"

"Either you leave or I leave. If I leave, I have to drag all this stuff back down the trail and I'm too tired to make the effort."

Nick stared at her, brows falling down tightly over his eyes. When he spoke next, his voice was gruff. "Get this straight. I don't have to explain myself to you. You're on my property, at my whim. I can kick you off this mountain at a moment's notice."

"Fine. So do it." Her eyes, full of challenge, met his defiantly.

Nick frowned.

"Come on," she prompted. "You're doing enough masculine chest-thumping here to make a gorilla proud. Am I leaving or not?"

There was a long silence.

His diamond-hard eyes drilled into her until she didn't think she could stand the pressure anymore. But then, just before she was going to cave in and look away, he did something totally unexpected. He leaned in toward her and reached out his hand. When he touched her cheek with a light caress, she flinched as if struck.

"What are you doing?" Carter demanded, craning her neck away.

"Getting that piece of hair out of your face." She noticed that his voice changed. It was softer, reflective. Seductive, almost.

Her heart began pounding.

His thumb stroked her cheek again and then drifted down to her jawline.

"Stop it," she told him. But the tremble in her voice weakened the command.

"I want to kiss you."

"What?" she sputtered.

"You heard me. I want to kiss you."

"No-you-don't." Her words came out in a rush.

"Yes, I do." His were slow and deliberate. "I've wanted to since you walked into my study."

"No-you-haven't."

"Yes, I have."

"I'm-not-your-type."

"I don't have a type."

"Yes-you-do." She just couldn't get words out fast enough.

"And you've come to this conclusion because?"

"That blond woman's a caricature if I ever saw one."

He laughed softly.

The sound gave her strength to fight. She wasn't going to be toyed with.

"Listen, Farrell, I'm not here for your amusement. I'm sure you're used to women throwing themselves at you but I'm not . . ."

He reached up and brushed back another tendril of hair from her face. As he tucked it behind her ear, his hand lingered on the skin of her nape. It was the softest of touches, the pads of his fingers just brushing over her skin.

Her mouth went dry. She licked her lips.

"I love it when you do that." His voice had grown thick with a rasp that went straight to her spinal column. As his thumb stroked across her lower lip, she noticed that there was nothing teasing or lighthearted about his expression. He was deadly serious as his fingertips followed a strand of her hair down to her collarbone. Through the thin cotton of her T-shirt, his touch burned.

Carter knew she should pull away. She reminded herself that she was mad at him. That he was a cruel bas—

With a flash of movement, Nick plucked off her baseball cap, causing her hair to fall free around her face. His eyes, sparkling with need, roamed over her as if he had a thirst to quench and she were the stream. In response, her body answered with a wave of desire for him so strong it threatened to topple her willpower. As time slowed, and then stopped, she wasn't sure how to handle the surging fever or the pounding anticipation that was coursing through her.

So she did the only thing she could think of.

She kissed him first.

Grabbing the front of his shirt, crushing the collar with her hands, she pulled him down to her mouth. Fusing her lips against his, she felt his tongue enter her mouth in a rush and his arms go around her waist. Melding together, their bodies were a perfect fit, her curves and his hard angles coming together seamlessly. His arousal was thick against her, pressing into her softness.

His hands raked through her hair, his fingers digging deep against her skull. She couldn't keep a moan of pleasure from escaping as her body swelled. Gripping his powerful shoulders so hard she knew she must be leaving marks, she wanted more of him. All of him. And it didn't matter that they were on the side of a mountain.

But then suddenly, she heard the sharp sound of a tree branch snapping and a rhythmic beating of the air. They pulled apart, shaken. Turning toward the noise, they watched as a hawk carried itself on great wings up into the darkening sky.

Nick stepped back, and she heard his labored breathing over her own. His shirt was veering at a crazy angle from her having yanked at it, and she flushed, wondering what in the hell had caused her to act so aggressively.

For a long time, he stared at her as if trying to come to terms with the passion that had exploded between them. He seemed as surprised by it as she was.

"I think I should leave now," he said finally.

As he turned away, she whispered, "Yes. So do I."

Nick left the campsite in a hurry. In the gathering darkness, there was still enough light so that the way down the mountain was obvious. He didn't need the help, though. He knew every bend in the trail, every boulder he walked past. The familiarity was comforting.

Because he sure as hell didn't know what had gotten into him.

How they had gone from arguing to that rousing kiss was a mystery. One minute he'd been angry with the woman and the next he'd been overwhelmed by how incredibly beautiful she was with the setting sun on her face. Then she'd kissed him and the whole damn world had caught on fire.

That mind-blowing intensity was not what he had intended.

He'd been attracted to her from the start, true. But he'd had no idea what it would be like kissing her. He hadn't been prepared for the feel of her body against his, her breasts pressing into his chest, her lips returning his kisses with a passion as great as his own.

It had been a long time since anyone had kissed him like that. Hell, no one had kissed him like that. No woman had ever gripped the front of his shirt like it was a pull chain and whipped his head forward to her mouth. She'd had him under her complete control in that moment.

His body throbbed just thinking about it.

Nick sped up his descent. He was not a man who got overwhelmed easily, and he sure as hell didn't lose control of himself that often. Certainly, never with a woman. Until now. With the mere touch of her lips, he'd felt as if he'd been thrown into a volcano. Out of control, burning hot, he'd had no defenses against the onslaught.

Hadn't been interested in mounting any, either.

Gritting his teeth against his need, he decided it had to be a fluke of nature. He hadn't been with Candace in a while, what with his Japan trip and then the headache. That had to be the problem.

That just had to be it, dammit.

Coming to the end of the trail, Nick walked out into the meadow and then across the lawn.

Before heading inside, he paused and glanced back at the mountain. Close to the summit, he could see the glow of a fire. He felt a strong urge to go back up there, as if he'd forgotten something important.

Nick cursed out loud before making himself go into his home. He went directly to his study and, with grim determination, picked up the phone.

He knew just how to take care of any unhealthy preoccupation he might have with that archaeologist.

When Candace's voice came on the line, he spoke clearly. "It's me."

"Hello," she said, surprised.

"I want you to come back up this weekend."

"Darling," she breathed, "I would love to."

"Come Thursday night. Stay for however long, through the next week if you want."

She positively cooed with pleasure. "I'd stay the whole summer, if you'd let me."

Nick didn't reply. He was too occupied by a sensation of strangulation that had come over him.

This was wrong, he thought.

"Nick?" she purred.

"What?"

"Does this mean you've given some thought to our conversation about the future?"

Oh, Christ. What was he doing?

"Of course I've thought about it."

"I knew you'd come around."

"I've got to go," he said quickly.

"See you soon."

Candace's voice was happy as they hung up.

Nick knew damn well why she was so pleased and surprised. He generally kept her down in the city, wanting to save the lake house for those times when he could really unwind. And he sure as hell hadn't ever given her an open-ended invitation.

Nick went over to his wet bar, poured a scotch, tossed it back, and poured another.

With a groan, he thought of Cort. He needed to go and talk with the boy, to try to bridge the gap that had been widened once again. But what could he say that hadn't already been thrown back at him a hundred times?

"Bloody hell," he said aloud.

Gertie poked her head in the door. She was buttoning up a yellow sweater and had a handbag with a big sunflower on it hanging from one arm.

"I left you a plate of dinner in the fridge. And before you ask, Cort's up in his room. Took his food upstairs."

Nick sent a weary smile her way. "How did you know I was thinking about him?"

"He was upset when he came in and, whenever you're wondering what to do about the boy, you always look like this."

"What do I look like?"

"Like your tail's under a rocking chair."

He finished the scotch. "I should go up and talk with him."

"Good idea."

As he put down his glass, Nick changed the subject. "I've asked Candace to come up here for a while."

Gertie said nothing; she just took out a scarf from her pocket and knotted it over her hair.

"No reaction?"

"I'll make sure everything is ready."

He frowned.

"Don't give me that look," she said curtly. "I can't make you feel better about doing something you know doesn't sit right."

He ran his hand through his hair as she shut the door quietly behind her.

Thank God Gertie was the only one who could read him so well.

At least no one else would know the kind of mess his life was in.

5

THE NEXT morning, Carter woke up to the sound of an alarm clock. This was a surprise because she hadn't brought one with her.

It took her some time to figure out that the staccato beats were coming from a woodpecker. As the relentless tapping droned on, Carter wrapped her pillow around her head, thinking if the bird didn't give it a rest, it was going to cure her of being a nature lover.

A little later, she pushed the pillow aside and tried to read the face of her watch. If she calculated it right, she needed three more hours of sleep to make up for the insomnia that she'd had the night before.

Fat chance of that as long as Mr. Snare Drum kept it up.

She unzipped her sleeping bag, thrust her legs out, and got up. After she changed into blue jeans, a turtle-neck, and a fleece pullover, she stepped into her boots and emerged from the tent to confront the noisemaker.

"I'm up," she barked. "You satisfied?"

The bird, startled by the sound of her voice, took flight in a fit of self-preservation.

"What a peckerhead."

Going over to the mess tent, she made some coffee. After downing a mugful, she began to feel a little more like herself and started to plan the day. Having spent so many hours in the dark probing why she'd kissed a man she should dislike, it was great to think about work. God knew, her midnight machinations hadn't gotten her any closer to some relief. Maybe she just needed to focus on other things.

Like the job she was there to do.

Going into Papercut Central, she picked up the definitive biography of General Farnsworth, a copy of his journal, and a pad and pen. She paused to fill up a thermos with more coffee and headed out to the big view. As she stepped free from the trees, she was astounded at the sunrise that greeted her. Pink and yellow streaks filled the sky, and down below, the water's calm surface reflected all the glory.

Now, this was worth waking up for, she thought.

Choosing a boulder with a flat top, she climbed aboard and sat cross-legged. The pine-scented mountain air was crisp in her nose and the sun's rays were warm on her face. Comfortable, satiated, and much happier than she'd been in her tent, she cracked open the larger of the books. Drinking her coffee and occasionally looking up to monitor the sun's progress as it rose, she reread parts of the biography to refresh her memory of the general.

Farnsworth was the illegitimate son of a British nobleman and he'd joined the king's forces because he had few other prospects. Embroiled in the New World's military conflicts, he rose to power fast, using a combination of scare tactics, bribery, and deadly force against anyone who stood in his way. Within two years, after numerous victories in battle, he was given command of Fort Sagamore.

In the fall of 1776, just after taking up his new post at the fort, he got himself into serious trouble during a trip to the harbor of New York. While there to develop military strategy with other British leaders, he took a fancy to a young barmaid and apparently wouldn't take no for an answer. The girl's father, a colonist with a lot of friends, caught the general brutally raping the colonist's daughter. When Farnsworth tried to flee the city, he was captured by an angry mob. Demanding his freedom and maintaining his innocence, he claimed he'd been seduced by the girl, a defense that would have been far more believable if she hadn't been found under him, bloodied and in shock.

The colonial community demanded his death. The British, however, had no intention of losing such a valuable military asset, and they had the perfect bargaining chip. Just weeks earlier, at the conclusion of a bloody skirmish up around Boston, Nathaniel Walker had been taken prisoner. One of the great colonial leaders of the Revolution, he was, ironically, ensconced in the dungeon of Fort Sagamore. After tense negotiations, a deal was struck between the two sides. A trade would be made.

Two colonial soldiers, who'd been farmers before the fighting, were chosen to escort Farnsworth upstat, where the swap would occur. They were joined by the Reverend Jonathan Winship, a close friend of Nathaniel Walker's, and a spiritual as well as community leader in the colonies. It was the expectation that his influence would temper the minutemen's hatred for the man they were escorting and thus assure the prisoner arrived for the trade alive.

The Winship party, as the group was called, retained an Indian guide to navigate the way north to the environs around Fort Sagamore. In spite of the risks, it was conceivable that the party could have survived both the trip into the Adirondacks and the exchange, despite being so close to the enemy's seat of power. They were all smart men who knew their way around a musket loader, including the reverend, and they were being led by an Algonquin Indian who had been born in the area.

What tipped the scales in their disfavor was that they weren't traveling light.

Revolutionary supporters in the city had laden the three colonists with gold. It was to be used for purchasing food and furs for soldiers who would have to brave the fury of the coming winter at strategic outposts along the Hudson River waterways. The plan was for the Winship party to link up with a band of militia close to the south end of Lake Sagamore and transfer the gold there, well before they got close to Farnsworth's fort. The thought was that transporting the precious metal with Farnsworth was advantageous because the Winship party held a kind of diplomatic immunity as long as the British leader was under their care.

All along, Farnsworth had planned to have the party ambushed. He wasn't a man who played fair to begin with, and he was looking forward to starving Nathaniel Walker to death in his dungeon. While the negotiations between his side and the colonists had taken place in New York, it had been easy to send word to his fort as to when and where to attack the party in the mountains. His plan was to slaughter the Americans, slowly, and leave their bodies to feed the bobcats.

But, as soon as the party started out into the wilderness, he realized he had the opportunity to come out of captivity a far wealthier man. His escorts were carrying a heavy load in a small strongbox and he knew there was only one thing that could make a man's shoulders sag like that: gold, and lots of it. When the colonists lingered for a night at Lake Sagamore, and then headed out still burdened and decidedly more anxious the next day, he realized he had a prime chance to better his financial prospects.

To the frustration of historians, the curtains on the drama were closed at this point. Farnsworth was the only one who made it out of the mountains. Severely injured, he dragged himself back to Fort Sagamore and collapsed outside of its stone walls. The only thing he had with him was his journal but he hadn't been able or willing to detail the final chapter.

While Farnsworth lingered near death, Walker escaped and came back with reinforcements. His attack on the British stronghold would become known as one of the major battles of the War of Independence, and Farnsworth died during the assault, at Walker's hand. As the general was heaving his last breath, Walker demanded to know what had happened to the reverend and the other colonists. Farnsworth told Walker of a murderous attack made by Red Hawk, their guide. A search for the killer ensued but the Indian was never found.

And neither was the gold.

From that point, the story drifted down to the present with the popular consensus being that Red Hawk attacked the party. The Native American had never been seen or heard from again so it was assumed that he had been killed in the process and that the gold was likely somewhere in the vicinity of Fort Sagamore. Beginning in the late 1800s, as the Lake Sagamore region was settled more densely, people drawn to the lore and by greed began to get ideas. That was when the digging started. Farnsworth's descriptions of the clearing in which the party had camped were pretty clear, and folks started to traipse up and down mountains on either side of the lake, looking for the precise spot. Nick Farrell's mountain was one of the favorites, and the fact that there were rumors of a ghostly Indian spirit who wandered around its summit only increased his property's allure.

But after generations of searching, no one had found the gold.

And the rest, as they say, was history, Carter thought, closing the book.

Bringing the mug to her lips, she grimaced at the last inch of coffee, which was cold and bitter. She emptied the mug with a quick toss and got off her rock. Already the temperature had come up ten degrees and it was going to be a beautiful day.

Heading back to camp on the little foot trail, Carter heard someone or something coming through the woods behind her. She tensed up. It was hard to know what would be worse, a bear or Nick Farrell.

When she realized it was just Cort, she let out her breath.

"Hey!" he called out, jogging over. He had a baseball cap on his head but hair still managed to escape out of the sides at jagged intervals. He seemed endearingly young in the early light, his brash, self-confident expression at odds with the hint of shyness in his eyes.

As she greeted him, she watched his face glow with a warm intensity that made her uncomfortable. She knew she was going to have to talk with him soon about the infatuation.

"So are you ready to get to work?" Carter asked as they walked the rest of the way to camp together.

"Damn straight. How was your first night up here?"

"I'm still in one piece."

She led the way over to Papercut Central.

"When do we start digging?" Cort began bouncing up and down on the balls of his feet, shadowboxing.

"Not until my team gets here."

His face fell as he stilled. "I thought it would be this morning."

"There's a lot of work that has to happen before the first shovel meets the ground. I also want Buddy's read on the site before we get going."

"So what are we doing today?"

"We've got to map the place first. I understand if you want to skip this part and come back when the fun begins." She picked up an empty duffel bag and put it on the table.

Cort shrugged. "That's okay. It'll be cool. Besides, I need to get out of the house."

"Why?" Carter went over to a toolbox. She flipped the metal latches free and popped open the lid.

"She's coming back."

"Who is?"

"My uncle's girlfriend."

Carter's body stiffened involuntarily, and she had to force her hands to rummage around. She was looking for the hammers, she reminded herself.

"Did you meet her when you were here last time?" Cort asked. "She's right out of Greek mythology. Has her hair done at a snake farm as far as I can tell."

Carter fought to keep her voice level. "I'm sure you're exaggerating."

"Not really. She can make waiters cry at the Plaza Hotel in New York. Seen it myself."

"There must be some redeeming qualities in the woman for your uncle to be in love with her." She found the hammers, tucked them under her arm, and shut the lid.

"He isn't in love. Or if he is, I don't want to be in love like that. Things are horrible when Blondzilla's here, horrible before she comes, too. Gertie gets tense and Uncle Nick turns into a crab. Not that he's much fun to begin with. That's why I can't understand it. I don't know why he invited her up."

"Invited?" Carter crammed the tools into the duffel with more force than necessary.

"Last night, apparently. At least that's what I overheard Gertie saying to Ivan."

Carter stared at the kid blankly as her mind seized up. It was hard to face the fact that the first thing Nick had done after their kiss was go call his woman. That what had kept her up all night was of such little consequence to him. That she was just one more pair of lips.

Although, as she thought about it, she figured she must be the most naïve person on the planet. The man had been linked with some of the most beautiful women in the world. The whole kiss-at-sunset thing probably happened to him all the time.

"So are we going to head over to the site?" Cort prompted.

"Yeah, sure."

"Carter?"

She shook herself. "Sorry. Let's get the stuff we'll need together."

Even though she'd been doing digs for almost a decade, she had to think about what they were going to need to chart the site. She retrieved four balls of white twine, three dozen wooden stakes, and a measuring tape. In a backpack, she put a camera, scissors, mapping paper and pencils, rulers, and some bottled water.

"What are all the stakes for? We hunting vampires?"

Cort started shadowboxing again and then mimicking stabbing motions in the air.

Smiling and shaking her head at the kid, she resolved to push the subject of Nick Farrell from her mind. Feeling a little stronger for the decision, Carter slipped the backpack on and straightened her spine.

It was simply mind over matter.

Make that mind over man.

As she and Cort headed into the woods, each holding one handle of the duffel, she told him what they were in for. "We're going to create a grid pattern over the site."

"Why?"

"When we excavate a site, we ruin it. The artifacts are significant in and of themselves but equally important is their relationship to each other. A well-mapped site and conscientious documenting mean that any archaeologist can re-create the dig from the records and come to their own conclusions."

They stepped inside the ring of stones and she took out her camera, offering Cort the job of photographer. He began to shoot, the sound of the shutter clicking away.

"Give me more," he vamped at the rocks. "I need to feel the emotion. That's it. A little more pout."

After ten minutes, she called out, "Hey, take it easy on the film there, Helmut Lang. We don't want to run out on the first day. How about trading in that lens for a hammer?"

"For you, anything."

Flamboyantly, he sashayed over to her and accepted the duffel bag of stakes.

"Put one of these every three feet around the interior, as close to the rock walls as possible."

While he went to work, she sketched the outlines of the site and then began to string twine between opposite stakes so that a grid pattern was formed about a foot and a half above the ground. In the middle where it sagged, they reinforced it with more wooden pickets.

"It looks like a checkerboard," Cort commented when the job was done.

He watched as she drew the grid on the map she'd sketched and then ran numbers down the left margin and letters across the bottom.

"Now, whenever someone finds an artifact, it gets entered on the site map. I'll create another map which will measure depth. On that, we'll record how deep the finds are underground. In addition, everyone who digs will keep a daily log of what area they excavated and what they found. These daily logs will be extrapolated into the excavation log that encompasses all the diggers' work and also details what the condition of the weather was, what the soil was like, in what order things were found."

Cort rolled his eyes. "It's a wonder you ever find anything with all that recording."

"Cross-checking is important and so is having a minute attention to detail."

"I'll bet being compulsive helps, too."

Carter smiled.

After lunch, they prepared a spot outside the circle of boulders where dirt would be passed through screens to make sure even the smallest finds would be retained. Then they took a break and did some exploring around the mountain.

It was late in the afternoon when they returned to camp. Cort's eyes were looking off into the distance when he said good-bye. "So, I guess I'll see you tomorrow?"

"Sure. Thanks again for all your hard work."

With an awkward wave, the kid disappeared into the woods. She was hoping that the day spent at work with her had discouraged his crush. After laboring in the dirt, she felt sweaty and disheveled and trusted that her current condition wasn't the stuff to attract the opposite sex.

Especially not sixteen-year-old boys who probably believed magazine models looked like they did without the benefit of airbrushing.

Carter picked up her site map and a pad and went back to the rock that she'd started the day sitting on. She was ready to spend the next hour or so working on dig strategy.

Should they do a few test pits or just start the excavation? The site was insular enough—

Nick had invited his woman up.

Carter looked around, as if she'd been struck by a spitball.

Frowning, she went back to the map.

The site was insular enough, sufficiently compact, and had had at least one artifact retrieved, Winship's real cross. Test pits were probably not necessary to—

She was jealous.

"I am not!" The sound of her indignant voice startled a nearby chipmunk who squeaked and scurried under a log.

She put her head in her hands. She and Nick Farrell had nothing in common. She didn't even like him. He was arrogant, sarcastic—

He was a terrific kisser.

"Oh, for heaven's sake," she muttered.

Even when things had been unbearably bad after her mother's death, even in those bleak moments when her world was spinning and shifting on its axis, even then, she'd been able to find some relief in her work. Certainly enough for her to get by. But now, as she looked down at the map with its static grids and alphanumeric coding, she couldn't see farther than the surface of the paper.

"Dammit."

With her head full of images of Nick Farrell, she wanted to run but had nowhere to go. And she found it hard to believe she could feel so suffocated in the great outdoors.

Carter left her perch and returned to camp. The change in scenery didn't help, so she dropped the map, as well as any thought of getting some work done, and took a walk over to the brook. When she got there, she crouched down and dropped a hand into the water. It went numb under the cold rush.

Exactly what she was looking for.

Stripping off her clothes, she stepped into the river. The cold took her breath away even though the water only came up to her thighs. Reaching down, she cupped her hands and carried the chill to her body, desperate to cleanse herself of her thoughts and the heat they generated. As the water streamed down her body in icy paths, she enjoyed the stinging sensation that lingered. Even if her teeth chattered, at least she wasn't thinking about Nick Farrell for the moment.

Through the trees, Nick watched her with complete absorption. The only thing that kept him from going over to her was his iron will.

Which was feeling less ironlike with each passing minute.

He'd come up the mountain to talk about their kiss and had waited until Cort had returned home so they'd be alone. He'd intended to have a straight-out conversation about what had happened the night before and was determined to put the event in its proper context. In the intervening hours since he'd felt her against him, he'd managed to convince himself that it had been nothing more than an impulsive mistake and he wanted to make sure she knew how he felt.

It was a damn good plan. Until he got knocked off his soapbox.

When he'd arrived at camp, he'd found it empty. After he didn't find her at the dig site either, he decided to check and see if she'd gone swimming.

That was when he took a turn off the high road.

When Nick got to the river, he saw Carter bending down to put her hand in the water. Her expression was grave, the moment private, so he thought he'd go back and wait for her at camp. That was when she began to unbutton her shirt, and Nick's feet had started ignoring his commands to get moving.

Leaning against a tree for support, he watched as, inch by inch, she opened her shirt and then peeled it from her shoulders. As the shirt floated to the ground, she turned to kick off her shoes and that was when he saw her breasts. Draped in sunlight, they were taut and perfectly proportioned, her nipples pink and small. Below the curves, her stomach was flat and toned.

Nick's heart started pounding like a jackhammer and he felt himself harden.

He told himself he should turn around and go. He was no Peeping Tom, after all. And he'd seen women naked before. It wasn't as if he didn't know the inventory of female attributes well enough, but somehow the familiarity didn't register. As he looked at her, it was as if he was seeing a woman for the first time.

And he liked what he saw. So much so, he could feel the images burning into his memory.

Her hands went to the fly of her jeans and she released the buttons. Gripping the waistband, she slid them free from her long legs. Her hips were a gentle swell, her thighs strong and shapely. When her simple white panties followed, Nick gripped a tree limb so hard he cracked it in half.

Carter froze and then looked in the direction of the noise.

Nick ducked for cover.

He waited a moment and peered around the tree again.

Carter had turned back toward the river and was stretching her arms over her head, arching her back.

"Oh, sweet heaven," he whispered, clenching his jaw.

In the course of his life, he'd lusted after companies, real estate, works of art. Even a few women. Nothing, however, came close to the throbbing urgency he felt while looking at her. As she stepped into the water and splashed herself, her neck arched as she looked to the sky, he was as close to desperation as he'd ever been.

Nick wrenched himself away from the scene, afraid if he stayed any longer he'd give in to his driving impulses.

That he'd step free from his hiding place and reveal his desire. That he'd take her down onto the bank of the river and enter her body in one deep thrust.

Lost on his own mountain, he struggled to find the trail back down.

6

THE DAYS before Buddy and Ellie Swift's arrival were a blur for Carter, and she spent a lot of time with Cort, who came up every morning. When he seemed to stop staring at her with hopeful eyes, she began to think he'd gotten over his crush and relaxed in his company. Together, they pored over Farnsworth's journal, speculated on the route used by the Winship party, and talked about Indian lore.

The only difficult part of it all was enduring the updates on how things were going down at the mansion.

According to the news bulletins, Candace had turned up with enough luggage to stay for the whole summer. In contrast to other visits, Nick seemed to be spending a lot of time with her, a sacrifice for which the rest of the household was paying dearly. Evidently, extended proximity to the woman put him in an awful mood and yet he still seemed determined to be with her.

The turn of events made everyone uneasy. Everyone, that was, except for Candace. She was cheerful and bubbly, according to Cort, apparently thanks to seeing marriage in her future. And, as a result, she was growing bolder with her demands. The woman had even gone so far as to inform Gertie that she needed to start coming to work in a uniform, as all housekeepers should.

That had just about done it. Needless to say, Gertie

was still wearing her own clothes. Nick had flown off the handle when he'd heard what had happened and had been driven further into his dark temper. But Candace had stayed on.

Carter tried not to show how much she cared. She laughed off the comments or gave noncommittal responses, but inside she felt a burning curiosity over what Nick was up to with his woman. She hung on Cort's every word and at night she tossed and turned, wondering what she'd done to deserve getting sucked into Nick Farrell's world. She just couldn't get him out of her mind.

Though she soon had another problem to mull over.

At the end of a long workday, she and Cort were sitting against two boulders, looking at the lake view and talking about colonial munitions, when the boy cleared his throat and blurted, "I was thinking maybe you and I could go to a movie tonight. If you want."

Carter glanced up in surprise. He wasn't looking at her. Instead, he was drawing on the ground with a long stick.

"The theater in town has two screens," he mumbled. "There's an action movie in one. And I think the other is a love story. It would take about a half hour to drive there. Each way. But I have my learner's permit. It could be like a date. Sort of."

Carter had no idea how to respond. She'd clearly read him wrong and was stuck scrambling to find the right words to let him down.

"So what do you think?" he prompted. His body was strung tight and his awkward expression had begun to fade into a worried look.

Carter ached for the courage it had taken for him to ask. And because there was no way she wasn't about to hurt his feelings.

"Well, thank you. But I don't think that would be a good idea," she said gently.

"No?" he croaked.

"No. I—"

"Don't you like me?"

"Of course I do. But—"

Ivan McNutt appeared in the clearing. He looked grim.

"What is it?" she asked anxiously. Going by his expression, she'd have thought someone lost a limb.

"Your team's here."

"Oh. Thanks for letting me know."

He grunted and disappeared back down the trail.

Getting to her feet, Carter brushed pine needles off the seat of her pants while offering Cort an apologetic smile.

"I think we better get going before Ivan decides to drag out his twelve-gauge welcome wagon. Buddy faints easily."

The teenager got up, his eyes drifting over the trees and the camp carelessly.

"Cort, I—"

"Hey, just think about it, okay? Don't give me an answer right now."

"But—"

He cut off the discussion by starting down the trail. With a heavy heart, Carter followed him. She felt as though she hadn't handled the situation all that well and struggled for a way to bring up the subject again. Cort, however, was walking ahead of her with a stiff back and didn't seem to be in the mood for talking. She let him have some space.

When they cleared the woods, they saw a Range Rover had pulled up to the mansion. A group of people were gathered around it, staring intently at the front grille.

Getting closer, Carter picked out Nick and Candace, and she had to groan as she took in the other woman's clothes and hair. With a hand lying possessively on her man's forearm, Candace was dressed in a pale yellow sundress that played around her ankles in the summer breeze. Her hair was loosely curled, falling onto her shoulders in pretty blond waves, and her face, which was tilted toward Nick, was discreetly made up. She looked like a golden statue.

Carter felt like a grunge ball in comparison. She figured her hair was probably stringy and wished she knew whether she had any dirt on her face. Glancing down at her shorts and her hiking boots, she noted they all needed a good cleaning. She wished like hell she'd taken a moment to dress herself up a bit.

Or at least hit the stream with a washcloth.

Nick looked over in her direction. His expression was remote, but what was behind his eyes was so shocking, she almost faltered. Passion, hot and hungry, seemed to be reaching out to her. Abruptly, she was taken back to what it felt like to be in his arms, his lips moving against hers, his tongue sliding into her mouth—

Carter caught the tip of her boot in a chuckhole and almost fell on her face. Cort's swift reflexes were the only thing that kept her from hitting the ground, and she flushed, feeling even more sweaty and disheveled.

As she pulled herself together, Candace flashed a condescending look her way. Watching as the woman nestled even closer to Nick, Carter thought morosely that the two belonged together.

But to her surprise, his penetrating gaze never wavered from her. As she walked up to the group, his eyes watched her every movement. Even when Candace frowned and gave him a nudge of protest with her arm, he wasn't diverted.

Flustered, Carter looked past the pair, to her friend who was standing by his car. It was such a relief to see him.

"I never saw it coming," he was saying while shaking his head.

"What happened?" Carter asked.

Buddy Swift broke into his trademark grin. Wide and friendly, it showed the small space between his front teeth and one gold cap that covered a back molar. Although he was tall and wore conservative, wire-rimmed glasses, when he smiled he looked more like a student than a professor.

"It's my favorite partner in crime!" He wrapped his long arms around her.

"I'm your only partner," she said into his shoulder. "You refuse to work with anyone else."

"That's because they're all stiffs."

Carter risked a glance in Nick's direction and was struck by the disapproving way he was regarding Buddy.

She pulled back and focused on the front of the car. "Good Lord, Swift, what did you do? And where's Ellie?"

"I had an unexpected communion with an oak tree. She's having the expected communion with some indoor plumbing."

The hood of the Range Rover was mangled and the front bumper was hanging by a prayer. Inside, the air bags had deployed and were lying deflated over the seats. She reached out and pulled a tree branch from the grille.

"Are you all okay?"

"Yup. Just an unforeseen trip into the bushes that ended a little too emphatically." He put his hand on her shoulder. "But your concern touches my heart."

"Hey, I've got a lot vested in your health and safety. Not everyone makes coffee like you do."

As Carter playfully elbowed him in the ribs, she noticed that Nick and Cort wore matching expressions of displeasure. Candace, on the other hand, was looking a little more relaxed.

"C.C.!" Ellie exclaimed. As she shot out of the mansion's front door, strawberry blond hair streamed behind her. She was wearing a cornflower blue sundress and had a pair of coordinated Skechers on her feet.

Carter laughed and embraced the girl. "So I see your father's driving hasn't improved."

"It's his second accident since he bought the car. Two months ago."

"That other one was just a fender bender," Buddy said pointedly.

"Dad, you hit a police car."

"It was in the middle of the road."

"It was parked on the shoulder. With the lights going." The girl turned back to Carter. "But this time he had a good reason. He swerved to avoid killing a deer and fawn who had wandered into the road."

Buddy laughed. "I thought for a minute we were going to end up as the Swift Family Robinson in the Adirondacks. I was prepared to build Ellie a house in the trees and live off boiled bark until we were rescued."

His daughter rolled her eyes.

Nick stepped forward, breaking the contact with Candace.

"You may want Ivan to take a look at it," he interjected darkly. "No telling what it's leaking. We can have it towed into town if we have to."

There was a cautious and assessing light in Buddy's eyes as he looked at the taller man. "Thanks. I'd appreciate any help you have to offer."

Carter turned to introduce the Swifts to Cort. "The demolition expert is Buddy, my partner. And this is his daughter, Ellie."

"Hi," the girl said, raising her hand and offering a tentative smile.

Cort nodded in her general direction. "There's a lot of stuff in this car. Should I get the four-wheeler?"

"That would be great."

She watched as he stalked off, his expression no more affable than his uncle's. With all the complicated emotions swirling in the summer air, she couldn't wait to get back to camp.

"I think you all should come to dinner tonight," Nick announced abruptly.

Carter swallowed a grimace.

"Yes, do come down," Candace said, stepping in close to Nick again.

"That'd be great," Buddy said happily. "Camp food is

okay but it gets old real quick. Might as well start out on a high note."

When Carter sent him a glare, he responded with a shrug.

"Darling," Candace crooned. "Shall we take that swim now?"

Nick nodded with distraction. His eyes were boring into Carter.

"I'll see you tonight," he said to her.

As soon as the pair were out of earshot, she hissed, "Nice move, Buddy."

"What?"

"Don't *what* me. You know exactly what you've done." When he feigned innocence, she grumbled, "And don't give me that look."

"What look?"

"That I-didn't-just-stir-up-trouble look."

"Who said there was trouble to stir? I didn't." But the smile he gave her was lopsided. "Although while we're on the subject, what's up between you and Farrell?"

She felt the blood drain out of her face and prayed that he didn't catch the reaction. "Nothing is up."

"That man looks at you like he's half-starved—"

"He does not! And you better enjoy this dinner because it's the only one we're having in that house."

"I'm thinking I will. Even if the food sucks, I'll bet you could pull up a chair and grab some popcorn for all the theatrics."

Carter hip-checked him. "You're officially being removed as the camp's social director."

"Does this mean I get to be head nurse instead?"

"Yes, and you can start by bandaging your own butt as soon as I'm finished kicking it."

He was still smiling when Cort pulled up beside the car in the four-wheeler.

"Hey, that's cool," Ellie said, looking at the machine. "Can I drive it sometime?"

Cort shrugged and turned away carelessly, missing the girl's hurt look.

With four pairs of hands, the back of the Rover was unpacked in short order, and Cort ran a couple of loads up the mountain. While he was on his last trip, Ellie changed into shorts and then Carter led the way to camp.

"Nice setup," Buddy said as he looked over the place. "Papercut Central is back in working order, I see."

"And ready for business."

"Good thing I packed all those Band-Aids."

When Cort was finished moving the Swifts' things, he gave the group a stiff nod and disappeared. Ellie watched him go and then said she was going to look for firewood.

"That boy takes after his father," Buddy commented as he and Carter faced the daunting mountain of bags. "Not exactly the warm and friendly type."

"He's Nick's nephew." Carter helped him pull out two tent rolls from the bottom of the pile. "He's a good kid but whenever the two of them are together he's different. I hope he and Ellie can become friends."

While Buddy smoothed the tent out flat on the ground, she got a hammer and started securing the corners with stakes.

"So, seriously, what's going on with Farrell?"

Carter missed what she was aiming for and nailed her thumb a good one. The curse that followed wasn't only because of her bad aim.

"You okay?" Buddy asked.

She was far from okay but nodded, raised the hammer again, and this time made sure her targeting was better. When the stake was in and she began wrapping cord around it, Buddy repeated the question.

She shot him a look. "Farrell owns this mountain and he's tolerating our presence. End of story."

"You sure about that? When I put my arms around you, I think that man's eyes burned a hole in my skull."

"Then it matches the ones you already have."

"Who's the blonde?"

Carter stopped what she was doing. "Since when did you get into sociology? I don't remember your ever being so interested in people before."

"I've never seen you attracted to someone before."

The bald statement made Carter feel like she'd bashed her thumb again. "What are you talking about?"

"Am I wrong?"

"Of course you're wrong!"

"What are you torturing C.C. about?" Ellie asked as she emerged from the woods. Her arms were filled with twigs and branches.

"Tall, dark, and hostile down there," her father replied.

"Oh, him." Ellie dumped the load in the vicinity of the fire pit. "He seems a little scary."

Mercifully, the subject was dropped when Ellie asked about the site. As Carter gave them an update about what she'd accomplished so far, the three finished setting up the new tents and then headed to the circle of stones. With the sun setting fast, there was only time for a cursory review before they had to head down the mountain. On the descent, Ellie and her father had a bounce to their steps.

Carter felt like she was dragging an anchor after her.

She couldn't believe she was about to spend the evening with a sixteen-year-old who had a crush on her, a man she'd kissed on a regrettable impulse, and the latter's socialite girlfriend whose nickname was Blondzilla.

Buddy was right. It was the stuff of a Monday Night Movie.

But the real problem was less the company she'd be in than the truth she couldn't escape. Seeing Nick Farrell again had been like getting whipped with a high-voltage wire.

She had to get a grip if she was going to make it through the meal. Desperate for some reasonable explanation for her feelings, she reminded herself that she hadn't had a date in God only knew how many years. Surely that had to count for something. The night she had kissed Nick had been the first time she'd kissed someone in ages. Of course she was going to feel something when she saw him again. It was called embarrassment.

Right?

And as for dinner, the minute it was over, she was going to hightail it up the mountain and not come down again until she could control herself.

It was only one meal. How long could it last?

Only a bloody lifetime, Carter thought later as she checked her watch.

The others around the dining room table had just polished off a strawberry mousse. She hadn't touched hers, however, just as she'd only picked at the rack of lamb. Her stomach had been in knots as soon as she'd stepped through the front door.

The evening had been grueling. Nick continued to give her most of his attention. He spent the remaining time shooting Buddy cold looks. At the head of the table, Candace chafed at the lack of interest being thrown her way and made increasingly obvious and awkward attempts to get it. The kids didn't seem to be enjoying themselves, either. Cort was stone-faced and silent and Ellie was quiet through the ordeal.

"I simply adore Paris," Candace was saying. "Don't you remember, darling, that wonderful weekend we spent there?"

Nick shrugged and took a drink from the glass of scotch he'd brought with him to the table. His eyes flashed to Carter and she looked away from him.

"We so enjoyed the shopping, didn't we? Darling?"

"Yes, you did," Nick countered.

Across the way, Ellie was nodding off in her chair. Buddy cleared his throat and dropped his napkin. When Carter glanced over, he nodded for her to lean down with him.

"We've got to get out of here," he whispered when their heads were together. "My daughter's melting."

"Right."

As they sat back up, Carter interrupted another one of Candace's earnest attempts at engaging Nick in conversation. "Thanks for a lovely evening but I think it's time we all headed back up the mountain."

"You're right, C.C.," Buddy chimed in. "We've got an early start planned for the morning and it's been a long day."

"I'd like to see you in my study," Nick said authoritatively as he got to his feet.

Carter was already out of her chair and halfway to the door when she realized no one was following her. Turning around, she saw all eyes were pointed in her direction. Nick had been talking to her.

"Can it wait until tomorrow?" she asked.

"No."

Candace inserted herself in Nick's line of vision. "Darling, do wait until the morning. You wouldn't want to keep me waiting, would you?"

Carter felt a pang of jealousy and waited for Nick to acknowledge the offer being pressed against his side. He didn't.

"My study," he repeated. "Now."

Carter frowned, angry at him and herself. Jealousy was not something she had any right to and she resented like hell his domineering attitude.

"Fine." Anger seeped into her voice and she struggled to get in touch with the emotion, knowing it would save her.

"We'll wait for you," Buddy offered.

"That's okay. I'll meet you up there."

Carter followed Nick out of the room, her heart beating triple time.

When they got to his study, Nick shut the door and poured himself another scotch over ice. Leaning against the bar with one hand planted firmly on the marble, he swirled the drink around but remained quiet. He was about to lose it and knew he needed a minute to calm the hell down.

Carter had been a source of torture from the moment

she'd walked into his house with the others. He'd spent the evening watching the candlelight play over her skin and seeing different expressions flare in her face. He liked the way she fidgeted in her seat and incessantly crossed and uncrossed her legs. She was so alive, so vibrant, that he just wanted to reach out and touch her. Among other things.

Thanks to his fantasies, he'd been in a state of rigid arousal for most of the evening.

All of his pent-up need made the very air Buddy Swift breathed aggravating. The bastard had been shooting Carter looks all night long, his eyes soft behind those stupid gold-rimmed glasses, his expression tender like he couldn't wait until they were alone. Nick wanted to toss the guy out on his ass.

Even worse to watch was Carter's response to the man. Every once in a while, she'd send her partner a glowing smile. It was obvious there was something going on between the two, and he couldn't believe they were carrying on in front of Swift's daughter.

By the time the mousse had arrived, Nick was seething and infuriated with himself for letting them sit side by side. He was also frustrated as hell that she was with that archaeologist instead of him.

"So what do you want?" Carter asked him.

He looked over his shoulder at her. Her hands were on her hips, a stance that pulled her shirt tightly across her breasts. He was instantly distracted by the memory of what they had looked like doused in sunlight and river water.

"I can't believe you're acting this way," he said gruffly.

"Excuse me?" Her expression was of total surprise.

She was a hell of an actress.

"You and that . . . Swift man." He had another word he'd rather have used. Quite a few of them, actually.

"What are you talking about?"

"You women," he derided, tossing the drink back and putting the glass down with a crack. He turned around. "You're all the same."

He watched as her anger grew. Her cheeks got a lovely brush of red across them and her mouth parted. He became consumed with the need to stroke her bottom lip with his tongue.

"Thank God that's not true," she huffed. "That blonde in there and I have nothing in common."

"No? She's had affairs with married men, too." Carter's expression of disbelief was so close to genuine, he laughed out loud. "Although I don't recall she's ever had the temerity to screw someone in front of his daughter."

"You think Buddy and I—"

"You're actually going to deny it?"

She shook her head with admirable conviction. "Where the hell did you get the idea we were—"

"Oh, I'm sorry," he bit out sharply. "I suppose people who grope under the dinner table are just trading napkins."

"What? I— He . . . Oh, that."

"Yes, *that*. And don't roll your eyes at me like it was nothing."

"I'll go one even further," Carter said, heading for the door and opening it. "I'm going to pretend this conversation never happened."

"Can't handle someone calling you on your actions?"

She wheeled around, her luxurious black hair swinging across her shoulders. Her face was flush with indignant rage, her eyes sparkling with hostility.

God, he wanted her.

"You are hardly one to talk," she bit out.

"I'm not complicit in adultery."

Carter marched back toward him. "Considering how you kissed me the other night, you might want to drop the holier-than-thou act. You're no poster child for monogamy."

"You kissed me first."

A hiss sounded from behind them. They turned and looked in the direction it came from.

Cort stood aghast in the doorway of the study. He

turned and looked at Nick with a combination of rage and pain.

"You kissed her?"

"Now, hold on a minute . . ." Nick raised a hand.

"I can't believe you," Cort spat. "Do you have to take everything away from me?"

In a flash, he tore off down the hall.

As Nick rushed out of the study and watched Cort run upstairs, he realized the kid must have a crush on Carter. He wasn't sure how it had happened but that didn't matter.

His vision receded to a pinpoint of light as irrational anger went through him.

In a rage, he turned on Carter, who'd followed him out into the hall. "I don't care what you do to that other family but I'm not going to let you ruin mine."

"What?" she asked, astounded.

"Stay the hell away from Cort," Nick growled. "If you want fun and games, pick on someone your own size. I can take it. He can't."

Carter stuttered in disbelief and then blurted out, "Are you out of your mind? I never intended for him—"

"What the hell did you think was going to happen?" Nick's eyes narrowed on her. "Dancing around in those damn shorts, flashing your legs, wearing those godforsaken little T-shirts. He's too young to know the difference between attraction and love, although you've just taught him a damn good lesson. What else were you planning on teaching him?"

Carter's pupils dilated. She raised her hand and slapped him across the face. His cheek stung as blood rushed to the skin.

"How dare you?" she snapped. "He's just a boy."

"Yeah, and thanks to you, he's taken one more step out of childhood. He's had his heart broken."

Nick was headed for the stairs, intent on finding his nephew, when she called out indignantly, "Assume what you will about my partner but I never encouraged Cort."

He wheeled around. "I don't think you know how not

to attract men. Magnetic north draws the compass arrow. It's a goddamn fact of nature."

His eyes roamed over her body, and he didn't bother to hide his lust for her.

"Don't look at me like that," she said, crossing her arms over her chest.

"So is that the kind of woman you are?" Nick laughed harshly. "It's all kicks and giggles until someone takes you up on your offer?"

"I'm not offering you a thing."

"That wasn't what it felt like the other night. I could have taken you, right then and there."

Her eyes narrowed with derision. "You vastly overestimate your appeal."

Nick moved so fast, she didn't have time to run away from him. Grabbing her hard around the waist, he dragged her against him and put his lips on hers in a blaze of frustration and hunger. She fought against him, struggling in his arms, until suddenly she opened her mouth and let him in, kissing him back with equal fury. With a groan of need rising from his throat, he buried his hands deeply in her hair and pressed her back against the wall. Her body was all delicious curves, and he moved himself against her, driven to be inside of her.

With disordered thoughts, he began to plot how they could make it into his study with their bodies still entwined. Behind his closed door, they could shed their clothes and fall onto his couch. He could cover her bare skin with his mouth, delve into her softest parts, make her moan under him.

And he *would* make her moan, he vowed. Until she forgot everything but him. Everyone but him.

"Let's get out of the hall," he said roughly, against her neck. "We can't do this here."

He felt her stiffen and then her hands pushed hard against his shoulders.

"Stop it," she told him breathlessly. "Stop this now."

He pulled away with grave reluctance.

When she finally spoke, her voice was dead.

"As long as you can kiss me like that with your woman in the next room, don't you ever talk to me of fidelity again."

She took off in a hurry, fleeing from him. From his house. From his fantasy of how the evening should have ended.

Nick swore out loud, planting his fist into the wall with a thunderous noise.

7

THE NEXT morning, Carter woke up to the smell of pancakes and coffee. Fumbling out of her tent, she took in with gratitude the sight of Buddy working a pan over the hot plate. After a night spent with an empty stomach and a head bloated by images that made her cringe, a big breakfast was just what she needed to start the day.

She shrugged her Windbreaker on and went over to the mess tent. "You're a saint—you know that?"

"Might as well make myself useful," he grumbled. "No sense trying to sleep."

"Tough night on the ground?" Carter helped herself to some coffee. As she poured, steam rose up from the mug into the cool air.

"You didn't hear that racket?"

She shook her head, taking a test sip. It was good and strong.

"Some ridiculous woodpecker was drilling for oil in the bedrock. Damn thing went on forever until I threatened to have him taxidermied and mounted on a wall."

"I must be getting used to him by now."

Ellie appeared, and Buddy put three plates of pancakes on the table. "Eat up, folks. It's not as fancy as what we had last night, but the company's bound to be more palatable."

"Dinner was weird," the girl said as they sat down.

"No one's very happy in that house. They didn't seem to like each other. Or us."

Carter's and Buddy's eyes met across the table.

"We don't have to go there again," her father said.

"Whatever."

They finished the rest of the meal in silence. While they were cleaning up, Buddy asked, "So what did Farrell want with you last night?"

Carter shot for a breezy reply and hoped he bought it. "Nothing."

"Nothing?"

"Well, something. Sort of. Not really."

She shook her head, thinking she really should keep to one-word responses when it came to Nick Farrell.

"He's not pulling the plug on us, is he?"

"I don't think so." But anxiety pegged her in the chest.

She hadn't considered the possibility he might kick them off the mountain. She'd been too busy thinking about how things had gone from her slapping the man in the face to . . . what had happened after that. All night long, she'd stared up at the nylon roof over her head, trying to sort it all out. Nothing was much clearer when the sun had finally come up, and now she had something else to worry about. What if all the fighting between them endangered the dig?

"So what did you talk about?" Buddy prompted, his eyes curious behind his glasses. "The guy must have had something serious on his mind. He was looking bound and determined when you two left."

"It was nothing important." She looked over at Ellie. "You ready to get to work?"

Carter knew Buddy wasn't fooled, but she was grateful he let the subject drop as the three headed over to the site. When they stepped inside the circle of stones, she heard him let out a long whistle.

"I reread Farnsworth's journal last night. For a sadist of the first order, he certainly had an eye for accurate description. Man, if this isn't the place, I don't know what is."

"I don't think we need to do test pits. Do you?" Carter was referring to the practice of random digging that was used to determine where artifacts might be concentrated within a given area.

"Nah. After reading through the primary source last night, I'd bet my firstborn this is where it all happened."

Ellie shot him a stern look. "One of these days you're going to lose and I'm going to end up someone else's daughter. Although now that I think about it . . ."

Buddy gave the girl's ponytail an affectionate tug.

"Let's fan out along the northern side and work our way south," Carter suggested. Within ten minutes, they'd retrieved tools and buckets and positioned themselves at regular intervals in the grid, ready to work.

Getting down on her haunches, Carter sifted through layers of pine needles until she got to what passed for top-soil on the mountain. Taking her hand shovel, she pushed it into the ground. The familiar scent of dirt rose up into her nose, and she started ladling earth into the bucket she'd put beside her. As soon as it was full, she would take it outside the circle and sift the contents through the screen for fragments. She knew these regular interruptions in digging, when she could stand up and stretch, would be appreciated as the day wore on.

They worked steadily on their hands and knees as the sun rose higher in a clear sky, breaking only for water and a quick lunch. Over the course of the day, Ellie found a couple of arrowheads and Buddy dug up some old animal bones. As the hours passed, Carter kept hoping Cort would show up, but he didn't.

Around three in the afternoon, she made up an excuse about needing something from her car and went down the mountain to find him. As she came out of the woods and walked through the meadow, she heard noises in the garage and followed the sounds of metallic clanking inside. Ivan was under Buddy's Range Rover, tools fanned out around him. The man was groping in the general vicinity of a screwdriver.

"You need that Phillips head?" she asked.

The grunt could have meant anything so she put the tool in his hand and stepped back. She didn't expect a thank-you and was surprised when the next snort sounded a little like one.

"I'm looking for Cort. You know where he is?"

After a resounding *clunk,* Ivan slid himself out from under the car. Oil was all over him, and his dark eyes were as sharp as one of the arrowheads Ellie had found on the mountain.

"Boy's probably down at the boathouse."

"Thanks."

"Hey," he called out as she turned away. "If anything bothers you up there, you let me know. I'll take care of it."

Carter was surprised at the offer. "That's nice of—"

"Been told I have to look after you," he said and then slid back under the car.

She thanked the woodsman again and walked back into the sunshine, relieved to be out of his way. The fact that taking care of them didn't seem to appeal to him wasn't surprising. What interested her was that Nick had thought about their safety.

Then again, maybe he just didn't want another party of people lost on his mountain.

Crossing the lawn and heading to the lake, she gave the mansion a wide berth, hoping not to run into any of its inhabitants. As she went past, it was hard to believe so much conflict resided inside such a peaceful-looking place. The home seemed like such a beautiful haven with its white siding gleaming in the sunshine, its porches full of inviting wicker chairs, its window boxes overflowing with flowers.

But then, Pandora's box had looked great from the outside, too.

Down at the water's edge, she stepped off the grass and onto the wooden dock that ran around the boathouse. As there were no immediate signs of Cort, she went inside. There were two boats tied in the slips. One was an antique wooden craft and next to it was a flashy ski boat. They were an incongruous pair, an opera singer tethered next to a rock star.

Still, Cort was nowhere to be found. She turned around to leave, resigned to checking at the mansion, when she heard a whistle that froze her in her tracks.

"It can't be," she murmured. But she heard it again and winced as memories came back to her. She saw her father as clearly as if he were standing before her, and the remnants of childhood joy burned in her chest.

Trains. Toy trains. They'd been a passion she'd shared with him.

As the whistle drifted down again, she noticed a narrow set of stairs in the back corner of the boathouse. When she reached the top of them, she saw that the whole second floor was devoted to a model train set. A model train kingdom, really. Stretching out on a raised platform that snaked through the room, the setup was one of the biggest she'd ever seen, rivaling even the one she and her father had put together so many years ago.

Cort was at the controls and, through the haze of her memories, she focused on him.

"This is quite an accomplishment."

He looked up in surprise and flushed. "What are you doing here?"

"I came to find you."

Cort fingered the throttle, sending the red engine and its trail of boxcars cruising faster along the tracks. The sound of tiny wheels clicking filled the room.

"I was hoping you'd come up this morning. We've started digging."

The train went speeding through the different regions of its world. The mining town, the mail stop, a grain filling station.

"I'm busy." Cort was standing at stiff attention, which was at odds with his floppy clothes. His shorts were riding low on his hips and he was wearing an oversized University of Kentucky basketball jersey. She noticed his hair wasn't as high or as spiky as it usually was.

In the tense pause that followed, the train disappeared under a mountain range and reappeared on the far side.

"Cort, I'm really sorry I hurt your feelings."

The boy powered up the engine, making the clattering even louder. "It's cool. Everything's fine."

"It doesn't feel fine to me."

He stayed silent.

"Cort—"

"I'm totally cool." He brought the train to a halt in front of him. "Will you just go?"

"You have to understand—"

He cut her off in an angry rush.

"All I know is that I liked you and I wanted to be with you and my uncle got in the way." He finally met her eyes. "And why him? Why did it have to be him? God, I'm so tired of having everything be about him. He makes me stay up here all summer, won't let me be with my friends, and then he takes you away, too."

"I haven't gone anywhere."

"Yeah, well, you aren't going anywhere with me, are you?" There was a wealth of bitterness in his voice.

"I'm too old for you."

"But you're just the right age for him?"

Carter took a deep breath. "I am not with your uncle."

"But you kissed him."

"Cort, I . . ." She shook her head in frustration. It was hard to find the right words about something she wasn't too clear on herself.

"Doesn't it bother you that he has a girlfriend?" His clear gray eyes, which were so like Nick's, challenged her.

"This isn't about your uncle. Someday, you'll understand—"

"Spare me, okay? I get enough of that 'when you grow up' crap from him."

"You just have a crush on me. It's not—"

"How do you know what I'm feeling!" Cort's hand slashed through the air with frustration. "Everyone's always so busy telling me what I feel, what to do, where to go. For once, why can't you people just accept me?"

Faced with his agitation, Carter wasn't sure where the lines of helping and hurting were.

"How long have you known me?" she finally asked.

"A week," he grumbled.

"Try five days, tops. Do you know what my favorite color is?"

"No, but why is that—"

"What about my religion?"

Frowning, he shrugged.

"How about where I come from, what my family's like, whether I like sushi or Tex-Mex? Do you know whether I'm a neat freak or a slob?"

With a defiant look, he said, "I know you're pretty and smart and have a good sense of humor. I know I like being with you. What else is there?"

Carter bit back a groan.

If only all men were so simple and clear with their affections.

"I'm flattered. I really am." She cautiously walked over to him. "But I hate to break this to you—I'm no saint. You haven't seen me when I'm cranky from stress, when I swear at other drivers behind the wheel, when I cry at old movies and Hallmark cards. You don't know me when I'm angry or depressed. I'd like to tell you that believing I'm pretty and smart is enough but it's not."

"Don't you like me?" The words were spoken softly and his face contracted as if he was preparing himself for a hit.

"Of course I do," she said gently. "But not romantically."

"But you like my uncle like that."

Carter couldn't answer him. She didn't want to lie, couldn't confront the truth.

"I'd like us to be friends," she offered.

"Yeah, sure."

"I mean it. I like spending time with you, too. And I'd like your help on the dig. I need your help."

"You have those other two."

"There's a lot of area to cover."

There was a pause.

"You really have started digging?" He looked up.

She nodded.

"Found anything?"

"Ellie dug up some arrowheads."

Cort started to fiddle with the controls, making the train go forward and backward.

"Look, we really could use an extra set of hands up there. Will you come join us?"

He shrugged. "Maybe. But I gotta work on my trains right now."

"Well, I hope we'll see you tomorrow."

"Yeah."

Carter left with an ache in her chest. She remembered getting her heart broken for the first time by a teacher she'd had a crush on. He'd let her down as gently as he could, but the sting of the rejection had been a terrible blow. It had never dawned on her that one day she'd be on the other side of that pain.

The experience from this end wasn't much easier, she thought, as she walked out onto the lawn.

She was passing the mansion, her head low and filled with heavy thoughts, when Candace appeared in front of her. The woman was wearing a short print dress that was bright pink and green—a preppy getup that teetered on being a Rorschach test. With a string of pearls and matching earrings, she looked like she belonged at a country club sipping iced tea and playing bridge.

Well, except for the expression on her face. That made Carter think of pro wrestling.

Candace jabbed the air with her forefinger. "I don't know what kind of game you're playing, but I won't let you come between me and Nick."

Carter took a deep breath. "I don't know what you are talking about."

She tried to step around the woman, thinking that she should have stayed farther away from the house.

Hell, she'd have taken a trip through another zip code if it meant avoiding this kind of confrontation.

"Don't play dumb with me." Candace's eyes were little slits in her pretty face. "I am going to be the first and *only* wife of Nick Farrell. If you think you stand a chance of getting in my way, you're in for a nasty surprise."

The woman paused, waiting for a response.

"Well, thanks for the warning," Carter said dryly.

Candace seemed momentarily nonplussed. "I don't think you understand. Nick loves me. You may be able to flirt with him across a table, but I'm sleeping in his bed."

Jealousy coursed through Carter. It was the kind of unconscious reaction that told her so much about what she was feeling. And it was one more reason she could have done without the altercation.

Before she could say anything, a screen door slapped shut and Nick rounded the corner. Candace's demeanor changed on a dime.

"Are we going for that sail?" she asked him serenely.

Nick looked through the blonde. "I just spoke with Ivan, who's called a tow truck. Swift's car needs to go into town."

Carter managed to reply evenly, "Thanks. I'll let him know."

She refused to meet his eyes. She wasn't proud of having slapped him the night before but was unsure how she could apologize without backing down from her stance. And she sure as hell wasn't going to get into it with him in front of Candace.

It was a relief to turn away from them.

"By the way," Nick called out, "I'll be coming up to check and see how things are going later."

"Don't hurry," she muttered, thinking that her life was suddenly overflowing with people and conflicts and drama. Where had all those calm hours spent with books and papers gone?

"What did you say?"

"Don't worry. Everything's fine."

*   *   *

Buddy and Ellie were on their hands and knees together when Carter stepped into the circle.

"Just in time!" her partner said, with a delighted grin.

"For what?"

"The grand unearthing."

Carter surged forward. "What'd you get?"

"It's hard to ID finds in the field, as you know," he said cautiously, "but offhand, I think it's the carburetor from a 'fifty-six T-bird."

Carter stopped short. "You're kidding me."

"Nope." He reached into the earth and pulled out a hunk of metal. "I never kid about auto supplies."

"What's it doing here?" Ellie asked as Carter laughed out loud.

Buddy turned the find over in his hands. "Some people have an odd idea of what needs to be interred. I once dug up a roasting pan that had a eulogy inside. A whole page extolling baked hams and turkeys."

"Ewww. That's creepy."

"Yeah, considering your mom's still using it."

"She is not!"

"Is too. With that kind of product endorsement, she had to try it."

Ellie muttered, "Why do you tell me these things?"

Considering the scene she'd just been through with Candace, Carter was so happy to be back around her friends and her work, she had an urge to hug both of the Swifts.

She smiled and put a casual hand on Ellie's shoulder. "I hate to break up this Martha Stewart meets *Night of the Living Dead* moment but the Range Rover is about to be towed into the nether regions of the Adirondacks."

Buddy got to his feet, looking resigned. "Ivan the Terrible couldn't fix it?"

"Guess not."

"Well, I better get down there." Buddy looked at his daughter. "You coming?"

"Aye, Captain."

After the two left, Carter settled down to work on her area, hoping to get in another two hours of digging before it got too dark. She found her mind turning back to her run-in with Candace.

Carter had never played the other woman before. Not that she was involved with Nick, she reminded herself. But she'd never been on the receiving end of another woman's aggressive turf protection. It wasn't a position she relished.

After all, she wanted Nick all to herself.

She groaned at the thought.

While she was fervently trying to talk herself out of such idiocy, her shovel hit something hard. Putting the tool aside, and thankful for the distraction, she peered into the dirt and was pleasantly surprised to see an arrowhead. She picked it up and was turning it over in her hands when she heard someone approach through the woods.

Nick's sail with Candace must have been cut short, she thought, tensing.

At least she was semiprepared for his arrival. On the trip up the mountain, she'd composed two speeches. The first was all about how they were going to keep things on a professional level from now on. No more arguing, no more clashes. No more kisses. What she had to say on this point was short and direct, although it made her stomach clench like a fist.

The other speech was longer and easier. She'd mentally reviewed what she wanted to accomplish in the next week and was prepared to bore him with technicalities. She figured this would discourage frequent updates. Her spiel would last about fifteen minutes and then, if she was lucky, she could get him to leave.

Bracing herself, she started talking before he even came through the boulders.

"About what happened last night—"

But it was Conrad Lyst, not Nick, who entered the circle of stones.

She fell silent and felt a needling sense of fear as she

realized how alone she was on the mountain. She hoped the Swifts would be back soon.

Lyst moved fluidly across the ground toward her. On someone else, the gait might have been seen as elegant. Considering the antagonistic way he was looking at her, however, it came across as sinister. His eyes, small and dark in his pale face, were predatory.

She shuddered.

"I suppose some congratulations are in order." He gestured around the dig site.

"What are you doing here?" She rose to her feet.

"I've come to see how the competition is getting along." When he settled against one of the boulders, she moved away.

"All your little string boxes. So neat and orderly," he murmured. "Has anything come of your efforts?"

"I think you better go." She was impressed with how strong her voice sounded.

"You seem rather eager to be rid of me. How about some collegial respect?"

Show me a colleague, then maybe I'll share a little, Carter thought.

"So I'm dying to know," he said in a slick voice, "how far did you have to go to get Farrell's permission to dig?"

The implication behind his words made her feel dirty, and she didn't like the drift of the conversation. Instinct told her to start looking for an escape route.

Where was Buddy when she needed him?

Lyst's eyes drifted over her body. "You know, I've always thought you were a woman with hidden talents. I wasn't able to get so much as an audience with the great Farrell much less permission to ply his soil, but here you are."

Carter took a step back, wanting to position herself so she was near an opening in the stones. From his casual perch, he tracked her movements.

"Okay, you're not willing to go into the specifics. I can understand that. Wouldn't want to kiss and tell. But have you found anything?" His false smile made his eyes seem more hostile.

"No."

He shrugged. "No matter. With your expertise, I'm sure it won't be long before you're pulling that gold out of the ground."

She shrugged and kept silent.

"You're awful quiet," he murmured. "Cat got your tongue?"

"I'm just waiting for you to leave."

Lyst looked up to the sky as if pondering a mathematical theory.

"You want me to go." Abruptly, his eyes snapped back to her. "I find the cross that brought you here, to this place where a fortune may be hidden in the earth, and all you can do is tell me to go."

"That cross was a fake."

In a flash of movement, he lunged at her. She turned and tried to escape but he grabbed her arm. Carter struggled, feeling his fingers digging into her skin, but not only was he faster than she'd thought; he was stronger, too. Panic, thick and suffocating, began to clog her throat.

"Without the cross," he snarled, "that bitch at the Hall Foundation would never have called you. You didn't even know about this place until I went to her."

He snapped her around to face him and she felt his breath on her face, hot and damp. "You may be planting shovels in the ground but this dig is mine."

"Let go of me!"

Lyst reached up and grabbed a fistful of her hair. With a yank, he wrenched her head back. As he held her in the awkward position, she watched in horror as his expression morphed into sexual anticipation.

"What did you give Farrell in return for permission to dig?" She struggled against his rough hold. "You've got a terrific body. I bet you know how to use it to get what you want."

She gritted out, "My credentials stand on their own. I don't have to lower myself to your level—"

He pulled her hair hard, and she had to bite her lip to keep from crying out. "You could work on being a little more complimentary—you know that? Considering what you owe me."

"I owe you nothing," she said roughly.

"Bullshit. You cheated me out of this." His eyes roamed over her face. "The least you can do is make good on the theft. And considering everything you have to offer, I think the pleasure of your company would be sufficient. At least, for the time being."

Carter thought with dread that Buddy and Ellie wouldn't be back for at least another hour and there was no one to hear her scream. She was going to have to save herself and the only option made her sick.

Her hand shaking, she reached out and touched Lyst's face. Affixing a smile to her lips that she hoped he'd fall for, she murmured, "I'm sure we can work something out."

Her voice was frail, but apparently his ego lent her words the credibility they otherwise lacked.

"How very wise of you," he said, looking at her lips.

She felt him let go of her hair and loosen his hold on her arm. Just as he was bringing his mouth toward hers, she shifted her weight, gripped his shoulders, and drove her knee up so hard she could feel the bones in his pelvis when she made contact.

Lyst crumpled like a paper bag, falling to the dirt and coughing. She didn't stick around to measure the damage. Racing out of the circle of stones, she fled toward camp, found the trailhead, and started barreling down the mountainside. With her feet pounding over the dirt and her arms flailing from side to side to keep herself from falling, she was dangerously close to losing control of her descent. Rounding a sharp corner, one that was perched on top of a high rock shelf, she skidded wildly and had to push herself off a sturdy pine to keep from going over the edge. At the last moment, she bounded back onto the trail.

Only to career into Nick.

She hit his chest with enough force to throw them both off balance. Grabbing onto his shoulders to keep from hitting the ground, she felt his arms come around her and the world tilt alarmingly as they started to fall off the trail. For a sickening moment, she thought they were going to end up tumbling onto the jagged rocks below.

But then he threw an arm around a thick tree trunk. Using all his strength, his muscles going rigid, he halted their free fall, righting them a mere foot from the ledge.

Carter took one look at where they might have ended up and buried her face in his shoulder. Numbly, she felt his arms wrap around her and bring her closer to his warmth.

"What happened?" When she didn't answer, he pulled back a little and looked into her eyes. "Good God, you're shaking."

"Nothing. Nothing. It was nothing." She nestled farther into his shoulder. The material of his polo shirt was soft against her cheek.

"It sure was one hell of a nothing. Are you okay?"

She risked a glance up at his face. His diamond eyes were sharp and concerned, and she got the sense that, as soon as he was sure she was all right, he was prepared to go after whatever had frightened her and beat it into a pulp.

She was surprised at how much this appealed to her.

"Was it an animal?"

Carter started to shake her head before finding the lie to her advantage. She was hesitant to tell Nick what had happened, afraid it would only muddy the waters further. And considering the bloodlust that had been on Lyst's face, she figured it wasn't that far from the truth.

"Er—yes."

"What kind?"

"Bear." It was the first animal she could think of.

"I'll get Ivan up here to find it."

"No, that's okay," she said quickly. "I think I scared him off."

At the very least, the bastard was walking with a limp now.

Carter's laugh was forced as she pushed some hair out of her face. "I'm just overreacting. I don't know where I was running to."

She looked up the trail, wondering when it would be safe to return.

"Forget about going back there," he said darkly. "You need to come down to the house for a little while."

Carter was tempted to argue, but the idea that Lyst might still be around kept her silent. "Okay."

He tilted her head toward him with his finger. "Are you sure you're all right?"

His eyes were impossibly tender, especially after what they'd been through the night before, and she struggled to comprehend the safe haven he seemed to be offering. It had been so long since she'd felt like someone was watching over her, someone who would be strong when she was weak.

The pad of his thumb brushed across her lips. In a rush, she became aware of how close they were. That the solid wall of his chest was against her breasts. That one of his legs was in between hers, tight against her soft core.

His smell, that combination of expensive cologne and something altogether more primal, filled her nose. Her heart started racing again.

And then he leaned forward and his lips touched hers softly.

The sensual contact brought her out of the trance and made her remember that he already had a woman to take care of.

Pulling away sharply, she turned from him. "I think we better get going. Don't you need to get back to Candace?"

Without bothering to see if he was following, she began walking, her head down, her eyes trained on the beaten earth of the trail. Distantly, she heard the sounds of him behind her and did her best to tune them out.

When they reached the mansion, Nick led her out to a porch that overlooked the lake. He suggested a sherry and she took it tensely, sitting down in a wicker rocking chair. As she took a sip, she watched from under her lashes as he leaned against one of the white columns. He was staring out at the lake when at last he spoke.

"I think you should stay down here. All of you." His voice was full of command.

She took another small drink from the glass and felt the sherry burn a path to her stomach. "We're fine."

"I don't like the idea that you could be in danger."

"I'm not and we're going to keep staying at camp."

She watched impatience flicker across his face. "Ivan will be able to tell if the site's in some mother's territory. You may not have a choice."

"He doesn't need to go up there," she said sharply.

The last thing Carter wanted was that woodsman poking around. She hadn't seen a bear anywhere in the vicinity since she'd arrived, and if Ivan the Terrible went up there, she knew he'd find nothing. Except maybe Lyst's footprints.

Nick frowned and narrowed his eyes.

"We're okay," she told him as she quickly finished the sherry. "I'm going to be fine."

She could feel him staring at her, testing her, and was relieved when all he did was ask if she wanted a refill.

She glanced down at the delicate crystal. "Yes, I think I do."

When he handed her the glass back, she immediately took another sip. Anything to keep herself busy.

From across the porch, Nick watched Carter closely, remembering what it felt like to kiss her.

Frustration mounted, tightening the muscles in his shoulders.

That comment she'd made about Candace, the one

that had separated them up on the mountain, had been apropos but sure as hell unwelcome. It pointed out a discrepancy he found intolerable. Having spent months with Candace, he knew damn well he didn't care about her and yet she was still in his life. Carter, the one he really wanted, was on the fringes. Nick was struck with an urgent need to reverse the circumstances.

He heard Carter sigh and had to grit his teeth as he took a seat.

She leaned her head back and began to rock herself, her eyes rising up to the porch ceiling. He'd never seen a more attractive woman. She was silhouetted against the lake view, her strong profile accentuated by the light coming down from the sky. Her hair fell around her shoulders in a shining black wave and, thanks to the sherry, the color was coming back into her face. His eyes traveled down the length of her and came to rest on her calves and thighs.

Feeling himself harden, he shifted in the chair.

"I owe you an apology for last night," she said, abruptly. She turned her head to look at him with hooded eyelids. "I'm sorry that I lost my temper like that."

He shook his head, ready to accept his own blame for the flare-up. "You don't have to apologize."

She swallowed the last of her sherry. "I don't usually behave like that. Never have, actually."

"Well, I deserved it. I can be a rude son of a bitch." He paused. "I *was* being a son of a bitch. Why are you smiling?"

He asked the question even though he really didn't care why. Just seeing her lips tilt upward and her eyes lighten pleased him.

"I didn't think I'd ever hear you admit something like that."

Nick shrugged and crossed his arms over his chest. "Yeah, you and a lot of people. Just keep it to yourself. I like to cultivate my mystique."

"You mean this tough-guy thing is just an act?"

Nick told himself that talking was good. Kissing her

was infinitely better, but at least if they were talking he had a good reason to look at her.

"Power is the sum of two things. Force of will and the impression of invincibility. If people know they can affect your behavior, they'll exploit the weakness. I don't give anyone tools to use against me."

Her eyes flashed to his again. There was an assessing quality to them and, behind that, a vulnerability that brought out both the predator and the protector in him.

"You're a very hard man."

He laughed softly. "I prefer the term 'realistic.'"

"And yet when Cort is around, you seem more . . ."

"Irritable?"

"Human."

He caught a subtle change in her voice, a slight lilt of approval in the words. He liked it.

"Cort is my family. And family is different." When she raised an eyebrow, he said, "You seem surprised."

She shrugged. "I'm glad you think your family is important. I imagine your life would be very lonely if you didn't have any ties to people at all."

Coming from anyone else, the comment would have been easy to turn away from. He'd dismissed statements like it before, usually as they were being thrown at him by women on their way out of his life. From Carter, though, it was impossible to push aside and he pondered his isolation for a moment. He was connected to Cort, Gertie, and Ivan. That was about it.

She was right. He did have a lonely life.

And instead of becoming defensive, he found himself liking her candor and insight.

"This is good sherry," she murmured. Lithely, she unfolded herself out of the rocker and crossed the porch. She poured herself another, her hands steady on the decanter and the glass.

"I talked to Cort," she said as she sat back down. "Tried to get him to see that I'm a fantasy to him, nothing more. As soon as he realizes I put my pants on one leg at a time like everyone else, he'll be fine. I hope."

"How was he doing?" Nick could feel his body tighten with stress.

"He's hurt. But I'm sure he'll get over it."

"I tried to talk to him last night but it didn't go well."

Carter glanced over at him, her lovely blue eyes full of conviction. "I know it's hard right now, but he's a very good kid and he's going to grow up into a very good man."

Nick released some of his frustration with his breath. "Yeah, well, I wish to hell it was because of me, instead of in spite of me. It feels like this fighting is all we've got."

"You're too alike to get along now and too alike not to get along later. Trust me, I know all about bad family dynamics. You two will figure it out."

"I hope you're right."

There was a long silence between them. A breeze drifted off the lake, wandered onto the porch.

Her lips tipped up at the corners.

"You're smiling again," he told her softly.

"Am I?" She tilted the glass and sipped a little more sherry.

"Could it be that you're enjoying my company?"

Carter leaned her head back again and stared at him. He thought there was a sensual speculation in her expression and relished the implications.

"I hate to disappoint you but it's probably the sherry," she said, looking away. "And the fact that I forgot to eat lunch."

But then her eyes drifted back to his and the heat was still in them.

"I think you're lying," he said huskily.

Her cheeks got more pink but she firmly changed the subject. "The dig's coming along well."

He frowned, unsatisfied and hungry, and had to force some enthusiasm into his voice. "Really?"

Carter launched into a detailed report, which he mostly didn't hear. He asked a couple of questions, to urge her on, but he was really concentrating on how he could make her stay for dinner and when he would see her next.

Alone, he thought, he wanted to get her alone. But how?

When her speech was over, Carter unexpectedly presented him with an opportunity.

"Today I was down at the boathouse. I saw your collection of boats," she murmured. "You've got all the bases covered. Speed, cruises, sailing."

"I like to be on the water."

"Me, too."

The soft purr behind the words made her sleepy expression downright seductive and turned the two words into an invitation he hoped to hell she meant.

"Would you like to go out on the lake?"

"I would." She smiled widely.

Nick's body became white-hot. He knew he was going to have her. His heart began to thunder and he struggled to keep his voice calm and measured.

"The wind's supposed to be good tomorrow through the beginning of next week. We could take a sail."

Her face changed and unhappiness flared in her eyes. "What about Candace?"

Nick wanted to curse.

"She's going to be leaving soon," he said roughly.

"Ah, but when will she be back?" Carter's laugh was bitter.

"She won't be." It was a vow and, after a moment, she nodded at him gravely.

When she spoke next, her voice stroked him as it rode on the summer breeze across the porch. "Then as soon as she goes, we'll head out on the lake."

Watching her mouth move, Nick was prepared to hunt the other woman down and send her bouncing out the door with her designer luggage that very afternoon. He wondered where Candace was and how long it might take to find her.

But then an unfamiliar car drove up and the Swifts got out. When Buddy saw Carter, he waved and came ambling over.

At the sight of the other man, Nick's anticipation

evaporated. He glared in her partner's direction and leaned in close to Carter.

"Tell you what," he growled. "You do a little cleaning up of your own and then we'll talk about going for that sail."

Nick was tempted to kick the man off his property. A part of him felt ridiculous at the surge of jealousy, but logic didn't stand a chance against the emotions he was feeling. Images of her with Buddy, the two entwined and twisted in a sleeping bag, made him want to pound the guy into the ground.

"I can't believe it," Buddy said when he got within earshot, "but I actually found a rental car in the Adirondacks."

The Swifts mounted the porch, their feet clapping against the boards. After Ellie headed into the house to use the bathroom, Carter started to get up out of the rocker and faltered. Both men reached out to steady her, but Nick shot a warning glare at her friend. The other man dropped his hands immediately.

"Whoa," Carter said, grabbing onto Nick's arm. She let go of it as soon as she had her footing. "I guess I had a little too much sherry."

"You don't drink," Buddy said, shooting her a curious look.

"And now I'm remembering why." Carter glanced up at Nick. "I think I better lie down for a minute. You got a spare bed in this ark?"

Nick nodded, willing to do anything to keep her from going up his mountain with another man.

The screen door opened and Ellie emerged with Cort by her side.

"I got lost," the girl said with a smile.

"And I found her." Cort wasn't smiling but he sent a long, measuring glance in Ellie's direction.

"We better get going," Buddy said to his daughter. "Carter's going to meet us up at camp later."

As the Swifts left, Cort lingered on the edge of the porch, watching them walk across the lawn.

"I think I'll come up to the dig tomorrow," he murmured before heading back into the house.

The screen door bumped shut, and Carter and Nick were alone again.

"Just point me in any direction," she mumbled, "and I'll do my best to get through your house in one piece."

"I'll take you upstairs."

He led her through the mansion, wishing that she'd stop brushing his hand away and take the arm he offered.

They ascended the grand staircase, and Nick took them down the hall to the bedroom with the best view in the house. It was a peach-colored sanctuary that faced the lake and had its own second-story porch. It also had a bed he thought she might like, a great canopied antique covered with floral bedding.

He imagined her lying naked on it.

"This is beautiful," she said reverently, going over to the stack of pillows. Her fingers were light as they brushed over them. "I'll bet these sheets are cool and will crunch like my grandmother's used to."

She checked the seat of her pants before she sat down and bounced a little on the soft mattress.

"You should be comfortable here." His voice sounded hoarse and he wondered if she noticed.

"Hard to believe anyone wouldn't be."

"And feel free to take a shower. It's through there," he said, pointing to a door.

"Now, that sounds like heaven." She began taking off her hiking boots.

Nick dragged himself over to the doorway. He knew he had to leave. His hand gripped the doorknob tightly.

"Sleep well," he said.

Carter nodded, already on her way into the marbled extravagance of the bath.

Nick stepped out of the room and closed the door but couldn't let go of the damn knob.

When he heard the water go on, he imagined her stepping beneath the jets, her back arching as she wet her hair. That was when he turned and went downstairs. He knew if he didn't get the hell away from the door, he was liable to try to get in the shower with her.

Heading to the kitchen, he went in search of Ivan and found the man taking his four o'clock tea with his wife.

"You get her settled?" Gertie inquired as she put a plate of shortbreads on the table in front of her husband.

"You knew she was here?" Nick took a seat and smiled as a cup of Earl Grey was slid in front of him.

"I figured that empty sherry glass on the porch wasn't yours."

"Something scared her off the mountain?" Ivan asked while picking up his teacup. His workman's hands gripped the dainty handle with care, the scars on his skin and his calluses seeming out of place on the fine Limoges. When he put it back down, it was without a sound, precisely in the center of its saucer.

Nick nodded. "She had a run-in with a bear."

"You want me to track it?"

"That'd be great. If you think there's going to be trouble, I'm going to yank them off the site, at least after dark. The last thing we need is to have a bunch of archaeologists served up as a midnight snack. During the day, at least they can see what's coming at them."

"I don't like having people up there," Ivan said, looking down into his tea.

Nick smiled. It was the closest the man would ever come to expressing disfavor with him.

"Then you'll be happy to know, they've already started digging. They may be gone in under a month."

He frowned, finding his own words disturbing. He thought of the woman upstairs, who had probably dried off and slid between the sheets by now. He didn't relish the idea of her leaving anytime soon.

Finishing his tea, Nick got to his feet.

"Like I said before, make sure she's safe up there," he told Ivan before nodding thanks to Gertie. "I don't want anything happening to her."

"Don't you mean them?" the woodsman asked.

"Yeah, right. Of course. Them."

Nick was aware that the McNutts were looking at him strangely, but he wasn't in the mood to answer questions. As he walked through the house, he thought it was probably better to keep to himself, at least until the hunger for the woman in his guest room passed.

Although on that logic, he thought grimly, he probably should lock himself up in his study until she left.

8

CARTER WOKE up in a dark, unfamiliar room and panicked. Her body was wrapped in a towel and she had no immediate recollection as to where in the hell her clothes were. It wasn't until she sat up and her head started to pound that she remembered where she was. And why.

Moving hair gingerly out of her face, she put both feet on the floor and stood up with a groan. The worst hangover she'd ever had was sitting on her skull like a piece of heavy machinery. A steamroller. Or maybe a dump truck.

How could something as highbrow as sherry, sipped from a little crystal glass, do so much damage? She'd have expected it from rotgut wine or a fleet of wretched, fruity cocktails drunk in some seedy bar. But sherry? On a porch?

Carter fumbled around until she found a lamp beside the bed and turned it on. The soft glow made her headache howl in protest. She switched the thing off and then realized she'd managed to blind herself completely.

Not a good call.

Moving in the direction she thought the bathroom was in, she knocked her shin on the leg of an armchair and almost went back to bed.

Of course, that would mean she might sleep through the night and have to see Nick in the morning. This wasn't a prospect she felt up to handling, especially if she was still hungover. She'd propositioned him for a date, for all intents and purposes, and followed that little ditty up by demanding that he get rid of his girlfriend.

As she remembered his response, though, excitement swirled in her stomach. It was a heady feeling that lasted until it occurred to her that she'd taken another step closer toward a man she'd resolved to stay away from. If she knew what was good for her, she'd stick to digging holes at the site and not go creating them in her own life.

Cursing and hobbling through the darkness, Carter eventually felt cool marble under her feet. The pile of clothes was where she'd left it on the counter, but before she attempted that obstacle course, she splashed her face and had two glasses of water. Both improved the headache some and she got dressed quickly.

After making the bed, she went over to the door. Opening it a crack, she waited for her eyes to adjust to the hall light. There was no one around, and she was relieved by all the silence. She stepped out and looked at the three different branches the corridor split into. The choices were overwhelming.

Thanks to the sherry-induced stupor she'd been in, she couldn't remember which way to go.

Picking a direction randomly, she went some distance and, when the stairs didn't appear, figured she was lost. She was about to double back when she heard voices.

"Why are my clothes in this guest room?" Candace's voice was soft and filled with hurt.

Carter froze. Down to the left, Candace and Nick were standing in a doorway.

"I asked Gertie to move you here."

"Why?"

"Because things have changed." Nick's tone brooked no negotiation, his face a mask of cold control.

"Changed?" Hysteria sharpened the word. "What do you mean changed?"

"Things are not working out between us."

"But you asked me up here." Candace sounded confused and disappointed but then stared at him in disbelief. "It's that ditchdigger, isn't it?"

Nick's silence was a powerful answer. Carter drew in a breath, unable to believe what was happening.

"Tell me the truth," the woman demanded. "Come on. I've seen the way you look at her."

When Nick stayed quiet, she straightened her shoulders and tossed her hair back. "Maybe I should just leave."

"Yes, I think that's a good idea."

She let out a gasp. "How can you be so cruel?"

"Candace, you knew from the start where things stood between us. I've always been upfront with you."

"But I love you. I thought we were going to get married. I thought that's why you wanted me to come here. To ask me to marry you."

"I never gave you that impression." Nick's head was moving back and forth grimly.

"You are breaking my heart." This was followed by a sad, choked sob that chilled Carter. "I knew I should have listened to my father, my friends. They warned me about you, about how you always do this. Whenever someone gets close, you pull away. I just never thought it would happen to me."

Carter wrapped her arms around herself. She had to wonder whether she was volunteering for the same fate if she went sailing with him. He was obviously pursuing her, but then, he must have done the same thing to Candace. If she gave in to him, she'd likely end up getting a similar brush-off, eventually.

"How could you?" the woman murmured and then let out a sniffle. When Nick made no move to comfort her, she grew angry and went back to glaring at him. "So how long is this new one going to last? Are you going to play her along like you did me?"

"You jumped to your own conclusions. I was very clear about what I wanted. Besides, I have every confidence you will rebound."

"I'm not one of your stocks!"

Nick's tone was close to bored. "Candace, I know you're seeing someone else in the city. You have been for almost two months now. I'm not holding the infidelity against you but don't try and play the ruined innocent, okay?"

There was a sharp intake of breath.

With that, Nick turned to go, only to halt when he saw Carter crouched for flight. As their eyes met, hers widened in embarrassment. He showed no reaction.

Candace seemed to take the hesitation as an encouraging sign.

"Darling, let's not fight." She reached out and touched his arm.

The sight of the woman's red nails on his shirt was the last thing Carter saw as she fled.

"There was no bear," Ivan told Nick the next day. The two men were in the garage, leaning against the tractor.

"I don't get it. She said she saw one."

"Don't know of no bear that wears sneakers and walks upright. Do you?"

Nick frowned in confusion. Are you sure there wasn't one?"

Ivan shot him a dry look.

"Of course, you are," Nick muttered. "Could the prints have been from one of the Swifts?"

"The new ones were man-sized and that Buddy, he wears hiking boots. Also, they came up from the back. Whoever it was used the rear trail that hooks down onto the road."

"Why the hell would she lie?"

With a sharp noise, the front door to the mansion slammed shut as Candace appeared. She was dressed in a dark blue linen suit, high heels, and plenty of gold jewelry. Her face was drawn in rigid lines.

"So she's going back to the city," Ivan commented.

"She is."

Nick wasn't looking forward to the trip to the train

station. It would take less than an hour but he had a feeling it was going to be an interminable drive.

"Is she coming back?"

"No."

Ivan nodded.

Nick glanced at the older man. "You never liked her, did you?"

"Doesn't matter now, does it?"

Nick shrugged and then got into the Porsche.

The excursion to town was every bit as awkward as he'd imagined but, when he deposited Candace at the terminal with her luggage, he wished her well. She didn't reply, just stared off in the direction the train would be coming from. Standing next to her monogrammed bags, she appeared to be a perfect lady, but he had a feeling she'd have tucked a live grenade into his shorts if she'd had the chance.

On the way back home, he thought of how Carter had looked when he'd caught her listening in on the breakup. Her face had been bright red as she'd wheeled around and hightailed it down the hall. He laughed softly at the memory.

He couldn't wait to be with her. An enthralling picture of the two of them naked in the river came to mind. He saw himself running water over her skin with his hands, kissing her neck and her shoulders . . .

Abruptly, Buddy Swift's face intruded on the fantasy, ruining it.

Cursing out loud, Nick stomped his foot on the accelerator and rocketed into a straightaway.

Fair was fair, he thought darkly. He'd gotten rid of his designer baggage, so Carter could get rid of her extra backpack.

This kind of stipulation was a new development for him. He wasn't typically one to demand monogamy in affairs. It hardly seemed fair since he was so uninterested in permanent ties. Besides, the women he'd been with tended to give him their fidelity with eagerness, figuring it was their best shot at the golden ring. If they did see other people, he didn't ask and they didn't tell.

But Carter was different. He wasn't going to share her with anyone.

"So, how'd you like sleeping in a real bed last night?" Buddy asked while shoving his trowel into the dirt. "That mattress feel good?"

Carter looked up from her work. With Ellie still asleep in her tent, they were digging at the site alone. "It was nice. The shower was the high point."

"I was surprised you didn't spend the whole night. Did Farrell turn into a bad host? Not that I can't imagine him being anything other than perfectly accommodating," he said sarcastically.

She wiped her brow with the back of her hand. "You don't like him, do you?"

"More to the point, he doesn't like me."

"Oh, come on. He's a little brusque to everyone."

"Brusque? I feel like the man's ordering my tombstone every time I see him."

"You don't get to the top of the heap on Wall Street by being a nice guy."

Buddy looked up with an incredulous eye. "Don't tell me you think this is just about his personality."

"I'm sure that's what it is," she said firmly, hoping he would take the hint and let the subject drop.

"Listen to me." Her friend's voice was serious as he wagged his trowel at her. "That man wants you, Carter. And he's not going to let anything or anyone stand in his way."

Rolling her eyes, while swallowing a secret thrill, she thrust her hand shovel into the ground. With a sharp sound, she hit something solid.

"What was that?" Buddy asked.

"I don't know."

She reached over for a more delicate tool. Moving more slowly, she brushed away the earth until a stretch of bone was exposed to the air. Digging around it, she found herself looking at a thighbone and hip socket.

"This looks human," she announced. Buddy immediately came over just as Ellie and Cort appeared at the site.

"What'd you find?" Cort asked excitedly.

"Someone's leg, I think."

The group clustered around Carter.

"How do you know it's a someone instead of something?" Ellie asked as she peered over for a look.

"Based on its shape and size." Carter highlighted the distinguishing features with the tip of her brush. "Considering the length of the bone and its angle into the joint here, I'd say this was probably a male, about eighteen years of age. I'll need to see the full pelvic area to be sure."

"Do you have to call the cops?" Cort asked.

Buddy nodded. "Even though these look like old bones and we have a permit to dig on this site, we'll need to have the state police come and confirm this isn't a crime scene. If this proves to be a Native American burial ground, which is unlikely given the lack of ceremonial artifacts so far, we'd also tell the appropriate tribal authorities. I'll go get on the horn right now."

As Buddy left for camp, Cort came in for a closer look. "How long ago did he die?"

Carter cocked her head as she considered the bones. "Going by the look of the bone and the composition of the soil, which was deep and seemed undisturbed, I'd say it was a long time ago. I'd also guess he'd been buried."

"Buried?"

"I suspect further excavation will show this to be a shallow grave. Someone either killed him or found him dead and rolled the body into a hole."

"Creepy," Ellie murmured. "What are you going to do now?"

"Nothing until the state police get here. It's tough not to keep digging, though. I'm really curious to learn more about this man. Hopefully, we'll be able to find some clues to his identity."

"Don't hold your breath for a driver's license," Cort said wryly.

Carter smiled. "Buttons, buckles, bullets, and coins will tell us a lot if we find them. If he's as old as I think he is, anything cloth or leather would have mostly rotted away, but the metal hangs around. Maybe we'll get lucky and find something personal."

She thought of Winship's cross.

To Carter's surprise and delight, it wasn't long until Ivan showed up at the site with two state policemen. They were strapping young men, dressed in gray uniforms, and they seemed to know Ivan really well. The staties made a thorough but expedient review of the find and declared that the dig could proceed.

"Thanks for coming so quickly," Carter said as they were about to leave. "I was thrilled you got here so soon."

The taller of the two smiled at her. "We'd do anything for Mr. Farrell. We take care of our own."

Her curiosity must have shown on her face because he explained, "I'm Gertie McNutt's nephew's kid and my partner's Ivan's second cousin once removed."

"We're just one big family up in these parts," the other officer said. "Say, you think you're going to find any other skeletons?"

She shrugged. "Maybe. I hope so."

"And what about the gold?" The guy's eyes lit up. "We've been hearing about that fortune all our lives. How it's up here somewhere."

Carter smiled. "Who knows? I'm really more interested in the people."

"Have you seen Red Hawk?"

The man's partner rolled his eyes. "Come on, McNutt. Of course there's hawks up here."

"I mean the Indian. My grandmother always said that Red Hawk haunts the Farrell peaks. During the day he flies in the form of a bird, but at night he comes as a ghost. I remember hearing stories about people coming up to this site and getting scared away by him. He doesn't like visitors, apparently."

"Aw, leave it, will you?" The taller one offered Carter a wink. "You just call if you find anyone else. We'll come running."

Carter thanked them again and waved as they left.

"They were nice," she said to Buddy. When she looked over at him, she was surprised at the frown on his face. "What's the matter with you?"

"No one told me about a ghost."

"Aw, come on. You don't believe in that kind of stuff, do you?"

"Maybe I do."

Ellie laughed. "C.C., don't get him started. He'll have nightmares."

Buddy shot his daughter a mock glare. After Ellie and Cort ambled over to where Carter had been digging before, he dropped his voice.

"Seriously, I've noticed that someone's been walking around camp at night. There are fresh tracks in the mornings."

Carter frowned while a stab of fear went through her. "Are you sure you know what to look for?"

Her friend shrugged. "Just keep on your toes. No telling who's roaming this mountain."

Carter was feeling disturbed as they all settled down with their shovels and their buckets. Soon, however, the find captured her full attention. Working steadily until the light dimmed, and pausing only to photograph her progress, she peeled away the skeleton's blanket of sweet-smelling earth. When she'd exposed the area from his feet all the way up to his sternum, she stopped. It was getting difficult to see and she was cramping up from her efforts. Besides, she didn't want to reveal the man's skull to the night. It just didn't seem right. He'd had enough darkness and deserved to be welcomed out of his rest by daylight.

Carter put her shovel and her brushes aside and surveyed her work with satisfaction. There were indications that the skeleton was from the Revolutionary period. She'd found brass buttons interspersed among the ribs and vertebra, which indicated the man had been a British soldier. They were lucky he'd been buried in his uniform.

"Bones are in good shape, aren't they?" Buddy commented.

"He is a fine one," she agreed, getting to her feet.

"So, what do you know?"

"The pelvic bone confirms it was a male and the metallurgic finds suggest he was a Brit. There's evidence here"—she leaned in and pointed to a part of the rib cage—"that he may have died of a stabbing. Either knife or bayonet. The rib pattern is disrupted and you can see several bones broken in a manner consistent with that kind of trauma."

Ellie and Cort wandered over.

"Did I hear something about a stabbing?" the girl asked.

Carter nodded. "It appears as if he might have—"

"Been murdered?" Cort interjected.

"Died by knife wound."

"Then he could have been murdered. By the Indian," he prompted urgently.

"You need a heck of a leap to get to that conclusion."

"But he was a British soldier—you said so. And from the Revolutionary period. So he could have been one of General Farnsworth's men." The kid was growing more excited with every word. "Maybe the gold's around here, too."

"Perhaps. But right now, we need to focus on what we've found. Will you grab that tarp? We better get him covered up."

Cort brought over a stretch of blue plastic, and they covered the exposed skeleton, nailing the corners into the ground with stakes.

"I wonder if he'll start haunting us because we disturbed him," Ellie said softly.

"You don't have to be afraid," Cort reassured her. "From all the stories I've heard, the dead don't hurt anyone. They just kind of float around."

"Actually, I was kind of looking forward to it. I may not like looking at the bones, but ghosts are cool."

Cort cocked his head, giving the girl serious consideration. Abruptly, the kid grinned, as if struck by a thought that pleased him.

"Well, if you do get scared, you can come down and stay at my house." He glanced awkwardly at Buddy. "All of you. I mean, now that Candace is gone, it's just me and him."

Carter, who had begun to pick up her trowels and other tools, struggled to keep moving naturally.

"Since when?" Buddy asked.

"Today. Uncle Nick put her on the train this morning. It was really sudden and she didn't look happy about it. I don't think she's coming back. Ever."

"What gave you that impression?"

"Uncle Nick came back whistling. He always does that, whenever he gets rid of them."

Carter forced her hands to continue their work, while wondering what in the hell she was getting herself into.

Nick was in the kitchen, eating with Gertie and Ivan, when Cort came through the back door.

"The skeleton's cool," the kid announced as he retrieved a glucose monitor from a special cupboard. Inside were syringes, test strips, and medicines. "And he may have been murdered."

"Good Lord," Gertie said, pausing with her fork in the air. "Who told you that?"

"Carter." He waited for the machine to calculate his blood sugar level and then injected himself with insulin. When he was finished, he took a seat in front of an empty plate. As Gertie passed a serving dish of lamb toward him, he shook his head. "No, thanks. I already ate. You know, Carter's totally cool. She knows everything. She's really smart. And you should see what the bones look like. They're really amazing."

Nick kept his voice noncommittal. "Maybe I'll go up and take a look."

Maybe? Hell, he'd been ready to head up the mountain as soon as he'd returned from the train station, but he'd forced himself to wait. He wanted to give her a day to set that Buddy guy straight.

Which meant at the crack of dawn tomorrow, he was putting on his hiking boots.

When Gertie got up to bring over an apple pie for dessert, Ivan and Nick helped clear their plates.

"That Ellie girl is very nice," she said while sitting back down. "She's your age, isn't she?"

"Yeah." Cort turned the color of cherries.

"Do you like her?"

"Gertie!" Ivan hissed, as he picked up the coffeepot and a few mugs. "You don't go intruding on a man's private thoughts like that."

His wife shrugged and put a slice of pie in front of her husband's seat. "If I hadn't cornered you in that diner, we never would have gotten married. You'd have pined after me for years, stuck in your seat at that counter like your pants were nailed down."

Now it was Ivan's turn to get red in the face.

"I would have said something eventually," he mumbled while filling his wife's mug.

"Deathbed confessions don't count."

"I don't know about that," Nick said, accepting his slice. "They're likely to be honest."

"Only way too late," Gertie argued.

Cort looked up at his uncle. "It matters more if you hear it sooner. My mom always told me she loved me. Except for that last time she left. She meant to, I think. But they were late and . . ." Everyone froze around the table. Cort glanced around, embarrassed. "Anyway, I'm glad she'd told me a ton before she didn't come back."

The kid looked down and played with the fork and knife in front of him.

Ivan reached over and gave Cort's shoulder a squeeze. If anyone else had reached out to him, he would have bolted from the table. They all knew it. The kid was strung like a wire but, after Ivan touched him, he seemed to settle a little.

Nick watched, envious. It was hell, being so far away from his nephew, not being the one to comfort him.

Sifting through the years, reaching back into the nether regions of his mind, Nick remembered when he'd been upset as a boy. Like Cort, Ivan's silent, powerful love had been the only thing he'd let touch him.

He'd been eleven at the time. His dog had gone after a porcupine and had been stuck by hundreds of quills. He'd found the mutt curled up against the garage, moaning out of a bleeding mouth. Nick had reached out a hand, desperate to help, only to be bitten hard. Recoiling, with tears rolling down his face from the pain in his hand and his fear for the dog, he hadn't gone to his father or mother. He'd gone looking for Ivan.

Nick glanced down at his palm, seeing the scars, which were now so faint. He'd needed stitches and the dog had needed Ivan's steady hand with a pair of pliers. After the ordeal was over and the quills were out at last, the mutt had come to lie next to Nick, who'd been put to bed. Seeking to comfort the animal, Nick had stroked the dog's head gently with his good hand.

As the evening wore on, Gertie had brought him dinner, which he couldn't stomach, and his mother had popped in on the way to a party, looking elegant and smelling good. As usual, her eyes had been empty when she'd kissed him on the cheek, but Nick hadn't cared. He hadn't wanted consolation from her anyway.

In the dwindling light, he'd been far more concerned about the arrival of his father. As soon as he'd seen the bite, his father had demanded that Ivan shoot the dog. With his hand still bleeding, Nick had begged him to reconsider but the man had pushed him away in frustration, saying that dogs could be replaced.

Nick had waited and waited for the end to come. He'd

barely been breathing, looking back and forth between the dog and the door.

When it finally opened, his eyes had gone wide. Ivan stood silently in the doorway.

Nick's throat swelled shut and he'd hardly been able to speak. "You gonna shoot him?"

"No."

There had been a long silence between them.

"You sure?"

"Yup."

As tears of relief fell onto his pillow, Nick had turned his face away. He hadn't wanted Ivan to see him cry, didn't want to seem like less of a man.

Ivan had shut the door and taken a seat in a chair across the room. He'd leaned back and crossed his feet at the ankles, like he had nothing else he needed to do, nowhere else he needed to be, even though it was late and he had a family of his own to get home to.

Trying to be as quiet as he could, Nick had kept on crying until he didn't feel so dizzy with relief. The dog was alive because Ivan had saved it and Nick felt saved, too. It was a miracle.

Still, he'd been ashamed of his weakness, of his tears.

When he'd woken up the next morning, Ivan was gone, but on the bedside table was an eagle feather. The symbol of courage. An Indian warrior's pride.

It was the kind of gesture a boy never thinks of again, but the man he becomes never forgets.

Coming back to the present, Nick focused on Cort. He wished, like nothing else, it could have been his hand that eased the boy's suffering.

9

THE NEXT day, Carter's trowel was steady as she carefully removed a wedge of earth. After she put it aside, she reached down and gently brushed off some loose dirt, exposing the graceful, pale arc of the skeleton's jawbone. She saw that the teeth were still anchored in their cavities, the bottom row uneven in the front.

"Cort, hold the chin here so it doesn't fall as I excavate the rest."

The kid put his hand where she told him to.

Working efficiently, she freed the bone until it was lying in Cort's hand. "Okay, you can remove it now."

Cort sat back, cradling the jawbone. His eyes were wide and he was barely breathing.

Ellie leaned over his shoulder. "Can I feel it?"

"Gently," Carter said, touched by their reverence. "Don't dislodge any of the teeth."

Ellie ran a finger over the joint. "I wonder what he looked like."

Carter pulled the baseball cap she was wearing down more tightly. In spite of the fact that the sun was beating down on her back, and she was in a cramped, unnatural position, she didn't feel any discomfort. Her focus on her work was enough to distract her from her aches and pains.

Although it didn't take her mind off Nick. She'd been

waiting for him to come up all morning, with an edge of impatience that made her uncomfortable.

"So what do you think?" Ellie prompted. "What was he like?"

Carter looked at the bone.

"We'll know more when we see the rest of the skull but, as I presumed, he was young, probably eighteen or so. You can tell by the amount of wear and tear on the molars in the back. In an older person, they'd be smoother. Also, if you look at the teeth in the front, some still have the serrated edges that helped the permanent teeth break through. Maybe he was closer to sixteen." She pointed over to a box. "Put the jaw inside there. We can reassemble him when it's time for the pictures."

It took her a half hour to uncover the skeleton's head in its entirety. When it was completely revealed, the whole group let out a collective gasp. There was a large, gaping hole in the cranium.

"And I thought the knife wound was bad," Carter murmured.

"What happened?" Cort asked incredulously.

"This man was struck on the head. From what I can see here"—she pointed to the wound—"I'd say it was done with a machete because the bone has broken away with clean edges. You need something sharp to get that effect."

"It must have been the Indian," Cort whispered.

Carter glanced to the sky, which was clouding up. "Let's get some pictures taken. I'd like to get him free from the ground before it rains."

While Cort took pictures, she got out a measuring tape and recorded the skeleton's various dimensions and the depth at which it was found. With the find fully documented, she began to remove the bones one by one and put them in a container that could be locked. She figured the skeleton would be safe there until she could get him over to her lab in Burlington. She'd just started on the rib cage when Buddy, who'd resumed digging, let out a low whistle.

Staring into the hole he was working on, he said, "We better call back the staties. Looks like we may have another one."

Nick was walking up the mountain, in a good mood. He was banking on the fact that Carter had spoken with Buddy and was looking forward to getting out on the lake with her. Alone.

When he got to the camp, it was orderly, as always. The mess area was spotless with any food stored in locked-down coolers and hold-alls. The dishes had been washed and stacked neatly on a small table and the fire had been banked. The three tents, nestled off to one side, had their flaps down and secured. The sight of these made him glower.

He pictured Buddy sneaking into whichever one was Carter's, and thought that goddamn professor better be staying in his own from now on.

Nick headed over to the dig site. When he stepped inside the circle of stones, he saw them all staring intently at the ground. Carter and Buddy were kneeling over a pit, close together.

"Did you find the missing link?" Nick asked, not bothering to hide the edge in his voice.

Everyone looked up and it gave him pleasure to watch Buddy move away from her.

"We've got two skeletons. Buddy just found another and I think it might be a colonist, based on this shoe buckle," Carter explained. Her eyes flipped up to his and then darted away as she flushed.

Nick joined them, looking away from Carter only long enough to glance at the ground. He saw part of a foot and an ankle in the shallow pit and, about five yards away, a completely exposed skeleton, part of which was missing.

"You've been busy," he said, leaning over Carter. Her eyes rose again to his, the blue in them deepening. In his mind, he took her into his arms, and she seemed to know what he was thinking because he saw her breath quicken. She stood up abruptly.

"I understand we're to thank you and Ivan for the prompt appearance of the state police yesterday," she said in a rush. "Any chance you two can work your magic again?"

"Maybe this time I can show them the carburetor," Buddy quipped.

Nick sent him a cool look. "You found a piece of machinery?"

The man nodded. "You never know what's going to come out of the ground."

"Yes, I imagine it all depends on what you bury." Nick's voice was dark.

Buddy frowned and got to his feet. "Kids, why don't we head back to camp and start dinner? Leave Carter to give Mr. Farrell the details while we make gourmet sandwiches."

Nick cocked an eyebrow at Buddy's swift departure, thinking the professor was one smart guy.

Immediately, Carter started talking to him about the finds in a serious voice. "The skeleton we have excavated fully appears to be that of a male, between sixteen and eighteen years of age, who died as the result of cerebral trauma and a penetrating wound to the chest cavity. Based upon . . ."

As she went on, Nick didn't want to hear about the dig. He was far more interested in talking about when they were going to be alone together.

He cut her off with some gentle teasing. "Are you purposely doing an imitation of Quincy or do all archaeologists speak like this when they're around open pits?"

She stopped talking and looked at him with wide, searching eyes. "Excuse me?"

"Quincy. You know, the medical examiner. I recall there being a lot of plaid going on in his suits, wide lapels, this kind of thing. Lived on a boat."

She flushed angrily. "And exactly what's the parallel between me and a 'seventies TV character?"

"You're so very serious," he said softly. He hadn't meant to antagonize her.

"Do you address your board of directors doing a Donald Duck imitation? This is my work. I take it seriously." She put her hands on her hips. "So are we ready to try again?"

Obviously, Carter was fully prepared to give him hell if he tried anything, and it made him smile. He didn't doubt for a moment she'd walk away if he didn't behave.

He found himself thinking there might be room in his life for someone who stood up to him.

"Now what's wrong with you?" Her voice was exasperated.

"Wrong?"

"You're smiling."

"You don't like me in a good mood?"

She cocked her head to the side. Slowly, as if it were going against her better instincts, she gave him a smile that made his heart stop. It was lopsided and shyly teasing. "It's like a plaid leisure suit. I never expected to see you in one."

Nick laughed, wanting to pull her close. "Thanks for the vote of confidence on the wardrobe, although I'm not sure I like what you're implying otherwise."

"Now, can we get serious for a minute?"

"You keep smiling like that and I'll do anything you want."

She blushed before leading him over to the fully excavated skeleton. He listened and was impressed with what she had to say. Her conclusions were measured and logical and he realized she was more of a scientist than he'd thought.

"So what are the chances these two were involved with the Winship party?" he asked.

"Strong. Farnsworth was escorted by two Americans as well as Winship and Red Hawk. The party was met by his own men from Fort Sagamore, and I believe this first one is a Brit. I've uncovered several buttons on him which are consistent with those found on British redcoat uniforms in the middle to late 1700s."

"What about his buddy?" Nick nodded over to the other remains.

"The bones appear to be at the same depth in the soil and they've aged in a similar fashion. It looks as if that body was also buried in a shallow grave. I'm really curious, but we can't excavate further until the staties come back."

"You said grave. Who buried them?"

"That's what I've been wondering. After the slaughter, everyone was supposed to be dead except for Farnsworth. Maybe he sent other soldiers up from the fort to dig the graves but I doubt it. With Walker escaping, the place would have been in an uproar and the last thing on Farnsworth's mind would have been burying some remains in the wilderness." Her face was rapt with enthusiasm. "Interestingly enough, this first skeleton shows no signs of disruption from scavengers, which would suggest he was buried soon after he died, before some animal got a chance to work on him. He also was laid to rest in his gear, if the pattern and number of buttons is anything to go by. This means he was buried by someone who was in too much of a hurry, or disinclined, to strip him of his clothes and munitions. If Red Hawk killed them—"

"Hey, I think we're being watched," Nick interrupted, as he caught a flash of movement.

Carter looked alarmed. "By who—"

He pointed up to a tree. Settled on a limb, a red-tailed hawk was peering down at them with unblinking eyes.

"I'm not superstitious," she whispered.

"Neither am I."

"And I don't believe any of those ghost stories about the Indian."

There was a moment of silence.

"You want to go back to camp and talk about this?" she asked, still looking up at the bird.

"Great idea."

Carter was surprised at the ease with which Nick accepted an invitation to have dinner with them. He seemed perfectly content to have a sandwich outdoors with all the bugs as opposed to something fancy in his formal dinning room. He'd even volunteered to put out the plates and cups and had helped cut up fruit for dessert.

Still, when he squeezed in next to her at the picnic table, she really wished he'd eaten somewhere else. Throughout the meal, their elbows touched and their thighs brushed. By the time she turned down the damn fruit, she was feverish from the contact with him and resentful that he seemed so unaffected.

She was ill at ease for another reason. The scene she'd witnessed between him and Candace was still hanging over her. Aside from the questions it raised about Nick, she wanted to explain why she'd been in the hallway but knew it was going to be tough to justify herself. There was no good excuse for her behavior. She'd been eavesdropping and was caught.

There was one more thing clouding her mind. She wanted to know whether or not he was going to follow through with that sailing proposition. Even though she was wary of him and the threat he represented, she wanted to be alone with him. Heaven help her, but she did. She wanted him to take her into his arms and slip his tongue into her mouth and rip off her shirt—

"Right, Carter?"

Startled, she looked across at Ellie. "What?"

"You've wanted to get out on the lake, too."

Carter blanched, wondering what she'd given away. "Yeah, sure."

Nick drawled, "Then I wouldn't be a good host unless I made that happen, would I?"

He glanced at her and, flustered, Carter stood and began picking up plates. When she reached in front of Nick, he got to his feet and offered to help.

"I've got it," she said quickly, balancing a load carefully and heading over to the river to rinse the dishes.

"Hey, you forgot these," Buddy called out, holding up some knives. When she said her hands were full, he followed her into the woods.

They were gone only a few minutes, but by the time they had returned, the mood at the campsite had changed. Nick was wearing a dark look and the kids were very quiet.

Frowning, Buddy told Ellie and Cort to go spread a tarp over the new find. After they disappeared into the woods, he turned on Nick, frustration evident on his face. "What the hell's your problem?"

Carter held her breath as she watched Nick turn on her friend.

"Seems like you're the one with the issue."

"I'm tired of getting measured for a shroud by you, Farrell."

"You know what they say," Nick growled back. "We're all dead men walking."

Carter started scrambling for a way to defuse the tension. "Why don't we all head over to the site and—"

"What have I ever done to you?" Buddy asked with exasperation. "Or are you such a miserable bastard you take on everyone this way?"

"You haven't done anything to me."

"Precisely my point."

"Although I'd be worried about what you're doing to your wife and daughter." Nick's eyes were fierce.

Buddy looked shocked. "What?"

"I don't know many men with the gall to sleep around under their daughter's nose. You're a depraved son of a bitch—you know that?"

Buddy blinked in confusion and glanced over at Carter. "Do you know what he's talking about?"

"I wouldn't know where to start," she said, throwing up her hands in defeat.

Buddy looked back at Nick. "You think she . . . and I . . ."

He started to laugh. It was a happy sound, completely at odds with the stress in the air. Buddy put a hand on Nick's shoulder.

"I knew it," he said when he paused for breath. "I knew it all along."

"Let's just leave this," Carter begged. "Forget all about—"

"I knew you were attracted to her."

Nick frowned at the smile shining up at him.

"Listen," Buddy said in a light, relieved tone, "Carter's the most wonderful woman I have ever met, apart from my wife. But I can swear on the life of my child that I have never, ever been unfaithful to Jo-Jo in thought or deed. Partially because she's got a lab full of dangerous chemicals in our basement, but mostly because I love her with all my heart. Not that it's any of your business."

Carter saw that Nick was watching the man carefully, weighing his words.

Still smiling, Buddy ambled over to the kitchen area and put away the utensils he'd washed. "Take it from someone who was lucky enough to find the love of his life and luckier still to have had the courage to do something about it. Time's passing and you should be spending less time glaring at me and more time alone with her."

With something perilously close to a chuckle, Buddy gave them a cheerful wave and left.

In his wake, they were silent for a time. Even though her friend had left in a good mood, Carter felt as if the friction had increased in his absence.

"Your Buddy's quite the philosopher," Nick said, eventually. "I suppose I owe him an apology."

"He's a pretty forgiving sort." Nervous, she began to babble. "I once dropped a sledgehammer on his foot and broke it in three places. His foot, of course, not the hammer. He got over it, although he still gives me a wide circle when I carry heavy tools . . ."

Abruptly, Carter clamped her mouth shut before more inane words tumbled out. She was trapped between wanting to run away from him and wanting to make plans for a good long sail over the water.

She heard him approach. When she looked up, she saw his pale eyes were no longer remote. They were burning.

"I guess I owe you an apology as well," Nick said, his voice a low rumble.

A shiver of anticipation went through her.

He reached out and tucked a stray hair behind her ear. "Since I've met you, I think I've apologized to you more than I have any other woman."

"If you're warming up to another one, it's only been twice."

"As I said . . ." His fingertips brushed over her cheek, down to her jaw. "I'm sorry I jumped to the wrong conclusion about you and Buddy."

"We've never been more than good friends."

"I can see that now. I'm just not used to women like you."

Her voice dropped to a whisper. "What kind of a woman am I?"

His eyes scanned over her face and a smile lifted the corners of his mouth. "Clueless."

She frowned. "Thanks. Remind me not to come here for compliments when I have body image problems."

Nick laughed and then grew somber.

"I don't think you have any idea how beautiful you are." His voice was hypnotic, a blend of rasp and purr that was making her temporarily forget her doubts about him. "And you've been keeping me up at night, wondering whether I remembered it right."

"Remembered what?" she croaked.

"That your lips taste like sweet melon."

Carter's heart leapt to her throat. He was going to kiss her. She knew it. Wanted it.

He stepped in closer.

"You're one hell of a woman." Nick reached his hand underneath the weight of her hair and stroked her neck. "But you're a rotten eavesdropper."

Carter flushed as the apology she'd been waiting to offer came out.

"I'm sorry about that," she mumbled. "I got lost trying to find my way out of your house and I didn't mean to intrude. I—"

"Did you enjoy hearing that Candace was leaving because of you?"

At the sound of the other woman's name, Carter pulled back sharply. With a few faltering steps, she took refuge behind the table and began picking up napkins.

"What's wrong?" he asked.

"I remember other parts of the conversation more vividly."

"Really?" His voice changed back to the laconic drawl she was used to hearing. She watched as the heat in his eyes dimmed and his cool remoteness returned.

While he waited for her to explain, she wondered how honest she should be. Did she want to admit she was scared of getting hurt? She didn't think so. She was already feeling vulnerable.

Then Nick spoke before she did. "I'm no angel, Carter, and I've never pretended to be one. But don't condemn me because I'm honest. There are no guarantees in any relationship. I believe in stating that upfront and getting out when things aren't working. It's better than living in a fantasy."

"But what about the women?"

"What about them?"

"They get hurt." I'd get hurt, she thought to herself.

"They know what they're getting into. Believe me, they're tough enough to handle it." His voice was jaded.

Feeling way out of her league, Carter looked down at the napkins she'd wadded up in her hands. "Are you still planning to ask me out for that sail?"

"Yes, I am."

"And what do you think we'll do when we're alone?"

"Eat, drink, swim. Enjoy the day." When she glanced up at his pause, he finished, "Make love."

Her heart began jumping around in her chest. It was what she wanted to hear but it also frightened her.

She took a deep breath. "And, in your spirit of honesty, would you like to tell me where all that is going to take us?"

The frown that appeared on his face wasn't encouraging. Neither was the long silence that followed.

Carter laughed stiffly. "If I go by those tight lips of yours and all this resounding quiet, should I take it the answer is *nowhere*?"

He wrenched a hand through his hair. "Of course not."

"So what are we doing?"

"I don't know." His voice sounded frustrated.

"No wonder your women get confused," she said gruffly. "Is this what you always say to them?"

"No. It isn't."

"So what is?"

He pushed his hands into the pockets of his khakis and looked uncomfortable. "I tell them not to get serious. That I'm not looking for anything long-term. That if they come across a better offer, they should take it."

Carter sighed and shook her head sadly. "I don't know why I asked."

"Do you want me to lie to you?" He raised his hands up with irritation. "What exactly are you looking for?"

"I'm not sure, but it's not what just came out of your mouth. I don't like being reminded how foolhardy it would be to get involved with you." She wrapped her arms around herself.

He shook his head back and forth. "I don't know what else to tell you. I'm sorry."

"That makes three."

He fixed her with a level stare, his eyebrows arched.

"Three apologies."

Nick's laugh was short but it reached his eyes. "I guess I'm beginning to make up for all those years of being an insensitive son of a bitch. Never thought that'd happen."

Their eyes met and held. When he spoke again, his voice had softened. "I don't want to hurt you."

"Good. I don't want to get hurt."

"And when I say I don't know what's ahead, I mean it's not clear to me how you fit in." His face was serious. She sensed he was giving her the best answer he could.

"Fit in with what?" she prompted.

"The way things usually go between women and me."

A spark of hope caught fire in her chest. "I suppose if your reputation is anything to go by, that's probably a good thing."

"I think it is." There was a lengthy pause. "So the weather's going to be good tomorrow."

"Really," she said cautiously.

"It'll be a good day to be out on the lake."

It was a long time before she answered him.

"All right. Let's go."

The next morning, Carter spent an hour pacing around inside her tent after breakfast. The problem she was facing, aside from the fact that she was about to be alone with Nick for the whole day, was that she had nothing to wear.

Which was laughable. She hadn't worried about her wardrobe in years. Yet there she was, on the side of a mountain, wondering which pair of khaki shorts would look better to a man she had no business getting involved with in the first place.

Reminding herself that it was just a boat ride and not the Oscars, she dropped to her knees and dug into her duffel again, fishing through the stacks of folded T-shirts and shorts, looking for an inspiration that remained elusive. The homogeneity of the whites, blacks, and khakis struck her for the first time as disappointing. She didn't have a wardrobe, she thought. She had a uniform.

Carter finally settled on a pair of shorts, changed into them, and put on a clean, white tank top that showed off her tanned arms. After running a brush through her hair, she filled her backpack with a pair of purple flip-flops, that mystery novel she'd almost finished, and her baseball cap. On a whim, she tossed the brush in and was about to step outside when she realized she'd forgotten her bathing suit. Wading through the bag, she searched in vain for the black one-piece.

"Dammit."

"What's wrong?" Ellie said, putting her head in through the tent flap.

"I'm late and I can't find my bathing suit."

"You can borrow one of mine."

Relief struck. "Thanks. That would be great."

Ellie disappeared and returned with a bundle wrapped in a towel. "Bathing suit, towel, and sunblock."

"You're a lifesaver." Carter crammed the wad into her backpack as the two went out into the sunshine.

"So I hope you have fun on your date," Ellie said with a teasing lilt.

"It's just a sail."

"Sure it is."

"Really." Carter tried to sound serious but, with all her nervous excitement, it was hard to pull off.

"Uh-huh. Like dinner and a movie is just food and a chance to take a load off in the dark?"

"See you later," Carter said firmly while trying not to grin.

As she raced down the mountain, she couldn't believe what she was doing.

The shock of it all didn't slow her down one bit, however.

When she approached the boathouse, she saw that the sailboat had been taken off its mooring and was tied to the dock. Its teak gunnels and brass riggings gleamed in the sun, and the thick wooden mast waved lazily to the sky.

She flushed as she saw Nick appear out of the cabin. He was wearing a Harvard sweatshirt and a pair of black trunks. His hair looked wet, as if he'd just been swimming, and he had on those dark sunglasses. With fluid power, he leapt off the boat onto the dock. His legs were tanned and muscular, clearly those of an athlete. With all that hardness and lack of spare fat, she knew he'd been doing some heavy-duty endurance training. She had to wonder when he found the time.

He bent down, picked up a picnic hamper, and casually hopped back on the boat. A tune, hummed under his breath, was carried up to her on the breeze.

"Don't just stand there looking good," he said over his shoulder. "Let's get going."

Carter blushed, wondering how long she'd been staring at him. How long he'd known she was there.

Stifling her embarrassment, she stepped onto the dock and said casually, "Nice boat."

Nick offered her a hand up but she jumped aboard without his help and caught his grin at the rebuff. She stowed her gear and then went over to the console that controlled the boat's discreet inboard motor.

"Shall we fire this baby up?" she asked. When he didn't answer, she looked over at him and felt a quickening deep inside her body. "What?"

"You know your way around a boat, don't you?"

"Of course. Now are we going to get going?"

He laughed. "Sure. Just make sure she's in neutral, pull the choke—"

She had the engine flaring to life before he finished the sentence.

"Cast off," she told him, looking out to the lake.

"Hey, who's captain here?"

"Who's at the helm?" When she glanced over her shoulder, they shared a smile. "Cast off, mate."

She grinned with satisfaction as Nick did as he was told.

10

NICK ENJOYED watching Carter at the helm. She had one hand on the boat's wheel, the other on the engine controls, and a big smile on her face. Putting them in reverse, she gave the engine some throttle, pulled away from the dock, and executed a perfect turn in front of the boathouse.

"Nice maneuvering," he said as she took them toward the open water.

"Thanks."

"You do this a lot?"

"Every chance I get."

"Me, too."

Confident in her handling of the boat, he went fore and hoisted the mainsail. When he was satisfied with his rigging job, Nick came back to the cockpit.

"Let's head south. We can tack over to a secluded bay that's got a great swimming hole."

"What's the temperature of the lake?"

"About sixty-five degrees. Not cold enough to turn you into a Popsicle, but it'll get your attention."

The sailboat rode through the choppy waves in the bay with water slapping at its sides and spray coming over the bow. Overhead, the sky was clear, except for an occasional cloud, and sunshine rippled across the lake with flashes of gold. It was a perfect day in late June and Nick felt downright jubilant.

As well as very attracted to the woman who stood before him.

When they were past the peninsula that insulated the boathouse, Carter cut the engine as the sail grabbed a gust of wind and the boat took off. Targeting the best trajectory for the wind's direction, she set them on an aggressive course that maximized their speed. The gurgling noise of their wake swelled, and Nick adjusted himself higher on the gunnels to compensate for the boat's lean into the water. She was in total control at the helm as she angled them farther into the gusts, ensuring that every square inch of the sail was filled with wind. The boat was tilted at a steep pitch, the keel almost out of the water, and still she pushed them harder.

Nick didn't look where they were going because he couldn't take his eyes off Carter. Her hair was billowing around in the wind, the dark strands whipping across her face in a lively dance. Her eyes sparkled as much as the sunlight on the water. Her joy was palpable.

"You're a terrific sailor," he said over the din. He was surprised as a shadow crossed her face.

"I spent a lot of time sailing as a child."

"Where?"

When she remained silent, he wondered if she'd heard him.

Finally she answered, "The Aegean Sea, Bahamas, off the coast of Brittany. On Lake Michigan here in the States." She hesitated. "My father taught me."

Nick's interest was piqued by the grudging admission, and he changed his position so that he was closer to her. "He taught you well. You see him much?"

Carter's head wrenched around and she immediately got defensive. "Why do you ask?"

"Pretty common question about someone's father, isn't it?"

There was a long pause as she seemed to struggle with anger and mistrust. "No. I don't see him."

"Ever?"

She shook her head.

"Mind if I ask why?"

He watched as her hands tightened on the wheel.

"I don't want to ruin the day with a conversation like that."

"You two don't get along?"

"No one can get along with a sociopath," she snapped.

"Sociopath? He's got a reputation for being fairly ethical."

Her eyes were wide, almost panicked, as they flashed to his. "How well do you know him?"

"I've met him a number of times." Nick made sure his words were gently spoken. "But that can't be a shock. He's a venture capitalist, too."

"I should have known," she muttered. "Two sharks swimming in the same water."

"Two men in the same line of business."

They were silent for a long time.

Nick's eyes never left her. He needed to know what had happened to make her hate William Wessex so much.

"Why are you staring at me?" she demanded impatiently, tightening her grip on the wheel.

"Why don't you want to talk about your father?"

"Oh, for Chrissakes." She shifted angry eyes to him. "Can't you just leave it alone?"

"Just tell me why."

"Because it's guaranteed to put me in a bad mood, as you can see. I didn't know you were so interested in family dynamics."

"I'm interested in you."

She stiffened. "Be interested in me in other ways."

"I am."

"Then be satisfied with what I'm willing to give you."

"I want more."

"Tough." Her voice was hostile.

"I want all of you."

Her blue eyes flashed to his. He saw alarm in them. And heat.

Nick was shocked by his admission, too. It had leapt

out of him with such honesty he couldn't have held it back if he'd wanted to.

"You can't blame my curiosity," he said, changing the subject. "One mention of your father and you're gripping that wheel like it's your last hold on sanity."

He watched as she forced her hands to relax.

"Did you ever get along with him?"

Carter stayed silent for a long time, and all that traveled between them was the sound of the water and the rush of the wind.

Then she said, slowly, "My father and I . . . When I was growing up, I worshiped him. He wasn't around a lot, but when he was my life got more stable and I was happy. Although that was all before I really knew the man. I miss the illusion of him."

"And your mother?"

"Dead. But then, you must know that, right?"

"I'm sorry. I know what it's like to lose parents. Were you close to her?"

Carter shrugged and focused on the horizon, though he doubted she was actually seeing what was ahead of them. "Mummy was beautiful. Far too young for Father. In the beginning, he cherished her like a doll and, because she craved attention, they got along rather well, or so I've heard. She had me when she was twenty-two, one year and two months after they married. Things began to unravel after that. She was far better equipped to be a child than to raise one. I grew up. I don't think she ever did."

Carter was talking to herself, he realized, and he didn't prompt her when she paused, for fear she would stop speaking altogether.

"They weren't a good match. My father was always gone and she didn't handle being alone well. Of course, she'd have handled it better if he'd been faithful while he was away." She stopped abruptly. "Isn't it time we come about?"

"A little bit farther," he said, holding off the flurry of activity that would come with changing the sailboat's direction. He knew the conversation would be lost. "When was the last time you saw him?"

"At her funeral," she said brusquely. "I think we should come about."

"Not yet. Another couple hundred yards. Does your father ever try to get in touch with you?"

"Coming about," she announced, and wrenched the wheel around. The boat swung hard, and Nick was thrown off balance. He recovered quickly and leapt to reel in the mainsail. When they were settled on their new course, Carter regarded him coolly.

"That's enough conversation about my past. I live in the here and now. That's all I've got and it's all I need."

She remained quiet as they traveled down the lake, but at least they fell into a good pattern. Carter would call the directional change and work the helm while he handled the sails. The easy rhythm went a long way to relaxing the tension that had sprung up during their conversation.

A while later, Nick pointed ahead.

"Head over to that island. The bay's behind it."

She piloted the sailboat easterly. The island was a quarter mile offshore and about the size of a football field. As they passed by it, they saw that none of the campsites dotting the shore was inhabited. After the Fourth of July, the official start of summer, they'd be in high demand, but not now, not quite yet.

"It's so peaceful here," she remarked.

Nick nodded, pleased she was talking to him. He'd pressed her too far on the topic of her family, but he'd learned some valuable information. The raw strength of her emotions about her father made him rethink the chance of a successful reunion between them.

"Did you ever camp on any of the islands?" she asked as they drifted by another empty dock, tent platform, and hearth.

"When I was young, it was high living to me. Taking a bedroll, a knapsack full of food, and heading out onto the lake with no particular direction. It was a great adventure."

When they cleared the island and breached the entrance to the bay, the sailboat's mainsail began to flutter. Nick took it down and secured it as Carter fired up the engine.

As she steered the boat deeper inside the secluded paradise, Carter was awed by the bay's beauty. The lofty mountain overhead charged down to the lakeshore in a series of jagged cliffs, but it wasn't all steep rocks and plunging vistas. In the far corner, there was an alcove that offered gentler slopes and a level place that would be perfect for sunbathing and picnicking.

Shutting down the engine, she let them drift silently. The water was calm and clear, the breeze soft and welcoming. Wood ducks, clustered in pairs, skimmed over the placid water, and somewhere in the background she could hear the call of a loon.

"This is spectacular," she murmured.

"One of my favorite places in the world," Nick said, reaching into a hold and taking out an anchor. "I've been to more five-star hotels than most travel writers, but I'd take this over any of them."

He tossed the anchor overboard in a single, powerful movement. It landed with a splash, kicking water up into the sunlight.

As she looked down into the lake and watched the ripples he'd created spread over the smooth surface, she regretted her revelations. She hadn't spoken of her father to anyone in a long time, and it had been hard to relive her feelings. Mixing her confusing emotions for Nick with her shadowy past was particularly disturbing.

And she'd have much preferred that the two men didn't know each other at all.

In the quiet that surrounded them, she felt pressured to make conversation, to bury what she'd told him about her family under mundane chatter. Subjects like the weather or interest rates seemed appealing, but she settled for tourism. It was less obvious and something she could fib her way through, which was more than she could say for Alan Greenspan's lot.

"Do you come here often?" She hoped her tone passed for casual.

Nick was standing on the bow, looking at the mountains, and he turned to talk with her.

"Only in the off-season. In July and August, this place is standing room only. It gets choked with tourists in powerboats. Ironically, they come to enjoy nature but instead end up in nautical gridlock, choking on exhaust fumes and drowning in noise pollution. It's a damn shame."

He paused and then took off his sweatshirt.

Carter didn't hear anything else he said.

Trying to appear as if she wasn't staring, she forced herself to murmur in appropriate places and hoped she nailed the right pauses. Seeing him naked to the waist had wiped out any coherent thought. His chest was wide and well muscled, his arms carved, his stomach a washboard of planes and angles. Lightly tan, his skin was smooth, with only a little hair marking his pecs and disappearing in a line under the waistband of his trunks.

"Hello?" he said in a sexy drawl.

"I'm sorry—what?"

Nick's smile was slow and full of promise. "Do you like what you see?"

Carter tried to swallow. "I told you, the bay is beautiful."

"I didn't think you were looking at the landscape."

He approached her with unmistakable purpose, and she took an involuntary step back.

"Of course, I was. The water, those ducks over there . . . the water . . ."

Carter panicked, overwhelmed by how good he looked and the fact that they were alone. That she wanted him badly and might actually have him.

"I have to go change now," she said quickly, skirting around the helm.

His laughter, deep and very male, followed her down into the cabin.

Hands shaking, Carter shut the door and collapsed against the wood.

Trying to pull herself together, she grabbed her backpack and fumbled with its zipper. When she finally got the thing open, she wrenched Ellie's towel free with more force than necessary and it unraveled wildly, throwing something to the floor in a flash of color.

Carter stared, dumbfounded, at what had popped out.

"You've got to be kidding me," she said aloud.

"What's that?" Nick asked from outside.

"Nothing."

Which was exactly what she was looking at. Two tiny pieces of pink fabric joined by a string and a larger piece the size of a handkerchief. She picked them up, wondering where the rest of the bikini was.

"Ellie, you're only fifteen," she said with exasperation.

"What?" he called out.

"It's so pristine down here."

"Thanks. I like to keep a neat boat."

Rolling her eyes, she sank down onto one of the bunks and looked around the cabin for a better option.

It was pristine, from the galley kitchen to the two sleeping compartments to the sitting area. Everywhere, wood and brass glowed with age and attention. It was luxurious and elegant, perfectly appointed.

But it sure as hell didn't offer up anything else she could swim in.

Carter glanced down at the pink slashes of fabric and then over to the kitchenette, wondering if she could make do with a dish towel or two. Hell, if he had any Band-Aids around, she'd use them. A box of those would cover more surface area. Stay in place better, too.

"You okay down there?"

"Fine," she called out and then muttered, "Just damn ducky."

She'd feel foolish reappearing on deck in her clothes but would feel like an exhibitionist wearing the bikini. The trouble was, she really wanted to go swimming. And besides, she had nothing to be ashamed about. Years of hard labor had honed her body into top condition. She was perfectly fit and, after all, she didn't have anything that he hadn't seen before.

Oh, that was a big help, she thought, imagining all of the women he must have seen naked.

Grimacing, she stripped and put on the bikini. With some artful arranging, she was able to cover the parts that would have gotten her arrested for indecent exposure, but she was far from feeling clothed.

Wrapping the towel around herself tightly, she emerged from the cabin, trying to look calm and composed.

Nick's sensuous smile greeted her. He'd taken off the sunglasses, and she watched his eyes go over her legs and linger on her thighs. "You want to swim first or have lunch?"

"Lunch."

"Picnic it is. Can you just reach down into that hold and grab the hamper? I didn't have time to put all the food in the fridge."

"Sure. No problem."

But the reality of bending over, picking up the basket, and keeping herself covered proved to be more than she could handle. Gravity won over coordination and the towel slid down to the deck.

She heard Nick hiss through his teeth.

When she looked up at him, he was staring at her with a look that took her breath away. In response, her breasts strained the bounds of the bikini, pulling against the fragile strings. As her nipples peaked, his face tightened with need.

"You are . . ." He didn't finish, just whispered, "Come here."

He held his hand out to her and, before she could think about what she was doing, she took it. As he drew her toward him, she felt his other hand slowly slide around her waist and settle onto the small of her back. His skin was warm on hers and her breasts brushed up against the faint hair on his chest.

"I've been imagining what it would feel like to have you naked, in my arms." His voice was very deep.

Carter felt his hands drift lower until they were on her

hips. They gripped her body urgently, and he pulled her all the way against him. When she felt the rigid length of him, her mouth opened with a gasp.

That was when he kissed her.

The contact was shockingly soft. Even though she could sense the urgency in his body, his lips were gentle against hers. Persuasive, cajoling, light. Teasing her with a patience that spoke to the depth of his self-control. She could feel herself relaxing, giving herself up to the sensation of his tongue in her mouth, sliding wet and warm inside of her, wrapping around her own.

Caught in the maelstrom, she forgot about everything.

When his fingers sought out the hard tips of her breasts, his touch as gentle as the sunlight that was warming them, she moaned into his mouth. Electrical shocks surged through her and she gripped hard onto his shoulders.

"Carter," he said against her mouth, roughly. "Will you let me make love to you?"

She knew the choice was up to her. He was giving her the power of their future.

Carter met his glittering eyes. They were nothing like the lucid ones he usually looked out onto the world with. Now they reflected a storm raging inside of him, an incandescent, swirling need that she knew she was responsible for igniting.

She took a step back from him and his face contracted in pain. But she wasn't turning away. Slowly, she reached behind and freed the strings of the bikini top, letting it fall to the deck. She watched as a shudder went through him, wracking his body. When she put her hand on his bare chest, he let out a groan.

This time when he kissed her, there was nothing soft about it. Desperation sent them careening into the cabin where he pressed her down onto one of the bunks and covered her with the weight of his body. As he removed the bottom to the bikini and his own trunks, her hands traveled the broad expanse of his back, feeling his muscles under smooth skin.

When he settled in between her thighs, she knew an erotic sensation so powerful that she felt as if she had left her body behind. She arched her back and his head came down to her. He kissed the skin of her neck, trailing small bites downward until he took the tip of a breast into his mouth, rolling it with his tongue.

Crying out, she thrust her hips into his, feeling him come up against her very core. But he didn't enter her, not yet. His hands and his mouth explored her body, learning the most intimate parts of her. Only when she could take no more did he come up over her and capture her lips in a kiss that was reverent. Slowly, he slid inside of her.

As he entered her, Carter moaned deeply. They began to move together, a rhythm that quickly grew to a frantic dance of sensuality. As they rose higher and higher, she was breathing heavily, hanging on to his surging body, her heart racing and her hips absorbing his thrusts, until she was bathed in white heat. His name left her lips, sailing up into the air, a hoarse cry, and she felt his powerful body shudder into her, his arms contracting around her.

After the tempest, Carter felt his head drop onto her shoulder, his breath coming in gasps. The sweat that covered his forehead was a delicious wetness against her skin. When he finally lifted his head, she was shocked by his expression. Gone were any traces of cynicism and hardness. It was a stunning transformation. He looked younger. Happy. Satisfied.

She smiled at him.

And the expression that came back at her was of such tenderness, she felt her heart ache.

He stroked away a lock of hair that had gotten tangled around her neck, and it seemed as if he was on the verge of a revelation. But instead of giving her words, he kissed her.

And the heat rose again.

After a fortifying lunch, they settled down on the deck in the sun. Nick positioned himself against the mast and

Carter put her head in his lap, promptly falling asleep while he watched over her.

Underneath the scant triangles of the bikini, her chest rose and fell with her delicate, even breaths. She looked vulnerable as she slept in his arms, and a strange feeling came over him. It was so powerful that he could decipher neither its cause nor its content, and his first thought was to run from whatever it was.

Except, as he looked down into her face, he didn't want to leave. Slowly, he tried to figure out what was bothering him.

After they'd made love that first time, and he'd fallen against her, utterly spent, he'd recognized that something dramatic had taken place. Something unparalleled in his life, something that had stripped him bare, exposed him in a way he'd never been before to anyone. And he'd wanted to tell her what he was feeling.

When he'd tried to marshal words, however, they'd refused to form cogent lines. His thoughts had splintered and fragmented in his mind until they didn't make sense, even to himself. That was when he'd kissed her again and tried to show her with his hands and mouth what he couldn't tell her.

But something had changed. As she lay sleeping, he now felt only panic. An urgent need to retreat from her and the closeness she represented.

Dimly, Nick noticed the breeze had caught a tendril of her black hair, whisking it over her nose. He carefully moved the errant strand away, not wanting her sleep disturbed. In response, she stirred in his lap, curling over on her side and tucking her arms around herself. The graceful curve of her cheek and her lips captured and held his eyes.

Love.

The word came to him like a ghost and, as it bounced around his brain, he thought of the past. There had been so few women he'd felt love for, and his own mother wasn't even one of them. When he considered it, he realized that Gertie and his sister were the only possible exceptions to the emotional distance he kept from the fairer sex. Both of them had loved him for who he was and had never looked for anything more.

Which sure as hell set them apart from most of the women he'd come across.

Would such simplicity and acceptance be Carter's way?

Yes, an insistent voice told him.

Except even as the thought occurred to him, he rebelled against its implications.

He wasn't ready to fall in love. Besides, he wasn't sure he knew how to love someone. He hadn't been close to his parents. Hadn't done enough for his sister when she'd been alive. And Cort? God knew that relationship was a complicated mess.

So what the hell did he have to offer Carter?

The answer that came back to him was painfully sparse. Almost every relationship he'd ever had with a woman had been merely physical. Looking back on it, his love life had been punctuated by scenes like the one he'd just been through with Candace. A long string of good-byes that had been easy for him to initiate.

He had quite a run going, Nick thought with disdain.

But now this beautiful, smart woman whom he'd just made love to, this woman he suspected he might be able to love, now she had come into his life and he felt at a loss. Instead of being grateful for the gift, he seemed incapable of accepting what she had to offer. He was a successful businessman, in his late thirties, who had no clue how to handle a serious, adult relationship with a woman. With an equal.

A wholly unfamiliar chill went through him. It was followed by a surge of irrational anger.

As if she'd felt the shift in his emotions, Carter opened her eyes and looked up at him.

In that instant, Nick went into hiding. He shifted his cold mask into place and watched from a distance as her expression lost its warmth and happiness.

"Where have you gone while I was sleeping?" she said softly.

"I'm right here."

"No, you're not."

"So your head's in someone else's lap?" His voice was sharp, close to combative.

As Carter sat up, he knew he'd ruined the afternoon. The sun was still washing over them, the bay was beautiful, but her eyes were dark.

"What's wrong?" Anxiety replaced the relaxation that had been on her face.

"Nothing."

"You're lying to me."

"Don't behave like a girlfriend. I don't do well with that kind of thing." Nick avoided her eyes, unable to stomach the dawning pain in them.

There was a wealth of confusion in her voice. "How does my asking you what's wrong equate to—"

"You see? Now you want to talk about what's wrong with my telling you nothing is wrong. These kind of conversations are pointless."

"I don't . . . understand." She shook her head, her hair flashing black in the sun. There was a telltale shine in her eyes that told him she was close to tears.

Seeing her hurt and knowing he'd caused it only made him more angry.

He lashed out. "With Candace gone, I was looking forward to a respite from getting poked and prodded by someone in a skirt. I guess the optimism was premature."

Carter gasped. "I can't believe you just said that."

Frankly, neither could Nick.

"Talk to me," she implored.

"What do you want me to say?"

There was a long pause and then, abruptly, Carter's expression changed from hurt to angry. She shot to her feet. "We're going back. Right now. Before I do something else I'll regret."

"Else?"

"Sleeping with you was clearly a mistake. I don't want to compound the error by trying to drown you." With a violent movement, she wrapped a towel around herself.

"You know, I never pictured you as the hysterical type."

She turned on him, emphasizing her words with clipped consonants. "This is not hysterical. This is pissed off. There's a big difference."

Nick watched her march down into the cabin and then cursed in frustration. The words that had come out of his mouth, the tone he'd used, everything about the fight was familiar to him. It was what he had done countless times before. The behavior felt oddly safe.

That was when something occurred to him. He knew what was coming next. Following one of these scenes, there was always relief. A sweet rush would course through his blood as he realized he was untouched, unhampered. Free.

Desperately, he waited for the salvation to come.

Minutes passed.

He took a deep breath, eager for the release.

It was ten minutes later that Nick wrenched a hand through his hair. His chest was still tight, his muscles rigid, his heart in a knot.

"Dammit," he said roughly, feeling cheated. He wasn't supposed to feel worse.

Then again, Carter never had fit into his pattern.

Getting up, he went over to the door she'd slammed shut. He was surprised at what he was prepared to do. Was he actually going to try to apologize? Yes, he was.

Nick hesitated. He wasn't sure what he was going to say. He knew only that he felt far, far worse after pushing her away, not better.

When the cabin door opened abruptly, he reached out for her.

"Carter, I'm sorry."

"Oh no, you don't." With an angry shove, she pushed him away. "Let me teach you the difference between pissed off and hysterical. The whole contrite thing works with hysterical. It doesn't do jack for someone who's pissed off. So you can take your apologies and go practice them in the mirror. No doubt, you'll need them for the next *skirt* who's dumb enough to fall into bed with you."

"Will you let me explain?" There was a pleading tone in his voice that he'd never heard before.

"There's nothing to explain. I saw what happened to Candace."

"You're not like her."

"That's not true. I was surprised when you pushed me away, too." She went to the helm. "Now, get the anchor out of the damn water and let's end this charade right now."

Nick stared at her for a long time, and she looked him right in the eye, all coldness and defiance.

"What are you waiting for?" she demanded. "If you think I'm going to let you walk all over me, you're out of your mind."

"Look, I'm not good at this—"

"Obviously. But I don't give a rat's ass. I want to go home. *Now.*"

Their eyes met.

He'd blown it. Big-time.

"If you're waiting for me to come around," she said in a brusque voice, "I might as well start swimming. Because you'll be in this bay 'til hell freezes over waiting for me to give you another shot."

"Fine." He turned away, scowling. "Start the engine."

"With pleasure."

11

CARTER WALKED up the mountain alone after shooting down Nick's offer to escort her up the trail. She couldn't wait to be by herself. The trip back from the bay had been one long, tense silence, punctuated by her terse commands from the helm and his tight responses. The whole time, she could feel his eyes on her, boring into her.

Considering the state she was in, she thought she'd done a bang-up job keeping her composure on the damn boat. Now that she was alone, though, she felt like collapsing. Her pride gone, her anger dissipated, all she felt was a sick ache. The fact that she should have known better was just one more shadow in the nightmare.

When she'd woken from her blissful doze and rolled over in his lap, she'd expected to see the joy and happiness she was feeling in his face. Instead, he'd been looking at her with a cold detachment. It had been a shock, to say the least, and then he'd followed it up by speaking to her in that condescending way. She cringed as she remembered what he'd said.

After making love to her like no one else had or probably could, he'd promptly reverted to type. He was a pursuer, she thought. And men who liked to chase things didn't find much amusement in keeping them. It was exactly what she had feared.

If only she'd listened to her instincts.

When Carter reached the summit clearing, she looked out over the lake and tried to pull herself together. She was bitterly sorry she'd let things go so far with him and felt like throwing her head back and screaming.

Instead of indulging the impulse, she looked toward the sunset, taking in the magnificent peaches and pinks that stretched across the horizon. It was what her grandmother would have called a lovers' sky. One so special, it had to be shared.

Be honest, Carter said to herself. What had she expected would happen when they made love? That he was going to miraculously change and become a sensitive, accessible, warm-and-fuzzy kind of guy? That Candace's fate wouldn't fall on her head? That they'd embark on a long, mutually satisfying relationship?

That she would be the exception?

Well, yes. And the other half of the problem was that she hadn't been thinking much at all. When he'd kissed her, she'd been lost to him. It was that simple.

Lovers' sky, my ass, she thought, turning away.

"Where's the printout of my daily log?" Carter asked the next day. She was talking to herself as she rooted around Papercut Central, weeding through loose-leaf binders, notepads, and files.

"It's right there, isn't it?" Ellie said, coming to help.

"It should be. I thought I put it here yesterday before I left."

"Could it be in your tent?"

Buddy poked his head inside. He hadn't shaved or brushed his hair yet, and his glasses were slightly off-center, but he was looking perfectly happy as he sipped his coffee. "You lose something?"

"I can't find the site records, either," Carter murmured.

Frowning, Buddy put his mug down. "They've got to be here somewhere. When we finished removing the second skeleton yesterday morning, I spent two hours writing it all up. I was sitting right here."

He looked through the piles of paper on the table and, when he came up empty-handed, they searched the whole camp.

When that yielded nothing, Buddy scratched his head. "Maybe someone was up here yesterday while we were gone."

"How long were you guys away?" Carter asked.

"We went to town. Did some shopping. Got the car back. Probably two, three hours."

"But how would anyone get up here?" Ellie interjected. "Ivan the Terrible knows where everyone is."

Her father shrugged. "There's the access road that Cort uses for the four-wheeler. It comes up the other side of the mountain. It's a lot less direct, but no one down at the mansion would know. Except what the hell would someone want with those records? They're hardly light reading. Who would care?"

"Conrad Lyst cares," Carter said softly. Buddy's eyes shifted to hers.

"Who's Conrad Lyst?" Ellie asked. "Is he a thief?"

"A loser, to put it in your terms," her father replied. "And a rotten archaeologist. He could dig up a landfill and not find any garbage. But he's not going to traipse all the way into the Adirondacks just to take a tutorial on digging strategy. Right, Carter?"

When she didn't answer, two heads snapped in her direction.

Buddy looked back at his daughter. "Hey, do you mind going to the site and getting—"

"Are you trying to get rid of me?"

"Not at all."

"Look, you should just say so," Ellie told him agreeably. "I'm going to wash up at the river."

After the girl left, Buddy frowned. "What haven't you been telling me?"

"He was up here before," Carter answered, feeling badly she hadn't told him sooner. "The day you and Ellie went to drop off your car in town."

"Good Lord. Why didn't you tell me?"

"I've been meaning to."

"And it just didn't come up?"

"It was no big deal." Her eyes darted away from the concern on his face. "He just played bull in the ring and pawed the ground a little." She could tell by his worried expression that Buddy didn't buy the lie.

"I wish you'd said something to me earlier. You tell Farrell?"

"No. I didn't think it was necessary."

"But now we've got papers missing. Farrell should know."

"No, he shouldn't." Carter's voice wavered at the mention of Nick, but she pressed on. "I've got the documents backed up on my hard drive, and I used my laptop this morning so I know it's still around. The missing printouts don't materially affect the dig."

"But this is serious. If Lyst came back and took the logs—"

"He'd have no idea what to do with them. That man's analytical skills are as sharp as bread dough, and besides, the finds are all still here and it's not like he can barge in and start digging."

Buddy frowned, pensively. "If he can't do anything with the logs, why would he want them?"

"Most likely, he wants to know if we've found the gold, and he probably kept them to send a message. He's the type who'd do it just to rattle our cage and make sure we knew he'd been here."

Her friend took off his glasses and rubbed his eyes. "You know, it's not just that I don't respect the man. There's something wrong with him."

You got that right, she thought.

He looked over in the direction of the stream. "I think I'm going to stick closer to Ellie from now on."

Carter watched him leave in a hurry and wished there was something reassuring she could say. Buddy had always watched over her, and she could tell he was worried not only about Ellie but about her as well.

She turned back to the piles of papers and files and

started straightening them. When she heard footsteps on the ground, she said, "Buddy, I should call the Hall Foundation and give Grace an update. She'll be thrilled about the skeletons."

"You can use the phone down at the house," Nick said in a level voice.

Carter swallowed a gasp and stiffened. She refused to turn around and continued to fiddle with the papers. "What the hell are you doing here?"

"I came to see you." His tone was low and quiet, as if he didn't want to startle her.

"Why?" Her hands were shaking as she picked up a file and pretended to sort through it. She wanted desperately for him to go away. She needed space to lick her wounds, not more injuries to fix.

"We need to talk."

She threw the folder down and glared at him. "I'm done talking. Now, if you'll excuse me, I need to get back to work."

"Can't you just listen to me?" She saw a flash of frustration cross his face.

Shaking her head, she didn't bother to keep the bitterness out of her voice. "I already *listened* to you yesterday. You were pretty damn eloquent with the put-downs and, because my short-term memory's working just fine, I remember every word you said. I don't need to hear it again, thank you very much."

"Oh for Chrissakes, Carter, will you give me a break?"

"Now you're the victim?" She laughed harshly. "You know, it's rare to be so deluded and not be on medication."

Nick pushed a hand through his hair. "I don't want to argue with you. I came up here to apologize and to see if we can start over."

"I'm not interested in starting over. One trip through the grinder with you has been enough. Besides, I know how you can't abide *hysterical girlfriends,* and we wouldn't want to upset you again, would we?"

She turned and started out blindly for the site but he caught up with her, taking her arm in a strong grip.

"Let go of me," she whispered urgently. "Please, just let me go."

His response was equally intense. "I can't do that. I was up all last night, thinking of you, regretting what I said."

With an achingly slow movement, he brought his hand up to her face and stroked her cheek with the pad of his thumb. She slapped his touch away.

"No!" she cried out, wrenching away. "I will not let you do this to me."

She took a few halting steps backward.

"Carter, please."

She shook her head fiercely. "I'm going to get to work now. Because the faster I'm through, the faster I can be free of you."

His eyes were unwavering on hers, the pale irises a vivid contrast to their black centers. There was a long, taut silence.

"Tonight, you will come down for dinner." His voice was low and steady. Commanding.

"No."

"Yes, you will. To report on the dig."

His abrupt change of direction surprised her. "No."

"I have a right to know how it's going."

"Then Buddy can—"

"Go to hell. I want you."

Carter threw a curse at him. He didn't flinch, just kept looking at her with single-minded determination.

He took his sunglasses out of the pocket of his Windbreaker and slid them on. "As you recall in the grant, you have an obligation to report to me when I wish. So I wish for a report. Tonight. At seven."

"You are a bastard."

"I know."

With those tight words, he disappeared down the trail. In the wake of his departure, Carter realized she was shaking from head to foot. She sat down at the picnic table and put her head in her hands.

The last thing she wanted to do was be alone with Nick and try to talk about her work. But what choice did she have? She wasn't going to risk losing the dig and she knew he was fully capable of following through on his threat to throw them off his property.

She was tempted to walk away from the project. Sorely tempted.

But then Buddy and Ellie came back from the river, full of talk about their work and what they'd found so far. As she watched her friends' excitement and enthusiasm, envying their carefree happiness, she didn't want to let them down.

She also didn't want to explain why she needed to leave.

Seeing that she had no choice, Carter resolved to go down a little early and call Grace. She needed to report to the Hall Foundation, but more than that, she was desperate for moral support.

Much later, as the sun was setting, Carter put new copies of the logs in her backpack and walked down the mountain with a heavy heart and a defiant attitude. She'd taken part of the afternoon off and wandered the trails for a couple of hours. She'd used the time to armor herself for the evening.

When she arrived lakeside, she saw the mansion glowing in the gathering darkness. Her feet slowed as she approached the front door. When she finally raised the door knocker and let it fall, she was thinking about the first day she'd come to Nick's house. It felt like years ago.

She was surprised when he opened the door. He had a glass of scotch in one hand and a portable phone up to his ear. As he motioned her to come in, a flash of heat surged in his face, only to be buried behind his reserve.

"Right," he said to whomever was on the line. He closed the door behind her. "Listen, you need to adjust the analysis to include debt service payments of up to $60 million a year, and you're wrong on the depreciation figures . . ."

He nodded for her to follow him. As they walked through the house to his study, his deep voice strung words together that made no sense to her whatsoever. It was a foreign language, full of numbers and percentage points.

"Listen, I've got to go. Call Ronning. Tell him the boat's sunk and you guys had better come back with something better. And get Ben involved. He's the best damn corporate lawyer in the city." He hung up the phone. "You're early."

"I need to make a call before I talk to you," she told him stiffly.

"Be my guest." Nick held the phone out.

Approaching him cautiously, she took it while being careful not to have their hands touch.

"You want some privacy?"

"Yes."

He gave her a long look and then shut the door behind himself.

Dialing a familiar number, Carter quickly updated Grace on the dig and the complications that had unexpectedly come into her life. Her friend's encouragement made her feel stronger and she was grateful for the boost. She hoped it would make the meeting with Nick easier to get through.

When she hung up the phone, she realized she'd taken a seat in his chair and was staring out over piles of documents. Idly, she looked over the fax machine, two other phones, and a laptop.

Procrastinating, she peered over at a stack of papers, seeing where he'd put notes down in the margins. The handwriting was bold and decisive, his comments direct. She thumbed through a couple of pages and kept seeing the name CommTrans. Something triggered in her memory but she couldn't quite recall where she'd heard the name before.

Enough, she thought, getting to her feet. She was just prolonging the inevitable.

Leaving her backpack and her notes behind, she went looking for him. When she got close to the kitchen, she caught a whiff of something that smelled like roasted turkey. Her stomach grumbled with approval.

As she opened the butler's door a crack, she saw Nick standing over the stove. He had a carving knife and fork in his hands.

"You eat yet?" he asked over his shoulder.

Carter was amazed he'd heard her. "No, but—"

"It's Gertie's night off. The plates are to the right of me. I think she left a salad in the refrigerator."

"I didn't come here to have dinner with you."

"Fine, then just get out one plate. You talk. I'll eat." When she hesitated, he looked across the room. His eyes held a frank challenge.

Girding herself, Carter marched over to the cabinet and took out two plates.

There was no damned way she was going to look weak in front of him. Even if it took every lick of strength she had, she was going to get through the meal, make the report, and then get the hell back to camp. Pride would carry her through, if nothing else.

Besides, she thought, the night was young. She'd still have plenty of time to lose it in her tent later.

"In here or the dining room?" she demanded. When he nodded toward the oak table, she took the plates over.

"Silverware?" she asked stiffly.

He glanced to his left. "Napkins are in the drawer under it."

Before she knew it, she'd set the table, he'd brought the turkey platter over, and they were sitting down across from each other in his kitchen having dinner.

While wondering how in the hell it had come to pass, Carter started eating. The food was good. The silence was awful. All she could hear in the kitchen was the sound of silverware hitting plates. Halfway through the meal she realized she couldn't take it any longer. She put her fork and knife down, knotted up the napkin, and was about to leave when his voice stopped her.

"The last woman I said the words to was my mother." Nick put a piece of turkey into his mouth.

"What are you talking about?" Her eyes narrowed.

In the ensuing quiet, Nick just kept eating. He had perfect table manners. Cutting the meat carefully, laying the knife down, shifting the fork to his other hand, lifting a piece to his mouth.

"The words *I love you.* Last time was to my mother. And I didn't mean them." His voice was characteristically direct. "I remember distinctly because I told myself I wouldn't say them again until I did mean them."

Carter held herself very still. "What does this have to do with me?"

"I'm . . . glad we made love." Heat flickered in his face and then impatience. "*Glad.* What a stupid goddamn word. Ruined, is more like it. All I've been thinking about since yesterday is how lucky I was to have been with you. And what an idiot I was to blow it all like I did."

A flush bloomed in Carter's body and she twisted the napkin in her hands. "I don't want to talk about what happened."

"Yesterday meant so much to me."

"I find that hard to believe."

"You are the first woman . . . to really have affected me." Nick wiped his mouth and leaned back in his chair. "I regret the fact that I couldn't put into words how much yesterday meant. And how damn scary it was for me."

She searched his face. He was regarding her with such frankness and honesty, she couldn't find a toehold to mistrust him. As hard as she looked for one.

This was how she'd gotten hurt, she reminded herself. By believing in him.

"I don't have to listen to this." She rose from the table and he stood up with her.

"Carter, I don't have a clue where this is going between us."

"Well, then let me spell it out for you. Try nowhere."

"I will not accept that."

"You don't have a choice!"

He brushed a hand through his hair. "This whole thing scares the hell out of me. I like to be in control and, when I'm with you, I'm not. I panicked and I said some really stupid, god-awful things."

When she didn't reply, he said roughly, "I'm a clueless son of a bitch when it comes to real relationships, but I'm willing to try harder. With you. You've got to believe me. No one has ever made me feel like you do."

Carter shook her head. "I'm not listening to this."

He reached out and took her hand. "I just want another chance."

Her body flushed as the memories of them making love came back. She found herself wanting to believe him. Heaven help her, she did.

"Nick, you hurt me."

"I know. And I'm so goddamn sorry."

Looking into his eyes, she saw torment and tenderness. "You're not an easy man to trust."

He opened up her hand and stroked the pad of his thumb across the inside of her palm. The sensation was hypnotic. Slowly, he raised her hand up and brushed his lips against her skin.

"Are you trying to seduce me?" she asked softly.

"Yes." The word hung between them.

When he drew her closer, Carter went reluctantly into his embrace.

"I want you," he groaned against her hair. "And I don't want to hurt you."

She pulled back and studied him closely. He looked truly contrite and seemed to understand, and regret, the pain he had caused. There was a vulnerability in him, too, as if he were unsure whether he would be forgiven.

She wanted him. And she wanted to forgive him even though she would remember the hurt. She made up her mind.

"If I give you my body, that doesn't mean I'm giving you my heart."

With those words, meant as much for him as for herself, she lifted her lips for his kiss. When their mouths met, she melted into his solid body.

"I hate this," she moaned as his hands cupped her breasts. "I *hate* you."

"I'll take it," he said hoarsely. "Whatever you'll give me, I'll take."

They stayed only a moment longer in the kitchen. Next thing she knew, they were fumbling toward the stairs and doing an awkward pas de deux to the second floor. As they made their way down the hall, pieces of clothing marked their path as shirts were stripped and then pants.

"What about Cort?" she mumbled breathlessly.

"Out at a friend's house. God, I need you so much," Nick growled against her mouth. His hands were under her bra, cupping her breasts, his thumbs brushing over the aching tenderness of her nipples, making her cry out.

They burst into what she assumed was Nick's bedroom. She had a fuzzy impression of deep red, royal gold, and dark green, but vision left her entirely as his mouth took her breast and he lifted her onto the bed. She felt the mattress come underneath her and then his weight on top of her. Carter raked her nails into his back as she felt his body press against her.

As he came up to kiss her again, she caught an image of the desperation in him. Whatever else was going on inside of him, he wanted her. That much she knew for sure.

Lips fused together, she removed what was left of his clothing by pushing his boxer shorts off his legs, and he did the same for her by flinging her panties to the floor. Hungrily, she kissed him and opened her legs so that he could come between them. When she felt his hardness brush against her, she cried out.

"I want to go slower," he groaned. "But I can't."

He drove inside of her and she held on tight as he thrust again. Wrapping her long legs around his hips, she urged him on with her own pumping. It was a dizzying, frenetic ride, born out of pent-up anger and frustration, and she called out his name as she was hurled toward the sky.

Afterward, he fell against her. His magnificent body utterly spent, she felt him relax as a peaceful euphoria passed through her as well.

When he lifted his head, his voice was grave. "I didn't sleep last night."

"No?"

"I shut my eyes but all I could see was you. I missed you. I couldn't stomach the idea that I'd never be with you again. That I had lost you." He kissed her, a long slow caress of lip on lip, tongue on tongue. Inside of her, she could feel him growing big again.

Rolling over and moving her on top of him, he stroked her with his eyes and his hands. With abandonment, she sat up, and he moaned as he cupped the weight of her breasts. This time, they made love more slowly, savoring the feel of the touching and teasing until passion won out over patience and they came together in an inferno of sensation.

As they lay together afterward, Carter felt an unexpected sadness. In spite of how close they had been physically, she still didn't trust him completely. The distance hurt but she wasn't going to talk about it. Words were not going to bring them closer.

Maybe time. Perhaps in time there could be trust.

"When does Cort get home?" she wondered aloud, looking toward the open door and the clothes strewn out into the hall.

"Eleven." Nick glanced over at the brass clock. "We've got ten minutes!"

Scurrying from the bed, they went after their clothes frantically, bending down, picking things up, switching boxers for panties, khakis for trousers, racing out into the hall after shirts. In a mad dash to the finish line, they came to a screeching halt before the front door just as the grandfather clock in the living room began to make its announcement of the hour.

"Your shirt," Nick said, as he was tucking his in.

Carter saw that her buttons were in the wrong holes and scrambled to reorder them.

When the clock fell silent, their panting breaths sounded loud in the quiet house.

"After all that, he's really going to get it for being late," Nick said dryly.

With their clothes back on, Carter felt surprisingly more vulnerable. She cleared her throat. "I guess I'm going to leave now."

His eyes locked onto hers. "You don't have to go."

She didn't answer the subtle inquiry in his eyes. She just turned and walked away.

"I left my backpack in your study," she said over her shoulder.

Carter went into the dim room and picked up her pack. Before she left, she wandered over to his desk, amazed at what had happened since she'd sat in his chair and talked to Grace. Her eyes passed over the papers and caught the word CommTrans again.

"You're looking at my desk as if it holds an answer for you."

She looked up, not hiding the uncertainty in her eyes. Nick was leaning against the door jamb, the light from overhead cascading down on him. It illuminated his high cheekbones, his strongly molded lips, and the rigid length of his jaw.

"Tell me, Carter, what answer are you looking for?" His voice was husky and she was reminded of what it sounded like in her ear as he drove into her body.

"The one that tells me who you really are." She shrugged on her backpack and started to walk out.

She passed by him only to be pulled into his arms. The kiss he gave her had an urgency that was not just about passion.

"You are different to me," he vowed.

Carter reached up to his handsome face and ran her fingers down his cheek. "Right now I might be. We'll see about later, won't we?"

And then she left the house.

Under the clear night sky, she walked across the lawn and through the meadow. It was chilly and she paused to get her fleece out of the pack before she went into the woods. As she was pulling it over her head, she heard a chorus of cracking twigs.

Cort came charging out of the brush at a dead run and careened into her.

"Carter!"

"Easy there, rough rider." She grinned as she helped steady him.

"What are you doing out here?"

"Just met with your uncle." She was grateful for the night's cover as blood rushed to her face. "What about you? I thought you went into town with friends."

"I did—for a little while. It wasn't much fun so I, er, went up to see . . ."

So she wasn't the only one blushing in the dark, Carter thought.

"Anyway, I think I'm a little late for curfew."

With a sheepish wave, the kid took off in the direction of his home.

"Yes, you certainly are late," she said softly.

Shaking her head, she took out her flashlight, shined a shallow beam in front of herself, and penetrated the forest.

As she followed the trail, she replayed the evening over and over again in her mind. The way Nick had spoken to her, the way he'd touched and kissed her. Her heart pounded as she hiked up to camp, and not just from exertion.

She was not going to fall in love with Nick Farrell, Carter promised herself.

Nick was sitting at the desk when he heard Cort come through the door. The kid called out but didn't stop and talk on his way upstairs. He was ten minutes late but Nick wasn't going to get on his case about it.

Feeling restless, Nick left his desk and walked out of the French doors onto the porch. Taking a seat in a wicker chair, he was watching the moonlight on the lake when he heard a voice drift down through the night air.

"Uncle Nick?"

Wicker creaked as he looked up at the porch ceiling. "Cort?"

"Can I ask you something?" The kid's voice was tentative.

"Of course."

It was a long time before Cort spoke again. "What do you do if you like someone?"

Nick was stunned. It was the first time Cort had ever asked him for advice.

But why the hell couldn't it have been about treasury bills? He'd gone to school to answer questions like that.

Trying to buy himself some time, Nick asked, "Do you like someone?"

"Maybe."

"What makes you think you do?"

"Whenever she's around, my head doesn't work right, my legs feel like I've run a sprint, and my stomach feels queasy. Like I ate too many tacos."

That about covers it, Nick thought.

"Do you think this person likes you back?"

"Maybe." There was a pause. "It's not Carter, you know. She's too old for me."

The edge was almost gone out of the kid's tone, and Nick was relieved they seemed to have weathered that crisis.

"So, what do you do?" Cort prompted.

Nick sighed. "Be yourself. Spend time with her. Listen to her. Make sure she knows how special she is."

Drive yourself nuts fantasizing about her, he added to himself. Brace yourself for a bout with insomnia. Get ready to put your foot in your mouth and have to beg for forgiveness.

"That wasn't how you were with Candace," Cort challenged him.

Nick winced. "I know. I didn't really like her."

"I don't think anyone did."

"Well, you shouldn't be with someone you don't really like."

"I know that. I didn't think you did, though."

Nick laughed softly at the boy's candor.

Funny, he thought, that it had taken him so long to learn the lesson.

Silence stretched out between them, the sound of waves against the shore marking the passing moments.

"I think you're right," the kid said with resolve. "I'm just going to be with her. Thanks."

"Cort?"

"Yeah?"

"I'm glad you asked me." Nick took care to make sure the words were spoken clearly and that Cort heard them.

There was a long pause.

"Yeah. Me, too."

Above, the door into Cort's bedroom was closed softly.

Nick, for once, didn't feel shut out.

Staying on the porch, he got lost in memories of Carter until he became so agitated he had to go back to the study. When he sat down in his chair, he picked some papers off the desk and tried to distract himself.

The deal for CommTrans was progressing nicely, he thought, as he reviewed the memorandum of understanding that had been faxed to him earlier in the day. If all went well, by the end of the month the transaction would be complete. Wessex would buy the company, then immediately sell most of it to Nick.

And at the end of all the paperwork, Nick's prey would have a new boss.

He smiled grimly. Payback was a bitch.

The year before, Nick had been forced to sell off some holdings because of antitrust concerns. Bob Packert, CEO of CommTrans, had bought the manufacturing companies and proven to be incapable of running them. He was so bad at it that the value of the rest of the man's holdings had been dragged down into the sewer. Share prices had plummeted and his stockholders had gone ballistic.

Instead of fixing the problems he'd created, however, Packert had gone to the press and alleged that Nick had falsified financial documents during the sale, making the company appear more healthy than it was. The man had declared loud and wide that fraud was the cause of the failure, not his own incompetence.

It was all lies and Nick wasn't one to let that kind of attack go without retribution. This was where William Wessex came in. Wessex was only too happy to buy up all of Packert's stock in a hostile takeover and pass the bulk of the holdings on to Nick for a fair price. To keep it all legal, he'd retain the manufacturing plants that Nick couldn't own because of the antitrust laws—a little reward for doing the favor.

Courtesy of the maneuvering, Nick was going to own Packert's ass, and his first move as the new chairman of the board of CommTrans was going to be discharging Packert from his own company for cause. The next step was going to be having him blackballed among Nick's friends on the Fortune 500 list so Packert wouldn't be able to get another high-paying, high-profile job. Then Nick was thinking about getting the man kicked out of the private clubs and golf courses he belonged to and ensuring that his wife found out about his various mistresses.

Wessex was critical to the revenge because, legally, Nick couldn't resume ownership of the manufacturing businesses and therefore couldn't be the front man in the CommTrans acquisition. The situation put the two raiders in a difficult position, however. Nick had to trust that Wessex would divest as soon as the ink was dry. Wessex had to have faith that Nick would pay him the agreed amount for CommTrans.

Even though they had interests that were aligned, the

deal was only as safe as any situation involving two hungry lions and one piece of meat.

This was why Nick had wanted to give the man a chance to meet with his daughter. Wessex's gratitude would have made Nick feel more secure about his position, and would have added a personal obligation to ensure that the professional one would be adhered to.

He shifted in his chair, feeling trapped by his own maneuvers. When he'd started down this road, he'd had no idea what would happen between Carter and him. Abruptly, the idea of leveraging her struck him as totally wrong.

Disturbed, Nick went to the bar, poured himself a scotch, and then walked over to the bookcase. He knelt down in front of a five-volume set of Victorian travelogues. With the flip of a lever, that part of the bookcase came forward and revealed a safe.

Turning the dial to the right, twice to the left, and then back again, he heard the tumblers release and then pushed down on the brass handle. Lights came on inside, something he'd always thought of as a nice touch, like the thing was just a really sturdy little refrigerator.

He was looking for the cross, knowing that holding it in his hand would give him solace. It was something he had done over the years when feeling conflicted.

But before taking it out, he was distracted by the familiar stacks of leather boxes containing some of his grandmother's jewelry collection. On impulse, Nick reached in and picked up a small one that was covered in Cartier's brilliant red. He unlatched the lid.

A diamond ring glistened in the dim light. The stone had been given to his grandmother upon her engagement to Rufus Lachlan Farrell. The ring had outlived both the giver and receiver, and Nick thought it was a shame that such a magnificent piece was locked up in a safe.

Nick remembered his mother coveting the diamond, not because of its size and quality, although it was stunning on both accounts, but because it had been worn by a woman she couldn't compete with. Nick's grandmother, known as Ma Farrell, had been a consummate hostess, a prize-winning gardener and, in an era when women like her were supposed to lead the inactive lives of "ladies," she was also a horsewoman, a poker player, and a swimmer. She was charismatic, charming, and loved by anyone who'd ever met her.

Nick's mother, Sarah, had been the opposite. She was willowy, not strong, and socially insecure and aggressive, not gracious and likable. She'd also suffered from a bottomless appetite for approval and had always been resentful because she never seemed to get enough. Making things worse, she'd had to endure the Oedipal hardship of knowing her husband, Ashland, infinitely preferred spending time with his own mother over her.

This burden might have been easier to bear if Ashland had had some bizarre attachment to Ma Farrell. Sarah might have been able to leverage an embarrassing pathology into guilt-induced fits of spending at Tiffany's. The truth, however, was both more prosaic and difficult. The man just liked his mother's company, and his wife had never forgiven him for the split of affections.

This had been the reason for Nick's birth, or so he'd heard. Sarah had figured that by becoming a mother, she could get her husband to stop fixating on his own. It proved to be an ill-conceived strategy. Ashland had made room for his son, right next to the mother he adored, and his wife, instead of finding herself in higher regard, was squeezed out even further.

Which was why Nick had always had the sense his mother despised him.

It was capricious cruelty, or perhaps mercy, that Sarah's life ended before the woman she had hated passed on. Ma Farrell survived her by almost a decade, and the diamond ring had gone on plying the dirt in the gardens at the edge of the lake. After his mother's death, Ashland had had the ring appraised and then put it in the wall safe. It hadn't been worn since.

Nick's favorite story about the diamond was one

Gertie had told him. Ma Farrell's active lifestyle had meant the platinum setting had taken a beating over the years. When Ashland took it back to Cartier to get it evaluated, the jewelers had offered to put it in a brand-new setting.

"You don't reset a life, gentlemen," Ashland had said. "That ring earned those nicks and someday, if it gets passed down, the woman who wears it is going to know exactly who put them there. It's a legacy to live up to, not something to be replaced."

Nick looked at the band, seeing the scratches in the surface of the metal, and was shaken as he imagined the diamond on Carter's finger. Returning it to its box, he was struck by the fact that he'd been in and out of the safe for years and had never bothered to look at the ring before.

Refocusing on a lower shelf, he rifled through stacks of money and shoved aside about $100,000 in gold Krugerrands that he'd pushed into the safe two weeks ago. Behind the largesse was the felt bundle he'd taken that day to Carter's.

Going over to his desk, he unveiled the cross. The aged wood, cracked in veins, seemed to glow.

A familiar feeling in his stomach returned, caused by the colliding of his family's private history with the history of his country. He thought once again of the men who had died on what was now his land. He was, as always, moved.

And then he froze.

That strange shift in gravity was how he felt when he was around Carter. How he felt when he thought about her.

This was what had always been missing. He'd never felt truly moved by a woman before. He could stand next to them and forget they were in the room at all, could leave the country without missing them, could walk away without second thoughts.

But Carter, she consumed him. Challenged him with her quick wit and her intelligence. And when they were making love, he felt whole.

Nick sucked his breath in as he struggled with that familiar fear of his.

Rolling up the artifact carefully, he realized something was changing inside of him.

And he was never going to be the same again.

12

Two WEEKS later, Carter and the team were on their hands and knees, laboring under a bright sun, when they hit the halfway point. In spite of the heat and their progress, there was no celebration over the accomplishment. They continued to work, steady and determined.

Carter noticed only because she paused to take a drink and saw how much distance they'd covered. The ground inside the circle of boulders was now split down the middle into a higher and a lower level. It was the result of countless hours of trowels slicing into the earth and dirt rushing into plastic buckets.

The site had proven to be a rich one, and many artifacts had been found, some more significant than others. Back at camp, collapsible containers had been expanded to accommodate all manner of arrowheads, pottery shards, and musket balls, and more kept coming. The day before, Cort and Ellie had found the remnants of a Brown Bess, the gun used by redcoats during the Revolutionary period. Luckily, the metallurgic appointments on the weapon were in good shape, and some of the wood had survived as well. It was quite a find, and everyone was thrilled that it might have been used by one of the men whose remains had been unearthed.

As for the skeletons, they had been removed from the ground, and the bones were now carefully housed in boxes stashed out of the sun's heat. As they were the most precious of the finds, Carter found herself increasingly anxious to get them over to the university where she knew they would be safe. She didn't want anything to happen before she had a chance to study them.

She glanced over at Cort and Ellie. The two were joking and laughing together, their eyes flirtatious as they jostled over a trowel. She thought back to Cort's early infatuation with her and was glad he had come around so well.

Her next thought was of Nick.

The night before they'd stolen off together for a midnight boat ride. The moon had glimmered over soft waves as they'd slowly cruised the shoreline, the sound of the Hacker's throaty engine and the call of loons accompanying their trip down the lake. She'd leaned against his chest, snuggling into his warmth, and felt a terrible temptation to believe that the warm summer evening was going to go on forever.

Although the physical pleasure Nick gave her was intense and satisfying, she did her best to keep her heart to herself. There were moments, particularly after they had a deep conversation about his past or her plans for the future, when she could feel him struggling. He would get a faraway look in his eyes, as if he were searching for an escape, and tension would run through his body. Even though he hadn't shown any inclination to follow through on the impulse, she remained wary.

There was another reason she wanted to keep a level head. She'd remembered where she'd heard of CommTrans, the company mentioned in the papers on his desk. The man who owned it had accused Nick of falsifying financial documents. It had been all over the news, to such an extent that even she, far away from the financial hubs of the world, had read about the soured deal and the ongoing investigation. Even though the drama had nothing to do with their relationship directly, the idea that he'd misled someone deliberately stuck with her.

And there was one other thing bothering her. Always

in the back of her mind were Conrad Lyst and the missing logs. The other morning Buddy had shown her a series of footsteps in the soft earth. Tracing the path, they'd weaved their way through the trees until they'd reached the back trail. There, like the wake of a small army, were so many more of the prints that they blended together in places, flattening the hard soil.

Ivan came up the back way on occasion but he'd never leave those kinds of footprints. She and Buddy and the kids used only the front trail. And considering the homogeneity of the tracks, it was doubtful the markings had been made by curious tourists. It just had to be Lyst.

As soon as they'd returned to camp, they'd both agreed the skeletons needed to be removed from the mountain in the next few days. Although the gold was what Lyst really cared about, there was no telling what he might do.

Neither she nor Buddy was going to take any chances with the man.

Carter pitched a shovelful of dirt into her bucket and noticed it was full. She was getting to her feet to empty it outside of the ring of stones when Nick stepped into the clearing.

A flush came over her body and she watched as the corners of his lips rose ever so slightly. It was a special smile, meant only for her.

"If this isn't a tribute to industry, I don't know what is." He casually walked across the site, but his eyes were on her. The others greeted him with various hellos.

"I didn't realize you'd made it this far," he commented when he was standing in front of her.

"Come and look at this," she said quickly, feeling awkward and excited by his presence. She went over to a box that housed a few shards of pottery. "We found these this morning."

As she put one of the pieces into his hands, her fingers touched the skin of his palm. His smile deepened.

"How old is it?" he asked as he examined the wedge of dull, baked clay.

"Over a thousand years, perhaps."

"Amazing."

"This has been a popular spot for people over the centuries. That fire pit has seen a lot of things."

Nick gave the artifact back to her, stroking her wrist as he did. "Have you found anything else from the Winship party?"

Distracted by his touch, Carter stumbled over her words. "Er—no, but we've still got a lot of digging to do."

"And there's no gold."

"No gold."

He walked over to where the fire pit had been before they'd dug it out. "How much longer until you're finished?"

"Three weeks or so."

"Then what happens?"

"I get to see my wife again," Buddy muttered.

Carter caught the approval on Nick's face as her friend mentioned Jo-Jo. To her relief, the two men had been getting along much better.

"As soon as we're done, we hit the lab," she replied. "There is going to be a lot of analysis to do. Then we write up the whole dig along with any conclusions we come to."

Buddy put his shovel down and got to his feet. "After that it's the rubber chicken dinner circuit."

"Making presentations at various universities," Carter amended, shooting him a mock glare. "Depending on what we find, that can last a short time or upward of a month or two."

"Is it a drag?" Nick asked.

"Hell no," Buddy said enthusiastically. "It's the closest thing we archaeologists get to being rock stars."

They talked a little more about the dig and then Buddy and the kids took a break and wandered back to camp for a cool drink. As soon as they were alone, Nick wrapped his arms around Carter. She breathed in his scent, catching his tangy aftershave.

"Hi," he said against her lips. "I've missed you."

Closing her eyes, she soaked in the feel of his body against hers. "You saw me last night. Or do I have to remind you what we did under all that moonlight out on the lake?"

He moved against her. "You want to show me again?"

His tongue slid between her lips and she arched toward him. Sliding her hands under his shirt, she stroked his skin until he groaned. The heat that flared between them made her think of the stream's rushing water, of having him naked with her in one of the pools.

She was about to suggest going over to it when they heard Cort and Ellie's laughter.

Reluctantly, they pulled apart.

"Too bad we're not alone up here," Nick said in a rough voice.

"I was going to suggest hitting the stream."

"We'll have to remember that for later."

The kids came through the circle of boulders and looked much cooler as they ambled back over to where they'd been digging. To Carter, the idea of settling back down to work wasn't as attractive as it usually was. She was distracted by Nick and what she wished they were doing together.

It sure as hell didn't have anything to do with shovels.

"So what's the technique here?" Nick asked, going over and picking hers up.

"You ever plant anything?"

"Once. It was some vicious gossip about a competitor to the *WSJ*. But the guy started it." He shot her a wink.

She couldn't help but smile up at him. "I was thinking more like lily bulbs."

"Then I'd have to say no."

"Ever play in a sandbox?"

"Nope."

"Okay, how about make a divot when you hit a golf ball?" She knew he was teasing her.

"That'd also be a no."

"You don't golf?"

"I don't divot."

Carter laughed.

"God, I love to see you smile," he said softly as he leaned over to her. "Among other things."

Carter snatched back her shovel and blushed. "Do you really want to learn how to do this?"

"If it means I can be with you, absolutely."

"All right, then, get on your knees."

"I thought you'd never ask," he drawled in a husky voice.

When Buddy returned, she and Nick had their heads in the dirt, examining a set of bones that appeared to be those of a deer.

"You find the missing link?" Buddy said cheerfully as he came over.

"More like what he had for dinner," Carter murmured.

"You having fun?" the man asked Nick.

"Absolutely. I find it . . . absorbing."

With a glow, Carter realized he was looking at her. She avoided his eyes, trying not to blow her cover around her team.

When they went back to work, Nick whispered in her ear, "So when do I get to see you again? Alone."

She glanced up, feeling a rush.

"Well, I'm going over to Burlington a couple of days from now," she said quietly. "You could come with me—"

"I don't know if I can wait that long."

"Forty-eight hours?"

"That's two days." He let out a groan.

"I see corporeal delights haven't compromised your math skills."

He laughed. "I'll go with you to Vermont, but only if you promise to not keep your hands to yourself."

"I think that can be arranged."

Nick reached out and stroked her cheek. The movement was lightning fast but poignant.

"I have to go. Business is waiting." He got up and stretched.

Carter smiled at him, sorry that he was leaving. "I'd hate to have dirt get in the way of progress."

"So would my shareholders."

With a last lingering look at her, he disappeared into the woods.

On the way down the mountain, Nick thought about how Carter could catch and hold him with just her eyes. It wasn't simply because they were beautiful, though their cobalt blue color was arresting. It was more the combination of strength and vulnerability that got to him. And that, when unguarded, she looked at him with an expression that made him feel like he could leap tall buildings in a single bound.

He was looking forward to the trip to Burlington like it was Christmas.

When he entered the kitchen, he saw Gertie was up to her elbows in dough. She was kneading the prenatal bread in a deep wooden bowl, and flour was pouching up in puffs of white smoke as she punched and folded, punched and folded.

As he used to do when he was a child, he leaned on a doorjamb, crossed his legs at the ankles, and wiggled the tip of his boot.

"What are you nervous about?" she asked.

"Who said I'm nervous?"

"You're waving that foot like it's a flag."

He stilled himself.

"I've been spending a lot of time with Carter. I'm growing rather . . . fond of her." He couldn't believe he was actually saying the words.

"Yes, I've noticed." Gertie pushed the bowl away, draped a dish towel over the top, and washed her hands. "She's a good woman. What are you all beside yourself for?"

Nick took a deep breath. "I don't know."

"Well, I hope you keep on seeing her." Gertie took her apron off, a gingham affair that had been washed so many times, it was a pale pink. "By the way, her father called today."

Nick stopped breathing. "What?"

"William Wessex called."

"How did you know he was her father?"

"I asked him because their last names are the same. He called to say he was coming up this weekend and bringing someone with him. Said you were going to want to see them. He seemed surprised to find out Carter was here." Gertie frowned.

"Did he say anything else?"

"Just that he wants to talk with you and he'd wait by the phone for your call." She looked at him strangely. "Are you okay?"

He nodded and left for his study in a hurry. He was not going to have Wessex up to the house. No way in hell. He wasn't going to jeopardize his relationship with Carter.

Nick had known all along that he'd have to tell her about the business with her father. And he was preparing to talk to her about it. He just wanted a little more time to figure out how to broach the subject, to construct the words in such a way so as to lessen the shock.

He was sure about one thing. Having the man just show up was definitely not the way Nick wanted it all to come out.

Sitting down behind his desk, he dialed Wessex's private line.

"Wessex." The man's voice was sharp.

"It's Farrell."

"Just tell me"—the words were clipped short—"when were you going to mention my daughter was on your mountain? Before or after I arrived?"

"Of course I was going to let you know," Nick answered evenly.

"How bloody thoughtful of you." There was real anger in Wessex's voice.

"Look, I was going to tell you. Although, considering that she's here, I think we should meet in New York."

"Well, it's too damn late. I invited Packert up to your house this weekend. We'll be arriving on Friday."

Nick's throat closed on him. "No, you won't. And what the hell's going on? We're not ready for the ambush yet."

"Packert's found out about our little side arrangement. He knows if you take control, he's out of a job. He says either he meets with you or he's going to the press again."

"Screw him. He's welcome to call every goddamn reporter on the street," Nick growled. "He's got nothing to say to them."

"Don't be so sure about that. He's prepared to let the world know you and I are skirting the antitrust laws. That we're double-dealing."

"He's out of his mind!" Anger curled Nick's hand into a fist. "Everything is perfectly legal. Does that guy have a death wish?"

"All I can say is that he's got a loud voice when it comes to making accusations, and you know how the reporters just love his sound bites. Even though everything about the deal is legitimate, in the court of public opinion, it's going to look bad. I don't want to take that kind of hit and neither do you. Especially after last year."

"I swear to God, I'm going to crush that son of a bitch." Nick pushed a hand through his hair. "But tell him we'll meet in New York. We can do it at my office. I'll fly down this weekend."

"Fine." There was a long pause and then Wessex asked in a low voice, "Now do you mind telling me what my daughter is doing at your house?"

Nick took a deep breath. "She's up on my mountain. Digging. When I spoke to you last, I had no idea she was going to be excavating on my land."

"How well do you know her?"

There was a pause. Nick didn't want to get into specifics with Carter's father. He had a feeling she'd view it as a betrayal. "Well enough."

"Personally?"

"Yes."

"How is she?"

There was a desperation behind the words, one that Nick didn't associate with the man.

"She's well."

"Has she told you why we're estranged?"

"Some."

A sigh of sadness and resignation came over the line. "It's hard to make up for the whims of fate."

Then, as if he were shaking himself out of the past, Wessex cleared his throat and said, sharply, "Anyway, I'll call Packert."

"You let me know when you need me down in the city."

After Nick got off the line, he picked up the Comm-Trans documents. For the first time, he saw them not as the key to winning but as nothing more than a stack of paper, held together at the left-hand corner by a black clip. Flipping through the document, he saw where he'd highlighted clauses, written notes in the margins, crossed out sections. The weight of the contract felt flimsy in his fingers.

He tossed the thing back down and thought of the way Carter's body felt. The way she moved under his hands, how warm her skin was, how she breathed his name against his neck as she climaxed. All of that seemed so much more important than the business deals cluttering his desk.

As he pictured the blue of her eyes, it suddenly dawned on him that maybe, all these years, he'd been hungering after the wrong thing.

"Let's go to Burlington," Nick said to Carter the next morning. They were alone at camp, the others having gone to the dig site.

"Now?" she asked.

Nick nodded as he sat down at the picnic table. The early morning was glorious on the mountain, the golden light filtering through the pine trees, the sky a vast, clear expanse.

"What's the rush?"

"It's going to be hotter than hell today. You'll be miserable out under all this sun."

It was only partially the truth. He wanted to spend the day with her and worried that he was going to have to go down to the city soon. He didn't want to miss the chance for them to be alone.

She came up from behind and offered him a mug of coffee. Before she could turn away, he grabbed her hand and tugged her down close for a lingering kiss. "Besides, I want to be with you. Soon."

He watched as she blushed and pulled back slightly, looking around to make sure they were alone.

"I guess there's no reason we couldn't."

"Then it's a date," Nick said with satisfaction.

When she sat down beside him, he pulled her into his arms and took her lips in a searing kiss. As he felt her indrawn breath, he thought that the day was full of promise.

13

Down at the garage, Ivan was cleaning a spark plug when Nick came in for the four-wheeler. "Is the monster gassed up?"

Ivan nodded. "Headed for the mountain?"

"I am." Nick didn't hide the pleasure in his voice. "We're going to be gone all day. Taking the skeletons to UVM."

A grunt came back at him. "Been a lot of foot traffic on the access road lately."

Nick halted. "More than usual?"

"Believe so."

"Since when?"

"Pretty recent. And there been no bears, either."

The men looked at each other.

"Could the tracks just be from our archaeologists?" Nick went over to the machine and straddled it, frowning.

"Nope."

"So we're talking tourists?"

"Tourist."

In the process of turning the key, Nick stopped. "Only one?"

"Up and down. Up and down."

"How often?"

"I'd say two times this week."

"Do the tracks go to the site?" he asked darkly.

"Yup. And they're the same ones I found when I went looking for her bear."

Nick tried to find a reason for Carter's lie. "I don't like this."

"Can't say I'm crazy for it myself considering who it is. I wish my aim had been better back in May."

"It's the one you almost shot?"

Ivan nodded.

"What the hell's he doing up there?" Nick demanded.

"Question's more, who's he seeing."

Nick started the four-wheeler with a roar. "Find that man and bring him down for a little chat with me."

"With pleasure," Ivan shouted.

As Nick raced down his driveway, he couldn't make sense of the news. He was wondering why Carter or Buddy would be spending time with a competitor, on a dig they'd gotten at the man's expense.

When he got to the main road, he traveled up a quarter mile and then took a hard left onto the access road. Zooming up the single lane, he spent as much time looking down as he did watching where he was going. Periodically, he slowed and searched the ground, seeing the tracks Ivan had described.

The back access road had always been a thorn in Nick's side because it made getting up Farrell Mountain so easy. Only a half mile away from it, there was a public parking lot off the main road that serviced the state-owned mountain next to his. All trespassers had to do was park there and take a short walk. If they knew what they were looking for, they could jump off the shoulder at the right place and have a clear shot up his property.

He'd posted plenty of No Trespassing signs, but Ivan was the first and best line of defense against the uninvited. The man took great personal enjoyment out of tracking his prey, and most of them didn't come back. One brush with the woodsman was usually enough to discourage subsequent visits.

But that other archaeologist was damn brazen, Nick thought. Or had a driving purpose.

Fifteen minutes later, he was close to the mountaintop but far from a satisfying resolution to his concerns. Moving past the circle of stones, he maneuvered the four-wheeler as close to the camp as possible and turned it off.

When he approached the tents, Carter looked up from where she was crouched by the fire pit.

"That was quick," she said, flashing him a smile.

He thought about the footprints and his instincts told him she was hiding something.

"Nick, is something wrong?"

He met her eyes, seeing nothing but honest concern. Still, he had to wonder if she was scamming him. He knew from friends in the art world that Lyst worked the black market like a good QVC host. If she did find the gold, he'd be the perfect conduit to turn it into cash, and money was usually a great motivator for people. She was, after all, estranged from her father and the income of an archaeology professor couldn't be that great.

And besides, going by the way the camp was decked out in high-tech equipment and supplies, she clearly knew how to spend a buck or two.

"Nick?" Anxiety darkened her expression as she rose.

Maybe Ivan had made a mistake, he thought, toying with the idea of letting the issue drop. He wanted her so badly it hurt. Footprints or no footprints. And there would be plenty of opportunities to talk about tracks and hypothetical bears later. There was no reason to waste a moment of the precious little time they had to spend alone.

"Everything's fine," he said smoothly. "You need help packing it all up?"

She gave him a strange look and then shrugged. "I'm all set, thanks. Let's put the skeletons on the back of the four-wheeler."

When they reconvened by Carter's Jeep, they loaded the skeletons side by side in the back so the cargo wouldn't shift too much on the winding road to the ferry. Then Nick took the four-wheeler over to the garage and Carter watched as he returned across the lawn. In the bright sunlight, he was looking happy again and she wondered what had been on his mind when he first got up to camp.

As he neared the Jeep, she teased, "You're looking awfully cheerful."

"Cheerful?" His eyes glinted while he smiled at her.

"Yeah, as in not dour."

Nick shot her a mocking look across the hood as they both got in the car. "I happen to be looking forward to spending the day with you."

Lightning quick, he reached across the seat and took her hand.

"Come here." He pulled her over and kissed her mouth firmly. "Let's get going."

He didn't have to ask twice. She turned the key, threw the car into gear, and took off down the drive. As she headed onto the main road, she could feel his eyes on her.

"What are you looking at?"

"You." The word came out of his mouth long and slow.

Carter blushed with happiness but held herself in check.

"Why do you do that?" he asked her softly.

"Do what?"

"Freeze every time I compliment you."

She wasn't aware that she did but she knew the cause of it. She was perilously close to falling in love with him and the feelings scared her.

"Let's just enjoy the day," Carter said. "Okay?"

She felt his frustration from across the seat. "I don't understand you."

Carter took a deep breath. It was hard living in a netherworld, between what she wanted and what she feared. She just didn't know how much she could give him of herself. How much she should give him.

Nick turned away, his face tightening.

Skirting over the main road, Carter had to navigate tight curves and was grateful for the concentration it required. The silence between them was awkward. She made small talk but he barely responded, just stared out the side window while rolling a quarter through the fingers of his right hand.

Twenty minutes later they pulled into the ferry docks. On each side of the lake, there were twin docks, paved parking lots, and identical restaurants. These eateries were nothing special on the outside but they served the best damn soft ice cream ever twisted into a cake cone.

Carter paid the toll and obediently took a place in the line that was forming for the next boat.

She glanced over at Nick, feeling trapped. He was still playing with the coin, and she wondered if he was ever going to say something.

When he finally did speak, she was startled by the sound.

"You want anything from the restaurant?" he asked, putting on his sunglasses.

"No, I'm fine."

He left the car and strode across the hot pavement, an incredibly handsome man whom people turned and stared at. He returned with a leaning tower of vanilla on a cake cone.

She watched with aching distraction as he licked the ice cream with his tongue. Heat pooled in her belly and she had to look away. In a halfhearted way, she noticed that it was a spectacular summer day, full of sunshine and blue sky. In contrast to the cheery weather, Carter felt ill, saddened by the silence with Nick.

"We're up," he said, biting into the cone part.

Snapping to, she started the Jeep and drove onto the ferry.

When they were parked again, she watched him polish off the last of the cone and wipe his fingers on a flimsy paper napkin. As soon as he was done, he looked at her. Their eyes held.

"I always did like vanilla best," he said.

Carter looked down at her hands. "The idea of you eating an ice cream cone would have seemed unimaginable when I first met you."

"Oh?"

"Much too simple a pleasure."

The ferry sounded its tinny whistle and lurched free of the dock. Engines, deep and throaty, churned propellers through the water.

Carter opened her door, eager for some fresh air. When she walked over to the rail, he joined her.

"So you thought I'd eat only canapés or frilly pastries?"

"Something like that." She offered him a smile and was relieved when he returned it.

The breezy quality of the conversation matched the wind coming across the lake, and she was relieved as some of the tension between them dissipated.

When Nick moved toward her, she was happy that he tucked her into his shoulder and put his arm around her waist. He kissed the top of her head.

"You're a piece of work—you know that?" he said against her hair. "Tough as nails but tender, too. You confuse the hell out of me."

"I don't mean to."

"I know. And that's part of why you get to me like you do."

His voice was gruff and, against her cheek, she felt the sound rumble deep in his chest. Under her rib cage, his hand was stroking her rhythmically. With the sun on her back and the shimmering water all around, she felt herself relax.

She craned her neck and looked up, seeing the cut of his jaw, the masculine planes of his face. Looking under his dark sunglasses, she watched his eyes scan the horizon, tracking the sailboats that dotted the lake.

"Now I get to ask," he said, looking down with a smile. "What are *you* looking at?"

"Nothing," she murmured, tucking her head back down against his chest.

He chuckled.

When the opposite shore grew dominant in the landscape, they went back to the car. With another lurch and squeal of rubber bumpers, the ferry docked and they disembarked, heading to the University of Vermont. With his help, they finished unloading the finds in under fifteen minutes.

"Thanks," she said, checking her watch. "We've made good time. How about lunch?"

He turned and smiled with a sensual spark. "How about picking something up and taking it back to your place?"

When they pulled up in front of her house, she shut the engine off and was about to get out of the car when Nick reached across the seat.

"Hold up." He removed his sunglasses. His eyes were somber and serious and his mouth opened and then shut a few times.

Anxiety curdled her appetite and she braced herself. He was a man who spoke his mind clearly and cleanly. Always. And she doubted his hesitation was a good thing.

Finally, he cleared his throat.

"I love you," he said gruffly.

In the silence that followed, Carter was dumbfounded. "You love me?"

"Yes. I do. I love you." He reached for her hand and opened it, kissing her palm softly and then placing it on his chest.

Carter searched his face. There was tenderness and reverence in it, not a hint of calculation. What stunned her, though, was the slightest hint of vulnerability in his eyes.

"Oh, Nick," she murmured as she reached out and touched his face. "I think I love you, too."

He gathered her in his arms and put his lips against hers softly, moving them sensually over her mouth. When his tongue dipped inside, she sighed as pleasure overwhelmed her.

"When did you know?" she asked after they pulled apart for some air.

"Despite my cynicism, I think I've always known you were out there. I just didn't recognize your face until you walked through my door."

After lunch, Nick was feeling very satisfied as they sat on her porch in the swinging bench. He kept the to-and-fro rhythm up with his foot, pushing against the deck with his heel. Carter was curled up in the seat, her knees tucked under her, her head in the crook of his arm. Her eyes were closed.

Looking up to the sky, he saw that the sun had begun its downward descent and he sorely regretted the day was coming to a close. Telling her he loved her had been much easier than he could have imagined. The words just felt right and he was glad he'd spoken them.

Though, they weren't what he'd planned to say. Not even close.

He'd meant to come clean about her father.

Carter stirred in his arms, a smile spreading her lips as she looked up at him. He reached down and stroked her cheek. There was an unmistakable glow in her eyes and he felt himself harden.

She uncoiled herself gracefully and then took his hand and led him upstairs to her bedroom. As soon as they ascended to the pine-scented space, he took her in his arms and kissed her while he undressed her. He took his time, savoring the feel of her skin and the way she looked in all the light. When she was gloriously naked, he tossed aside his own clothes and laid her down on her bed. Her smile of anticipation took his breath away.

His hands drifted across her breasts and stroked her flat stomach. As he kissed her and swallowed her moans of pleasure, as he plied her moist secrets, he felt as though she was really letting him in. Again and again, he pleasured her, driven to make her feel the love he had for her so she would remember it always.

When he entered her slowly, an aching tenderness in

his heart, he watched as her head arched back and her mouth parted. Her nails bit into his back and he threw himself into her again and again, until they were wet with passion. When he released, it was with a hoarse cry like nothing he had ever heard come out of his mouth before.

They lay together, still joined, for the longest time, until he felt a new wetness against his neck and pulled back. Carter was crying, fat tears rolling out of the corners of her eyes and strolling down her cheeks onto the white pillow.

He wiped one of them away, concerned.

"Don't mind my leaking," she said in stilted tones.

"Did I hurt you?"

She shook her head. "I just never expected . . . this. You."

Nick wiped away another tear and kissed her eyes. The tears came faster and he held her close. Rolling them over, he rocked her side to side, stroking her back.

After her crying eased, Carter pulled back from him. Her eyes glistened from her tears, the blue in them as deep and dense as the midnight sky. She had an embarrassed smile on her lips.

"I must be a mess to look at."

"You couldn't be more beautiful," he whispered.

Bringing her to him, Nick kissed her long and slowly, tracing the edge of her lips with his tongue. Her soft sigh of pleasure drifted up into the air.

"I'm going to do my best not to ever hurt you," he told her solemnly.

"God, I hope so," she murmured with a tremor of fear.

"Trust me."

"I'm going to try."

He pulled her to him, kissing her with heartfelt intensity. When they took a breath, she was smiling.

"So tell me, Mr. Fancy Pants," she said in a husky voice. "You ever been in a cramped shower stall before?"

He laughed softly. "Teach me, Master."

After the shower, which had much more to do with making love than it did with soap and water, they closed up the house and headed back to the ferry. While they were waiting to get on, Nick hopped out of the Jeep and returned with two ice cream cones, which they ate while perched on the front bumper of her car. During the trip across the lake, they sat on the upper deck, holding hands and watching boats head home for the evening.

Just before they returned to the car, she looked at him and said, "Thank you for a wonderful day."

"You'll stay for dinner, won't you? I've got a dessert in mind I know you'll like."

Carter flushed. "Does it come with whipped cream?"

"Only for you," he said, leaning in and putting his lips against hers.

The bump of the ferry coming into the dock separated them.

While they were speeding over the mountain, Carter looked over at him. Her eyes were joyous, full of a light that hit him square in the chest. "I'm sorry this day is over."

"We should do it again."

"Fall in love?"

"No, we've already done that. I was thinking about getting away."

Carter was beaming as she turned off the main road and onto his driveway.

"I think we should go to Montreal for dinner," he suggested. "We could drive up to the Ritz—"

Nick frowned as they rounded the final turn.

In front of the mansion was a black stretch limousine.

"Expecting company?" Carter said, coming to a halt behind it.

The front door of the house was wide-open and, as they got out of the car, they could hear voices.

When Nick saw Bob Packert's round face and stocky body emerge from the interior darkness, his heart went cold.

When no one followed the man out, Nick's hopes soared. Had Wessex stayed behind?

Then her father walked into the sunshine.

Nick turned in slow motion and saw Carter blanch, wobble in her boots, and reach out a hand blindly. He took it, steadying her.

"Well, how do you do, Nick Farrell?" Packert asked in his broad Texas accent. "I guess you weren't expecting us all until tomorrow. You're gonna have to forgive my jumping the gun, but the three of us have a lot to talk about. Best to get started early—you know what I mean?"

Nick didn't even acknowledge the man. He watched as Carter pulled away from him, horrified.

"Why is he here?" she said softly as she lurched backward.

"Carter—"

Packert spoke up. "Wessex, is this your little girl, the one you were nattering on about? Real nice of Farrell here to get the two of you together again. You owe him one now, don't you?"

Carter spun on Nick, her eyes widening with alarm. He reached out to her, taking her arm.

"I didn't mean for this to happen."

She pulled herself free from his grasp. Her head was shaking back and forth, her face a tight mask of horror. "Don't touch me. Don't you ever come near me again."

She ran off toward the mountain, leaving the doors of the Jeep wide-open, the key in the ignition, and her backpack on the seat.

Nick swore, long and hard.

"Well, that's a fine hello," Packert commented.

Nick wheeled on the man, about to vent his fury when Wessex, who was looking shaky himself, stepped between the two.

"How about a tour of the house?" the man offered the Texan.

"Mighty fine idea." Packert leaned in close to Wessex and said in a stage whisper, "This man looks like he's got a burr in his shorts. Best give him a little time to cool off."

As Packert ambled inside the house, Wessex hung back.

Nick fixed the man with a deadly expression. "What the hell are you doing here?"

"I tried to call it off. I really did. But Packert was determined to come up here. He called while he was in the air, heading to Albany. I had no notice. I was on the phone all day trying to warn you but you were out."

Nick's eyes flashed up to the mountain.

"Occupy that asshole," he said tersely. "I'll be back."

14

CARTER HAD no recollection of her trip up the mountain. One moment she was looking into her father's eyes for the first time in two years and the next she was in her tent, packing. Even though her mind had shut down, at least her hands seemed to know what to do. They had pulled out a bag and started to stuff clothes into it.

Progress was slow, however, on account of the great rolling sobs coming out of her.

Suddenly, the tent flap was pulled aside.

"We found another one!" Ellie announced.

Carter hid her face from the girl and wiped her eyes. "Another what?"

"Skeleton! Quick, come see— What are you doing?"

Carter searched for a convenient lie. Nothing came to mind. "I have to go."

"Why?"

"I just have to go." Carter resumed the frantic packing, not noticing as Ellie disappeared.

Minutes later, she heard Buddy's gentle voice. "Carter?"

"Go 'way."

"What's going on?" He started to open the flap.

"Don't come in," she said in a choked rush. "I don't want you to see me like this."

His soft laugh preceded him into the tent. "I've seen you after a week without a shower. In the morning before you've had your coffee. And what about in that god-awful Bo Peep costume last Halloween? Nothing's going to scare me."

Carter tried to keep up the pace by grabbing another bag to pack. It kept slipping out of her hands.

"Talk to me," he begged. "Please."

But she just shook her head and began to disassemble her cot. Buddy stopped her by putting his arm around her and sitting her down.

"Take a deep breath and tell me what's wrong."

"I have to leave." The words came out disjointed and rough.

"Okay. Why?"

"I— He's here. He invited him, here. Purposely." Desperation and hurt caused her voice to waver.

"Who's here?"

Carter sagged against her friend's shoulder. "Oh God, Buddy, he used me. He knew exactly what he was doing. The whole time we . . ."

Stroking her hair and murmuring softly, Buddy let her ramble until she exhausted herself.

When she finally lifted her head, he tucked a strand of hair behind her ear and said patiently, "Who's here?"

"My father."

His eyes widened. "Good Lord. Why?"

"Nick invited him."

Buddy frowned. "Does Farrell know how it is between you two?"

"I told him. He knew weeks ago." She wiped her eyes. "What a fool I've been."

"You aren't a fool."

"What else do you call someone who throws herself at a master manipulator? Brilliant sure doesn't fit." She got to her feet. "Nick engineered his visit. On purpose. As a favor to my father."

"You don't know that."

"Yes, I do. I watched as he tossed Candace out like garbage. Why am I surprised to be treated just as badly? He's a born liar and a knee-jerk opportunist."

"Carter, you're rambling. If you could just calm—"

"He's got a hell of a track record with women. And I knew that going in. God, I can't believe I let myself get involved with a man like that."

"I don't understand." Buddy's eyes crinkled from thought. "What would he get out of inviting Wessex up here?"

"My father is a powerful man and would do anything to see me. He'd owe Nick a hell of a favor for pulling off a stunt like this." Carter started pacing. "I just need to get out of here. I need to go. You finish the dig if you want but I'm through."

"Hold on." Buddy put out his palms in a show of caution. "Just slow down a minute. Stop and think about what you're doing."

"Believe me, I am."

"Carter, I want you to do whatever you think is right, but your name's the one on the grant. You walk and the dig is over."

"So go to Grace and replace me as the principal investigator. I don't care."

"But we can't leave the site unattended, even if it's just for a day so I can go meet with the Hall Foundation board. Whoever made off with the logbooks could pick the site clean, Ivan or no Ivan."

"Christ, Buddy, what do you want me to do?" She threw her hands up. "I don't care if they take the whole mountain away in pieces. I can't stay here and pretend everything is okay."

"You don't have to pretend." His eyes were unwaveringly sympathetic but firm. "I don't want to come across as insensitive but you should finish what you started."

"I just can't," she cried.

"Look, it's only a couple more weeks. You think you're going to feel any better prowling around your house? Stay up here and bury yourself in the work. I'll take care of everything else. You won't have to leave the mountain until we pack up and go."

Carter pictured her house, which had now been contaminated by memories of Nick. Her porch where they had sat and talked about the renovations she'd done. Her bed, where they had made love. Her shower, for God's sake. Suddenly, the idea of going home and being alone with her memories seemed worse than staying at camp with her friends.

Besides, no matter where she went she knew there'd be no escaping from the hurt. She had been betrayed by Nick, used as a pawn in the business world he dominated. No change of zip code was going to make that go away.

She struggled to hold on to her composure. "I don't know how to get through this. Here or anywhere. God, I knew I should never have trusted him."

Buddy stood up and put his arm around her. "I'm on your side. Anything you want or need, I'll make it happen."

She raised troubled eyes to him. "Can you make it all go away? Can you change him into who I wanted him to be?"

He shook his head sadly. "I wish I could."

Nick was striding across the lawn, with Carter's backpack and keys in his hand, when Ivan stepped in his path.

"Storms are comin'," the man said. "Gonna be some bad ones."

"When are they going to hit us?" Nick asked numbly. He felt as though they had already arrived.

"Tomorrow afternoon. They'll last into the night."

Nick looked up at the high, thin clouds. "Looks fine now."

"Things change. Anyway," Ivan continued, "I'll be settling the boats real good tomorrow and pulling in the lawn chairs. May even batten down the shutters on the north side of the house. Hey, you all right?"

"No, I'm not. I'm not okay at all." Nick started across the meadow, feeling bereft and pissed off at himself.

He scaled the mountain quickly, thinking only of

Carter. He was worried that she might bolt from the dig. Disappear from his life altogether.

He was glad he knew where she lived.

When he got to the campsite, he didn't see anyone around. He was about to head over to the dig when she appeared out of her tent, a logbook in her hand. She stopped short when she saw him, and he watched as anguish flared in her face. It was covered quickly by anger.

"For Chrissakes, can't you just leave me alone?" Her voice was strong and sure.

He approached cautiously. "Carter, please. Let me—"

"Why did you bother coming up? You want to pick over the carcass?" She marched over to the office area and started rifling through papers. "I'd have figured mowing me over would have been sufficient. Usually drivers don't back up to make sure roadkill isn't moving."

"Let me explain."

"Wait. I know. You've come to make sure the job is finished." She gave a bitter laugh. "Just in case I survived the first set of tires. As a matter of fact, we've already been through this whole apology thing a few times before. It never seems to stick, does it?"

"Carter, you have to believe that—"

She wheeled around. "I don't *have* to believe anything that comes out of your mouth. I was naïve enough to fall for the I-love-you crap. I'm not going to make that mistake again."

"I do love you."

She talked right over his words. "One of the first things I ever said to you was that I don't believe in conversions when it comes to people like yourself. I should have listened to myself."

"I didn't know that he was coming today. I'm sorry—"

"I don't care that you're sorry! You want to make things right, then tell me you didn't engineer a reunion between my father and me so he'd be in your debt."

Carter stared at him as he tried to find the right words.

When he didn't immediately offer a denial, she shook her head.

"You did, didn't you? You set the whole thing up. That's why you let me come here and dig in the first place, wasn't it? That's why you changed your mind."

Nick made sure his voice was even. "Look, in the beginning, I admit that I thought it was potentially beneficial to try and bring you and your father together. I knew he missed you and—"

Carter slammed a folder down on the table. "My family is—*was* none of your business. My father can go to hell and take you with him."

"Listen to me. As soon as I realized I was falling in love with you, I knew I had to call the whole thing off. I didn't want to jeopardize us."

"Then why didn't you tell me before?"

"I was going to today but I didn't want to ruin everything." Nick stepped forward, and when she started to look around wildly for an escape, he froze.

"What could your father possibly have done to deserve this?" he murmured.

"My mother is dead because of him!" she shouted. "Is that enough for you? Enough to justify to the great Nick Farrell why I choose not to speak to the man?"

"Carter, I—"

"But wait. Mr. Farrell wants the details." Her eyes were burning as she spoke in a shrill voice. "My mother and I lived alone while he traveled the globe racing after business deals and other women. His life was a revolving door of socialites only too eager to be with a man who had plenty of connections and a lot of money."

She pegged him with a hard look. "Remind you of anyone?"

Nick flinched.

"Two years ago, after I'd moved out and my mother had no one but servants in the house with her, she decided to reach out to him. They fought because he refused to stay home and talk with her about their marriage. He had to rush to Paris for a *really important meeting.* After more than twenty years together, you'd think he could have put off one lousy appointment, but he was far too busy for that. His driver took him to the airport and my mother got in a car to go after them."

Abruptly, Carter's voice grew quiet. "It took me three hours to get to her bedside at the hospital and I was almost too late. I watched her die and her last words were about him. How she loved him."

Her blue eyes were so full of pain that it hurt to look into them. He didn't turn away.

"You want to know where my father was when she died? Over the Atlantic Ocean. By the time he had the jet turned around and headed back, she was gone." Carter pushed a hand through her hair. "My father had the gall to want to give the eulogy but I refused. I wasn't going to have a philanderer speak in front of my mother's casket. The last time I saw him up close was when I left him at the grave site. Until today."

Nick was stunned by the story. "I'm sorry."

"Oh, no, you don't." She shook her head vehemently. "You don't get to be sorry. I'm not going to make it so easy for you. You don't get to apologize. You don't get to explain. I didn't give the man who put my mother in the ground a chance to and I don't feel inclined to grant you special privileges. Anymore."

"Carter, you've got to let me talk." His voice was urgent as he prayed she'd find faith in the better side of him. "I never meant to hurt you—"

"Yeah," she shot back harshly, "I believe that. You've always been too distracted taking care of yourself."

"Can't you let me get one word in here?"

"I have to go back to work." She picked up a clipboard from the table and held it against her chest. "You know, you and my father are a lot alike and I'll bet you've done some terrific deals together. Screwing people comes naturally to you both."

Nick swore in frustration and was about to launch another protest when he froze. Her eyes were looking straight through him, not even registering his presence. That, more than anything else, scared him most.

Carter squared her shoulders. "I'm going to finish the dig. Not because I have something to prove to you but because I have something to prove to myself. I've been doing pretty well living alone. I like my life. And I'm not going to lose any part of it just because you turned out to be exactly who I thought you were."

"I'm not like your father."

"Then maybe you need to get to know yourself a little better. You've lived up to your reputation admirably, and have made me remember why it's important not to trust people. I'd forgotten, you see."

"I'm going to tell your father to go."

"Don't bother. I won't be coming down off the mountain again until we're through."

Without a backward glance, Carter walked away, leaving him standing next to the cold fire pit.

It wasn't supposed to happen like this, he thought. The end wasn't supposed to come this soon. Or even at all.

He stood next to the cluster of gray embers for a long time, looking around the campsite. He noticed odd things, like how the ketchup bottle on the mess table was half empty and that there was a pair of sunglasses dangling from the clothesline.

When he couldn't stand it any longer, when his regrets and recriminations threatened to overcome him, he went back down to the mansion. He thought about getting in his car and driving somewhere. Anywhere.

But as soon as he walked in his front door, he heard Packert's voice calling out for him.

Smelling blood, Nick went out onto the porch.

"So it's the master of the house," Packert said, holding a short cigar in his right hand. "You ready to behave civil-like now?"

Nick smiled with vengeance as he embraced the cold emotion. "If I were you, I wouldn't be so worried about manners."

"My mother raised me right."

"Perhaps, but you've got other things to agonize over," Nick drawled. "Trust me."

As Packert squinted up at him, Nick sought out Carter's father. He was sitting in a wicker chair, dressed coolly in a white linen suit. He was a very elegant, powerful man, who seemed to have aged twenty years in the last two hours.

Packert puffed on the nub of his cigar and offered Nick a conciliatory grin. "Say, why don't you take a load off? You look worn-out, old man, and we've got a lot to talk about."

"Worn-out?" Nick leaned against a column. "That's funny. I'm feeling rather aggressive."

Nick shot a dark glance across the porch and the man's overconfident smile faltered a bit.

"Well, I think that's just fine. I like a strong opponent." A cloud of smoke was pushed out of Packert's lips. Behind it, the man's eyes grew sharp. "So, boys, what do you say you all fess up to what you're doing?"

Nick's voice was bored as he answered. "CommTrans is in trouble."

"Trouble?" Packert laughed. "We've had a couple of challenges over the last year but the company's doing just fine. No thanks to that dog of a manufacturing division you off-loaded on us."

"I don't think you want to bring that up, do you?"

Packert's eyes darted away to the end of the cigar.

Nick continued, his words clipped and clear. "Your company's overvalued, undercapitalized, and debt-heavy. You're sinking fast."

"I don't recall opening myself up for insults."

"Those are facts, Mr. Packert, not insults."

"So what are you gonna do? Buy up my company and kick me out?"

"That's the plan."

Packert was taken aback. "You're serious."

"I am," Nick said darkly. "I don't take my reputation lightly. You dragged my name through the mud because you failed to manage your own organization. I can't let that go, can I?"

"Now, hold up there. I did no such thing."

"Then you must have interpreted those front-page articles in the *Wall Street Journal* differently than everyone else did. You remember, the ones where you accused me of fraud? I have copies of them, if you need a refresher. And there's the investigative demand the attorney general of the State of New York served on me. You've heard about that, too, haven't you?"

Packert began to look truly panicked.

"So how about dinner?" Nick said. "I think we're having fresh meat."

After a tense silence, the other men followed him to the dining room where three places had been set at the end of the long, elaborately dressed table. It was an awful meal even though Gertie's food was perfectly cooked. Packert was subdued and neither Nick nor Wessex was in the mood for conversation.

After the Texan had grabbed a bottle of bourbon and gone upstairs to bed, Wessex followed Nick into the study.

As soon as the door was closed, the man asked, "What did she say?"

Nick sat down at his desk. "She doesn't want to see you. Or me, for that matter."

"Is she okay?"

"No." He glanced up at Wessex, recalling what his daughter had said about him.

"You're looking at me strangely," Wessex murmured. "She told you everything, didn't she?"

"It's none of my business." And Nick wished he'd figured that out much sooner.

"Things didn't happen as she thinks they did. That's what I've wanted to tell her." Wessex stared into space, as if he were reliving the past. But then his eyes shifted over and met Nick's. "You're in love with my daughter, aren't you?"

Nick's eyebrows rose but he didn't hesitate in his answer. "I am."

At that moment, the door was flung open with such force, it ricocheted off the bookshelves with a crack.

"What the hell did you do to Carter?" Cort demanded.

15

NICK TURNED to Wessex and said grimly, "Allow me to introduce my—"

"I don't want to meet another one of your stuffed shirts," Cort spat. He was practically vibrating with anger.

Nick frowned. "You want to try that again?"

Cort shot the other man a cutting glance. "Do you mind beating it? No offense, but can't you go shuffle papers somewhere else?"

Wessex's eyebrows launched upward but he replied in an even tone. "If you're going to talk about my daughter, then no, I don't want to go 'shuffle papers somewhere else.'"

Cort's eyes widened.

"This is Carter's father," Nick said tightly. "Now, how about an apology?"

"Er—sorry." Seeming confused, Cort rubbed the top of his head, making his hair climb to new heights. "But what are you doing here?"

"Are you always this blunt?" There was an indulgent cast to Wessex's face, one that surprised Nick.

"When someone's been trampled by my uncle I get kind of mad. Since he does that a lot, I guess you could say it's an *always* kinda thing." Cort turned to Nick. "So what did you do to her?"

"Nothing that concerns you."

The kid linked his wiry arms over his chest. "You mean you don't want to talk about it."

"That's right."

Nick could feel his temper rise. He was upset as hell at what had happened with Carter. The last thing he needed was another fight with his nephew.

Cort huffed. "Just because you don't want to admit to yourself or anybody else that you're a heartless—"

"Enough!" Nick slammed his hands down on his desk and shot to his feet. "Do *not* push me on this one!"

Cort stepped back, dazed by the reaction.

Nick took a deep breath and sat down, regretting his explosion and feeling ragged.

"I didn't know you cared so much . . . about her," Cort mumbled while looking at him with wide, cautious eyes.

Nick pushed a hand through his hair. "Yeah, well, I do."

Cort's head tilted to the side and the kid looked at him closely.

In the silence that followed, Wessex got up and poured himself a brandy from the bar.

"She has a lot of people who care about her," the man said as he sat back down and swirled the glass in his palm.

Cort glanced over at him. "You look like her—you know that?"

"I know."

"She's really upset." The kid looked back and forth between the two older men, who were quiet. He finally settled on Wessex. "Hey, you're her father. You should go talk to her. That's what my dad would've done if I were upset. Whenever I woke up from a nightmare, he was always there. It made me feel better."

Cort started shifting his weight back and forth, as if he expected Carter's father to leap out of the chair and leave the house.

"So you should go to her," he prompted.

"You're right," Wessex allowed. The hopeless desolation about him was at odds with his sophisticated dress and polished voice.

"So why aren't you going?"

"It's a long story."

"But it's just a short walk up the mountain."

Wessex, still staring into his glass, did not reply.

Cort shrugged awkwardly. "Well, do what you want. But I'd go up there if I were you. Who doesn't want their father when they're feeling bad?"

Nick watched as the man stiffened.

"So . . . ummm . . . good night, Uncle Nick."

"Good night," Nick returned softly.

Cort left the room, closing the door quietly.

"God, I wish I had done so much differently," Wessex said. "And if only I could walk up that mountain and sit her down, talk to her, and have her listen."

Nick leaned back in his chair, stretching his arms over his head and thinking that he and Wessex were in the same boat.

"Maybe you should try," he suggested. "You never know. Time changes things."

"Did you see the expression on her face? I don't think time has worked in my favor." The man swallowed the last of his drink and got to his feet. "Good night, Farrell."

Nick nodded.

Left alone, he stared into space. An hour later, he got up from his desk and headed upstairs himself. He went to his suite of rooms, took a shower, and got into bed with no illusions that sleep was going to come easy.

Lying flat on his back, with his eyes clamped shut and his body rigid under the sheets, he waited for hours to lose consciousness. When sleep did come, it teemed with nightmares in which Carter was in danger and he could not save her.

The next morning, Carter watched the sun rise over the mountains from her favorite boulder overlooking the lake. She stayed there, witnessing the day come alive, with little enthusiasm. She was waiting until she could handle facing Buddy and Ellie but, as the sun got higher and she didn't feel any better, she gave up.

It was going to take a hell of a lot longer than a matter of hours to feel like herself again.

As she approached camp, she saw Buddy lighting the fire. Unable to bear his mute concern, she told him to meet her at the site.

Inside the circle of stones, she went over to the newest skeletal discovery and pulled back the tarp. With it they'd found Revolutionary-period military buttons and the bayonet of a Brown Bess, all of which marked the man as a Brit. This meant, with three-quarters of the site excavated, three other people from the party were still missing. Winship, one other patriot, and the Indian. Her gaze skipped across the undisturbed ground, all that was standing between her and freedom.

How long would it take to finish? she wondered listlessly.

Getting down on her knees, she reexamined the remains. The skeleton was almost completely revealed, and she went to work on the man's feet.

Despite the bucolic sounds of birds and the scent of pine in the air, she was anything but at peace. In the morning light, she found it next to impossible not to think about Nick and her father. Even though she'd spent all night dwelling on their betrayals, there seemed to be no end to her mind's desire to rehash what had happened.

When Buddy appeared with some coffee, she took a mug from him with an attempt at a smile.

"You don't need to pretend around me," he said, putting a hand on her shoulder.

"No, but right now I feel like I need to pretend around myself."

By the time Ellie showed up, the skeleton was completely exposed and Buddy was taking pictures.

"Do you think we'll find the others?" the girl asked, dancing around the pit. She'd pulled her hair back in a ponytail and it bounced up and down with her.

Watching the girl's enthusiasm, Carter was overwhelmed with sadness. She was years and miles away from that kind of carefree happiness, feeling old and beaten down in comparison.

"We'll have to wait and see. First, we've got to get this skeleton out of the ground." She looked around for one of the larger containers. "Hey, does anyone need anything from the site? I'm going back to get a storage bin."

"More coffee," Buddy answered from behind the camera.

Carter picked up the thermos and walked into the trees.

Nick was pulled out of a restless sleep by someone banging on his bedroom door.

"Go away," he called out.

The knocking didn't stop.

"What the *hell* is the problem?" He shot out of bed, grabbing a sheet and pulling it around his waist. When he wrenched the door open, Wessex jumped back.

"Sorry to wake you."

The man looked as if he hadn't slept well either.

"S'all right." Nick rubbed a hand over his eyes. His voice was a hoarse growl. "What time is it?"

"Before eight. What size shoe do you wear?"

"Eleven." Nick answered on instinct before wondering why the guy cared. "What's up?"

"I need a pair of hiking boots."

Nick came fully awake.

"I spent most of last night thinking about her," Wessex explained. "I have to try or I will never forgive myself. To be this close and not reach out . . ."

"I'll meet you in the kitchen," Nick said quickly. He shut the door, dropped the sheet, and began pulling on clothes.

When he got downstairs, Wessex was pacing back and forth in front of the refrigerator. Now that he was more awake, Nick noticed that the man had on another elegant linen suit. The fact that he wasn't wearing a tie seemed like Wessex's only concession to leisure.

"I keep the hiking gear in the mudroom," Nick told him. "You want to borrow some clothes?"

Wessex seemed surprised and looked down at what he was wearing. "This is comfortable enough."

"When was the last time you went up a mountain?"

"Summer camp, perhaps. But I'll be fine."

Nick kept his doubts to himself and led the way to a room off the kitchen where the sports equipment and foul-weather gear were kept. He handed over a pair of hiking boots that Wessex put on.

"So how do I get up there?"

"Come on. I'll show you the way to the trail." When they were outside, Nick pointed at the forest's edge. "You go through that break in the woods—"

"What break?" Wessex squinted.

"Here, I'll take you over." Hell, Nick was prepared to drag Wessex up the mountain if he had to. He was hoping for the best. If her father could somehow get up there and talk to Carter, if somehow a miracle happened . . .

"I say, Farrell, are you sure there's a trail in these woods?"

If somehow the man didn't get lost and end up in Canada.

"Why don't I walk you up part of the way?"

"That would be most appreciated."

The two men entered the forest and were silent for a while. Then Wessex spoke up.

"When Carter was young," he said, as if talking to himself, "I was gone a lot. Actually, that was true when she was grown, too, but I regret more my absences when she was little. Anyway, in those early days, she would wait for me to come home well into the night. No matter how late I was due to arrive."

The trail began to incline and Wessex started to breathe heavily. Nick slowed the pace, concentrating on the man's words.

"The house she grew up in, the one I still live in now, has a tremendous front hall with a grand staircase. It's cavernous, really, and must have been quite spooky for a small child in the dark. Inevitably, though, I would come through the door and there, curled on her side in her pj's, would be Carter asleep on the stairs. It couldn't have been comfortable."

Wessex cleared his throat between pulling in lungfuls of air. "She was . . . so tiny in that space, so very small."

Nick paused so Wessex could catch his breath. As they stood in a cool draught of air that was funneling down the mountain, the man took out a handkerchief and wiped his brow.

"I would open the iron-latticed door and, even though it never made a sound, she would come awake instantly. I don't know how she knew it was me. She just did. She would leap up and run into my arms, throwing herself at me. There was . . . such love in her eyes. In all my life, no one has ever shown me that kind of love."

They started walking again. Nick's heart ached as he remembered Carter's eyes looking at him with such warmth.

"When she got older and went off to boarding school, I would come home, open the door, and be looking forward to seeing her. It took years for me to remember she didn't live with us anymore. I tell you, that front hall never looked emptier than in the moments when I would realize she wasn't waiting for me."

The man fell silent for a while, breathing so hard he couldn't speak.

This time when they stopped, Nick settled on a rock so Wessex wouldn't be embarrassed by his lack of breath. Sinking gratefully against a boulder, Carter's father leaned down and braced his hands on his knees.

"I filled it up with art, you know. The lobby. It's hung with old-world masters. Changed the rug, too. It used to be pale to match the white marble. Now it's red." He looked up at Nick. "It still feels cold, though."

They resumed the hike and Nick took him to within a hundred yards of the clearing that faced the lake.

"Keep heading this way," he said. "You'll get to an

open stretch with a long view and the trail keeps going behind it. The campsite is to the left. You'll see it clearly."

"Thank you," Wessex murmured and started off by himself.

Nick watched him disappear into the trees, wondering what had really happened the night Carter's mother died. He had no idea whether the man who had just limped up the mountain was cruel or simply fallible. His emotions, however, had been obvious. He missed his daughter and would do anything for a second chance.

Nick knew exactly how that felt.

16

CARTER WAS rummaging around Papercut Central when her father emerged from the trees. She stopped moving as she looked into his face. She told herself she shouldn't be surprised that he'd come up. But she was.

He looked older than she remembered, less vital. The dirt smudged on the legs of his pants and the twig hanging off one shoulder added to the perception.

"Hello, Carter."

As soon as she heard his voice, she became angry again. "What are you doing here?"

"I wanted to see you."

She realized numbly that his inflection was as she remembered, carrying just the hint of an English accent. The tone was off, though. It was more hesitant than she was used to.

Carter resumed searching for the storage bin. "Then you've wasted the trip up and ruined an expensive suit."

He didn't leave, just stood on the fringes of camp.

"I've missed you," he said softly. "It has been very hard . . . to be away from you."

"Good." She stood up, having found the container. "I hope it hurts like hell. Now go away."

She started toward the site.

"Do you want to know why I send you the watches?"

She wheeled around, her tone combative. "Because

your secretary doesn't remember what she sent me the year before?"

"I buy them myself. I keep meaning to get you something else but the watches seem so appropriate. The time passing . . . It's been so long."

His sad expression as his words trailed off made her pity him for a brief moment. It was an unexpected emotion. But then images of her mother's funeral surged forward, cutting through any compassion she felt.

"Then you should keep the damn things. I'm not marking time. I left you behind for a damn good reason and I haven't looked back."

The words were a low blow and Carter knew it. She watched as he winced.

"I know you haven't," he said slowly. "But the watches, they're . . . my waiting, my hoping."

There was a long pause as their eyes, identical blue, met across the distance between them.

"Carter, I have a lot to apologize for. I never really thought about what or who I'd left behind for all those years. I never knew how hard it must have been until I was left behind by you." Her father took out a handkerchief and blotted his brow. "Do you know what I miss the most? The way we could speak without talking. You and I, we were so alike."

"I am nothing like you." Every syllable was enunciated, her distaste for him coming out clearly. She found it confusing, however, that she had to force the animosity a bit.

Her father nodded gravely. "Yes, I think you're stronger. You were always stronger than both your mother and me. Certainly, you were able to handle her far better than I could."

Carter's first instinct was to scream that he had no right to bring up the unspeakable. Furious, she opened her mouth but then hesitated as her father recoiled. The show of fragility halted the tumble of words in her throat.

She thought back to her childhood. How, in that mansion full of grown-ups, she'd always felt like the only one who knew what was really going on. Her father was either gone or in the process of leaving and her mother was . . . in her own world. Other memories started to bubble to the surface, scenes in which her mother flew into fits over trivial things. Carter saw her younger self hiding until it was safe to come out again.

Why had she forgotten these things?

Then she stopped herself.

"Don't you dare blame Mummy for the fact that you were never home. That was your choice, not her fault."

"She was sick, Carter." His eyes reached out to her, looking for understanding.

Her laugh had a sharp edge. "Because you left her alone in that house while you danced your way into the bedrooms of God knows how many other women."

"I never," he emphasized softly, "*never* was unfaithful to her."

Carter opened her mouth to fight him but he cut her off.

"No matter what she told you, no matter what she believed of me, I was never with another woman."

"I don't believe you." Carter shook her head vehemently. "She said you—"

"Your mother was mentally ill."

Carter threw down the storage bin, balling up her fists. "How dare you! How stable would you be if you were left alone all the time?"

"She wanted it that way."

"She *wanted* it? She was miserable!"

"Carter, she wouldn't go out of the house."

"I never saw you ask her to," she ground out bitterly.

"That's because I gave up hope before you were born."

Carter began pacing as memories came to her, memories of her mother's distress and sadness. "No, that's not right. She said you didn't want her around. Said you wouldn't take her places because you were ashamed of her."

"Untrue. She was her own jailer. And I wasn't going

to become a prisoner of her illness. By the end, she hated me for that freedom." He lifted his hands up, his voice gentle. "I begged her to go see doctors. She wouldn't go, at least not until they started prescribing things for her. Then she went all the time. Then I couldn't keep her away from them."

Carter thought back, remembering the bottles of pills that were always around her mother. By her bedside, next to her reading chair in the conservatory, in her knitting bag. Why hadn't that seemed odd?

"Mummy couldn't sleep," she protested. "It was nightmares of you that kept her up."

Her father went over to the picnic table and sat down. He put his head in his hands. "My biggest regret was that I left you there. That was no place to grow up. I should have . . . You shouldn't have had to deal with her by yourself. I knew the staff were there but you were so alone. I tried to take you with me once but she threatened to . . . It seemed more dangerous to take you away from her. I was a coward."

The self-hatred in his voice resonated in Carter's ears, and she couldn't shut out his pain.

"The night she died," he said in a voice that cracked, "I should have known she'd overdosed. She was out of control but I couldn't distinguish the effect of the drugs from what might have been just another of her episodes. It never occurred to me she would get into a car. I didn't think she could even drive. When I got the news, all I could think of was you. I raced back to see you."

Carter recalled him coming to the hospital and the scene that had followed.

Her father looked up, eyes pleading. "I have plenty to apologize for. There's so much I should have done differently. I've spent the past two years chronicling my failures as a parent and a husband and I still have a long way to go. If I'd been more courageous, if I had taken drastic steps like getting her hospitalized, maybe she'd have gotten the help she needed." His voice dropped. "But I didn't and she's dead and you're gone."

When Carter simply stared at him, his shoulders sagged. With a lurch, he got to his feet. "I exhausted most of my married life trying to get away from the loneliness and isolation she lived in. Courtesy of running from it, I'm exactly where I never wanted to be."

A stiff breeze blew through camp, ruffling the edges of the tarps and making the pines whistle. Her father looked at the sky, the wind lifting up the tails of his jacket.

"That's all I wanted to say." He spoke softly. "Except that I love you and always will. And I'll stop with the gifts, too. It was never my intention to antagonize you with them."

He lifted up his hand but then dropped it and turned to the trail.

Carter stared at his back as he left, engulfed by memories.

She was surprised to see him so emotional. She'd always known him as uniquely stoic and strong. Untouched by the chaos created by her mother. Above it all. To see him so frazzled, so human, was a shock.

Carter felt her knees buckle and she let herself fall into a folding chair. She was still sitting like that when Buddy came back to the site a half hour later.

"Hey, I was getting worried about you."

"Sorry. I got . . . distracted."

Buddy looked up at the trees, which were beginning to sway in the wind. "I think there's a storm coming."

Carter glanced heavenward. The sky had darkened dramatically, the sun shut out by purple clouds.

She took a deep breath. "We better tie everything down and get those bones out of the dirt. Why don't you finish up at the site and I'll get to work here."

After Buddy left with the container, Carter moved around in a daze. She checked all of the tent and tarp lines and gathered up anything that could blow away. By the time the Swifts returned, the wind had intensified further.

"Site's secure," Buddy said, putting the skeleton under cover in Papercut Central. "Looks like this storm's going to be a real humdinger."

Suddenly, from out of the trailhead, Cort came running toward them. He was wearing a yellow slicker and looked worried.

"You need to come down. There's a severe storm warning out and you really should stay at the house tonight. Even Ivan said so."

Carter and Buddy traded anxious looks.

"But we can't leave all this equipment unattended," she said to her partner.

"Then you and Ellie go. I'll hold down the fort."

Ellie shook her head firmly. "Dad, if you stay, I stay."

"I don't want you up here if it's going to be dangerous."

"Ditto," she challenged him.

"I'll stay," Carter cut in. "I want to stay."

They all looked at her dubiously.

Buddy frowned. "I don't want you up here alone."

"Please, how bad could it get?" When their expressions didn't change, Carter rolled her eyes. "Come on, people. I'm not a sissy. I can handle it."

No one moved.

"Go on." She nudged Buddy's arm. "Worse comes to worst, I'll tie myself to a tree so I don't blow away. God, will you guys give me a break? I'll be fine."

Bob Packert and Nick were standing in the leeway of the house, watching the lake grow gray and choppy. They were waiting for Wessex's return.

Packert's eyes were calculating as he spoke. "Farrell, if I went to the papers and cleared your name, would I still have a job if I sell to you and Wessex?"

Nick cocked an eyebrow. "You aren't selling. We're making an offer your shareholders are going to jump at. As for getting the truth out, it's a little late for that and it wouldn't make you a better businessman."

Packert snorted indignantly. "I don't appreciate your attitude."

"The truth hurts."

There was a moment of silence. "At least you can tell me when you're planning on making the offer."

"You'll know as soon as your shareholders do." Nick was bored by the conversation, bored by the man. What he was really thinking about was how Wessex had fared with Carter. The man had been gone for some time, which meant one of two things. Either she'd turned him away immediately and he'd gotten lost on the way back down, or they'd actually talked.

"Look here, boy, my company's one of the hottest properties on the street. I've got more of you raider types beating a path to my door than Gorton's has fish sticks. You and Wessex aren't the only ones interested."

When Nick didn't reply, Packert burst out with strained laughter. "You're a cold one, ain't you? The word on the street about you is right."

"I'm so relieved to live up to my reputation."

The first raindrops began to fall.

Packert cleared his throat, changing his approach. "Say, now, this rain's making me thirsty. What say we have a drink? Maybe we can get to know each other a little better."

"I'll show you to the bar but you'll have to excuse me." Nick turned away from the lake. "I've got work to do."

After dumping Packert off in the library, he went to his study, ostensibly to check his messages. Instead of picking up the phone, however, he walked out onto the side porch and looked at the lake again. The storm seemed to be preparing for a major onslaught, Wessex was nowhere to be found, Cort had disappeared up the mountain, and Carter and the Swifts could be in danger if things got bad at the summit.

He heard the first thunder roll through the sky. The sound made up his mind.

Nick was heading to the mudroom when he caught sight of Wessex, Cort, and the Swifts jogging through the rain to the house. He searched for Carter in the crowd of slickers. She wasn't with them.

As the motley group came through the back door, he met them with a steely eye.

"Where is she?"

Everyone looked at Buddy.

"She's staying at camp," he answered grimly.

"You left her up there alone? Are you out of your mind?"

"I don't like it any more than you do." Buddy glanced over at his daughter. "I would have stayed but . . ."

A streak of lightning flashed across the sky and flickered in through the windows. They fell silent, waiting for the storm's answer. After a pause, thunder came bounding through the lake valley.

Wessex paled beneath his tan. "Perhaps you could persuade her to come down?"

Nick was already changing into hiking boots. As he got to his feet, Packert rounded the corner with glass in hand.

"Hey, it's finally a party!" The man sidled up to Wessex, yanking the man's wet and dirty jacket. "What the hell happened? You look like crap."

When no one paid any attention to him, he spoke up.

"So what do you all have planned tonight? A little charades? From the excitement I've seen around here, this place might as well be a nursing home." He laughed. "Well, I'm sorry that m'pal Wessex and I'll miss all the excitement but at least there's a bar in the limo. It's gonna be a long trip back to the city."

"Unfortunately, you aren't going anywhere," Nick said briskly. "If these storms live up to their advertising, they're going to wash out the mountain roads. You're stuck here until they pass."

Packert digested the information and then grinned. "Guess I'll be drinking your scotch instead of Wessex's."

With a cheeky salute, the Texan went back to the bar.

Nick pulled on rain gear. "We've got plenty of bedrooms and bathrooms upstairs. Find Gertie and—"

"I'm right here." The woman put an arm around Ellie, who was looking distressed.

"What's going to happen to Carter?" the girl asked.

"I'm either going to drag her down off that mountain or sit on her like an egg." Nick wrenched open the door. "Either way, she's not going to be out in this alone."

Carter was at the rock ledge overlooking the lake as the storm came in, and she welcomed its fury. The rushing wind and frantic waves down on the water fit her mood. She was tossing and turning in her own skin, shaken by memories of her past.

Growing up, it had taken her a long time to realize that not everyone's mother roamed around at night, checking and rechecking locks on doors and windows. The rhythmic *click, click* as latches and bolts were tested for safety again and again was a noise that she learned to associate with the night, like the cicadas in the summer or the rustling of dry leaves in the fall. Her bedroom had been off a corridor with many windows, and she would fall asleep hearing her mother go through the ritual, the clicking getting louder as she approached and fading as she went away.

Once, Carter had slipped from bed and peeked out of her door. She'd watched as each window was put through an exercise, the bolts shifted four times fast, one time slow. The problem appeared to be that locked was never locked enough. Carter had gone back to bed confused and wondering what was wrong with her mother. Couldn't she see that everything was okay?

But relentless vigilance wasn't her only oddity.

Her mother's eating habits had been equally peculiar and vaguely threatening. She regarded everything on her plate with suspicion, as if it might be spoiled or contaminated. If a lettuce leaf was wilted, or there was a spot on a boiled potato that caught her attention, her foot would start pumping the hidden bell under the table as she frantically summoned the staff. More times than not, she would send back what was served. Growing pale, furious that her fears had been triggered by a careless cook, she would reach into her pocket and out would come the pillbox.

The pills.

How could Carter have forgotten the pills?

On her last visit home before her mother's death, Carter had gone into the master bath, looking for something to calm her stomach. Opening the medicine cabinet, she'd stared in shock at the vials of prescription pills that lined the shelves, precisely arranged so that the labels faced outward. The names of the medications were alphabetized. One by one, she'd read the little black print on the bottles until her back hurt from leaning forward for so long. From codeine to Valium, they represented efforts to control anxiety and were a testament to the turmoil her mother struggled with. Instead of relief, however, they appeared only to have created a rousing chemical dependency.

An image of her mother in death's cold hands blinded Carter. She saw beautiful skin, pale and flawless from years spent inside. Those stunning features, unmarred by time's passage. The long brunette hair, lying against the hospital bed's coarse white pillow.

She'd known bitter anger at that moment and, in the hours that followed, the emotion congealed into hatred for her father. As soon as he had arrived, she had hurled terrible words at him and he'd taken the onslaught with a silence that had enraged her further. When she'd stormed off, she'd taken his lack of response as confirmation of his heartlessness.

She contrasted his blank face then with the aching pain she'd seen earlier in the day, and she was struck by the difference. Had he changed in the intervening years? Or was he only now showing her what he was feeling?

Carter's eyes drifted to the trail that led down the mountain. She thought of Nick and a stinging pain lanced through her chest. An image of him as they'd pulled up to his house the previous day came to mind. It had been just before her father had come out of the house. Nick had turned to her and smiled, his eyes warm and contented.

She realized that she missed him and pushed the feeling aside. What she missed, she told herself, was an illusion. Nothing more.

With a light touch, the first drop of rain fell on her hand and, when she looked up, others hit her cheeks. Getting off the rock, she took a last glance down at the lake and thought that tragedies were a lot like storms. They blew through people's lives and sometimes, if they were bad enough, nothing ever looked the same again.

A gust of wind pushed at her and she turned away.

But things grew back, didn't they? she mused. There was always some kind of healing.

By the time she got back to camp, the rain had stepped up its tempo and, after rechecking the tents and tarps, she went into hers and zipped up the flaps. Outside her shelter, the wind began to rage, and the thin nylon keeping her dry trembled in the gusts. She took off her wet fleece and lay down on her cot, feeling tired but restless. There was nothing to do except wait the storm out, and she was wondering whether she could get some sleep when she heard the first crack of lightning.

It hit somewhere close by. She knew because she heard the thunder immediately and could smell the sting of the hit in the air. The first fingers of fear tickled her spine.

The bolt had hit somewhere very close by.

Lightning flared again, turning the dark green of the tent into neon lime, and another snap and roll of thunder drowned out the sound of the rain. Great gusts of wind pushed against the mountain. Suddenly, with a mighty crack, she heard a whole tree fall.

It hit the ground right beside her tent.

Carter leapt off the cot, shaking from fright at the near miss, and put on her Windbreaker. As soon as she got outside, the hood she'd pulled up was ripped from her head by the wind. Rain, cold and invasive, trickled down her neck as she surveyed the damage. A massive pine had been struck by lightning, and the impact had cracked the trunk in half. The magnificent tree was lying on its side.

Its resting place: Papercut Central.

Carter groaned.

Fighting her way through the wind, she hoped the newest skeleton hadn't been crushed. Her next worry was that the tarp, which had insulated the work area from the elements, could be a real danger. The heavy cloth, with its metal rings, was flapping around violently. Catching an edge without getting injured took several tries, but she managed to tie the loose end to the doomed tree. With it secured, she went searching through the damage.

When she found the skeleton's container, she was partially relieved. It was dented badly but not crushed. Unfortunately, the seal had been broken and water was already beginning to get inside. Reaching between the branches, with rain dripping into her eyes, she grabbed one of the handles and pulled hard, but the container didn't move. Trying again, she threw her whole weight into the effort but got nowhere.

Another lightning strike brought Carter's head up in alarm. She thought for a moment about retreating back to her tent but the flimsy shelter offered only dryness, not any real protection. Anyway, the idea of sitting inside the nylon bubble while the world raged around her seemed more terrifying than being out in the storm. At least outside, she could see what was happening.

And she also had to keep the skeleton from drowning, she thought with gallows humor.

Heading over to the mess tent, she rifled through the supplies until she found a handsaw. Back at the tree, she put the blade against the smooth bark and pumped her arm until the branch she was working on fell even closer to the earth. She stretched her back and went to work on another one that was blocking the way.

Carter was drawing back the blade when the saw slipped and streaked across her left hand, which she'd been using to leverage her strength. Pulling back with a curse, she let the tool fall to the ground as she cradled the wound close to her chest.

It didn't so much hurt as it burned and, at first, she thought she'd gotten away with a minor scratch. Then she noticed a dark trail snaking its way into her sleeve and knew she'd done more serious damage. Abandoning the skeleton project temporarily, she retrieved the first-aid kit from the mess area and returned to her tent.

What she saw in the dim light of her gas lamp made her stomach sink. The cut was deep and long, running through the valley between her thumb and forefinger. Tentatively, she wiggled the fingers and was relieved to find there didn't appear to be any tendon damage. Still, it seemed far more serious than what a Band-Aid could handle.

Picking up some bottled water, she leaned out of the tent to clean the wound and then doused the gaping cut with hydrogen peroxide, swearing as it stung. As soon as she wrapped her hand, she found a ski mitten to keep the bandages dry and went back out for the skeleton.

This time working with the saw was harder. Without a counterforce to pull and push against, the job was next to impossible, but she persevered until the limb was severed. She was bending down to try to pull out the container when she heard a new noise cut through the wind and rain. Busy with her work, she ignored the sound and continued struggling to free the skeleton from its trap.

When a hand grabbed her arm from behind, she screamed.

17

"WHAT THE hell are you doing!" Nick yelled over the din of the storm. As lightning sliced through the sky, she saw his face was tight with rage.

Carter was momentarily stunned that he'd come all the way up the mountain in the lashing rain and wind. And then the hurt and anger returned.

"Let go of me!" She wrenched her arm free.

"We're getting off this mountain—now!"

"I'm not going anywhere with you!" she hollered back.

She reached down for the container but he grabbed her arm again, his eyes focusing on the ski mitten. To distract him, she gave him an order. "Can you pull this out?"

"What?" he shouted.

She pointed at the container. "Pull! It needs to go under cover."

Scowling, he wrenched the skeleton's case free and gave her a pointed look.

Carter glowered but started walking. When they got to her tent, she held back the flap as he stepped in. She hesitated before following him, trying to think of the fastest way to get him off the mountain. She peered inside and saw a determined look on his face.

This was going to be a long argument, she thought.

As soon as she stepped out of the rain and started zipping up the flap, he began shouting again.

"Don't bother closing this thing up! We're not staying!"

"You mean, you're not staying!" She shrugged off her coat.

"Do you want to get killed up here?"

"I'm just fine," she yelled. "And I sure don't need you to try and take care of me."

Her defiant answer seemed to infuriate him even more. His jaw muscles clenched. "You know that tree over there? The one lying on the ground? That could have landed on you!"

"Well, it didn't. Now, leave me the hell alone!"

"You're coming with me!"

"No, I'm not!" She didn't care if she was in the path of a tornado.

"Yes, you are!"

Carter crossed her arms and stuck out her chin. "What are you going to do, carry me down? Because that's the only way I'm going anywhere with you."

Nick seemed ready to launch another offensive when he suddenly calmed down.

"What did you do to your hand?" He was looking back and forth between the open medical box and the ski mitten.

"It's nothing." She put her arm behind her back.

"Let me see it."

"No." Carter took a step away before remembering there was nowhere to go.

Nick reached forward, clamping a hold on her free arm.

"Stop manhandling me." She yanked back hard. His grip was like iron.

"If there's nothing wrong, then show me," he said darkly.

She wanted to fight him off but she was beginning to worry about the cut herself. It had started to throb badly. She also had the sense she was fighting a losing battle.

His face held the kind of determination that had no doubt crushed any opposition he'd ever faced.

When she reluctantly removed the glove, she saw that a red spot had come through the bandage.

Nick's eyes became grim. "What happened?"

"I cut it with the saw," she admitted.

"How badly?"

"Not bad."

"Then why is it still bleeding?" She didn't have a good answer for that one. "Let me see it."

Gingerly, she removed the bandages. When the wound was exposed, more lightning flooded the sky. As the flash of light hit his face, she saw real concern mixed in with his frustration.

"We need to get you to a doctor."

"I don't want your opinion," she countered, desperate to push him away. His anger she could handle but his concern threatened to overwhelm her.

"Carter, let me help you."

"No, thanks." She began wrapping the bandages back up. "Knowing my luck with you, they'd end up amputating the whole damn arm if you're involved. Now, if you'll just get out of my way, I can start rescuing all of the things getting soaked out there."

"You're behaving like a child."

"So maybe you should just teach me a lesson and make me fend for myself. How's that sound?"

Nick swore loudly. "Why can't you let me take care of you?"

Eyes clashing with his, she could barely speak through her clenched teeth. "There is nothing wrong with protecting yourself from people who hurt you. Sensible folks would see that as a sign of healthy self-preservation."

"You've got all the answers, haven't you?" he said bitterly. "You know just what everyone is thinking and feeling and all of their motivations."

"No, I just know a bastard when I see one."

Nick stared at her for a long time and she waited for him to toss some scathing comment back.

Instead, he just calmly opened the flap and left without a word. As he zipped her in, she felt something surprisingly close to contrition.

Which was nuts.

How dared he make her feel guilty? she thought, starting to pace in the cramped space. *He* was the one who'd hurt her, not the other way around. The man had no right to make her feel like he was in some way injured.

She went back and forth a couple more times.

Cursing a blue streak, she wrenched open the flap, intent on catching up to him on the trail and telling him how unfair it was for him—

Carter halted as soon as she stepped outside.

In the midst of the storm's fury, Nick was in the middle of Papercut Central, hip deep in the debris, picking up her printer. When he turned and saw her, he showed no surprise. He marched by without a word and went over to Buddy's tent. He came out empty-handed and went back to the fallen tree.

Carter's righteous anger disappeared. His hair was plastered against his skull, he must have been soaking wet under his thin Windbreaker, and yet he just continued working.

As he returned to the ruins, she stepped in to help him. Her hand rendered her all but useless so she acted as a scout, searching out things that needed rescuing, which he would then remove to safety.

When the work was done, Carter didn't know how to thank him, wasn't sure what to do next.

Their eyes met through the sheets of rain and rushing wind.

When there was another crack of lightning close by, he grabbed her arm and they hustled into her tent.

Once they were inside, she forced herself to look him in the eye and say, "Thank you."

He nodded. There was an awkward silence as she waited for him to go.

"So I guess you'll be leaving now?" She glanced meaningfully at the zippered flap.

"What gave you that idea?"

As she stared at him in disbelief, he started taking off his jacket and looking around for a place to sit.

Panic flared in her chest. She didn't want to spend the rest of the night with him in her tent. Couldn't possibly. "But I thought you were leaving . . ."

"That so?"

"But you were angry and . . ."

He shook some of the rain out of his hair. "I'm going nowhere. Unless you have in mind a drier, more reasonable place to spend the night? You could end our misery right now, just by agreeing to come down to the house with me."

His eyes were utterly calm, with a vast reserve of determination behind them, and Carter lost the will to fight. Maybe it was simple exhaustion. Maybe it was the injury. Maybe she was just sick and tired of being on an emotional Tilt-A-Whirl.

"Okay," she said in a low, resigned voice. "Suit yourself."

As her teeth began to chatter from the cold, she knew she had to get rid of her wet layers of clothing. Moving cautiously, so as not to bump her hand or inadvertently touch him in the confined space, she took off her Windbreaker and her soggy fleece.

But that didn't go far enough. Her jeans were soaked and her T-shirt was a transparent sheet against her body. She was trying to think of a solution that didn't involve her changing in front of him when she noticed Nick had fallen still. She looked over at him and realized why.

His eyes, hot and piercing, were focused on her nipples, which were peaked and straining against the wet cotton of her shirt. When she caught what he was looking at, she flushed and turned away. Grabbing a dry sweatshirt, she was about to put it over her head when he spoke in a low and husky voice.

"Don't be ridiculous. That's just going to get soaked from your shirt." He opened up the tent and the wind rushed in. "Holler when you're done changing."

After he disappeared, the hunger on his face lingered in her mind and she felt heat pool in her stomach. She was sorely tempted to pull him back inside and press her lips against his.

But that just wasn't going to happen, she resolved. If she'd learned anything over the past twenty-four hours, it was that the cost of having him was too high.

Pushing aside memories of them making love, Carter began to strip while trying not to hurt her hand. When the T-shirt was off, she shrugged on a dry one and reached for the top of her blue jeans.

Button fly.

Cursing, she tried to manipulate the fastenings but couldn't make them work. Repeated attempts yielded no success and, aware that Nick was getting soaked, she finally gave up and called him back in.

"What's the matter?" he said, looking at her wet pants.

"Nothing," she muttered as she put on the sweatshirt.

"The last time you said that, you were hiding a bandaged hand."

Her eyes flashed at him. "Why are you being so nosy?"

"Because you're being so evasive." He took off his jacket and began to unbutton his shirt.

"What are you doing?" Alarm sharpened her voice.

"Getting out of these clothes. I'm all for protecting your virtue but not at the expense of getting pneumonia." He looked over at her as he peeled the shirt from his body.

Gritting her teeth, Carter tried to ignore him. She sat on the cot and examined her fingernails with determination. As she heard his shirt hit the floor in a wet flap, then the sound of his pants being peeled off his legs, she remembered every part of his body. The feel of his tight stomach, the way his legs were hard and strong. It seemed a cruel fate to still be so attracted to him.

"You got any man-sized clothes around here?"

Now, there was an idea. Getting him covered was really appealing.

She leapt up from the cot, not caring if she had to wrap him up in the damn sleeping bag.

Going over to the duffel bags, she pulled out the biggest T-shirt she had and an oversized Irish knit sweater. Tossing them blindly across the tent, she rummaged around until she found a pair of pink drawstring hospital scrubs that she used as pajama bottoms.

When it seemed safe to, she risked a glance and couldn't help but laugh out loud. He looked ridiculous. The scrubs, which covered her feet when she wore them, ended in the middle of his calves. The shirt and sweater, both of which hung loosely on her, ended north of his belly button. He looked like a bad cross-dresser.

"I know I'm not a fashion plate," he said with a half smile. "But at least I'm dry."

Carter covered her laughter with a frown and then sneezed.

"You sure about those jeans?" he asked.

With longing, she looked over at some dry khakis just within her reach. As another shiver wracked her body, she stiffened her resolve and, turning from him, began to fumble with the fly again.

"You want help?"

She jumped. His voice was very close to her ear and she realized he'd come up behind her.

"No." She tried to move away. "Do you mind?"

His brow arching, he sat down on the cot.

After a few more failed attempts, and at least one other sneeze, she gave up.

Shoring her resolve, she confronted him. "Could you . . . er—"

"What?"

His expression seemed uninterested but his eyes told another story. They were filled with a brooding sensuality.

"Er—could you . . ."

"Take off your pants?"

Before she could tell him to forget it, he was standing in front of her and reaching out his hands. His fingertips brushed against the skin of her stomach as he released the top button and, when she sucked in her breath, he paused.

"Do you want me to stop?"

He was so close to her now, his lips almost on her ear, his body bent over hers.

"Just hurry up," she muttered tightly, focusing on the ground.

Nick went back to work and, with each button, his hands moved lower. The tugging and pulling was unbelievably erotic, and her lips parted as she let out a ragged breath.

When he reached the lowest one, his fingers lingered. He brought his head lower and his breath brushed over her neck.

"You make me burn," he whispered, pulling her hips into his. She could feel his arousal, thick and hot against her.

Her head fell back.

Lightning flashed, white and jagged.

When thunder bellowed in response, the noise broke through the fog in Carter's mind. She pulled away, stumbling.

"Don't do that," she said hoarsely.

Their eyes met and she thought he was going to fight her. But then he shrugged with nonchalance. His face closed up and the heat was replaced by disciplined composure. As he sat down on her cot, he seemed to be in total control of himself.

Carter, on the other hand, was feeling a messy tangle of desire, resentment, and self-loathing.

She turned away from him and began to shrug out of the jeans. When she finally stepped free and struggled into the khakis, she was afraid to turn around. She didn't know what to say or where to sit or what to do.

"There's plenty of room over here, you know."

Carter turned to him. His face gave nothing away and, in the end, she joined him, staying as far away as she could.

They sat in silence, listening to the raging of the wind and rain.

"How much longer can this go on?" she asked.

"Well into the night."

Under her lashes, she glanced over at him. His big body was folded up, his arms resting on his knees, his shoulders wide and straining the sweater. His eyes were trained ahead of him and, though it appeared that he was staring at nothing in particular, he had an expression of intense concentration.

Another bolt of lightning struck close by. She jumped.

When he spoke in the aftermath of the thunder, his voice was softer than she'd expected. "You really were going to stay up here all by yourself, weren't you?"

"Of course," she said tightly. "Buddy and Ellie had to be together. I'm just . . . me."

"And you would have spent all night cleaning this place up. Even with your hand."

She frowned, wondering what he was getting at. "Yes."

"Would it ever have occurred to you to ask for help?"

"From whom?"

There was a pause and then he said dryly, "Me, for instance."

She shook her head. When he let out an irritated noise, she countered, "Can you blame me?"

His smile was not cheerful. Silence fell between them but then he laughed softly.

"You're real tough. At least on the outside." She heard a thread of something sounding like respect in his voice.

"Look, I don't want to talk," she said roughly. "I'm not capable of making sense right now."

Her eyes lifted to his. She was stunned to find tenderness in them.

As she looked away, Carter put her head in her hands. "Can you not do that?"

"Do what?"

"Look so damn . . . compassionate."

He laughed shortly. "You like my acerbic side better?"

"It's easier to dislike you that way."

"I don't want you to dislike me."

They were quiet for a long time. At one point, he shifted positions and she jerked.

"I'm not going to jump all over you." Bitterness shortened his words.

When she glanced at him, he seemed really out of sorts. "You get angry when you don't get what you want, don't you?"

"You know anyone who doesn't?"

Carter shrugged. "Some people are worse than others."

Out of the corner of her eye she saw him rubbing his neck. As if some of his tension had been released, he said in a more even voice, "My sister was much more even-keeled than I ever was. A peacemaker."

Wistfulness softened his features, and she was sorely tempted to ask him about the woman.

"Was she younger or older?"

"Younger. My mother's last-ditch attempt to get some attention. She stayed in bed the whole nine months even though she was perfectly healthy. Melina was born by C-section so Mother got to creep around for a month afterward, dramatizing the event so much you'd swear she'd been cut in half and left for dead."

His stark tone resonated with Carter. It reminded her of the way she talked about her father. "Did you and Melina get along?"

"She and Gertie were my saviors growing up. My mother didn't really care for me all that much, and my father was better at numbers than relating to people. It would have been very easy for me to pull away from everyone and I think Mel knew that. She was always careful to be around when I needed her even though I can't say I repaid the honor adequately. That's one of the reasons why, when she died, I wanted to take Cort in so badly."

He cleared his throat and Carter sensed that he didn't want to talk about his family anymore. It was hard not to relate.

"My father came here today," she blurted out abruptly.

She felt rather than saw his head turn.

Feeling vulnerable, she tucked her legs under her. She regretted bringing the subject up, but at the same time she felt good about it. Like she had somehow taken control of the situation that had hurt her.

"He was very different than I remembered. I was surprised to see how much regret he carries with him."

"Of course he's sorry. He loves you."

"Yeah, I think maybe he does. I almost feel like it's a good thing he came up." She saw surprise and hope flare in Nick's face and she quickly tacked on, "But I'm still angry as hell at you for using me."

Frustration surged in his voice. "I did not use you."

"Yes, you did."

"For Chrissakes, Carter, if you and your father end up reconciling, that's between you and him. I'm not going to leverage it to my advantage and I sure as hell regret I ever contemplated doing that."

She just shrugged, trying not to get pulled in.

"God, I just want to strangle you sometimes," he muttered.

"I know what you mean," she shot back. "I feel exactly the same way about you a lot of the time."

They glared at each other, anger and passion flaring, and she was struck by how similar they were, both fighters to the end. She thought of how absurd it was to be arguing in a tent in the middle of a storm when they could be struck by lightning at any moment.

She started to laugh. She couldn't help it. And after a moment, he joined her. Their hilarity mingled, rising up through the tent walls, drifting out into the storm.

Wiping a tear away, she mumbled, "You'd almost think we were meant to be together."

Nick's laughter rolled to a stop. "We are meant for each other."

Her eyes flew to his. The air between them changed, growing solemn.

"I meant it when I said I love you. Carter?"

She looked over to him reluctantly.

"I wish you and your father happiness. You know that, don't you?" In the silence that followed, he said, "And I'm sorry that I hurt you. I told him not to come and, while we were in Vermont, I was trying to find a way to tell you. I wanted to tell you everything."

Thunder tumbled through the air, through the tense silence that followed.

"Doesn't that mean something to you?" he asked.

She shrugged. "It doesn't change where we are. Who you are."

"Why do you find it so hard to believe I love you?"

"I don't doubt you think you love me."

"So what's the problem?"

"I don't . . . I can't trust you."

Nick swore under his breath and then, moving so fast she didn't have time to pull away, he took her into his arms. His mouth came down hard over hers and, after struggling for a moment, she gave in to him. The sounds of the storm faded and all she knew was the feel of him against her, of his hands in her hair and his tongue sliding over hers.

Abruptly, he pulled back. "Can't you trust this?"

Slowly she shook her head. "Only a fool relies on a forest fire for warmth."

He let her move away.

After that, they didn't say much else.

Throughout the night, storms kept barreling down the lake valley. Neither was able to sleep. When the fierce weather finally left the area in the early morning, the quiet that reigned in its wake was disorientating. As dawn arrived, Carter found herself listening to water droplets falling on the ground and the roof of the tent. There was a lovely rhythm to the soft sounds.

Nick got up and put his jacket on. "I'll be right back."

After he left, she lay down, keenly aware of the throbbing in her hand. Grateful to be stretched out, she closed her eyes and sank into a dreamless state of exhaustion.

Outside, Nick walked around and surveyed the damage. The camp was a wreck. All of the other tents had collapsed, the tarp over the mess area was lying in a tangled heap, and there was mud everywhere.

He went over to the stream. It was twice its normal size and rushing down the mountain in a torrent of white spray. Kneeling down, he splashed his face. With water dripping into his eyes and off of his chin, he went out to see the sunrise over the lake.

He watched as light exploded into the sky and wanted to go wake Carter up. He knew he couldn't, however. So he stood alone for a long time, staring out over the view, missing her though she was only yards away.

When he returned to camp, he stuck his head into the tent. In the dim light, he could see Carter's chest rising and falling. Her dark hair was spilling over the pillow and she had one leg kicked out to the side. He was watching her sleep when she woke up.

"What are you standing there for?" she asked in a groggy voice.

"We need to get you to a doctor."

With a groan, she sat up. Her hair fell over her shoulders in waves that he wanted to run his hands through.

"What time is it?"

He didn't have to check his watch. "Early still. But we should go."

With a grimace, she got to her feet. Instead of arguing with him, she simply put on her coat and walked out of the tent. That's when he knew she was in pain.

In the fragile light of dawn, they took to the trail. It was god-awful to watch her move stiffly and hold her arm away from her body as if she was afraid of knocking it. He wished like hell there was something he could do to make the trip easier on her. Between the fallen tree limbs, the residual flooding, and Carter's quiet suffering, he thought they would never see the mansion.

As soon as they broke out of the woods, Buddy, Ellie, and Cort came rushing across the lawn. They were smiling with relief, but the happy group stopped short when they saw the bandage and Carter's tense features.

"What happened?" Buddy asked.

"Run-in with the handsaw," Carter muttered through pale lips. She quickly told them what had happened.

"I'm taking her into town," Nick said. "Do me a favor—have Gertie call ahead. She knows who we're going to see."

Nick packed Carter into his truck, threw a chain saw in the back, and then eased them out onto the main road. He was careful to drive with a steady hand.

All around them, the devastation was formidable. Streams flooded the road, tree limbs were down, and at one point, there was a fallen oak blocking their way. Using the chain saw, he deftly cut the tree into hunks that he tossed over to the shoulder. When he was back in the cab, he saw Carter was wearing a sad smile.

At his look of inquiry, she explained, "I was remembering the first picture I saw of you. It must have been when I was still in college. You'd just started to make a killing on Wall Street." A short laugh left her lips. "You were considered one of the most eligible bachelors in America."

He eased the truck back on the road.

"I don't remember that one," he said, hoping she'd keep talking.

"It was on the cover of some finance magazine. You were staring out at the camera and your expression was brutally serious. You looked much older than someone in his late twenties, which was how old the article said you were. I remember that a group of girls was crowded around the magazine. They thought you would make a dream husband."

"What did you think?"

"I wasn't so sure. But the reason I smiled was because

I never would have imagined that the same man would be bent over a fallen tree in the middle of the Adirondacks, wearing my pink scrubs, clearing the way for me to get to the doctor."

He shot a long look in her direction. "I'm glad you're letting me help you."

Nick waited for a response but she didn't answer him. Instead, she just put her head back against the seats and closed her eyes.

18

AFTER BEING treated by the town's doctor, Carter was feeling relieved and considerably more comfortable as Nick pulled the truck back into the garage. She was also exhausted.

"Would you like some breakfast?" he asked.

"Actually, I could use some shut-eye."

"I've got plenty of beds."

She thought about the wet campsite, her muddy tent, the stiff cot, the fact that she was so tired she could feel the fatigue in her bones.

"Thanks. Something soft and dry sounds great."

Once she'd had something to eat, Nick led her back to the bedroom she'd used before. He lingered in the doorway.

"Do you need anything?"

She shook her head. "Gertie's French toast can soothe a multitude of ills."

"Good napping, then."

Carter offered him a small, tight smile. "Thanks again for your help."

"You're welcome."

She tensed as Nick breached the doorway and approached her. His hand came out and rested on her shoulder.

"What is it going to take to get you to believe in me?"

She shrugged sadly, having little faith in his voice.

His eyes searched hers and then he dropped his hand. His expression hardened.

"I can't keep apologizing to you. I'm just not going to keep doing this," he muttered.

As he turned away, the warmth left his face.

"Enjoy your solitude." He shut the door sharply behind him.

Carter sank down on the bed.

She recognized the look on his face. It was the one he'd worn when they'd first met. Impregnable, remote, fierce.

It was over, she realized, going numb. He was going to give her what she asked for. He was going to walk away.

So why didn't she feel relieved? This was supposed to make her feel better. Ease the torment. It was exactly what she wanted.

Dragging herself to the bathroom, she shed her clothes and got under the shower. As hot water beat down on her, she bowed her head, letting it run over her shoulders.

She had to wonder why making the right choice hurt so much.

Wessex went in search of Nick, having heard that Carter and he had returned from the doctor's. When he found the man in his study, barking orders into the phone, he noticed the change in his business partner immediately. Farrell looked positively dark.

Wessex paused in the doorway and wondered what had happened. Nick had seemed so concerned when he'd gone up the mountain to get Carter. Now all that warmth had vanished, as if it had never existed, and the man seemed colder than ever before.

When Wessex was ushered in by an impatient hand, he shut the door and took a seat. He listened as Nick spoke in short bursts of well-chosen words.

"So I'll leave for Japan in two days, then," the man

growled. "Let them try and turn the terms down to my face. I'll eat them alive in their boardroom and they damn well know it."

Nick hung up the phone and shifted opaque eyes across his desk.

Wessex hesitated. There were many questions on his mind, particularly about his daughter, but he had a feeling he wasn't going to get answers to them. Nick didn't look as if he'd be open to personal discussions of any kind.

"So, what are we going to do about Packert?" he asked instead.

Nick leaned back in his chair, crossing his arms over his chest. "I'm looking forward to crushing him and then breaking up CommTrans."

"You're going to sell it off?" Wessex was taken aback. "But that wasn't part of the plan. I'll grant that Packert's been a fool but why—"

"Because I feel like it. CommTrans is going to be a distant memory in one year's time. Packert's legacy is going to be dust."

"But you don't need the money and it's—"

"Getting squeamish all of a sudden?"

Wessex stared across the desk and found himself wondering how someone that young got to be that hard.

"So are you in or not?" Nick's words were curt.

"I'm in," Wessex answered slowly. "But I do think you should reconsider—"

"Whatever I do to the damn thing after I own it is no one's business but my own."

Nick picked up the phone and Wessex knew he'd been dismissed. As he stood up and straightened his blazer, he wished there was some way to reach out to the younger man.

"Have a good trip back to the city," Nick told him as he dialed. "And you should remind Packert to enjoy the limousine. When I get done with him, he'll be lucky if he can afford cab fare."

Wessex was deep in thought as he left the study, wondering what had happened between his daughter and Nick. Going by the vengeful expression on the man's face, it seemed unlikely things had been resolved.

As he turned the corner into the dining room, he ran into Packert. Looking into the Texan's eyes, he winced a little, thinking about what was coming the man's way.

"What's wrong with you?" Packert asked, carrying a plate laden with food from a buffet set up on the sideboard.

Wessex wasn't about to explain that the man's net worth was about to go to zero.

"Forgive me," he replied evenly. "I'm a bit distracted."

"Well, cheer up! We're getting out of here today." The Texan clapped him on the shoulder with a meaty hand. "Say, you're a little on the thin side. You best eat up before we head off."

Wessex became aware of a pounding between his ears and decided that lunch with Packert wasn't going to improve the headache. Making an excuse, he escaped out a side door into the balmy, summer air. With no particular destination in mind, he headed down to the lake and found some solace in the sound of the waves lapping against the rocky shore. In the aftermath of the storm, everything smelled fresh and lush, and he took deep breaths as he walked along the shoreline. When his wandering took him over to the boathouse, he went out onto the dock, his sleek loafers clipping against the damp wood. Clasping his hands behind his back, he leaned forward and looked down into the water.

As the fish swam by, he was thinking of the past. And wondering with a sad ache whether he would see his daughter again.

Up at the mansion, from the porch outside the bedroom she'd been given, Carter watched her father's promenade.

Despite her exhaustion, she'd been unable to sleep. She'd stayed in bed until frustration had gotten the best of her. Opening a pair of French doors wide, she'd stepped outside, taking her discontent with her into the sunlight.

The first thing she'd noticed was her father's slow progress down to the shore. With his hands linked behind his back, and his head down as if he were deep in thought, he strolled over the grass. She'd watched as he went out onto the dock.

Carter made up her mind. Moving quickly, she went inside, got dressed, and made up the bed. She was out of the house a moment later, treading over the same lawn her father had just crossed.

He turned when he heard her footsteps on the dock. Surprise and hope flickered over his features.

"The water is really clear, isn't it?" Carter said casually as she came up beside him.

"Yes. Quite remarkably so." His smile held a tentative welcome. He glanced at her hand. "How does it feel?"

She wiggled her fingers. "As well as it could, I suppose."

She wasn't sure what to say next and neither was he, apparently. They stood a few feet apart and looked into the water.

"You're going back to the city now?" she asked in a soft voice.

"As soon as Packert is finished with lunch. He has the alarming alacrity of a fast eater but the portion control of a gorilla. It could be a while."

Carter smiled slightly, glancing over at him.

"I was very worried about you last night," Wessex told her after a pause.

"I can't say I enjoyed the experience, but it turned out all right in the end." Abruptly, she was struck by an idea. "Have you seen what's upstairs here?"

"No."

"You've got to take a look at this," she said with sudden urgency, leading him inside the boathouse and up the cramped set of stairs.

When they got to the second floor and he saw the train set, Wessex let out a delighted whistle.

"I had the same reaction when I first saw it." Carter went over and flipped the master switch.

The miniature world came to life. Lights glowed in shop windows. Steam began to come out of tiny smokestacks. Water started to trickle down the mountainside. Fingering the controls, she sent a train along the tracks.

They fell into talk about the cars and the setup, a relaxed conversation that surprised her. It made her remember how easy talking to her father had once been. And it made her miss him.

They enjoyed the grown-up toy until she noticed that the sun had spun over to a much lower angle.

"Do you know what time it is?" Carter asked.

Wessex glanced at a gold watch on his wrist. "Good Lord, it's past three. I should have been getting into the limo with that odious man hours ago."

Carter drew back on the throttle, bringing the engine to a smooth stop in front of her. She didn't want to turn the power off. She didn't want to leave the room. She didn't want to go back to the way things had been.

But she wasn't sure where to take them.

As the twinkling lights went out, her father said, "This has been wonderful."

She found herself agreeing with him. "Are our trains still in the billiards room?"

"They are. Just the same as when you ..."

He didn't finish.

"I remember the way they looked," she said, wanting to pull him away from painful memories. "Is that mountain range still halfway done?"

"Yes."

The two headed down the stairway.

"Maybe I should come by sometime, when I'm in the city."

Her father's steps faltered. "I would be so happy to see you."

Carter smiled in the dim light.

Together, they stepped out into the sunshine. As they

walked toward the mansion, their steps were slow over the grass.

Abruptly, she stopped and faced her father. "I'm glad you came up yesterday."

She watched, stunned, as a shine of tears appeared in his eyes. Instinctually, she reached out to comfort him. As her hand settled on his arm, he held on to it.

"Do you know that your mother and I loved you? As best we could? That I still love you so much now?"

"Don't cry," she told him softly as he fumbled for his handkerchief. While he wiped his eyes, she could feel some kind of thread taking hold between them. Some kind of gossamer-thin tie. They stood together for a long time, silently coming closer.

When they finally went into the house, they found Gertie arranging flowers in the front hall. She informed them that Packert had already left for the city and Wessex would have to take the train back. Carter offered to drive him to the station.

While her father went upstairs to get his things, she watched Gertie's gnarled hands work some fragrant lilac blossoms.

"He's a good man, your father," the woman pronounced, "from what I've seen of him. You two get to spend much time together?"

"It'll be more now." Carter was amazed that she wanted to see him again. It had seemed like such an impossibility just days before and yet so much had changed. Everything, it seemed, had changed.

Her father reappeared with his black, monogrammed suitcase. "Where's our host?"

"Behind you," Nick said, materializing in the foyer. He was dressed in a tuxedo but wearing boat shoes.

Carter jerked at the sound of his voice and searched out his eyes. They passed over her as if she wasn't there, and that hurt, even though she told herself it shouldn't. She also couldn't help noticing how wide his shoulders were underneath the black jacket, how the white of the shirt contrasted with his tanned skin, how tall and imposing he was.

"A bit formal for a sail, don't you think?" Wessex offered a smile that wasn't returned.

"There's a benefit tonight at Winnie and Curt Thorndyke's down the lake. I told Curt I'd help with roasting the pig. Man wouldn't know a good pit from a pendulum."

The words were casual but cold.

"I know Thorndyke," Wessex said. "His wife is very horsy. Members of the Borealis, aren't they?"

"That's the one." Nick stretched out a hand. "Safe trip. I'll be in touch."

"Thank you . . ." Wessex hesitated as they shook, glancing over at Carter. "For everything."

With a harsh smile, Nick turned away. "My pleasure."

As the door shut, Carter watched him through the screen. He pushed his hands into his pockets and sauntered down to the lake, looking as if he didn't have a care in the world.

She felt bereft at his nonchalance, at the sense that she was so utterly forgettable.

Which was ridiculous, she told herself angrily. Now was hardly the time for her ego to raise its head. Self-preservation had to trump the id. It just had to.

Still, she found it hard not to curse as she and her father went out to the Jeep.

While they were scaling the mountain roads, he asked about the dig and what they were trying to find. She was relieved by the distraction.

"We're investigating the Winship party."

"Quite a piece of American history. How much longer will you be up there?"

"A couple of weeks. Maybe less." She wondered whether her father had picked up on the ache in her voice. She sure had heard it.

"Do you love him, Carter?" The question was spoken with softness and compassion.

She looked across at her father, meeting his vibrant blue eyes. "I don't have a lot of experience with being in love, but I've got to imagine it's the only thing that hurts this much."

His expression grew thoughtful. "I've known Farrell personally for the past few years, known of him since he came to Wall Street. He's a hard man," Wessex reflected. "A good one, I believe, but very hard. It would take an extraordinary woman to capture his heart."

Pain seared at the thought of the next woman Nick was going to have. "Well, I'm sure she's out there somewhere."

"He thinks he's already found her."

Carter shook her head. "Not anymore. I cured him of his misconception. He'll move on. I'll . . . get through it somehow."

Carter changed the subject, feeling grateful when her father let it drop.

When they pulled up to the train station, she waited with him on the platform until the 4:19 pulled in with a squeal of brakes and a hiss. Suddenly there wasn't any more time.

In a rush, she wrapped her arms around her father, holding him close.

"I had almost given up hope," he said as he held her tight.

"Bye-bye," she said softly as they parted. "I'll see you soon."

Wessex closed his eyes, as if a wish of his had been granted. Then he kissed her on the forehead and mounted the three steps into the railcar. As the train pulled away, Carter watched him settle in a seat next to the window. She waved back at him as he disappeared down the tracks.

19

WHEN CARTER returned to the ruined campsite, her strength drained out of the soles of her feet. Everything was in disarray, soaking wet, and covered in mud. Tree limbs were down or hanging at crazy angles and the big pine was already wilting.

She looked at her bandaged injury and felt handicapped.

As she was wondering where to start, Buddy, Ellie, and Cort came back from the circle of stones.

"Looks like you had quite a party up here last night," her partner quipped. "So what'd the doctor say about your hand? Are you okay?"

"I'll be good as new in a couple weeks." She looked around the campsite. "Which is a shame because I need the thing to work right now. We've got some serious digging out ahead of us."

Cort beamed. "With all the mess up here, I guess you're going to have to stay down at my house for a while."

"You think your uncle will mind having two beautiful ladies under his roof?" Buddy asked.

"Two?" Carter interjected sharply. "Make that one. I'm staying up here."

Her friend frowned. "Don't be ridiculous. You're injured."

When Carter shot him a determined look, Buddy hitched up his baggy pants with a playful snort and turned to the teenagers. "Looks like the little woman and I are going to have us a talk. While we're gone, why don't you pour out the tents and hang up everything you can."

"We don't need to talk about this," Carter protested. "I've made up my—"

"Shall we?" Buddy offered her a long look and his arm.

With a side comment about heavy-handed men, Carter shrugged him off and marched into the woods.

When they were out of earshot, she put her hands on her hips. "We can't leave this place unattended—you know that. And Ellie needs you."

"She was worried about the storm last night but she'll be fine as long as we don't have any more typhoons." Buddy's voice was level, sensible. "Look, I know sleeping down there is not the best because of . . . but I'm worried about your health. That's a hell of a cut and you should really think of yourself as down for repairs."

"I'll be fine up here," she countered doggedly.

"With that injury, you're useless if anyone comes poking around. It really makes more sense for me to stay. It's safer for everyone."

As creative as Carter was, she couldn't argue with that one. What was she going to do if someone—if *Lyst*—came up in the middle of the night? Scare him off with some flashy, one-handed moves with a thighbone? If she did go down to the mansion, at least she could sleep in a real bed and take long showers to ease all her aches and pains.

Well, at least the ones in her body.

She thought about how Nick had looked at her in his foyer. His eyes had been so aloof, and her disappointment was both inappropriate and disconcerting. What did she expect? She'd pushed him away, for all the right reasons, and he'd gone back to being the cold man she'd met when she first walked into his house. What did she think was going to happen? He was going to keep pining away for her forever? Rot in a chair in a darkened room from heartbreak?

Yes, Carter thought. That was what she wanted him to do. She wanted to know that he was suffering like she was or at least for him to look as if he were having a hard time. She didn't want him wearing a tuxedo and going to a party. It just wasn't fair. Her life was a mess and he was going to go roast a damn pig.

Buddy snapped his fingers in front of her. "Hello? Anyone in there?"

"All right. I'll go down," Carter grumbled, resigning herself.

"Good. By the way, do you mind if I sleep in your tent? Mine is mercifully leak free, but we're not going to be able to move the stuff out until we resurrect Papercut Central."

"Fine with me."

When she and Buddy returned to camp, Cort and Ellie had turned the place into a laundry room. Sleeping bags, towels, and clothes were hanging from lines they'd tied between trees, and the tents had been resurrected.

"Interesting decor," Buddy cracked. "Early clothes hamper tinted with a whimsical vision. I like it."

They were talking about what to tackle next when Cort checked his watch and grew grim. "I have to go."

Ellie smiled at him. "If you can wait a little while, I'll just finish—"

"No, I have to go now. I'll see you down there for dinner."

After he left quickly, Ellie looked over at Carter with disappointed eyes. "I just don't understand men."

Carter put a sympathetic hand on the girl's shoulder. "I'd like to tell you that wisdom comes from experience with them."

"But you'd be lying?"

"Precisely."

"Now, wait a minute," Buddy countered. "As the lone representative of my gender, I have to take umbrage at that. Trying to figure you women out is impossible. Like picking linguine off the floor with a magnet."

"Dad, that metaphor sucks."

Carter smiled. "Ellie, I'd also like to tell you that wisdom comes to them with experience."

"But it doesn't, right?"

"Precisely."

The three of them spent the remaining daylight tackling the mess at Papercut Central. Thanks to a chain saw Ivan had lent him, Buddy cut up the pine tree and cleared it into the woods. When he was finished, Ellie and Carter helped rehang the tarp. Although the table was in bad shape, they managed to hammer it back into usable condition.

When they finally went down the mountain, they were greeted at the house with a meal prepared by Gertie. Cort, who looked happy to see Ellie, made a point of sitting next to the girl. After dinner, the two went to watch the only TV in the house, and Buddy headed back up to camp.

Left to her own devices, Carter retired to the peach bedroom and changed into silk pajamas, a rare luxury on a dig. Experience had proven that there was always one point in any project when living in the dirt and sleeping on the ground got to be too much. Tonight was the night, and she figured she deserved the treat after all she'd been through. Before she turned in, she stepped out onto the porch to look at the stars.

The night air brushed against her skin and she watched as moonlight danced across the lake. A whippoorwill, tripping through his solo and starting over, again and again, made her wish she had someone to share the moment with.

But not just anyone.

Where was he now? she wondered. The image that came to mind, of him holding some other woman close, made her wince.

Leaving the doors wide-open, she went back inside and crawled between the butter-soft sheets. She closed her eyes. Fidgeted. Tossed. Punched the pillow with her good hand. It was a long time before she fell asleep.

The steady hum of the Hacker's engine dropped to a low pump as Nick pulled into the boathouse. After he shut it off, he stepped from the gunnels onto the dock. As soon as his feet landed, he looked down at the decking, wondering why he felt like he was still on water.

Air, he thought. He needed air.

Or maybe he could've used less scotch over the course of the evening.

That was probably it.

With more care than usual, he tied up the boat and started on the walk up to the mansion. He discovered that as long as he kept his head level, the weaving and dizziness went away. The night chill seemed to help clear his mind, so he loosened his bow tie and opened up his starched collar. When that made him feel better, he took off the tuxedo jacket and slung it over his shoulder.

What a horrible evening, he thought. The Thorndykes were nice enough, but they'd invited Candace's father, not knowing about the breakup. The man had railed at Nick for an hour about how deplorably his daughter had been treated and how fortunate it was that she'd moved on to someone better.

Nick had started in with the scotch as soon as Hanson had started in with him. He'd kept drinking right through the roasting of the pig, which had not gone well. Thanks to his desire to keep emptying his glass, the entrée had emerged from the ground petrified into a pig chip half the size of what it had been going in. After attempts to carve the roast broke one knife and dulled two others, Thorndyke had given up and served his high-class guests hamburgers and hot dogs. As Nick was leaving, he'd been informed his services as pig-sitter wouldn't be needed in the future.

He stopped walking and looked toward the mountain. Squinting through the darkness, he tried to see if there was a fire going at the campsite.

Was Carter sleeping? he wondered. Curled on her side, breathing deeply and slowly, her lashes against her cheeks?

He cursed out loud as his mood deteriorated further. He'd been berated by Hanson, had failed at his assigned task of roasting that frigging pig, and was now staring down the barrel of a royal hangover. But worse, he was mad as hell at Carter and she was going to be leaving soon.

Nick raked a hand through his hair as he started for the house. He noticed there were lights on in the guest wing. The Swifts were down for another evening, obviously.

His eyes, more alert, shifted back to the mountain.

He changed direction.

Going past the house, he moved quickly through the meadow to the edge of the forest. Locating the trail in the dark, he scaled the mountain with growing conviction. As he made his way to the summit, he practiced his speech. About how closed-minded she was, how intolerant, how unfair . . .

When Nick got to the campsite, he saw a glow in Carter's tent and marched right on over. Wrenching back the flap, he pronounced, "Woman, you need to listen to what I have to—"

Buddy Swift looked up from a comic book, surprised.

Nick blinked, nonplussed.

A chuckle was sent his way. "I've been called a lot of things, but 'woman' is a first."

"Where is she?" Nick demanded.

"Down at your house."

"Oh." Nick weaved slightly.

As Buddy looked at the man who had interrupted his reading, he had to hide his smile behind Superman #7. It wasn't all that often he saw a billionaire disheveled and a little tipsy.

"You okay?"

"Damn right I am." Farrell's voice was gruff and his

eyes were dark with displeasure. He also looked as if he were going to fall over.

"Say, you want to take a load off? You look like you need a minute to gather yourself."

"Not a bad idea."

"Here." Buddy got up from the cot. "Why don't you sit down. I was just going to get up and check the perimeter."

It was something he'd been doing throughout the night, catnapping and then walking around between the campsite and the circle of stones. He was trolling for midnight intruders except, instead of finding one, one had found him.

As he went about his route, Buddy felt sad for Nick and Carter. They were both struggling, and he wished that the circumstances around William Wessex's arrival had been different. Carter had been so happy right before her father had come. She'd looked young and carefree for the first time since he'd known her. Truly happy.

When he didn't find anything out of the ordinary, he went back to camp. As soon as he stuck his head inside the tent, he groaned.

Snoring like a bulldog, Nick Farrell was asleep, one arm cast aside and hanging off the bed, the other tucked into his neck.

The guy was going nowhere tonight, Buddy thought.

Figuring he had no choice, he shrugged out of his jacket and rolled it up to make a pillow. He was hoping the ground was still soft from the rain and that the tent floor was free of leaks.

The next morning, Carter got up early, eager to get out of the house without running into Nick. She made the bed, put on shorts and a sweatshirt, and went down to the kitchen. There, she found Cort and Gertie with their heads together, working at something. They quickly put whatever it was away.

As Carter murmured a greeting, Cort grunted and

pulled his bathrobe around him. He looked like he'd just rolled out of bed, with his hair matted instead of sticking straight up and his eyes half closed into slits.

"Go take a shower and wake up," Gertie said, shooing at the boy. "You're making me tired just standing there."

"Mornin', Carter," he mumbled, shuffling past her.

"Rough night?"

"We watched *Jaws*."

Carter smiled, imagining they'd had a good time together. "Wouldn't think that would tire you out so much."

"We saw it three times." He yawned.

"Ah."

He turned around. "So, Gertie, can we go?"

"You'll have to ask your uncle."

Carter stiffened and looked over her shoulder as if Nick was going to appear any moment. She began to inch her way to the door.

"Where is he?" Cort asked.

Gertie shrugged. "Haven't seen him. Maybe he's still sleeping."

"Naw. His bed's made up. I know 'cause I walked by and the door was open."

Gertie frowned. "Didn't he come home last night?"

Carter's stomach heaved and she turned to the door. Gertie, however, stepped into her path and pressed a mug of coffee into her good hand.

It was Cort who made it to the door. "I'll go down and check to see if the boat's back."

After he left, Gertie shot her a pointed look. "I'm sure there's a perfectly good explanation. Nick knows this lake like the back of his hand and he isn't one for fooling around, if you know what I mean."

Carter offered a strained smile over the rim of the mug as she tried to drink the coffee quickly. She was wondering what was worse, him not coming home because he'd been in an accident or because he'd spent the night with someone else.

Now, those were two great choices. Like getting to pick between a broken collarbone and a dislocated shoulder.

"It's none of my business," Carter said with finality. "He's a grown man, free to do what he pleases."

The pounding between his ears woke Nick up and, at first, he thought it was another migraine. Then he remembered the scotch.

He rolled over, groaning.

"I can assure you," a dry voice said, "I don't like waking up to you much, either."

Nick's eyes snapped open. Even though they refused to focus, he managed to make out Buddy Swift's wry grin. The man was lying on the ground with his head resting on a rolled-up parka.

"What the hell are you doing here?" Nick demanded, his voice full of gravel.

"The same could be asked of you."

The guy had a point, Nick thought, looking around the tent. "What am I doing here?"

"Don't know. You showed up in the middle of the night."

Both men sat up slowly. Nick noticed that Buddy's grimace matched the one he felt on his own face.

"Does this mean we're going steady?" the guy asked with a gamine smile.

"Sorry. We're one-night-stand material only. What time is it?"

"Must be almost seven."

The two struggled to their feet. When they emerged from the tent, Nick's eyes strained against the bright light and the promise of the day. He noticed Buddy didn't seem any more eager to be up and around.

When the other man stretched, his body let out a loud crack of protest and he groaned in response. "Hard to imagine there was a time when my back could handle anything I threw at it. What the hell was I thinking, tackling that tree by myself?"

"It's arrogance." Nick rubbed his eyes. "Same thing that had me drinking half a bottle of scotch."

"I feel like I've been in a car wreck."

"I feel like I am a car wreck."

"You want coffee?" Buddy went over and fired up the propane stove.

Nick nodded. Carefully.

While it was brewing, Buddy said evenly, "So I guess I wasn't who you were looking for last night."

Nick sat down at the picnic table. "Wasn't looking for anybody. Just out for a midnight stroll."

"In a tuxedo?"

"It was after five."

Buddy laughed. "You sure seemed disappointed to find me in Carter's tent."

Nick reached his arms out over his head and bent side to side. "Last night was scotch-fueled folly averted by dumb luck. It was a good thing you were in there."

Buddy came over with two mugs, passing one across the table as he sat down. "You sure about that?"

"Sure enough." Nick took a sip and winced. "Good God, this stuff could wake the dead."

"Considering the state we're in, I think it's just the ticket."

The two sat drinking in silence, until Buddy said cautiously, "I've known Carter a long time. She seemed happy with you."

"That's changed now."

"I know. And I wish it hadn't."

"You and me both." Nick put down his half-empty mug.

"You want more coffee?"

He started to shake his head but stopped with a grimace. "No. I don't want to risk having a seizure."

Buddy took a big gulp of his. "What a lightweight."

With a sardonic smile, Nick got to his feet. "Well, thanks for a lovely evening."

"You're welcome. But tell me, when will I see you again?"

"I'll call."

"Sure, you will." With a saucy wink, Buddy waved and went back to his coffee.

Nick headed for the trail, hoping he'd make it down the mountain in one piece.

20

CARTER SWALLOWED the tail end of her coffee, burning the roof of her mouth. She had no interest in hearing confirmation that Nick hadn't come home. She'd already made up her mind about what he'd been doing in the dark hours.

"I think I'll head up the mountain," she said to Gertie, trying to force nonchalance.

"Will we be seeing you for dinner?"

"I don't think so. Things should be dry enough up there now."

And even if she had to eat cold corn out of a can and sleep in a puddle, she was going to stay at camp.

"You shouldn't be worried about Nick. As I said, I'm sure there's a perfectly good reason behind it all."

Of course there is, Carter derided. Like he met up with a six-foot-tall model with hair the color of the sun and bee-stung lips that could suck-start a Harley. The two were probably planning their wedding in Majorca right now.

"He wasn't with a woman," Gertie said evenly, as if she'd read her mind.

Carter shrugged. "If he was, it's all right. I have nothing to do with his personal life. It's just business between us."

At Gertie's look, she tacked on, "Really."

"You two are so alike," the woman said ruefully.

"We're both mammals, that's true, but then, so are elephants and dolphins." Carter opened the door and was almost outside when she remembered the clothes she'd left upstairs. Bolting through the house, she ran up and grabbed her bag. She was flying back to the stairs when she saw Nick come through the front door.

She skidded to a halt, teetering on the top step.

With a jolt, she saw that he was looking incredibly sexy in a disheveled kind of way. His tuxedo jacket was slung over one shoulder and his shirt was open at the collar. Those gray eyes were heavy-lidded and his hair looked as if it had had fingers running through it.

Whose fingers? she wondered.

"Good morning," Nick said as he looked up at her.

She shot him an angry look. Shoring up her load, she started down the stairs. When she got to the bottom, he blocked her way.

"Sleep well?" he taunted.

"Unlike you, obviously," Carter snapped. "You look like hell."

"It was quite a night." He had a sly smile on his face. "Unexpected, to be sure."

"I hope you enjoyed yourself." She put the bag between them and tried to push by him but he refused to move. "Do you mind?"

"I hope you have a good day at work," he said in a mocking voice.

"You bet I will. The faster we get finished, the quicker I can get away from here."

"The accommodations on my mountain and in my house aren't to your liking?"

"More the host," she hissed, shoving him hard.

He finally stepped aside and she rushed out the front door.

Carter's walk up the mountain was punctuated by a lot of curses and some fast footwork. She made it to camp twice as fast as she usually did.

Buddy was trying to light a fire when she arrived.

"Food," he said by way of greeting. "We need more."

Carter collected herself with difficulty. "With the way you pulled down dessert last night?"

"That's why they call the mouth a piehole. I was just following the owner's manual." He got to his feet. "We're running low on just about everything. I was thinking I would go. Ellie and Cort can stay up here with you."

Carter frowned. "I don't need them as babysitters. I have a cut on my hand, not a neurological deficiency."

Buddy's brows rose at her sharp tone so she took a deep breath and tried to smile. "So how was the night up here? Quiet?"

"No," he said with a grin, "and courtesy of the interruption, I'm stuck figuring out how to tell Cort I'm dating his uncle."

"Excuse me?"

"Last night, the big man and I shared a tent. Your tent."

She felt her jaw open. "Nick?"

"Yup."

"He was up here? With you?"

"Yeah, and he snores like a wounded badger. Did you know that?"

She started to shake her head in disbelief. "But why did he come up here?"

"Why do you think? Too much scotch, not enough of you. He was all ready to give a big speech. You should have caught the look on his face when he saw me." Her friend chuckled.

"You're not serious."

"The hell I'm not."

"I can't believe it," she murmured while sitting down.

Buddy sighed theatrically. "He even stayed for a cup of coffee this morning. Such a gentleman."

"Why didn't he tell me?"

"When?"

"This morning. He made me think he was out with . . ." She shook her head. "I guess it doesn't matter."

Buddy took a seat next to her. "Aw, come on, a billionaire stumbles up a mountain, in the middle of the night, wearing a tuxedo, just to find you. I think that means something."

"Yeah," she grumbled, trying not to be pleased. "That he's nuts."

"Right."

Carter shot her friend a long look and then cracked a smile. "Buddy, don't tell me the car is a lemon when you're trying to sell it."

"I'm nuts and you've put up with me."

"I'm not in love with you," she countered evenly.

Buddy's face assumed a hopeful cast. "Does that mean—"

"No, I'm not in love with him either. And don't give me that look."

"What look?"

She rolled her eyes. "Shouldn't we talk about getting back to work instead of my nonexistent love life?"

Buddy put his arm around her shoulders, his expression serious. "You should go talk to him."

She shook her head. "There's nothing more to say."

"I think you're scared."

"Damn right I am."

"You're crazy about him and, after last night, I'd bet the farm that he feels the same way," her friend said gently.

"Buddy, you live in university housing in Cambridge. You don't have a farm to bet. And let me get this straight. You think it's wrong to stay away from a ruthless man who has a reputation for treating women like disposable napkins?"

"That goes a little far, don't you think?"

"Come on, he's the poster child for 'use once and discard.'"

"Don't be absurd. And anyway, you're different." The conviction in Buddy's voice tore at her, reminding her of all she wanted to believe in. "You aren't one of those dime-a-dozen socialites who exists on a liquid diet of

Chardonnay and has her palm out for clothes money all the time. You're a real woman."

Carter stood up, trying to find the resolve she needed to let the subject drop, to let Nick go. "I'm not convinced the problem is with the women he picks. Now can we stop talking about this? It was old days ago when I lost my illusions about him."

Buddy reached out and took her hand. "Carter, how long have we known each other?"

"Jeez, I don't know. Six years? Something like that."

"And have I ever given you a piece of bad advice?"

She had an urge to send back a flippant response, but she saw that his eyes were grave. She shook her head. What he said next surprised her.

"I know he hurt you. Badly. But you know what? The course of love is never painless and people do stupid things. They make mistakes. And trust me. I know a man in love when I see him because I've been one. What showed up in your tent last night was a guy who was missing his woman. It wasn't a slick operator intent on getting laid. He loves you. I just know it. So think about giving him a chance. Okay?"

"But what if he hurts me again?"

Her friend's smile was full of wisdom. "He will. And you'll hurt him. And the two of you will make up. That's how it works."

She snorted. "There should be a better way."

"If you find one, let me know. But I'll tell you this." His eyes were full of reminiscence and love. "Jo-Jo and I have battled and made up for almost twenty years and I wouldn't trade one moment of it."

Her friend stood up. "So I've said my piece. Let's go see how the site is."

As they went over to the circle of stones, she had a lot to think about.

When they got there, they assessed the soil drainage, which had been much better than expected, and decided they could start working again. Still thinking of Nick, Carter settled down in the last square she'd been working in. She found it harder to dig with only one hand but managed as best she could. Using her trowel awkwardly, she was surprised when she hit something in the earth a little while later. It felt like bone.

"I think we've got another one," she called out.

Buddy came over and helped her uncover what turned out to be a set of ribs. Among the bones, they found a few metal buttons that were characteristic of the meager colonial army.

"Looks like it may be another revolutionary." Carter sat back on her heels, pleased with the new find. "So we've got two of them and two Brits."

"This one's only a few feet away from the redcoat we just dug up. Someone may have buried them where they fell after the fighting."

"Assuming this one is another minuteman," she hazarded, "then part of what's in Farnsworth's journal is likely correct. He was taken through the mountains by two militiamen and he was met by a pair of his own men who should have had Nathaniel Walker with them."

"But didn't because they were going to ambush the party."

"A fight ensues."

"Red Hawk kills them all except for Farnsworth."

"And then disappears with the gold," she finished. "So where's the reverend?"

The two looked over at the remaining, undisturbed ground.

Together, she and Buddy worked fast over the skeleton, and by the time Ellie and Cort arrived just before lunch, they'd freed much of the upper torso.

"You got another one!" Cort exclaimed. "Do you think it could be Winship?"

"I doubt it," Carter said, getting up for a stretch. "He was known for not wearing a uniform. The buttons here would indicate the man was a soldier on the colonial side."

"So where is the reverend?" the girl prompted.

"And where's the gold?" Cort chimed in.

"I don't have an answer for either of those." Carter ran an eye over the whole site. "But I don't think the gold is here. If someone took time to bury these bodies, I find it hard to believe that they wouldn't have taken it with them when they left."

For the next few hours, the group made a concerted effort to unearth the skeleton. Enough progress was made so that Carter was confident they could have the bones and ancillary artifacts photographed, out of the ground, and safely stored within a day. Just as the sun was taking a downward turn, Buddy uncoiled himself with a groan, stood up, and announced he was heading into town.

"I'll go with you," Ellie said. "Cort, you want to come with?"

"Naw. I think I'm gonna stay."

Ellie looked momentarily disconcerted but then lifted her chin and followed her father.

When they were alone, the kid spoke up in a soft voice. "Are you doing okay?"

Carter was concentrating on the arm bones of the skeleton. "Of course. It's awkward with only one hand but—"

"I was thinking about your dad."

She looked over at Cort. His eyes were firmly trained on where he was digging. He was working intently, as if he hadn't said anything at all, but there was a watchfulness about him.

She smiled, touched by his awkward concern. "Yeah, I'm fine. It was good to see him."

"Cool."

"And thanks for asking."

They'd been working steadily when they heard something rustling through the trees, coming from the back trail.

Carter tensed as Cort looked up. It couldn't be Buddy, she thought. That left possibilities she didn't like to consider. Nick. Lyst.

"It's probably just a deer," she murmured.

"That doesn't sound like Bambi."

"Maybe it's a tourist poking around. Or maybe it's Ivan."

"Naw. You can't hear him coming through the woods at all. Even if it's fall and the leaves are down." Cort went back to work.

The sounds grew louder. As a premonition of danger swelled in her chest, Carter got to her feet. At that moment, Conrad Lyst walked into the circle of stones. Her breath caught.

"Don't stop on my account, Carter," Lyst said in a mocking way. "So who's your new digging partner?"

Before she could head him off, the kid leapt up. "I'm Cort Farrell. Hey, I know you. You're the guy Ivan chased off from here before."

"Ah, the master's son," Lyst muttered as he leaned back against one of the larger stones. His eyes focused on Cort as if he were memorizing what the kid looked like.

"I'm his nephew."

"Indeed."

Cort puffed up his chest and demanded, "What are you doing here?"

Lyst's gaze slid over to Carter, caressing her in a way that made her feel stained. "I just couldn't stay away from my . . . friend over there."

"Maybe you should have made more of an effort," she said in a low voice as Cort looked at her with confusion. She was worried about him and trying to think of a way to get him the hell off the mountain.

Lyst began to smile.

"I've missed you deeply, Carter." There was a lover's tone to the words. "I've just hated being away."

Cort's eyes narrowed and Carter could only imagine the conclusion he was jumping to. She couldn't figure out what Lyst was doing. He seemed hell-bent on creating some kind of fiction about the two of them. Or maybe he actually was attracted to her.

She thought of the many times she'd bathed naked in

the stream and felt ill at the idea he might have been watching her.

"So I see you've found another skeleton. You're up to four now, is it?"

"I think you should go," she said evenly. "Mr. Farrell's made it clear you're not welcome on his property and we're expecting him soon."

It was a total lie and she hoped Cort wouldn't refute it as he looked over at her sharply. In her mind, she was madly calculating when Buddy was due back. It would be another hour, at least.

"I should like to see Farrell again," Lyst murmured and then surveyed the site. "You've been busy here. Not much further to go."

There was a tense pause and then he pegged Cort with an insincere smile. "Would you mind my having a minute alone with my friend? We have some things to discuss that are ... personal."

Cort hesitated.

"It's okay," she told him quickly. "Why don't you go and tell Gertie I'll be down for dinner soon?"

Her eyes were shooting a command at him and she prayed he wasn't going to argue. Cort opened his mouth as if he might but then rushed out of the circle of stones. She felt a measure of relief.

"What an attractive young man," Lyst said, stepping closer to her. "He seemed confused about the nature of our relationship, however."

"What are you talking about?" she hissed, trying not to show her fear as she took a step backward.

Lyst frowned. "I've watched you with Farrell, you know. I've seen the way you look at him. If I were another kind of man, I'd take it as a betrayal."

Carter looked down at the trowel she'd left in the dirt. She decided if he lunged at her, she was going to grab for it. It was the only thing around she could turn into a weapon.

"And what have you done to your hand? I leave you unattended for a couple of days and there you go, injuring yourself. Good thing you bandaged it all up. It's really important to take care of things that bleed like that."

Behind her mask of composure, it occurred to her that, by assuming Lyst was merely unethical, she might have vastly underestimated him.

"Not much more room to find my gold," he said, moving closer to her.

She wasn't about to argue over the pronoun. "I don't think it's up here."

"No? Well, I do, and I'm rarely wrong about these things. It's here, somewhere." His eyes traveled down her body. "I can smell it. Maybe not in this place but somewhere else on this mountain. Where will you dig next?"

"This is it. After we're done here, I'm leaving."

"Are you sure about that? I'm depending on you to do the work that Farrell has prevented me from accomplishing."

"I'm not doing anything for you."

"No? I should think you'd be more motivated. You've got a lot to lose. That barn in Burlington you've spent so much time working on, for instance. Fires frequently occur in the home, you know. Or what about that lovely young man. It would be terrible if something happened to him. Some kind of accident, maybe a fall in the woods? Teenagers can be so careless."

A cold sweat came out over her skin. "Don't you dare go near him."

"God, you're so protective. It's positively maternal." Lyst took another step closer. "But the one who really strikes my fancy is that young girl. Such beautiful red hair and pale skin. The things I could teach her."

He held out a hand to stop her from speaking.

"I know, I know—don't go near her," he quipped, mimicking her voice. "The question is, what are you willing to do to keep them safe?"

Urgent voices came through the woods, the sweetest sounds Carter had ever heard. She sagged with relief.

Lyst shot an angry glare in the direction of her Samaritans. "Here's what you are going to do. You will fin-

ish digging this sandbox out, and if you find the gold,
you're going to give it to me. If you don't find it, you're
going to stay up on this mountain until you do."

"You're out of your mind."

Lyst cocked his head. "Funny. I'm feeling quite lucid."

The voices grew louder.

"Your friends are worried about you," he said. "I'm
sure you'll be tempted to tell them all about our little
agreement, but let's just keep it between us, shall we?
For the sake of the children."

He laughed and grabbed her, moving in a fast streak.
Pushing her cap off, he pulled her hair back until she
thought her neck was going to crack. His eyes roamed
over her face.

"I know you've been with Farrell. He's quite a pack-
age and I like women who aim high." Black eyes scanned
her face. "I don't mind the infidelity, you know. As long
as you think of me when he's inside you."

Carter winced and looked away, but his hand clamped
on her jaw and forced her to meet his eyes.

"I'll see you soon," he said, inches from her lips.

"Try to kiss me and I'll bite your lip off."

"Promise?" he whispered.

And then he was gone.

Carter staggered back against one of the boulders just
as Cort and Ivan appeared.

"'Scuse me," Ivan said, going into the woods. He had
the shotgun on his shoulder.

"Did he hurt you?" Cort ran over to her.

She shook her head, wondering how long it was going
to take until her hands and feet stopped tingling.

"I didn't know you knew that guy." There was a hint
of suspicion in the kid's voice.

"I don't."

"He made it seem like the two of you—"

Carter shook her head adamantly. "I don't know what
that was all about. I hardly know him."

Cort relaxed a little. "He looked scary. That's why I
got Ivan."

"Don't worry about Lyst. He's harmless." She tried to muster a reassuring smile.

"He didn't look harmless to me."

"Hey, I'll bet the Swifts will be pulling in soon. Let's go down so we can help lug groceries."

Cort shot her a knowing look, as if he didn't buy the act, but he followed her to the trail. Before they started down, she looked at him seriously. "I want to be the one to tell Buddy about this, okay?"

"I figured you might. And I don't want Ellie to get scared."

When they arrived at the mansion, Buddy and Ellie were unloading supplies.

Carter resolved to put on a good face, and it was in a cheery voice that she greeted her friends. "It's great to know that the hunting and gathering instinct hasn't been lost in the modern world."

"That's quite a haul," Cort said, going to Ellie's side. She gave him a reserved nod.

Buddy emerged from the back of the Range Rover carrying plastic bags full of food. "Hey, Carter, can you take this one in to Gertie?"

She went over and accepted the load of rhubarb and strawberries. "What's all this for?"

His grin held a wealth of anticipation. "Some find pie-making in their hearts. Others have it thrust upon them."

Carter turned away, struggling with her emotions. Underneath her facade, she was having trouble recovering from the fear she'd felt up on the mountain with Lyst, and she knew she was going to have to talk with Buddy. Soon. The threat Lyst represented was very real and she wasn't sure how to protect herself or the Swifts.

As she went through the back door into the kitchen, the heat of the afternoon was replaced with the mansion's cool balm. She took a steadying breath and smelled apples, spying a big bowl of Granny Smiths sitting on one of the counters.

That was when she saw Nick standing by the sink. She stopped in surprise.

"I thought you were in a hurry to leave," he said roughly. With his hands, he was working one of the apples with a paring knife, peeling the brilliant green skin off in one long strip. Carter put the bag down on the table.

"We are." Her voice was admirably even, she thought.

"That's a lot of food for a short stay." His expression was remote as his hand wielded the knife.

"Buddy was probably hungry when he shopped."

"I understand Ivan headed up the trail with his shotgun," Nick said casually. He finished removing the skin, put the knife down, and bit into the apple with a crack. "Having problems up there?"

Carter's thoughts tangled. The last thing she wanted was for him to get further involved with the dig. If he knew Lyst had returned, he was territorial enough to patrol the damn site himself.

She wanted to see less of the man, not more.

"Not really," she answered.

"So he just felt like accessorizing with a firearm? Usually he's not so fashion forward." Nick took another bite, his sharp, white teeth cutting through the crisp flesh. "Were you harassed by someone?"

"Just a tourist. It was no big deal." All the tension in the room was making her want to scream. She turned and started walking away.

"You're lying to me."

Carter froze with her hand on the door.

"Cort told me who it was. And you lied about the bear, too, didn't you?"

She paused, wanting to kick herself.

"Isn't there something you want to say to me?" Nick's voice was cool. Stripped clean of any emotions.

She turned to him slowly, trying to frame something intelligible in her mind.

In the silence that followed, he polished off the apple and pitched the core into the trash.

"No," she said finally.

"No?" He crossed his arms over his chest. "A man

shows up at the site, who I've had kicked off my property, you lie about it twice, and you don't think you owe me an explanation?"

"I didn't ask him to come up. I don't want him at the site."

Carter sent him a taut look and then stepped outside. The screen door slapped shut behind her.

When she heard the sound again, she knew he was coming after her.

Nick's voice carried across the lawn. "You and I aren't done with this. Not by half."

Carter wheeled around. As she looked up at him, she was reminded how tall he was. "There's nothing more to say."

He pegged her with hard eyes.

"You spend a lot of time talking about trust," he said bitterly, "considering you haven't proven to be trustworthy yourself."

She opened her mouth but he cut her off.

"Are you collaborating with Lyst?"

"Good God, no!"

"So you want to try and explain why you're keeping his visits from me? Are you sleeping with him?"

Carter inhaled sharply. "How dare you!"

"You're protecting him. There has to be a reason."

"Well, I can assure you it's not because . . ." She shuddered. "And I'm not protecting him."

Nick jabbed a finger at her. "I don't like playing the fool. If I find out there's something going on between you two, I'm going to see to it that you lose your grant on the grounds of fraud."

"There's nothing between us." Carter shook her head. "Look, Lyst is desperate because he's got more ambition than talent. He'll do anything to get ahead, but I'm not doing a thing to help him."

"And what about the lying?"

"What about it?"

He threw his head back and laughed. It wasn't a happy sound.

"I should have known better than to have expected an apology from you. You only know how to turn them down." His voice was taut with anger. "Just do me a favor. The next time you condemn someone for lying through omission, remember this little episode so you don't turn yourself into a hypocrite again. *Trust.* Christ, to think I beat myself up over you."

With that, he turned on his heel and went over to the garage.

Carter could only stare after him. As the implications of the double standard occurred to her, she felt a stinging regret. He was right. She had lied to him and, in retrospect, her reasons for the deception seemed hollow.

The fall from self-righteous indignation was a hard one, she thought.

As she rejoined the group hovering around the Range Rover, she was preoccupied with the mess she'd created.

"So, you all are going to come to dinner, right?" Cort was asking.

Carter stiffened.

"I've already put in a request for pie," Buddy said from next to the four-wheeler. He was tying down supplies with a bungee cord.

"Wait 'til you try her cobbler. Ivan swears it's the best," Cort said, straddling the machine. "Ellie, do you want to come with me?"

Even though the girl looked hesitant, she hopped on behind him. As the two went roaring down the drive, Ellie's strawberry blond hair waved behind them in the summer breeze.

"Young love," her father murmured with a grin. "Almost as good as pie."

After slipping on backpacks, Carter and Buddy headed across the meadow.

Traipsing through the long grass, Carter felt as though her life was unraveling and wondered how it was all going to come together again.

If it was going to come together.

"You're awful quiet," Buddy observed.

She looked over at her friend. Thinking of what Lyst had said, she resolved to tell him about the man's most recent appearance. "I think Ellie should sleep down at the house."

"So she can watch more horror flicks with Cort? I wanted her to learn something this summer but the history of slasher cinema wasn't it."

"Lyst came back."

Buddy's steady pace faltered. "When?"

"Today."

Alarm flared in his face. "You saw him?"

She nodded, keeping her expression calm.

"Were you alone?"

"Cort was with me."

"What did he want?"

"I think Ellie should stay down at the house." Carter's soft words carried a wealth of meaning.

Buddy stopped altogether. "What the hell happened?"

"He was just poking around to see what we've come up with."

"So why do you want Ellie off the mountain?"

Carter forced her voice to remain even. "I just think it would be safer that way."

Buddy's eyes grew wide behind his glasses. "She should go back to Cambridge, shouldn't she?"

Carter nodded.

"Then she leaves tonight."

When they resumed walking, their pace had quickened.

21

Nick was approaching the garage when Ivan emerged from the darkness. "I was just coming to see you. What the hell is going on up there?"

"I got a little present for you inside."

"Oh?" Nick's voice was grim.

"Caught us a roadrunner."

"Is it Lyst?"

"Don't know the name but his backside was the one I chased off before."

Ivan led the way into the garage and over to a far corner where Conrad Lyst was tied to a lawn chair with a frayed water ski rope.

"I'm going to sue you for false imprisonment—" the man began yelling.

Nick crossed his arms over his chest and leaned casually against the hood of the Porsche. "Ivan, did you have to use the ski rope? I thought we agreed that trespassers were going to get the barbed wire."

"Must have slipped my mind."

Lyst's face was glowing with anger. "I'm going to call the police and the newspapers and—"

"Do what?" Nick interrupted. "Explain to the world why you've been running all over my property?"

"I was savagely mauled by your . . . this . . . groundsman and tied up like a dog!"

"Ivan, did you maul him?"

"Nope."

"Too bad." Nick turned back to Lyst. "Now, tell me, what were you doing on my mountain? Again?"

"I was visiting a colleague." With a subtle leer the man added, "At her invitation."

Nick ground his teeth. "Oh really? I wonder why she didn't mention to me you were coming?"

"That should be obvious. She enjoys my company on a . . . personal level. Immensely. Our meetings have been of a private nature."

Nick approached the tethered man and rested his hands on the arms of the chair. Leaning in close, he said, "I'm feeling generous today so I'm willing to make you a deal. You stay off my property and the hell away from her and I'll consider letting you walk out of here without a neck brace."

"I can't believe you're threatening me, Farrell. Because you don't need any more bad publicity, do you?"

Nick glanced over at Ivan. "I offer the guy a good shake and he throws it back in my face."

"Not much for gratitude, is he?" Ivan said with a wide grin.

"Either that or he's stupid." Nick's gaze snapped back to Lyst. "Surely you couldn't be that dumb. You couldn't actually want to provoke me, could you?"

"You can't keep me away from her."

Nick's eyes trained on the man's jugular. "Want to try that again?"

"You're playing against type," the man shot back. "You aren't known for being possessive, at least if the tabloids get their facts right. I know she's good on her back but—"

Nick's hand went around the man's throat like a vise. "I'd be very careful about the next lie you tell."

Lyst choked out, "Let go of me."

"Why? I'm having a grand old time." Nick's eyes met Ivan's. "Besides, weren't you telling me the other day I needed more upper-body conditioning?"

"That I was. Those sails can be heavy lifting. You need to be in shape."

"See?" Nick tightened his grip even more, watching the man's eyes bulge. "You could become part of my regular workouts. We could keep you here in the corner. Hang you from the ceiling and use you as a punching bag."

"Go . . . to . . . hell . . ."

"So, tell me, how does hypoxia feel? I imagine your vision's beginning to get blurry and your extremities are going numb. Your lungs have got to feel like they're on fire."

"Supposed to be just like drowning," Ivan supplied helpfully.

"Let go . . ." Lyst's voice was a strained whisper.

"I want you to stay the hell away from me and mine."

"Fine," Lyst croaked.

Nick released his hand and the man collapsed, gasping for breath.

"Here's the deal," Nick told him forcefully. "If you go to the newspapers, if you come onto my property again, if you go anywhere near Carter, even after she leaves here, I will hunt you down and make your life more miserable than it already is. Got it?"

Lyst's head lolled around his shoulders but his eyes rose with challenge. "What if she wants to see me?"

"I doubt that will be a problem."

"You can't control her."

"Then you better pray she doesn't want anything to do with you. It'll greatly increase your chances of survival." Nick turned to Ivan. "Get this piece of crap out of here."

"What?" Ellie exclaimed indignantly.

She couldn't possibly have heard her father right.

"You've got to go," Buddy repeated gently.

"What are you talking about? No, I don't!" The girl flushed.

She just couldn't leave, not when things with Cort

were looking so promising. He'd even opened up the night before and told her about losing his parents. They were getting close, real close. Boyfriend and girlfriend close.

Her father put a hand on her shoulder, his expression a mixture of concern and resolve that made her feel like she had a noose around her neck.

"We're almost done here."

"Almost," she snapped. "So why do I have to leave?"

"There's a train that will take you to Albany and a bus will get you from there to Boston. I'll call your mother to pick you up."

Ellie's eyes narrowed and she searched his face. "You're not telling me something."

Her father shrugged. "There's nothing much left to do. If you go back now, you can still get into the summer program at Harvard."

"I've worked as hard as everyone else has and I deserve to finish the project. I want to stay here." She glanced over at Cort.

"You can always have visitors back home," Buddy said softly.

"I'm not going!"

"I'm sorry . . ."

"There's nothing to apologize for. I'm staying."

Unexpectedly, her father's voice dropped an octave and became something close to a growl. "Pack your bags or I'll do it for you."

Ellie was speechless. He never sounded that authoritative unless there was something really wrong.

She had a right to know whatever it was, she thought.

But before she could say anything else, she caught Cort's eye. He gave her a brief nod that seemed to say, *Just agree and we'll figure something out.*

"I can't believe you're being like this," she grumbled. When she went into her tent to start packing, Cort followed her inside.

It was gratifying to see the distress in his face as they sat down on her cot.

"I don't want to go," she whispered. "What are we going to do?"

"Can't you talk him out of it?"

Dispirited, she shook her head. "I've seen him like this once or twice before. He's not going to budge. I wish we knew what started all this."

"I'll tell you about it later. Can you call your mom? Maybe she could change his mind."

"No. She was upset I was going to be away for so long to begin with. She'll be thrilled to get me home."

"Could Carter talk to him?"

"Maybe. But I doubt if even she could change his mind." Ellie stared into space, hoping that a solution would come out of the air.

Cort took a deep breath and then blurted, "Okay, so we're going to get out of here."

Ellie looked at him with surprise. "What are you saying?"

"Let's go away. Just the two of us."

"You can't be serious."

"I sure am."

"Wait—That's crazy." She shook her head. "Where would we go? And they're just going to find us anyway."

"So let them. At least we'll have a couple of days to ourselves. I'm tired of being watched all the time, and they aren't going to change. For once, let's make them work for it. If they want us, they can come after us."

The growing confidence in Cort's voice made the idea seem not so ridiculous.

"But when? I'm supposed to leave tonight."

"Tell your father you want to stay for a final dinner. After we eat, we'll say we want to go say good-bye. They'll let us. We'll sneak out of the house and head up the mountain. We can hook up with the old logging trail that'll take us around the summit and down the other side. From there, we can go to my friends' house. The Canton brothers know how to deal with this kind of stuff. They do crap like this all the time. They'll help us out."

Fear and excitement made Ellie's heart race. She'd never disobeyed her parents before but an adventure, with Cort, was too tempting to turn away from.

"What if we get lost on the mountain?"

"We won't. I've been hiking this monster for years."

She thought for a moment. "But what about Ivan? He'll be able to track us."

"I overheard him talking to Gertie. He's going fishing tomorrow, which means he'll be out after night crawlers tonight. They'll have trouble finding him and that'll give us some time." Cort took her hands, holding them tight. His eyes had a soulful glow in them that made her light-headed. "I'll take care of you. I promise."

His conviction was rock solid, and she was ready to believe in him completely. All those times he'd gotten his distant look and disappeared, all the wondering whether he liked her as much as she liked him, all the ambiguities seemed clear now. They would go off together, be together.

"Okay. Let's do it," she said breathlessly.

Just after sunset, she and Cort went down on the four-wheeler with two duffel bags full of her clothes. Before they left, Cort distracted the grown-ups while she hid a pack in the woods beyond the fringes of camp. Inside, she'd stashed money, some food, and clothes. After they made their getaway, they would swing through and retrieve it as well as her sleeping bag, which was still spread out on the floor of her tent.

While she and Cort raced down the mountain, she held on to him really tight, thrilled by all the possibilities before them.

"I can't wait for tonight," she said in his ear as they zoomed over the trail, speeding headlong into the gathering darkness.

Dinner was served in the formal dining room despite the fact that everyone was in shorts. It was a tense, silent meal. Repeatedly, Carter could feel Nick's eyes pierce through the still summer air in her direction. When he abruptly threw down his napkin and left the table without a word, she let out the breath she'd been holding.

Buddy looked at his watch and then his daughter. "We need to leave soon."

"Will you let us say good-bye?" Ellie's voice was clipped short.

After he nodded, the two teenagers left. In their wake, Buddy pushed his plate away and sat back in his chair. "Not exactly a great example of family-style eating, was it."

"You want dessert?" Carter asked as she got up and went to the sideboard.

"Yeah. I might as well self-medicate with cobbler. And don't go light on the whipped cream."

She brought him a plateful and they sat quietly under the sparkling chandelier while Buddy devoured dessert. She fiddled with her cobbler until he ate it, too.

"I better go get her," he said when he was done.

Carter stayed behind to clean up and she'd just finished taking the plates into the kitchen when Buddy came back in.

"Has Ellie been through here?" he asked tensely.

"No."

"I can't find them."

"You try down by the boathouse?"

Buddy's face registered relief. "Maybe that's where they are."

But when he returned wearing a look of alarm, Carter began to feel sick to her stomach.

"Cars are here, boats are docked, and the four-wheeler's in the garage," he reported.

"Would they go back to camp?"

"I can't think why."

"You take the four-wheeler up and check," she said briskly. "I'll tell Nick."

When Carter got to the study, the door was open a crack. She knocked and when there was no answer, she pushed the door open and went in.

"Nick?"

The room was empty. She was about to leave when something on his desk caught her eye. On top of the sea of white papers, there was a color photograph.

Of her.

Carter's breath caught.

It was a picture Cort had taken, back when they had found the second set of bones and right after she and Nick had gone on their sail. She had a wide-open grin on her face from laughing at one of Buddy's calamities.

"Looking for something?" Nick spoke sharply.

Startled, she bolted upright. "Cort and Ellie are missing."

His expression didn't change but she caught the tightening of his mouth. "For how long?"

"Twenty minutes or so."

"You check the house?"

She nodded. "Everywhere except for upstairs. Buddy's gone up the mountain."

Nick shrugged. "Maybe they just went for a walk."

"She was leaving."

Nick's brow came down over his eyes. "Leaving? To go where?"

"Home."

"Why?"

"I don't have time to explain. We've got to find them," Carter said urgently.

Worry surged through the harsh lines of his face. "You look down in the boathouse?"

She nodded.

"Then let's check upstairs."

The two made quick work of the second story and came up empty. By that time, they could hear the sound of the four-wheeler coming back. They met Buddy at the front door.

"She's gone," he said desperately. "And her sleeping bag is missing. They must be on the mountain."

Nick went to a phone. "Gertie? I need Ivan, now."

The pause that followed was too long to be good news.

"All right. When you get him, tell him that the kids are missing. We need him on the mountain." He hung up with a scowl. "Ivan's out looking for bait. She's going to try and find him."

Abruptly, Nick went to the kitchen and Buddy and Carter followed. They watched as he walked over to the sink, bent down, and pulled out the trash bin. When he emptied it on the floor and began searching through the garbage, they could only watch in confusion.

"Thank God," Nick said, holding up a resealed hypodermic needle and an empty glass vial.

"What's that?" Carter asked.

"Cort's a diabetic. He's taken his shot tonight. We've got some time."

Carter felt like she'd been hit with ice water. "My God, I had no idea."

"He prefers to keep it quiet," Nick said as he stood up. "His mother was one, too."

"How severe?"

"Bad enough." He walked over to a cabinet. After looking inside, he took a deep breath. "Good boy. He's taken plenty of insulin with him."

When Nick turned around, he was visibly calmer.

22

"WE'LL START at the campsite." Nick quickly kicked off his loafers and put on hiking boots. "You two take the back trail on the four-wheeler. I'll run up the front."

He couldn't get the laces tied up fast enough.

As he got to his feet, he looked at Carter. In the midst of his fear, he was struck by the tender concern on her face. It shored up his strength, enabling him to focus.

"Nick, I . . ." Her voice trailed off as Buddy raced out the door.

She took a hesitant step forward, raising her hand as if she was going to touch him, but then she hesitated. As she turned away, he grabbed her and pulled her against his body. Burying his face in her hair, he felt her arms come around him.

"I don't want anything to happen to him," Nick said softly.

"We'll find them."

Nick pulled back and brushed his hand down her cheek. For a moment, he felt the tension between them dissolve.

Then she tore out of the house and he heard the four-wheeler roar off into the night.

Hastily, he scribbled a note to Gertie with the time and the areas they were going to cover. He knew she and Ivan would come as soon as they could. Picking up a flashlight, he leapt outside and broke into a jog. Halfway across the meadow, he wheeled around and returned to the house. A moment later, he reemerged and began running.

The trip up to the campsite was a blur. Visions of Cort lost in the wilderness spurred Nick on, carrying him up the mountainside. When he arrived, he found Carter and Buddy walking around, their flashlights trained on the ground.

Carter updated him. "There was no sign of them on the back trail. We've been trying to figure out which way they went but it's impossible with all the footprints around here."

Nick searched the dirt himself to no avail. There were prints coalescing at the camp from everywhere: the dig, the river, the clearing. It was like trying to read Braille, and he was losing hope when Ivan materialized like a ghost out of the woods. Everyone breathed a sigh of relief.

The woodsman said nothing. Using his flashlight, he trained his eyes downward and circled the camp once. Then he pointed west. "They went to the river. Smart kids. Knew they'd be harder to track that way."

The search party headed deeper into the mountain, flashlights scanning the night. When they met up with the river, they followed it at a steady pace, directed by Ivan's eagle eyes. They had been going along for about twenty minutes when they heard the first cry cut through the night.

"Help!" Ellie's voice was hoarse and frayed.

The grown-ups surged forward, flying over the ground to find her. Coming around a bend in the river, they saw Ellie bent over with her hands on her knees, drawing in great gulps of air. When she saw them, she burst into tears. As soon as Buddy reached her, he took her into his arms, but she pushed him away. Her eyes were wild with panic.

"Cort," she choked out. "He's sick."

"Where is he?" Nick asked with cold dread.

"Up the river. I don't know how far." The girl panted between the words. "I marked the place with a yellow shirt in the trees. He's in a cave, under the rocks."

Without another word, Nick and Ivan took off up the river. Carter made sure Ellie wasn't hurt and then ran off after the men.

In front, Nick was running flat out, his eyes searching for a streak of yellow.

It was a lifetime and a little longer until he saw the shirt.

"Cort!" he called out.

There was no answer.

Scanning the vicinity, he saw a group of rocks and ran over to an opening in them. Inside, slouched against the stone, Cort was soaking wet and unconscious. Nick collapsed by the boy's side. Reaching out with shaking hands, he picked up the boy's flaccid wrist and felt for a pulse. It was there, beating beneath the skin, but it was way too fast.

Nick reached into the pockets of his coat and took out a glucose meter. He thought he knew what was wrong but he wasn't going to chance it. If he guessed incorrectly, he could kill the boy on the spot.

Trying to ignore the screaming panic in his head, Nick pricked Cort's finger and spread the drop of blood on a chemical strip. The reading confirmed what Nick suspected. Unlike hypoglycemia, which could make Cort demented and combative because of the lack of sugar in his blood, this attack was caused by ketoacidosis, the result of his body being choked with sugar. They'd been through this before but never in such an isolated place.

As he fumbled in the pockets of his coat for the insulin and the hypodermic needle, he thanked God he'd decided to go back for the supplies, just in case.

Just in case had turned out to be just in time.

Flashing the light on the vial, he double-checked that it was the right one, stuck the needle through the rubber seal on the top, and drew out the correct amount of insulin into the belly of the syringe. The moment the injection was done, he picked up the boy and carried him out of the shelter.

Carter and Ivan were standing in the cool night air, and he felt their concern reaching out to him through the darkness.

"I'll take him down on the four-wheeler." Nick barely recognized his own voice for the urgent fear in it.

"I'll call the ambulance," Ivan said, taking off.

As she walked behind Nick, Carter stayed silent, trying not to be overwhelmed with dread. It was close to unbearable watching Cort's listless head flopping in the crook of Nick's arm. When the footpath to camp finally appeared, she felt like they'd been granted a small miracle.

As they entered the campsite, Buddy and Ellie ran up to them. As soon as the girl saw Cort, she gasped and tried to reach out to him. Her father held her back.

"Let Nick take him down," Buddy said, searching Carter's face.

She met his eyes sadly, having nothing to tell him.

Nick didn't stop to talk. As he headed off to the four-wheeler, Carter said to his back, "We'll see you at the hospital."

He didn't show any signs of having heard her.

Ellie began crying, and her father wrapped his arms around her. Her sobs were loud until the four-wheeler started up in the distance and drowned them out.

"We should go," Carter said gently.

When they got down the mountain, there was a note tacked onto the windshield of the Range Rover from Gertie, telling them where Cort was being taken. The Swifts and Carter scrambled into the SUV and flashed out onto the main road. As they hurried along, Carter turned and saw that Ellie still had tears rolling down her cheeks. She reached out and took the girl's hand.

"We didn't mean for this to happen," Ellie mumbled through her sniffling. "We never should have left. I don't know what we were thinking."

"It's all right," Carter said, rubbing cold hands in hers.

"I didn't know he was a diabetic! We stopped to rest and I opened a bag of cookies. We were eating them, and . . ." Ellie looked up with pained eyes. "What if he dies?"

The quiet, shattering words lingered in the speeding car.

Burlington Hospital, which was situated on the outskirts of town, was the biggest medical center in the area. In the darkness, its lighted entrances and windows glowed. Carter saw them as beacons of hope.

They found Gertie and Ivan in the emergency department's waiting room. Together, they passed the time restlessly while Cort was admitted to a bed on the med/surg floor. As soon as they found out the room number, they went upstairs but were turned away. A nurse informed them that there could be only one visitor at a time and Nick was already inside. When she left, the group traded stares.

Carter thought of Nick, standing vigil by himself, and was overwhelmed by a need to go to him.

"Unless any of you want to head in, I'm going to," she said in a strained voice.

The others looked at her and then, one by one, urged her inside.

But when she walked into the room, she debated whether to turn back. Nick was standing over the bed with his back to the door, a tall, dark figure hovering over a young body that was too still. He seemed totally absorbed and she was about to leave when he said her name. She looked up and saw him staring at her reflection in the window across the room.

"How is he?" Her mouth was dry.

"Stabilized. At least that's what they tell me." The breath that left Nick was ragged. "He hasn't come to, though."

Carter went to the bedside, reaching out for Cort's hand. It was warm but he didn't respond to her touch.

"I'm sure he knows you're here," she whispered.

"Does he?"

"I think so."

Nick wrenched a hand through his hair, his eyes wide and aching as they rested on his nephew. "So what should I do? Am I supposed to pour my heart out, tell him how much I love him? Or do I tell him what I'm really thinking? That I'm so mad I don't know what to do with myself."

Carter stroked the boy's hand, in case he could hear the anger in his uncle's voice.

Nick's expression was strained by grief. "How could he have taken a chance like that? Going off into the night, without telling anybody. And where was his medication? He obviously didn't use it. He was irresponsible, utterly irresponsible. This is exactly what I don't want for him. This horrible situation is so damned avoidable."

He began pacing.

"I keep telling him he has to be careful. Over and over again until it makes us both hate me. And then he goes off half-cocked and nearly gets himself killed." Gray eyes sought her out. Nick's brow was drawn tight and his mouth was a straight, hard line. "Dammit, the kid's not old enough to handle this illness and I can't get him to take it seriously. For Chrissakes, he could have died out there."

"But he didn't," Carter said softly.

"This was just one more in a series of near misses." Nick's eyes narrowed as he frowned. "I spend my life wondering where he is and who he's with and what happens if he collapses. I go insane worrying whether anyone would help him, if they'll know what to do, if—"

"Stop it," she commanded. As Nick fell silent, he regarded her with open hostility.

"Take a deep breath and calm down." Carter walked over to him. "You're scared out of your mind and you're rambling."

Tentatively, she touched his forearm. It was like rock from the tension in his body.

"Listen to me." She made her voice drop in volume.

"I know you've done everything you can think of to keep him safe, but you know what? It didn't work."

"Thanks for the recap," Nick shot back. "It's so damn helpful."

"You standing over his hospital bed ranting and raving isn't going to help. It's not going to get him to wake up faster and it's not going to make you feel better. It's only going to heighten the stress and make you more overprotective when this is all over."

"So what do you suggest?" Nick demanded hotly. "Assuming that chaining him in the basement isn't a solution."

"You two need to sit down and talk. You need to tell him what your fears are. Maybe that way he can see you as something other than a warden. And he's got to explain to you why he ran away and what he feels like. Unless you two can learn to communicate, you're going to end up going in separate directions. You can lose him forever even if he lives a long, healthy life."

Nick looked over at the boy.

"Trust me," Carter insisted. "I've wasted two years being angry with my father just because I didn't want to hear what he had to say. That's a lot to lose for silence."

She watched as Nick's face hardened, and she thought he was going to tell her to leave. With each passing moment, he seemed to get more rigid. His jaw became clenched tight and his lips all but disappeared. She was about to turn away when a single tear dropped from his eye.

"I can't lose him, too," Nick said hoarsely. "Melina's already gone. He's all I have."

Carter's heart swelled and she put her arms around him. He seemed to collapse into her, as if he needed every bit of the strength she was offering him.

"I'm not dead, you know," came a croak from the bed.

Carter and Nick looked across the room in surprise.

Cort's eyes were half-open and he was blinking slowly.

Nick wiped his cheek with the back of his fist and went to the bed.

"How are you feeling?" he asked in a husky voice.

The boy's eyes struggled to focus. "I'm fine. You don't look so hot."

"I'm better now that you're back."

"Uncle Nick, I'm so sorry." He began to get agitated. "I—"

"It's okay. You're awake and that's all I care about."

Cort's gaze drifted away. "I cause a lot of problems, don't I?"

"I don't care."

"No?"

Nick shook his head. "I don't know what I would do without you."

Similar gray eyes met and held.

"Even with all your business stuff?" the kid prompted.

"Especially if that's all I had."

"Even with the slamming doors?"

"Yes."

Cort was silent for a while. Then he asked, "Why?"

"Because you're my family." Nick sat down on the bed. "And that means you're everything to me."

Carter quietly backed over to the doorway.

Cort began to ramble, tripping over his words. "I took my insulin with me. I put it in my bag but I lost it in the river when I fell in. I shouldn't have eaten anything, but . . ."

"Shhh," Nick said, trying to soothe him.

"I didn't leave without it. I took plenty. And I had turned us around because I'd lost it."

On her way out the door, Carter saw Nick reach down and stroke the boy's forehead.

"Uncle Nick, does this mean I'm grounded?"

"You betcha." The two laughed. "But if you're stuck in the house, maybe we could watch some movies together."

"Yeah?"

As the door shut silently, she could hear Cort's voice getting stronger. "We could start with the *Evil Dead* series. Bruce Campbell is awesome and I want to be like Sam Raimi when I grow up . . ."

*   *   *

After she'd told the others that Cort seemed to be on the mend, Carter decided to go home. With all that had happened between her and Nick, she didn't know where she belonged in the aftermath of the drama, and she needed some time alone. Buddy and Ellie stayed behind with Gertie and Ivan.

Sitting in her friend's car, with hands resting on the steering wheel and the key in the ignition, she became lost in thought.

She'd felt, for that time she had held Nick in her arms, that the distance between them had evaporated. Now she missed him more than ever.

But she had no real role to play in his life, she told herself. They were less than friends. Ex-lovers of the briefest variety was more like it.

Forcing herself to start the car, Carter headed out to the road that would take her back around the tip of the lake. As soon as she pulled the Range Rover in front of the mansion, she headed for the mountain.

Moving through the night mist, she crossed the meadow to the trailhead. Before she disappeared into the forest, she turned back and looked at the majestic house. It was illuminated brightly from lights left on inside, and its golden halo spilled out onto the lawn.

Soon, she would be gone.

As she faced the prospect of never seeing Nick again, her heart ached.

Slipping into the forest, Carter scaled the mountain and found the campsite draped in moonlight. She went to her tent, settled herself on her cot without changing her clothes, and pulled her sleeping bag over her legs. Exhaustion overcame her and she fell into a deep sleep.

She was awoken in a rush when her tent flap was wrenched open.

"What the hell are you doing?" Buddy demanded.

Carter shot up, going breathless from shock. When she'd recovered sufficiently, she said dryly, "I was enjoying a dream where I was rich and famous until you woke me up."

"I thought we agreed you wouldn't be up here alone. What if Lyst had been here when you returned?"

"He wasn't. Where's Ellie?"

"Taking a shower down there." Buddy's expression softened. "She's still pretty shaken up."

"I don't blame her. When's the next train?"

"There's one at noontime. I came up here to get the stuff she left behind by the river. You want to come?"

Carter stretched. She hadn't slept for long enough but knew there would be no more rest for her. "Yeah, sure."

"Here." Buddy handed her a thermos. "I brought this coffee for me but it looks like you need it more."

"Thanks."

He grumbled and went back outside.

Carter changed between slugs of coffee, and then they walked up the river to the place where Ellie's yellow T-shirt was still hanging from a tree limb. With memories of the night before chilling her, Carter put her head inside the small cave.

"It's pitch-black in here. You bring a flashlight?"

"Jeez, I didn't think to. But I have some matches."

"Well, you still get points for showing up with the caffeine."

Buddy handed the box to Carter, who lit one and leaned into the space.

"You see my kid's backpack?"

"No, but, man, it smells bad in here."

"Rotting earth?"

"With a strong undercurrent of soggy dog. Ouch!" Carter exclaimed, flapping her hand. She struck another match and took a step inside. The paltry light was sucked up by the pervading darkness. She was peering around when the flame reached her fingers again.

When she swore out loud, Buddy laughed lightly. "I'm beginning to see a pattern. There's got to be something we can light on fire around here."

"You mean besides my fingertips?"

When Carter came out swearing one more time, he stuck some brush in her hand and they lit it on fire. The dry leaves and thin network of branches threw off more light and promised to have better staying power.

Moving in through the entrance, Carter looked around, holding the branch in front of her. She saw the backpack and went toward it, only to have the light catch on something farther back. Leaning down and squinting, she saw a dark shape in the far corner.

"Did you find it?" Buddy called out.

"Yeah. But there's something else."

"Don't tell me it's alive and has claws."

"I don't know what it is."

She heard a rustling behind her and then Buddy's voice was close. "What is it?"

Unfortunately, the makeshift torch was losing its strength. In the flickering glow, Carter reached out to the object she'd caught sight of.

"It looks like an old munitions box."

About two feet long and a foot wide, it had leather handles on the ends that had mostly rotted away. Covered with dirt and moss, it looked as if the earth had a jealous hold on the thing.

Before the light went out, Carter put her hand on top of the box. It was cold to the touch.

"Metal," she said, wondrously.

And then they were surrounded by blackness.

"Great," Buddy muttered. "You think a big rock ball is going to come rolling down on top of us now?"

"You know that only happens in the movies. You got more matches?"

He struggled to light one but by the time Carter had knelt down, it was out.

"Maybe we should come back with a flashlight," Buddy suggested.

"No way. Go find some more brush."

She heard him moving around and then a muffled thud was followed by a curse that came out loud and clear.

Carter pivoted around in the darkness. "You okay?"

"Backpack got me."

As she heard the sound of his boots shifting more slowly across the floor of the cave, her fingers searched for the box again. She was exploring the shape of it and wondering what period it dated from when there was a click and the space was flooded with light.

She looked into the source of it, reaching an arm up to shelter her eyes. "How did you—"

"I love my daughter," Buddy said cheerfully. "Such a good little packer."

Shining the light on the box, he stood behind her as she inspected it.

"The top's been corroded shut. This is old, Buddy. This is very old."

She was inspecting the object from every vantage point when Buddy sucked in his breath.

"Holy Moses," he murmured in astonishment.

"What?"

He nodded at the wall.

She looked up.

In rough strokes, a cross had been drawn onto the stone by something that looked like black ashes. It was barely visible against the lichen-covered walls but it glowed in the light, a holy marker.

And then Carter heard a grunt of pain and Buddy collapsed on top of her.

23

It was late in the morning when Nick softly shut the door to Cort's bedroom. He felt like he was surfacing from a nightmare, surprised and relieved to find everything was as it should be.

The kid had rebounded with vigor. After sleeping for a couple of hours, and with his blood sugar level stabilized, he'd been released after breakfast. Although Nick was glad to get him home, the kid's ability to recover quickly had always been a concern. It made him worry that Cort wouldn't respect the gravity of his condition.

But he had hope now. Courtesy of what they'd shared at the hospital, Nick felt as if they were coming together to face the diabetes. Two against one. More of a fair fight.

They'd gotten even closer after returning home. Once back at the mansion, they had gone up to Cort's bedroom and spoken for the first time about the deaths that had brought their lives together. It had been a halting talk, full of long silences and awkward hand-offs as questions were asked and answered. For the first time, Nick had the chance to share some of his bittersweet memories of Melina with her son. Cort had listened raptly, soaking in the descriptions of summer days on the lake, of Christmases in New York, of his mother's debutante ball.

"Mr. Farrell?"

Nick turned to see Ellie standing in the hallway.

"Is he going to be okay?" she asked anxiously. "I know they said so but . . ."

"Yes, he is. He's resting now but you can call him when you get back to Cambridge. He'll be anxious to hear from you."

"Yeah?" Hope and warmth flared in her eyes.

"Told me himself."

There was a long pause.

"Is there something you need, Ellie?"

"Have you seen my dad?" There was subtle worry in her voice.

Nick shook his head.

"He's supposed to take me to the train station. He was going up the mountain to get my backpack while I took a shower. That was around nine."

From downstairs, they heard the sound of the front door open.

"Ellie?" Buddy's voice drifted up from the foyer.

Nick saw relief surge into the girl's face.

"I'm up here," she called out and started walking down the hall.

"Do you know where Mr. Farrell is?" her father asked, the words spaced carefully.

Nick frowned. Something was wrong. He could tell by the sliver of fear in the man's words. "I'm right next to her."

"Could I meet you in your study? Ellie, I'll be with you in a sec."

Coming to the head of the stairs, Nick caught a glimpse of Buddy's back as he disappeared around the corner.

Why was the man covered in dirt? he wondered.

"What about my train?" Ellie murmured.

"Stay up here."

When he got to the study, he found Buddy standing in the middle of the room, glassy-eyed from shock and bleeding from a head wound.

"What the hell happened to you?"

"He took her."

Nick's heart stopped pumping. "Carter?"

"We need to call the police."

"Who?" Nick was struggling to make his mouth work. "What?"

"We went to get Ellie's backpack and found something else in the cave. Carter and I were in there trying to figure out what it was when someone hit me over the head. I woke up she was gone. I think it might have been Lyst."

Nick felt the world start spinning on its axis again.

"Any idea how long you were out for?"

"An hour. Tops. But it was long enough for him to make it down the mountain with her."

Carter's head bumped on something hard and the pain woke her up. As her stomach rolled in a queasy swell, she took a deep breath and smelled oil and gasoline.

Christ, she was in the trunk of a car.

Opening her eyes, she couldn't see anything and realized that she had some kind of sack over her head. She began flailing around and found out her hands were tied. She strained against their hold, getting nowhere.

She remembered crouching down in the cave, reaching out to the strongbox, and then being crushed by Buddy's weight. The flashlight had rolled aside and she'd seen a dark shape coming toward her. She'd struggled with her attacker, then felt something come over her face. The moldy odor of the cave had been replaced with a sickeningly sweet smell and then all had gone black.

Where the hell was she being taken?

Panic made her start yanking at her hands, twisting them madly to try to get free. Choking on fear, she felt the heat of her own gasping breath flood the inside of the sack. And then she returned to the darkness again.

The next thing she knew, hands were coming under her body. She was being lifted out of the trunk and put on her feet. Her knees sagged and she was propped up against the car. Fresh air seeped through the bag and she could see a lighter glow. It was still daylight.

Her heart began to beat in a rapid fire as her mind grappled with the facts. There was only one person she could think of who would kidnap her.

"Feeling better now that you're out of the trunk?" Lyst mocked, as if on cue.

"They're going to find you," she said inside the sack.

He pushed her roughly off the car. "Shut up and get moving."

He elbowed her again and she took a step forward, stumbling because her feet were loosely tied. After a few yards, Lyst jerked her to a halt and she heard a door creak open. As she was shoved inside, her boots caught on something and she started to fall, only narrowly saving herself. The door was shut.

She was forced into a chair and Carter felt the tie around her neck loosen. The sack was stripped off her head. She blinked myopically, adjusting to the dim light. Ahead of her, wilted curtains were drawn, shutting out the daylight. She was in a cheap hotel but, not knowing how long she'd been out cold, she wasn't sure which state she was in.

She could hear Lyst breathing behind her and felt true terror. She wondered in a surge of panic if he was going to kill her and prayed that Buddy had made it down the mountain to find Nick. That they were searching for her.

That they would find her, somehow.

Tears came to her eyes but she was determined to remain calm. Lyst was a sick bastard and she knew he would feed off any weakness she showed. If she was going to make it through this, she would have to be strong. At least on the outside.

"They're going to catch you," she said defiantly. "They're going to find you and—"

Lyst stepped in front of her and calmly slapped her across the face. Her head snapped back in the chair and she felt a stinging pain in her cheek.

"Don't piss me off, okay?"

As scared as she was, the assault galvanized her. Instead of cowering, Carter's eyes rose and met his with hostility. He seemed surprised and somewhat pleased by the reaction.

"You're one tough broad." He smiled.

Lyst's hair was messy and his clothes were dirty and disheveled, with darker patches of dried sweat staining the shirt. She realized that he must have carried her off the mountain.

He sauntered over to the phone. "Now, we're going to reach out and touch your lover. You better hope he's concerned with your physical safety."

Lyst's eyes trained on her, searching for a reaction. She refused to show him any fear.

"I don't know why you're doing this," she said evenly. "We haven't found the gold."

"Don't be naïve." He waved her comment away impatiently. "I don't give a shit about the gold. What I need—want—is money."

Carter's eyes narrowed. There was something behind the slip he'd just made and she wondered if it held a clue as to what was driving him.

He picked up the receiver. "If Farrell wants to keep you alive, he's going to have to be really generous. What's his number?"

Carter drew a blank. "I don't know."

"I'm sorry. I didn't hear you correctly." Lyst's eyes lashed at her.

"I don't have it."

With a speed that frightened her and made her rethink whether she might be able to overpower him, he bolted from the bed and came up to her. He grabbed a handful of her hair and yanked hard. "Tell me the goddamn number."

Through gritted teeth, Carter got out, "I've never called the man before. I don't know it."

Towering over her, his face pressed in close to hers, she saw sweat on his upper lip and a twitch in his left eye.

Desperation had come out in his face, making his eyes too wide and his mouth tight.

"Do not fuck with me," he growled, giving her hair another pull. When she just continued to stare back at him, he let go and returned to the phone, apparently to call information.

Carter had to swallow hysterical laughter. She'd been kidnapped, taken to some seedy hotel room, and the lunatic was calling 411?

The thought didn't strike her as funny anymore when it occurred to her that Nick might have an unlisted number. Fortunately, Lyst scribbled something down on a pad and then dialed again.

There was triumph in his voice when he said, "Farrell? I think I have something you want."

When Nick's angry response came over the phone loud and clear, she almost wept with relief. She knew, as soon as she heard the resolve in his voice, that he would do everything in his power and more to come get her. It was gratifying to see a little of Lyst's confidence drain out of his face.

Carter took a deep breath, the first one since she had been captured. Nick was going to come for her. She knew it as plainly as she recognized the danger she was in, and the realization was an antidote to her fear. One way or the other, Lyst was going to be brought down. She just knew it.

She frowned, surprised by the measure of calm that had come over her. That feeling was about trust, she realized with astonishment.

Trust.

She thought back to the way Nick had come up to get her on the mountain during the storm, how he had driven her to the doctor, taken care of her. Why hadn't she recognized his actions before for what they were? As proof that he cared for her, was willing and able to take care of her. She'd been so scared of getting hurt, she hadn't seen in his actions what she had been looking for all along in his words.

Regret burned as she thought of what she might have lost forever. Images of Nick and her together came in a painful flood, and the distance between them struck her as a misguided waste. She'd never given him a chance to really explain about her father's arrival. She'd pushed him away because of her problems with her family, because of her vulnerability and her fear of him and his past.

But he was coming for her. Even still, he was coming for her.

It gave her hope that there was still a chance for them.

Carter glanced over at Lyst.

Assuming Nick got to her before the other man did something really horrific.

"Now, Farrell, there's no reason to get nasty," Lyst was drawling into the phone. He shot her an outrageous wink. "Here's our *new* deal. You're going to give me five million dollars and I'm going to give you your girlfriend back in one piece. Nice and simple. Here's the account I want you to put the money in. When I get confirmation of the deposit, I'll call you back and arrange for the return of your little piece of ass."

He read a series of numbers out. "Now, don't get to thinking independently and going to the police. Let's just keep this gentlemen's agreement between us. It will be better for her that way. Oh, and Farrell? If you dawdle, I'm liable to get bored and there's nothing to do in this fleabag motel except her—you know what I mean? So let's be quick about this. I'll call you back in an hour."

He hung up the phone with a triumphant smile. "Well, that went nicely. You'll be pleased to know, no doubt, that Farrell is extremely worried about you. That's a good sign."

Lyst reclined on the bed, pushing his legs out in front of him. "He seems awfully attached to you. Maybe I should have asked for more money."

Carter stayed silent and shifted in the chair to try to ease her stiff muscles. The movement also gave her a pretext for trying to work her hands against the rope in hopes of loosening it. She didn't get far with the effort. The skin at her wrists had already been shredded and she suspected the new wetness she felt on her palms was her own blood.

She stilled herself and noticed Lyst's eyes traveling over her, hot and speculative.

"How do you like being tied up? Does it turn you on?"

With a shudder, she attempted to distract him. "I thought you were after the gold."

He shrugged. "I was. But events have— Let's just say, I need to go on a long vacation. And I don't have time for you to find that treasure."

Carter felt a surge of hope, thinking he might have already gotten himself in trouble with the authorities. Had some of his black-market deals come back to haunt him? Maybe the police were already after him.

"You can't honestly believe you're going to get away with this," she said stridently.

"Oh, I'm feeling pretty good about things. And five million goes damn far in a third-world country. I'll live like a king." He got off the bed and approached her. "Which makes me think. Perhaps I should take you with me. I imagine you'd make the nights much more interesting."

He brushed his knuckles over her cheek and she turned away. Lyst captured her chin and forced her head in his direction. "This hard-to-get act is wearing thin."

Carter blanched as he bent down toward her.

As soon as he hung up the phone, Nick had to fight to control his raging emotions. Fear and anger hit him hard, making him feel as though someone had shot him in the chest. He looked across the desk at Buddy.

"Lyst has her. He wants money." Nick wrenched a hand through his hair, his eyes going blurry. He focused on the ceiling, willing his vision back. "But at least we have something to tell the goddamn police now."

Nick picked up the phone again, rubbing the back of his neck as he dialed. "Freddie? I need you to arrange a wire transfer of five million dollars to the following account at Credit Suisse. But don't execute. Just be ready. And get me the number of John Smith. Thanks."

Nick hastily scrawled a number down on a sheet of paper. John Smith was a specialist in messy events, a tough man whose U.S. Marine and intelligence background had been useful to many Wall Street kingpins. As soon as the guy's voice came over the line, Nick quickly relayed the status of events.

Smith got right to the point. "I'll call my buddies in the FBI immediately, and I'll put an electronic trace on the account. You talk with the state police yet?"

"They're already up on the mountain and we've got a couple in the kitchen coordinating with some of the local sheriffs. Lyst warned me not to call anyone but they were already here."

"Good. Tell them everything, in spite of what the guy said. You're going to want their help. Did they set up a wiretap on your phones?"

"It's almost ready."

When Nick hung up, he looked at Buddy and the statie who was finishing up with the wiretapping. A thought occurred to him. Lyst had said something about a fleabag motel, and lodging was pretty scarce so far north. Considering the amount of time that had passed, he might have her close by.

Nick went to the kitchen where several armed policemen were at the table, making calls and speaking into walkie-talkies. He told them what Lyst had said and his theory. After mentioning the FBI had been contacted, he went back to his study. Although he appreciated everything the authorities were doing, he was frustrated. He wanted Carter back, wanted to take her into his arms and feel her safe against him. Anything short of that was a failure.

Checking his watch, he guessed it would be another forty minutes before Lyst called back. It seemed like an eternity.

When the phone rang, his head snapped to the sound

and he picked it up in a flash of movement. It was Freddie, calling to confirm that the transfer was all set and that Smith had connected with her. The trace was ready on the account.

As Nick put the receiver down, the policeman who'd been working on his phone line stood and closed up his tool case. "If he calls again, keep him on for as long as possible. We can find him now."

Nick nodded tightly and stared at the phone, willing it to ring.

He thought over the conversation with Lyst, wondering how the man would have gotten Carter inside a motel without being noticed. He'd have to have her tied up or have forced her into the room with a gun or knife. You do that in the light of day and you'd get seen, somehow, by someone. Unless it was a hotel set far back from the road. In the woods. Nick started to review all the places he could think of.

The phone rang again.

Nick snatched it to his ear.

"I know I'm a little early but how are we doing?" Lyst asked. The cockiness in his voice made Nick want to reach through the phone and put his hands around the man's throat.

Instead of yelling, which was what he wanted to do, Nick nodded to the policeman, who activated a machine and put earphones up to his head. As calmly as he could, Nick said, "We're ready but I want to talk to her first."

"That wasn't part of the deal."

"It is now." Nick's tone brooked no argument. "How do I know she's still alive?"

Lyst laughed. "She almost bit my lip off when I tried to kiss her. I can assure you, she's doing just fine."

Nick gripped the receiver so hard, the plastic creaked in protest. Through gritted teeth, he said, "I talk to her or you don't get the money."

There was a long pause while Lyst breathed into the phone. "Fine. Make it short."

There was a rustling noise.

"Nick?" Carter's voice was painfully thin. She was trying to be strong, he could tell, but she was scared. His heart pounded.

"I'm going to get you out of this. Are you okay? Has he hurt—"

Lyst came back on. "Like I said, she's just fine. Now wire the money and I'll call you with further instructions."

"No. Tell me now."

Lyst's voice was sharp. "You are not in a position to be making demands. Wire the damn money."

Abruptly, a third voice came on the line. It was that of an older woman and she sounded confused. "Hello, Jeanie? Oh, have I interrupted another call?"

Then the phone went dead.

Nick hissed in surprise, meeting the state policeman's eyes.

"I know where he has her," he said urgently, throwing the phone down. He ran through the house while talking, the state policeman and Buddy right on his heels. "She's at the Forest Ledge Cabins. They have a party-line system there, which means that all the phones are on one wire. Anyone can pick up at any time and interrupt someone's conversation. Old Mrs. Cullay just got on. They're only twenty-five miles from here."

As Nick sprinted into the kitchen, he knew the local cops had come to the same conclusion he had because they were grabbing for their hats and keys as well.

Before racing from the house, he got his .357 Magnum out of the locked gun closet in the mudroom. With deft movements, he threw a clip into the butt of the gun and cocked it. When he emerged, strapping on a shoulder holster, none of the state police stopped him from getting armed or coming with them. They weren't going to stand in his way.

Nick ran to the Porsche and gunned the car out of the garage. As he shot out onto the road with three state police cars behind him, he wracked his mind for what he could offer God in exchange for Carter's safety. Except for plenty of cash, he came up woefully short on trades.

You sure as hell can't put salvation on a credit card, he thought grimly.

So he made a promise to himself. If she came out of this alive, he was going to spend the rest of his life convincing her he loved her. Nothing would ever keep them apart again.

It took only twenty minutes to reach Forest Ledge Cabins, a conglomeration of small, dark green structures, the Adirondack version of bungalows. Nick knew that they would get whatever help they needed from the proprietors.

He wrenched open the screen door of the office and the officers followed him inside.

Mrs. Cullay, a spry older woman, was already looking up in surprise, having obviously seen the rush of cars pulling in. "What's going on?"

Nick spoke urgently. "Have you rented out a cabin to a guy who's about six feet tall, black eyes, whip thin—"

"Sure did. He wanted one way in the back. In the woods."

"Which one?"

"Number nineteen."

Nick stormed out, running fast over the grass and dodging trees.

When they got to cabin nineteen, he crouched behind the thick trunk of a pine and the police fanned out around him. It was dark underneath the canopy of the forest and he was grateful for the protection the dim light offered.

Up ahead, he saw a white Lincoln parked close to the door.

Nick was wracking his brain for what he should do. He kept coming up with Hollywood scenes, like him bursting through the door and knocking Lyst out, taking Carter into his arms, and holding her. The trouble was, real life couldn't be scripted and he was smart enough to know it. He wasn't sure how they were going to get in there without spooking Lyst and endangering Carter's life even further.

And then, unexpectedly, the door to the cabin opened a crack.

Nick peered through the shadows, watching as Lyst stuck his head out, looked in both directions, and cautiously went to the car. He was carrying a suitcase and seemed to be in the process of leaving.

That was all it took.

Nick sprang into action, leaping forward and running full tilt at the man.

Lyst couldn't have known what hit him. He looked up just as Nick tackled him and laid him out flat with one punch to the face. As Lyst went slack on the ground, Nick yanked him up by the shirt. He was ready to hit the man again and again when the officers pulled him off.

In an instant, the anger left him and he was filled with a desperate need to find Carter.

He broke free and raced through the door of the cabin. As his eyes adjusted to the darkness, he saw a vision that broke his heart.

She was sitting in a stiff-backed chair, her hands tied behind her at an awkward angle. Her face was red on one side and he watched as tears started to fall from her eyes as she looked up at him. Crossing the room in two strides, he fell to his knees and reached out to her, needing to touch her face, her arms, her body, to reassure himself she wasn't injured.

"Did he hurt you? Are you hurt?" He kept repeating the words.

With Nick actually in front of her, Carter couldn't find her voice. She shook her head, trying to speak and struggling to free her hands. All she wanted to do was touch him. He went to work freeing her and, when she was able to put her arms in front of her, she saw his eyes grow stark with grief. He was looking at her wrists, the skin torn and bleeding.

"Oh, God," he moaned, carefully bringing her hands

to his lips. He kissed her palms and then buried his face in her lap. Wrapping his arms all the way around her body, he held on to her and she clutched at him in return. She felt him shaking, or maybe it was her.

"I was terrified I wouldn't be able to find you," he said, lifting his head and staring into her eyes with love. She felt a warm rush replace the cold numbness in her body. Brushing aside a strand of her hair, he kissed her softly on the lips, as if he was afraid of hurting her.

As he pulled her to him, she felt the rough brush of his cheek against hers and smelled his aftershave. The familiar scent made fresh tears come to her eyes.

The gratitude and relief she felt to be in his arms was more than she could express. She'd been saved and he was with her. That made them both more than lucky.

"Blessed" was the word, she thought.

His hands, always so sure and steady, were trembling as he pulled back and stroked her face. "Are you okay?"

"Just hold me," she whispered. She didn't want to talk, just wanted to be near him. She'd had enough distance from him to last her a lifetime.

"Ma'am?" one of the state police said. "Ah, excuse me."

They reluctantly pulled apart. It was only then that she realized Nick was armed.

"Are you going to need medical assistance?"

She tried to steady herself with a deep breath. "I think I can take care of my wrists."

"Well, the paramedic is here if you want her to check them out. And we'll need to take a statement from you."

"Can't it wait?" Nick demanded protectively.

"I'm afraid not. She'll have to come back to the sheriff's office."

Carter shuddered.

Nick got to his feet, putting himself between her and the officer. "The hell she is. You can come talk to her later."

The other man didn't argue.

When Nick turned back to her, his eyes were gentle. With the help of his arm, she rose stiffly to her feet. Together, they walked out into the daylight, holding on to each other. There were police cars everywhere, and she and Nick watched as the first of the TV crews arrived.

"How did you find me?" she asked.

Abruptly, a man moving fast and low to the ground burst in front of them and blinded Nick and her with a camera flash. The state police were on him at once, but the picture had been taken.

"We've got to get you out of here," Nick said urgently, shuttling her over to the Porsche. He slid in next to her and got out his keys. Before he started the engine, she put her hand on his arm and stopped him.

"Nick?" Her voice was soft and low. His eyes, alert and worried, met hers. "I need to tell you something."

"What is it?" He seemed to stop breathing.

"I knew you were coming for me. Deep inside, I knew that you would do everything in your power to get me out of there."

Her eyes drifted over his handsome face, his features showing the strain he'd been under. She reached up and ran her forefinger along the length of his solid jaw.

"It takes courage to love." Her voice was a mere whisper. "It wasn't until today that I realized how much I could trust you. How much I should have trusted you. I'm so sorry I doubted you."

Nick leaned in and brushed his lips over hers. "Don't worry about that now."

She shook her head, needing to say her piece.

"I was looking for excuses to push you away because I felt so out of control. I was afraid of being hurt. I was looking for us to fail." Her eyes flashed up to his and she was touched by his tender expression. "I want to start over, Nick. Start again."

When he shook his head, her heart dropped.

"We don't have to," he said. "As long as you're beside me, now and in the future, that's all that matters. I don't give a damn about the past."

He brought his mouth down and captured her lips in a kiss that was both heartfelt and a promise of passion.

Reaching up behind his neck, she pulled him closer to her until she could get her arms around his big shoulders. When they parted, she smiled.

And then yawned widely.

"You need food and a rest," he said briskly. "I'll bet Gertie's been cooking up a storm."

As he sped toward home, Nick was thinking how much he loved life. And how much he loved Carter. His feelings for her were big, noisy ones, like cymbals crashing in his chest, trumpets blaring in his head. He didn't mind them in the slightest. He felt no urge to run from them, no panic to get away. They felt just perfect to him.

A goddamn symphony he could listen to forever.

Nick grinned.

And abruptly decided he couldn't wait any longer. Even though he told himself he should give her some time to recover, he couldn't hold back what he needed to say. A defining moment in his life was about to occur and, if the last twenty-four hours had taught him anything, it was that you didn't wait on the important things.

As he went to open his mouth, he became surprisingly nervous. His voice was rough and he rushed through the words. "Carter, you know I love you."

He paused.

"Will you marry me?"

In the silence that followed, he felt tension growing in his gut until he couldn't stand it any longer. He glanced over at the woman he loved.

Carter's head was back against the seat rest and her expression was one of utter relaxation. Her mouth was open sweetly, like a child's, and her eyes were firmly shut. She was out cold.

He couldn't believe he'd just proposed and she'd slept through it.

Nick laughed out loud. He never thought he'd love a woman so much that he'd ask her to marry him. And he sure as hell never figured she'd sleep through it when he did.

God, he thought with a smile, had one hell of a sense of humor.

Nick reached out, taking Carter's hand in his, and she roused briefly. Just long enough to squeeze back.

He was still grinning when he pulled up to the mansion. Because Carter was dead to the world, he opened her door, picked her up, and carried her to the front door. She only murmured a little, snuggling closer to him.

As they came inside, Buddy, Ellie, and Cort burst into the hall, looking alarmed.

"Is she okay?" Buddy's face was showing the worry they had all felt.

Carter stirred in his arms and opened her eyes.

"Hey," she said in a groggy way. "What happened to the strongbox?"

"You're kidding me." Buddy laughed in a short burst. "You get kidnapped and the first thing you think of is some old tin can in a dark cave?"

"Is it still there?"

"I guess so."

"Buddy, you have to go up and get it." She lifted her head and spoke with growing urgency. "Photograph the heck out of it and bring it down to the house. I don't want it left unattended. Ask Ivan to help you."

"Listen to you, barking orders," Buddy said with obvious relief. "I guess you're all right, after all."

"Thank the Lord, yes," Nick interrupted. "Now, I'm taking her right upstairs."

"Don't forget about the box," she called out, waving to the teenagers.

As Nick started up to the second floor, she looked at him from under her lashes. "You know, I could have walked up these myself."

"Where's the fun in that?" he teased gently as he took her to the bedroom she'd been using.

Kicking the door open, he settled her on the bed. As he pulled back, she said, "Please don't go."

"I'm not." He took off her shoes and then his own,

and lay down next to her. She moved in close and he kissed the top of her head. "I'm never leaving you."

A muffled response was spoken into his shirt.

In the quiet that followed, Nick took a deep breath. He wanted to savor the moment, store it in his mind forever, soak in the perfection of her warm body against his. The incredible gift of having her safe and in his arms overwhelmed him.

So this is redemption, he thought, stroking her shoulder as he closed his eyes and fell asleep.

24

CARTER KNEW whom she was with and where she was before she opened her eyes. She could feel Nick's arms wrapped around her, his body pressed in close, his heart beating against her own. She could hear the sounds of water lapping against the shore and the high-pitched, sweet calls of songbirds. In the soft summer air, she caught the delicate scent of lilacs.

It was exactly where she wanted to be.

As she looked up into Nick's face, she saw that he was staring down at her, those diamond eyes of his soft and warm. Oh, so warm.

Her lips found his.

"Make love to me," she whispered against his mouth.

She felt him shudder with need as her words sank in, and then he was on top of her, pressing her into the bed, his body a weight she couldn't get enough of. She peeled his shirt from his shoulders and went after his belt while he unbuttoned her top and released the clasp of her bra. When his mouth found her breast, she arched up, swept away in the wildness between them.

Clothes were pushed and pulled away, thrown to the floor, lost in the sheets, wedged into pillows. She felt his hands traveling across her skin, into places that made her sweat and moan and sway against him. He was raw with need, rough but tender, his powerful body swollen and throbbing with a passion she knew only too well.

"I have to be inside you," he groaned.

His fingers tangled in her hair, pulling her head back for his kiss, and her nails bit into the smooth skin of his back in response. She felt his rock-hard muscles straining under her hands, the ridges and valleys testaments to his strength.

His knee came up to part hers and he nestled in between her legs. When he settled over her, suspended by his powerful arms, he hesitated. She reached up, cupping his face in her hands, stunned by the pain in his expression.

"I love you," she whispered.

"Oh God, I needed to hear you say that."

And then he slid into her and swallowed her cry of ecstasy. Moving as one, they rose and rose until the explosion came and they fragmented at the same time, falling to the earth like snow.

They were lying together, taking deep breaths, when Nick rolled to the side and braced himself up on one arm. With his free hand, he stroked hair out of her face. In his eyes, she saw a solemn light.

"You seem so serious," she murmured.

"Carter," he began. "I have something I need to say. I tried on the drive home but . . . You know I love you?"

"Yes."

He reached over, kissed her slowly and whispered against her lips, "Will you be—"

"Well, jeez, Gertie, which bedroom are they in?" Buddy's voice drifted in through the closed door. There was a frantic note in it. "That Wessex guy's been calling all morning. He's gotta have tendinitis from dialing the phone. There's a knot of reporters on the front lawn that your husband keeps threatening to pick off like tin cans on a fence, and I need to show Carter what we brought down from the mountain last night."

Gertie's voice, also muffled, was more reasonable. "They're here somewhere. Hopefully in a bed together."

Carter blushed.

Nick rolled his eyes and got up, pulling a sheet around himself. He opened the door a crack.

"We're in here," he said quietly. "Tell Wessex we'll call him soon and remind Ivan it's against the law to shoot at people, even if they're reporters."

"Here are some clean clothes for her," Buddy said with a grin of satisfaction, as he pushed a duffel bag through the door.

"You want breakfast?" Gertie asked.

"That would be great," Nick replied.

As the shower came on behind him, he shut the door on their knowing looks.

Squaring his shoulders, ready to propose marriage to the woman he loved, Nick dropped the bag and the sheet and marched into the bathroom. He found Carter under the water, arching her back to wet her hair. Her breasts were taut, her stomach flat, her hips a gentle curve that made his eyeteeth ache. As soon as he joined her, his lips went to her mouth.

Carter picked up a bar of soap, lathered her hands, and began to work over his skin until he was gripping the glass shower door with such force his arms hurt. With a punishing attention to detail, she went over every inch of him, teasing and tantalizing him. With his heart pounding and his lungs screaming for more air, his muscles strained to the breaking point as he begged for a release she wouldn't let him have. He'd never felt so out of control, had never loved the torture of being denied so much. When she finally allowed him relief by wrapping her legs around his hips and taking him into her, he was wild.

After the fury of passion she'd unleashed was spent, he sagged against the shower's wall, feeling like he'd been wrung out. Sometime later, he heard the water being turned off, and forced his eyes to open.

Carter had an extremely satisfied expression on her face.

"Hi," she said.

"G'd mging," was all he could manage.

Her smile got even brighter. Moving with enviable ease, she popped out of the shower, grabbed two towels, and passed one to him. He took it but couldn't seem to lift the damn thing. It just hung down from his hand, the ends getting wet.

"Let me help you with that," she offered happily. She tossed the one he'd let get damp aside and coaxed him out of the shower. He stood still while she dried him off, tied the towel around his waist, and pushed him toward the bedroom door.

"Can you make it to your room?"

Nick nodded and began to walk away, backward. He couldn't take his eyes off her.

He murmured, "I don't think I'm ever going to look at a bar of soap in the same way again."

"There's more where that came from," Carter said. Her husky voice traveled through his ears to his very core.

As he stepped out into the hallway, Nick's body was already stirring again.

Looking down at himself, he said wryly, "Haven't you had enough?"

When Carter appeared downstairs, she was wearing a fresh pair of jeans and a crisp white polo shirt, and she felt like a new woman. She didn't bother to hide her glow of happiness.

Ellie rushed around the table and into her arms while Buddy leaned back in his chair and gave her a knowing grin. "You're looking awfully . . ."

She shot him a warning look over the top of his daughter's head.

"Clean," he quipped with a wink.

From across the table, Cort was smiling at her and she said to him, "You're looking better."

"So are you."

Gertie bustled over and put a plate of fruit and a cup of coffee on the table.

"Eat," the woman said, pointing to an empty chair.

Carter sat down, did as she was told, and was about to ask for a refill of both when Nick ambled into the room. His eyes sought her out and he looked at her with such tenderness and love, she felt her heartbeat quicken.

Cort frowned at his uncle.

"What?" Nick asked him.

"You look funny."

Nick's eyebrows arched as he sat next to Carter. He smiled a thanks at Gertie as breakfast was pushed in front of him.

"How do I look funny?" he prompted the kid.

"I dunno. You look kinda . . . loopy."

Laughter broke out in the room and Ivan wanted in on the joke as he came inside.

"What's the laughing for?" he asked.

"Uncle Nick," Cort explained. "He looks different, don't you think?"

Ivan glanced at the man. "'Course he's changed. He's in love."

Everyone in the room froze.

Except for Nick. He reached over, took Carter's hand, and brought it to his lips. "That's right."

"You know," Cort said, tilting his head to one side. "You keep smiling so much, you're going to have to get your driver's license picture updated. No one'll recognize you."

When Nick rolled his eyes, the kid laughed with delight.

While he ate, Nick was strategizing about the proposal again. If he could get Carter out on the boat, he thought, that would be perfect. The lake, the sun, a gentle breeze.

The ring.

When he jerked like someone had kicked his chair, Carter glanced over at him. "You okay?"

He nodded with distraction. He didn't have a ring. He was supposed to have a ring. She deserved a ring.

Carter gave him an odd look but then pushed her plate away and stared at Buddy purposefully.

"Where's the box?" She wadded up her napkin. "You brought it down, didn't you?"

The man nodded and disappeared into the mudroom. When he returned, he was carrying the tin construction in his arms, his shoulders hunched from its weight.

"I photographed everything before I removed it from the cave," he noted as he put the box on the table in front of her. The kids squirmed in their seats, eager for it to finally be opened.

Carter stood up and fingered the edge of the top. "The metal's fused into a tight seal. There's also a lock. We're going to have to cut this thing open."

"I got the right tool for it," Ivan said. He returned with a small, battery-powered Sawzall.

"Do you want to do the honors?" Carter asked Nick.

He shook his head. "I wouldn't want an archaeologist doing my taxes. I don't think you want a finance guy playing around with that thing."

Cocking a smile at him, Carter fired up the tool and cut a line around the edge of the lid. When she was finished, she wrapped her hands in two cloth napkins and got a grip on the sides.

Lifting slowly, she said, "Now, let's not get too excited. This could just be more auto parts."

But then the unmistakable glow of gold was revealed.

"Good Lord." She exhaled as a swell of surprise and delight filled the room. "Someone get a camera."

Nick was stunned. Never in his life had he thought that the fortune would be found. For all his years, he had refused to believe it was still on his land.

He looked at Carter and was thrilled that she had discovered it. She was wearing an expression of rapt excitement as she cautiously put her hand into the magical jumble and lifted up handfuls of the precious metal. There were coins, pieces of weighty necklaces, earrings with the stones removed, heavy signet rings.

He couldn't have asked for a better outcome, he thought.

"Wait a minute," she murmured. "There's something else in here."

She burrowed into the box and slowly pulled out a small book. Leather-bound by hand, it was about five inches square, a dull brown in the midst of the radiance. There was a cross drawn on the front.

Delicately, she slipped her forefinger under the front cover and lifted.

"J. Winship. Year of Our Lord, 1775," Carter read. "It's Winship's missing journal."

As everyone cheered, the exuberant sound reverberated throughout the house.

By early afternoon, Carter had finished reading the entire journal. Nick had given her free run of his study, and she'd spent hours curled up in the chair behind his desk, reading as the sun streamed in through the open windows.

It was the perfect way to decompress from her harrowing experience. Losing herself in the reverend's words helped her to feel safer and more grounded. She knew it would take time before she fully recovered from the abduction, but being with Nick and her friends would undoubtedly help. She'd also spoken with her father, who'd been overjoyed at hearing her voice, and that, too, made her feel more steady.

When she came to the end of the journal, she closed the cover and placed it on the desk. Twirling the chair around, she stared out a window, watching butterflies flirt among the wildflowers in the meadow behind the mansion.

The artifact was priceless, she thought, one of the most significant finds from the colonial period in the last decade. It told more of Winship's reluctant but patriotic involvement in the Revolution and everything about the fateful trip into the Adirondacks that had cost him his life.

It also solved the mystery of who had killed the men.

Carter got out of the chair, left the journal on the desk, and went in search of the others. She found them down by the lake. Ellie was sunbathing while Cort was snorkeling at the shore. Nick and Buddy were cleaning the sailboat's decks.

"What's the verdict?" Buddy asked as he caught sight of her.

Nick looked up, a slow, sensual smile coming over his face as their eyes met. He was wearing only swimming trunks, the same black ones he'd worn before, and his body glistened with sweat from his labors in the sun.

She felt herself warm up considerably.

"It's a remarkable story," she said as Nick came up to her. In front of everyone, he bent down and kissed her on the lips.

"Tell us everything." His voice was low and inviting and she could feel the blood surge to her face as she blushed. She couldn't help but remember the things he'd whispered to her while they'd been making love.

She cleared her throat and told them what she'd learned.

"Jonathan Winship was an amazing man. Reflective, serious, and indignant over the British government's remote control of the colonies. He was an unlikely war hero, a student of the Bible, not a fighter. Still, he had a strength of purpose that was indomitable." She looked out across the lake. "According to Winship, General Farnsworth was pure evil. He tells everything about how the man was arrested in New York for raping and beating that woman.

"After the exchange for Nathaniel Walker was worked out, the Winship party headed into the Adirondacks with Red Hawk in the lead and the general in shackles. They were carrying the gold for the troop supplies with them. When they got to the base of Lake Sagamore, they were supposed to hand the strongbox over to other revolutionaries. Their compatriots never showed, however, and they were forced to take the fortune with them.

"As they made their way toward the fort, Red Hawk

took good care of his charges, leading them through the mountains by the most direct route possible. When he got them to the place designated for the trade, the guide disappeared into the woods, having discharged his duty. Soon thereafter, the party was ambushed. The two minutemen and Reverend Winship were no match for the well-trained redcoats who attacked them. The American soldiers were killed, and Winship was stabbed in the belly by the general, a mortal wound as things would turn out.

"Farnsworth was about to finish the job on Winship, had a bayonet poised over the reverend's head, when Red Hawk came back. Materializing, as if from the ether, as Winship put it, the Indian fell upon Farnsworth, injuring him badly. Five British soldiers set upon the Algonquin, but with what Winship termed a terrible grace and power, the Indian killed two outright and the other three scattered through the woods."

"Holy sh—" Cort stumbled. "I mean, cool."

"While Farnsworth lay bloodied on the ground, Red Hawk came to Winship's side. The reverend asked to be helped up and went around to the fallen men, including the general, and performed last rites. He knew time was of the essence. The three Brits would return with reinforcements, and he had to hide if he had a chance at surviving. Red Hawk helped him through the wilderness to the cave and then went back for the gold. After the Indian returned with the strongbox, he asked if the reverend, who was clearly dying, had any last requests. Winship asked that the bodies of the dead men be buried and a cross placed at the head of each grave. Red Hawk left and Winship never saw him again."

There was a long silence and then Carter finished the tale. "The reverend knew he wouldn't survive and his last entry in the journal was barely legible."

"What was it?" Ellie asked softly.

The words had been burned into Carter's memory because she'd read them over and over again. They left her lips as if she'd known them all her life. "'A stronger nation shall be lifted high on the backs of men united by honor and the grace of God. For all who know love for their fellow man shall be as one under the heavens. Brothers are found not of the same womb but of similar hearts. Thank you, Red Brother.'"

"So Red Hawk was a hero," Cort whispered in awe.

Carter nodded.

"What happened to him?" Ellie asked. "He must have been killed."

"No, he wasn't."

Curious eyes looked Carter's way.

"The reverend's final entry wasn't the last one. Red Hawk's was. It was hard for me to decipher the language but I believe the saying can be translated as, 'So the Hawk flies from the earth, to the Great Spirit and beyond, as does the man. Be at peace, pale Father.'"

"That's incredible," Buddy said solemnly. "The find of a lifetime."

"I have a feeling," Carter said, "that Red Hawk came back, buried Reverend Winship in the cave, and etched that cross in the stone wall over his grave."

"So we should go excavate," Buddy prompted.

"No. I think we should just leave him be," Carter said slowly, shaking her head. "He should be left in peace. We have the diary. That's enough of him."

Nick nodded. "I agree."

Carter stood up from her perch. "And now I need to go to the university. I want to get my colleagues started on conserving the journal. I don't want any more deterioration to occur and it needs to be copied as soon as possible." She turned to Nick. "And we should probably lock up the gold somehow. It needs to be studied, too, but I'm not sure where I can put it at the university."

"You can use my safe until you get that figured out."

"Thanks," she said and gave him a look from under her lashes. "Would you have any interest in a drive across state lines?"

"You better believe it, woman."

As they went up the lawn, their hands caught and held. She couldn't keep the smile off of her face.

When they got to his study, Nick went down on his haunches and opened the safe.

"I don't have room for the box itself," he said with his head wedged into the wall of books. Inside, he was shuffling the contents around, making space. He took out the cross and handed it to Carter.

She unwrapped the felt and stared at the old wood. "What an amazing story."

When Nick looked up at her, his eyes were tender.

"What?" she asked him shyly.

"You're one hell of a woman—you know that? You come up here, find the missing gold, discover the reverend's final resting place, and get his diary. And then you go and do something truly amazing."

"What was that?"

"You get my heart, as well." He smiled. "Which I had no intention of losing to someone."

Carter grinned and wrapped the cross back up. "Sometimes you get what you're after. Even when you don't know you're looking for it."

Feeling quite delighted, she wandered over to a window. When she frowned, he asked what she was looking at.

"There's a . . . This is ridiculous." She leaned forward a little. "There's a red hawk in that tree."

"What's it doing?"

"Just sitting up there. Staring at us." She cleared her throat and looked over at Nick, who'd put his head back into the safe. "Do you believe in that ghost stuff?"

"That Red Hawk haunts my mountain?"

"Yeah."

"I don't know. Sometimes when I'm up there, I feel like someone's watching me. Why?"

"I swear that hawk is staring at me as if it knows . . . Never mind . . ." Carter laughed awkwardly. "I'll go get the gold from the kitchen. And, later, I'll have my head examined for delusional tendencies."

While she was gone, Nick finished reordering the contents of the safe and was about to take his head out of the wall when his hand brushed against the small red box that held his grandmother's diamond. He took the leather case out and flipped the lid open. The diamond gleamed and his eyes flared.

Bingo, he thought, slipping it into his pocket.

They were traveling toward the ferry on the highway when Nick looked over at her. "I've got something I've been meaning to ask you."

"Really?" Carter smiled, thinking that life didn't get any better. The summer sun was streaming down on them, the air was blowing her hair in a soft swirl, and the sexiest man she'd ever seen was looking at her like she was the center of his world.

"It's been a little hard to get through," he said dryly.

"Oh?"

"I figure I better do it now while we're alone."

She felt the car slow and then heard the crackle of loose gravel as Nick pulled over to the side of the road. He'd stopped in the middle of a valley framed by majestic mountains. Fields of grass and wildflowers backed up on either side of them and chickadees and red-winged blackbirds flirted in the still, hot air.

Nick took her hands in his and he leaned in close. There was a long pause. She'd never seen him so serious.

"Carter . . . ." he began. But then he pulled back. "Wait. This isn't right."

Her heart lurched.

"Get out of the car," he commanded, wrenching open his door.

Confused and more than a little curious, Carter did the same.

They came together in front of the Porsche and she watched in shock as he got down on one knee.

"Oh my God," she said breathlessly.

There was only one reason a man got down into that

position, she thought with a jolt. And it sure as hell wasn't to shine her shoes.

"Carter—" Nick paused, his eyes shining up at her. There was amusement in them and far more solemn, warm emotions. "What's your middle name?"

"Middle name?"

"You know, the extra one between your first and last," he chided gently.

"Carter is my middle name. My first name is Cordelia."

He cleared his throat.

"Cordelia Carter Wessex, I love you. I want to build a life with you. I want you to be my partner and the one who challenges me and the one who sleeps by my side. I want you to hold and care for and live with. Will you be my wife?"

With her heart pounding, she choked out a yes as she bent down and put her lips against his. "Yes, yes, yes . . ."

Still on his knees, Nick embraced her around the waist. They held on to each other for a long time until she felt him laugh. As he looked up at her, she ran her hand through his thick, dark hair.

"What?" she inquired gently.

"Do you realize I've been trying to ask you to marry me for about a day now?"

"You have?" She laughed with astonishment.

"I gave it a shot in the car on the way home yesterday but you slept through it. I was going to ask you this morning in bed but Buddy interrupted. I was completely prepared heading into the shower but we got . . . distracted. Then I was going to get you on the sailboat but with the gold and the journal . . ."

Carter grinned as Nick got up. He pulled her to him and took her lips in a searing kiss. When they parted, his hand disappeared into his pocket and he took out a small leather box.

"I understand it's customary to give a ring." He turned the box to face her and opened the lid.

Carter gasped at the diamond. With rainbow flashes, it twinkled in the sunlight.

As she looked at the ring, she tried to comprehend her luck and good fortune. She'd come to Farrell Mountain to solve a mystery and had found so much more than she could ever have imagined.

She met Nick's eyes. "It is utterly beautiful."

"It was my grandmother's. She was a lot like you. Fiery, independent, smart. And before you turn it down because you spend your days digging in the dirt, you should know that this ring survived fifty years of aggressive gardening and held up just fine. I'd like it to be yours. And I think she'd have approved as well."

Carter smiled and put out her hand. She felt the weight of the stone settle on her third finger. It fit perfectly.

Nick tenderly brushed her cheek and then kissed her, his lips soft and lingering against hers.

Suddenly, a rumble sounded through the valley, starting low at first and then growing in urgency. They parted and looked to the noise, watching as an eighteen-wheeler came barreling down the highway. As the truck approached, the driver released his air horn, pumping a high, roaring whistle at them. Carter and Nick laughed and waved as the man gave them a thumbs-up while going by.

Their laughter took on a bewildered tone when they saw what was on the side of the truck.

In wide, bold script, the lettering said, *Red Hawk Freightlines.*

And then the picture of an enormous red-tailed hawk, soaring with wings outstretched, streaked by them.

Read on for a sneak peek of
another contemporary romance by
New York Times bestselling author
J. R. Ward writing as Jessica Bird

LEAPING HEARTS

Available from Signet.

FROM THE fringes of the crowd, Devlin McCloud watched the scene unravel with cynical eyes. He'd known exactly when the horse was going to bolt. The stallion's massive haunches had tensed hard before the animal sprang forward and he picked the perfect time to make his move. At that exact moment, the groom holding the lead had let his attention lapse, looking in the opposite direction and laughing at someone behind him. Like a flash, the horse took off and, courtesy of his distraction, the young hand had been dragged through the dirt and almost trampled. By the time the kid let go of the lead, he looked like a breaded cutlet.

All around, people started scrambling to get out of the way, but Devlin, with his bad leg, wasn't able to move as fast as the rest of the crowd. Relying on his cane, he made his way to the edge of the ring in the awkward gait he despised, all the while keeping his eye on the horse.

He didn't stare just because he wanted to avoid getting run over. He was captivated. The stallion moved with a grace and force Devlin hadn't seen in a long time. It reminded him of—

He blocked the thought of Mercy. It had been almost a year since the accident, nearly a year since he'd had to put her down, but the pain was still unbearable. Once more, he wondered how long it was going to take to get over his grief, and feared the ache in his chest, like the one in his leg, was never going to go away.

When he finally reached the rail, he ducked out of the ring and then watched as order disintegrated. The crowd was still milling about like lemmings looking for water and he watched with amusement as several men tried to corral the horse.

The stallion's too smart for that trick, he thought, not at all surprised when the animal bolted at the men.

Devlin shook his head.

If someone could get a handle on that horse and channel all that energy, they'd have a hot ticket on their hands, he decided. It'd be like harnessing nuclear fission but the potential locked in the beast might just make the risk of getting burned worth it.

The stallion flashed by him, head held high, tail cocked and billowing in his wake.

Devlin thought about the horse's new owners. He hoped Sutherland Stables knew what they'd signed on for but doubted they were up to the task. The stable had a lot of money, great-looking tack and a swimming pool to play in, but he knew more about their toys than their feats of training. He had a feeling the stallion was going to put them to the test.

With an echo of remembered passion for his career, he thought how much he wished he could tackle the beast. As envy burned in his veins, he looked down at his leg with disgust. He was used to being in the ring, not at ringside. The distance between the two was vast and, after a year, he was still an uneasy traveler of the stretch of emptiness that separated where he'd been and where he was.

His gaze shifted back to the chaos and then sharpened as he watched a young woman step into the ring and approach the horse. She was tall and thin but her body was strong and he forgot all about the stallion. He couldn't see her face so he moved to try to get a better look. He wondered who she was. A groom? One of the auction's hands? He knew if he'd seen her before, he'd remember. There was something about the way she moved that was unforgettable.

Devlin watched as she walked toward the stallion with confidence, her hips swaying, her long legs carrying her across the ring. He felt like he'd been kneed in the gut as a strange ache settled into his body. He couldn't look away from the woman and his hand gripped his cane as she stopped in front of the stallion. Unlike the stable hand, her focus on the animal was unwavering and she was calm as she put her hands in her pockets.

Atta girl, Devlin thought with approval. Nice and slow. No big movements.

He watched the horse and the woman size each other up. The contrast between the two was striking. The animal, dark and fierce. The woman, slender and steady. Still, as she talked to the great black beast, it was immediately apparent there was something special happening between them. And then the stallion blew off her hat, clearly fishing for some sort of reaction, and, when he got none, dropped his head. It wasn't a surrender, more like an accommodation that was freely revocable. The instant her hand took the lead, Devlin, like the rest of the crowd, let out a sigh of relief.

He was really impressed. Like all daredevil feats, it had taken courage and stupidity for her to get that close to the stallion. Granted, she'd been smart in the way she did it, showing the kind of sense a person gets only after they spend a lifetime around unpredictable animals. The danger had been there all along, however, and Devlin was glad she hadn't been hurt.

And then the real miracle happened.

The stallion let her lead him. Feigning boredom, so he didn't appear to be giving in, the giant horse had let her take him from the ring. It was a small pledge of trust.

As the crowd dispersed, Devlin limped out to the center of the ring. Bending down, he picked up the woman's hat. The stately logo of Sutherland Stables, two Ss intertwined with ivy, was embroidered on the front.

He went in search of the woman.

*   *   *

"I'm not going to let you bring him back to the stables," Peter was saying to A.J. as they stood in front of the stallion's stall.

While her stepbrother continued yelling at her, she was absorbed by Sabbath, who had his head out in the aisle. The stallion seemed to be regarding Peter with the same level of interest she was. Which wasn't much.

"For heaven's sake," she finally broke in. "Sabbath is coming home and everything is going to be fine as soon as you drop this nonsense and get out of my way."

"That horse is not boarding at the stables."

"What are you suggesting—I bring him to the house? Your mother will hate the hoofprints all over those Persian carpets she insisted on buying. And besides, I don't think they make an equine equivalent of a doggie door."

She and Peter had been back living at her father's mansion since they'd both graduated from college. It created an awkward situation because of the strain between them but the location was conveniently close to the stables for her and luxurious enough to satisfy Peter. She knew her father wanted them home but his second wife was less magnanimous. Regina Conrad, Peter's mother and Garrett Sutherland's wife for the past eighteen years, always wanted her son close by but was less than enthusiastic about A.J.'s presence in the elegant home.

Peter pushed his chin forward. "I'm not going to argue about this. I warned you not to buy him. I've tried to be reasonable with you but, as usual, I'm getting nowhere."

A.J. was beginning to lose composure as frustration got the better of her. Struggling not to lose her temper, she brought a hand to her throat where a diamond solitaire dangled from a slender chain. It was the one thing she had of her own mother's, and as she rubbed the glittering stone between her thumb and forefinger, she tried to calm down.

"Peter, trust me. I can turn him around. I'm going to work with him, one-on-one."

"Not if I refuse to pay for him, you won't."

She turned her focus on Peter. "You can't be serious."

"One phone call to the office here and you're off the charge account."

"You can't do that."

"Try me."

"Well, then I'll just write a check from my personal account."

Peter paused, weighing his next move. "Your father isn't going to let you ride that stallion."

"He never interferes with my training."

"I'll bet that changes when I tell him all about your little friend's reputation for throwing riders. Not to mention his skills at crowd control."

"Look, you don't have to blow this out of proportion." A.J. let the stone fall back against the skin of her throat. "He'll be one horse out of fifty at the stables. You'll barely know he's there."

"It's not the ratio that bothers me. This animal is malevolent and dangerous. I don't want a mass exodus out of the barns. I have to protect my business."

"Let me remind you: Sutherland Stables is half mine."

"You do the riding part. I handle the business. And that's thirty thousand dollars of money I'm in charge of that you just threw out a window."

"In stud fees alone, this stallion will make thirty grand look like couch change."

"For what? The dubious pleasure of his company? I doubt it."

"When he's a champion, you can bet he'll be profitable."

"You don't know if that horse can compete in anything other than a bowling tournament. Knocking down people seems to be his forte, not jumping fences."

"He's been shown before."

"Only to be a horror in the ring. That's hardly a recommendation for a stud."

"It's in him."

"She's right."

A J. turned to see who had agreed with her and found herself looking at a legend.

Her breath caught in her throat as her body temperature soared. With her cap in one hand, Devlin McCloud was standing close enough for her to see the flecks of green in his hazel eyes. Her heart started to pound as she responded to an electric current that flared when they looked at each other.

Although she knew his face well from all the press he'd received throughout his career, it was the first time she'd ever been up close to the man, and she was stunned. If the champion was devastatingly handsome staring out of the cover of a magazine, he was downright mesmerizing in person. Her body began to tingle.

My God, he's beautiful, she thought.

The man was just over six feet tall, with broad shoulders, strong arms and a stance that was tough and confident. He looked out on the world from a pair of deep-set, highly intelligent eyes which were at the moment trained on her like searchlights. His hair was dark and brushed off his forehead, thanks to a cowlick that was in just the right place, and his skin was tanned from time in the sun. Unlike Peter, he was dressed as she was, in blue jeans and a work shirt, but with the command he held himself, he could have been wearing a dishrag and he'd have looked like he owned the place.

It really was *the* Devlin McCloud.

There were few in the equestrian world who didn't know him. He was a maverick, a national sports presence, the former captain of the Olympic Equestrian Team, a multiple gold medal winner and one of the best show jumpers the country had ever produced. And if he hadn't been known because of his accomplishments, his tragedy would have sealed the buzz on him. A.J.'s eyes flickered over his legs and she saw his flash of annoyance as he caught the glance.

"I believe this is yours." He held out her cap.

His voice was deep and sensuous and had a kind of gravel in it that reverberated through her ears and down into her spine. Although he'd been interviewed on national TV and radio numerous times, it was the first time she'd heard him speak live. Even though she knew so much about him, and his private stable was not far from the Sutherland compound, she'd never spoken with him before. That wasn't unusual. The man let few people get near him.

Aware she was staring, A.J. took the hat and confronted Peter. "You see? If anyone is likely to know a champion, it's him."

"I didn't say he was going to be a champion."

She turned back around in surprise. "But you agreed with me."

"I think he's got jumping in his blood. Being a champion is something else entirely."

That voice of his sounded delicious and she found herself preoccupied with the way his lips moved over the words. They were perfectly molded lips, she decided, the lower one more full, the upper curling over straight white teeth. She struggled to keep her train of thought.

Read on for a sneak peek of
New York Times bestselling author
J. R. Ward's Novel of the Fallen Angels

ENVY

Available from Signet.

Two houses down from Detective Thomas DelVecchio's, Internal Affairs Officer Sophia Reilly was behind the wheel of her unmarked and partially blinded.

"By all that is holy . . ." She rubbed her eyes. "Do you not believe in curtains?"

As she prayed for the image of a spectacularly naked colleague to fade from her retinas, she seriously rethought her decision to do the stakeout herself. She was exhausted, for one thing—or had been before she'd seen just about everything Veck had to offer.

Take out the *just*.

One bene was that she was really frickin' awake now, thank you very much—she might as well have licked two fingers and shoved them into a socket: a full-frontal like that was enough to give her the perm she'd wanted back when she was thirteen.

Muttering to herself, she dropped her hands into her lap again. And gee whiz, as she stared at the dash, all she saw . . . was everything she'd seen.

Yeah, wow, on some men, no clothes was so much more than just *naked*.

And to think she'd almost missed the show. She'd parked her sedan and just called in her position when the upstairs lights had gone on and she had gotten a gander at the vista of a bedroom. Easing back into her seat, it hadn't dawned on her exactly where the unobstructed view was going to take them both—she'd just been interested that it appeared to be nothing but a bald lightbulb on the ceiling of what had to be the master suite.

Then again, bachelor pad decorating tended to be either storage-unit crammed or Death Valley–barren.

Veck's was obviously the Death Valley variety.

Except suddenly she hadn't been thinking about interior decorating, because her suspect had stepped into the bathroom and flipped the switch.

Hellllllllo, big boy.

In too many ways to count.

"Stop thinking about it . . . stop thinking about—"

Closing her eyes again didn't help: If she'd reluctantly noticed before how well he filled out his clothes, now she knew exactly why. He was heavily muscled, and given that he didn't have any hair on his chest, there was nothing to obscure those hard pecs and that six-pack and the carved ridges that went over his hips.

Matter of fact, when it came to manscaping, all he had was a dark stripe that ran between his belly button and his . . .

You know, maybe size did matter, she thought.

"Oh, for chrissakes."

In an attempt to get her brain focused on something, anything more appropriate, she leaned forward and looked out the opposite window. As far as she could tell, the house directly across from him had privacy shades across every available view. Good move, assuming he paraded around like that every night.

Then again, maybe the husband had strung those puppies up so that his wife didn't get a case of the swoons.

Bracing herself, she glanced back at Veck's place. The lights were off upstairs and she had to hope now that he was dressed and on the first floor, he stayed that way.

God, what a night.

Was it possible Veck had torn apart that suspect? She didn't think so.

But he did—even though he couldn't remember a thing.

Whatever, she was still waiting for any evidence that came from the scene, and there were coyotes in those woods. Bears. Cats of the non–Meow Mix variety. Chances were good that the suspect had come walking through there with the scent of dried blood on his clothes and something with four paws had viewed him as a Happy Meal. Veck could well have tried to step in and been shoved to the side. After all, he'd been rubbing his temples like he'd had pain there, and God knew head trauma had been known to cause short-term memory loss.

The lack of physical evidence on him supported the theory; that was for sure.

And yet . . .

God, that father of his. It was impossible not to factor him in even a little.

Like every criminal justice major, she'd studied Thomas DelVecchio Sr. as part of her courses—but she'd also spent considerable time on him in her deviant-psych classes. Veck's dad was your classic serial killer: smart, cunning, committed to his "craft," utterly remorseless. And yet, having watched videos of his interviews with police, he came across as handsome, compelling, and affable. Classy. Very non-monster.

But then again, like a lot of psychopaths, he'd cultivated an image and sustained it with care. He'd been very successful as a dealer of antiquities, although his establishment in that haughty, lofty world of money and privilege had been a complete self-invention. He'd come from absolutely nothing, but had had a knack for charming rich people—as well as a talent for going overseas and coming back with ancient artifacts and statues that were extremely marketable. It wasn't until the killings had started to surface that his business practices came under scrutiny, and to this day, no one had any idea where he'd found the stuff he had—it was almost as if he'd had a treasure trove somewhere in the Middle East.

He certainly hadn't helped authorities sort things out, but what were they going to do to him? He was already on death row.

Not for much longer, though, evidently.

What had Veck's mother been like—

The knock on the window next to her head was like a shot ringing out, and she had her weapon palmed and pointed to the sound less than a heartbeat afterward.

Veck was standing in the street next to her car, his hands up, his wet hair glossy in the streetlights.

Lowering her weapon, she put her window down with a curse.

"Quick reflexes, Officer," he murmured.

"Do you want to get shot, Detective?"

"I said your name. Twice. You were deep in thought."

Thanks to what she'd seen in that bathroom, the flannel shirt and academy sweats he had on seemed eminently removable, the kind of duds that wouldn't resist a shove up or a pull down. But come on, like she hadn't seen every aisle in his grocery store already?

"You want my clothes now?" he said as he held up a trash bag.

"Yes, thank you." She accepted the load through her window and put the things down on the floor. "Boots, too?"

As he nodded, he said, "Can I bring you some coffee? I don't have much in my kitchen, but I think I can find a clean mug and I got instant."

"Thanks. I'm okay."

There was a pause. "There a reason you're not looking me in the eye, Officer?"

I just saw you buck naked, Detective. "Not at all." She pegged him right in the peepers. "You should get inside. It's chilly."

"The cold doesn't bother me. You going to be here all night?"

"Depends."

"On whether I am, right."

"Yup."

He nodded, and then glanced around casually like they were nothing but neighbors chatting about the weather. So calm. So confident. Just like his father.

"Can I be honest with you?" he said abruptly.

"You'd better be, Detective."

"I'm still surprised you let me go."

She ran her hands around the steering wheel. "May I be honest with you?"

"Yeah."

"I let you go because I really don't think you did it."

"I was at the scene and I had blood on me."

"You called nine-one-one, you didn't leave, and that kind of death is very messy to perpetrate."

"Maybe I cleaned up."

"There wasn't a shower in those woods as far as I saw."

Do. Not. Think. Of. Him. Naked.

When he started to shake his head like he was going to argue, Reilly cut him off. "Why are you trying to convince me I'm wrong?"

That shut him up. At least for a moment. Then he said in a low voice, "Are you going to feel safe tailing me."

"Why wouldn't I?"

For the first time, emotion bled through his cool expression, and her heart stopped: There was fear in his eyes, as if he didn't trust himself.

"Veck," she said softly, "is there anything I don't know."

He crossed his arms over that big chest of his and his weight went back and forth on his hips as if he were thinking. Then he hissed, and started rubbing his temple.

"I've got nothing," he muttered. "Listen, just do us both a favor, Officer. Keep that gun close by."

He didn't look back as he turned and walked across the street.

He wasn't wearing any shoes, she realized.

Putting up the window, she watched him go into the house and shut the door. Then the lights in the house went out, except for the hallway on the second floor.

Settling in, she eased down in her seat and stared at

all those windows. Shortly thereafter, a massive shadow walked into the living room—or rather, appeared to be dragging something? Like a couch?

Then Veck sat down and his head disappeared as if he were stretching out on something.

It was almost like they were sleeping side by side. Well, except for the walls of the house, the stretch of scruffy spring lawn, the sidewalk, the asphalt, and the steel cage of her Crown Victoria.

Reilly's lids drifted down, but that was a function of the angle of her head. She wasn't tired and she wasn't worried about falling asleep. She was wide-awake in the dark interior of the car.

And yet she reached over and hit the door-lock button.

Just in case.

#1 *NEW YORK TIMES* BESTSELLING AUTHOR

J. R. WARD

WRITING AS

JESSICA BIRD

An Irresistible Bachelor

Art conservator Callie Burke's new assignment is restoring
a masterpiece owned by ruthless, wealthy, and sexy
politico Jack Walker. When she's persuaded to move into
Jack's sprawling estate to finish the job, a mere business
proposition turns into something far more
complicated—and passionate.

"A love story too beautiful for words."
—Best Reviews

**Available wherever books are sold or at
penguin.com**

facebook.com/LoveAlwaysBooks

S0372

Max Apple

The Oranging of America

and other stories

"The Oranging of America"—every story in this book, in fact—is fiction, and its content derives entirely from my imagination. Where I have used real names or what seem to be physical descriptions of real people, it is done purely in the interest of fiction. In any serious sense any similarities between these stories and the real lives of any person living or dead are unintended and coincidental.

—Max Apple

*This low-priced Bantam Book
has been completely reset in a type face
designed for easy reading, and was printed
from new plates. It contains the complete
text of the original hard-cover edition.*
NOT ONE WORD HAS BEEN OMITTED.

THE ORANGING OF AMERICA AND OTHER STORIES
*A Bantam Book / published by arrangement with
Grossman Publishers
A division of The Viking Press*

PRINTING HISTORY
*Grossman edition published December 1976
2nd printing . . . February 1977*
Some of these stories originally appeared in American
Review, Esquire, The Georgia Review, New and Experimental
Literature, *and* Ohio Review.
Bantam edition / January 1978

ISBN 0-553-10992-8

Published simultaneously in the United States and Canada

Bantam Books are published by Bantam Books, Inc. Its trademark, consisting of the words "Bantam Books" and the portrayal of a bantam, is registered in the United States Patent Office and in other countries. Marca Registrada. Bantam Books, Inc., 666 Fifth Avenue, New York, New York 10019.

*In memory of my father
and my grandmother*

and for Ted Solotaroff

Contents

The Oranging of America

From the outside it looked like any ordinary 1964 Cadillac limousine. In the expensive space between the driver and passengers, where some installed bars or even bathrooms, Mr. Howard Johnson kept a tidy ice-cream freezer in which there were always at least eighteen flavors on hand, though Mr. Johnson ate only vanilla. The freezer's power came from the battery with an independent auxiliary generator as a back-up system. Although now Howard Johnson means primarily motels, Millie, Mr. HJ, and Otis Brighton, the chauffeur, had not forgotten that ice cream was the cornerstone of their empire. Some of the important tasting was still done in the car. Mr. HJ might have reports in his pocket from sales executives and marketing analysts, from home economists and chemists, but not until Mr. Johnson reached over the lowered Plexiglas to spoon a taste or two into the expert waiting mouth of Otis Brighton did he make any final flavor decision. He might go ahead with butterfly shrimp, with candy kisses, and with packaged chocolate-chip cookies on the opinion of the specialists, but in ice cream he trusted only Otis. From the back seat Howard Johnson would keep his eye on the rearview mirror, where the reflection of pleasure or disgust showed itself in the dark eyes of Otis Brighton no matter what the driving conditions. He could be stalled in a commuter rush with the engine overheating and a dripping oil pan, and still a taste of the right kind never went unappreciated.

When Otis finally said, "Mr. Howard, that shore is sumpin, that one is um-hum. That is it, my man, that is it." Then and not until then did Mr. HJ finally decide to go ahead with something like banana-fudge-ripple royale.

Mildred rarely tasted and Mr. HJ was addicted to one scoop of vanilla every afternoon at three, eaten from his aluminum dish with a disposable plastic spoon. The duties of Otis, Millie, and Mr. Johnson were so divided that they rarely infringed upon one another in the car, which was their office. Neither Mr. HJ nor Millie knew how to drive, Millie and Otis understood little of financing and leasing, and Mr. HJ left the compiling of the "Traveling Reports" and "The Howard Johnson Newsletter" strictly to the literary style of his longtime associate, Miss Mildred Bryce. It was an ideal division of labor, which, in one form or another, had been in continuous operation for well over a quarter of a century.

While Otis listened to the radio behind his sound-proof Plexiglas, while Millie in her small, neat hand compiled data for the newsletter, Mr. HJ liked to lean back into the spongy leather seat looking through his specially tinted windshield at the fleeting land. Occasionally, lulled by the hum of the freezer, he might doze off, his large pink head lolling toward the shoulder of his blue suit, but there was not too much that Mr. Johnson missed, even in advanced age.

Along with Millie he planned their continuous itinerary as they traveled. Mildred would tape a large green relief map of the United States to the Plexiglas separating them from Otis. The mountains on the map were light brown and seemed to melt toward the valleys like the crust of a fresh apple pie settling into cinnamon surroundings. The existing HJ houses (Millie called the restaurants and motels houses) were marked by orange dots, while projected future sites bore white dots. The deep green map with its brown mountains and colorful dots seemed much more alive than the miles that twinkled past Mr. Johnson's gaze, and nothing gave the ice-cream king greater pleasure than watching Mildred with her fine touch, and using the original crayon, turn an empty white dot into an orange fulfillment.

"It's like a seed grown into a tree, Millie," Mr. HJ liked to say at such moments when he contemplated the map and saw that it was good.

They had started traveling together in 1925: Mildred, then a secretary to Mr. Johnson, a young man with two restaurants and a dream of hospitality, and Otis, a twenty-year-old busboy and former driver of a Louisiana mule. When Mildred graduated from college, her father, a Michigan doctor who kept his money in a blue steel box under the examining table, encouraged her to try the big city. He sent her a monthly allowance. In those early days she always had more than Mr. Johnson, who paid her $16.50 a week and meals. In the first decade they traveled only on weekends, but every year since 1936 they had spent at least six months on the road, and it might have gone on much longer if Mildred's pain and the trouble in New York with Howard Jr. had not come so close together.

They were all stoical at the Los Angeles International Airport. Otis waited at the car for what might be his last job while Miss Bryce and Mr. Johnson traveled toward the New York plane along a silent moving floor. Millie stood beside Howard while they passed a mural of a Mexican landscape and some Christmas drawings by fourth graders from Watts. For forty years they had been together in spite of Sonny and the others, but at this most recent appeal from New York Millie urged him to go back. Sonny had cabled, "My God, Dad, you're sixty-nine years old, haven't you been a gypsy long enough? Board meeting December third with or without you. Policy changes imminent."

Normally, they ignored Sonny's cables, but this time Millie wanted him to go, wanted to be alone with the pain that had recently come to her. She had left Howard holding the new canvas suitcase in which she had packed her three notebooks of regional reports along with his aluminum dish, and in a moment of real despair she had even packed the orange crayon. When Howard boarded Flight 965 he looked old to Millie.

His feet dragged in the wing-tipped shoes, the hand she shook was moist, the lip felt dry, and as he passed from her sight down the entry ramp Mildred Bryce felt a fresh new ache that sent her hobbling toward the car. Otis had unplugged the freezer, and the silence caused by the missing hum was as intense to Millie as her abdominal pain.

It had come quite suddenly in Albuquerque, New Mexico, at the grand opening of a 210-unit house. She did not make a fuss. Mildred Bryce had never caused trouble to anyone, except perhaps to Mrs. HJ. Millie's quick precise actions, angular face, and thin body made her seem birdlike, especially next to Mr. HJ, six three with splendid white hair accenting his dark blue gabardine suits. Howard was slow and sure. He could sit in the same position for hours while Millie fidgeted on the seat, wrote memos, and filed reports in the small gray cabinet that sat in front of her and parallel to the ice-cream freezer. Her health had always been good, so at first she tried to ignore the pain. It was gas: it was perhaps the New Mexico water or the cooking oil in the fish dinner. But she could not convince away the pain. It stayed like a match burning around in her belly, etching itself into her as the round HJ emblem was so symmetrically embroidered into the bedspread, which she had kicked off in the flush that accompanied the pain. She felt as if her sweat would engulf the foam mattress and crisp percale sheet. Finally, Millie brought up her knees and made a ball of herself as if being as small as possible might make her misery disappear. It worked for everything except the pain. The little circle of hot torment was all that remained of her, and when finally at sometime in the early morning it left, it occurred to her that perhaps she had struggled with a demon and been suddenly relieved by the coming of daylight. She stepped lightly into the bathroom and before a full-length mirror (new in HJ motels exclusively) saw herself whole and unmarked, but sign enough to Mildred was her smell, damp and musty, sign enough that something had begun and that something else would therefore necessarily end.

II

Before she had the report from her doctor, Howard Jr.'s message had given her the excuse she needed. There was no reason why Millie could not tell Howard she was sick, but telling him would be admitting too much to herself. Along with Howard Johnson Millie had grown rich beyond dreams. Her inheritance, the $100,000 from her father's steel box in 1939, went directly to Mr. Johnson, who desperately needed it, and the results of that investment brought Millie enough capital to employ two people at the Chase Manhattan with the management of her finances. With money beyond the hope of use, she had vacationed all over the world and spent some time in the company of celebrities, but the reality of her life, like his, was in the back seat of the limousine, waiting for that point at which the needs of the automobile and the human body met the undeviating purpose of the highway and momentarily conquered it.

Her life was measured in rest stops. She, Howard, and Otis had found them out before they existed. They knew the places to stop between Buffalo and Albany, Chicago and Milwaukee, Toledo and Columbus, Des Moines and Minneapolis, they knew through their own bodies, measured in hunger and discomfort in the '30s and '40s when they would stop at remote places to buy land and borrow money, sensing in themselves the hunger that would one day be upon the place. People were wary and Howard had trouble borrowing (her $100,000 had perhaps been the key) but invariably he was right. Howard knew the land, Mildred thought, the way the Indians must have known it. There were even spots along the way where the earth itself seemed to make men stop. Howard had a sixth sense that would sometimes lead them from the main roads to, say, a dark green field in Iowa or

Kansas. Howard, who might have seemed asleep,
would rap with his knuckles on the Plexiglas, causing
the knowing Otis to bring the car to such a quick stop
that Millie almost flew into her filing cabinet. And
before the emergency brake had settled into its final
prong, Howard Johnson was into the field and after
the scent. While Millie and Otis waited, he would
walk it out slowly. Sometimes he would sit down,
disappearing in a field of long and tangled weeds, or
he might find a large smooth rock to sit on while he
felt some secret vibration from the place. Turning his
back to Millie, he would mark the spot with his urine
or break some of the clayey earth in his strong pink
hands, sifting it like flour for a delicate recipe. She
had actually seen him chew the grass, getting down
on all fours like an animal and biting the tops without
pulling the entire blade from the soil. At times he
ran in a slow jog as far as his aging legs would carry
him. Whenever he slipped out of sight behind the
uneven terrain, Millie felt him in danger, felt that
something alien might be there to resist the civilizing
instinct of Howard Johnson. Once when Howard had
been out of sight for more than an hour and did not
respond to their frantic calls, Millie sent Otis into the
field and in desperation flagged a passing car.

"Howard Johnson is lost in that field," she told the
surprised driver. "He went in to look for a new location
and we can't find him now."

"The restaurant Howard Johnson?" the man asked.

"Yes. Help us please."

The man drove off, leaving Millie to taste in his
exhaust fumes the barbarism of an ungrateful public.
Otis found Howard asleep in a field of light blue wild
flowers. He had collapsed from the exertion of his run.
Millie brought water to him, and when he felt better,
right there in the field, he ate his scoop of vanilla on
the very spot where three years later they opened the
first fully air-conditioned motel in the world. When
she stopped to think about it, Millie knew they were
more than businessmen, they were pioneers.

And once, while on her own, she had the feeling too. In 1951 when she visited the Holy Land there was an inkling of what Howard must have felt all the time. It happened without any warning on a bus crowded with tourists and resident Arabs on their way to the Dead Sea. Past ancient Sodom the bus creaked and bumped, down, down, toward the lowest point on earth, when suddenly in the midst of the crowd and her stomach queasy with the motion of the bus, Mildred Bryce experienced an overwhelming calm. A light brown patch of earth surrounded by a few pale desert rocks overwhelmed her perception, seemed closer to her than the Arab lady in the black flowered dress pushing her basket against Millie at that very moment. She wanted to stop the bus. Had she been near the door she might have actually jumped, so strong was her sensitivity to that barren spot in the endless desert. Her whole body ached for it as if in unison, bone by bone. Her limbs tingled, her breath came in short gasps, the sky rolled out of the bus windows and obliterated her view. The Arab lady spat on the floor and moved a suspicious eye over a squirming Mildred.

When the bus stopped at the Dead Sea, the Arabs and tourists rushed to the soupy brine clutching damaged limbs, while Millie pressed twenty dollars American into the dirty palm of a cab-driver who took her back to the very place where the music of her body began once more as sweetly as the first time. While the incredulous driver waited, Millie walked about the place wishing Howard were there to understand her new understanding of his kind of process. There was nothing there, absolutely nothing but pure bliss. The sun beat on her like a wish, the air was hot and stale as a Viennese bathhouse, and yet Mildred felt peace and rest there, and as her cab bill mounted she actually did rest in the miserable barren desert of an altogether unsatisfactory land. When the driver, wiping the sweat from his neck, asked, "Meesez . . . pleeze. Why American woman wants Old Jericho in such kind of heat?" When he said "Jericho," she understood·that this was a place where men had always stopped. In dim antiquity Jacob had perhaps watered a flock here, and not far away Lot's wife paused to scan for the last time the city of her youth. Perhaps Mildred now stood where Abraham had been visited by a vision and, making a rock his pillow, had first put the ease into the earth. Whatever it was, Millie knew from her own experience that rest was created here by historical precedent. She tried to buy that piece of land, going as far as King Hussein's secretary of the interior. She imagined a Palestinian HJ with an orange roof angling toward Sodom, a seafood restaurant, and an oasis of fresh fruit. But the land was in dispute between Israel and Jordan, and even King Hussein, who expressed admiration for Howard Johnson, could not sell to Millie the place of her comfort.

That was her single visionary moment, but sharing them with Howard was almost as good. And to end all this, to finally stay in her eighteenth-floor Santa Monica penthouse, where the Pacific dived into California, this seemed to Mildred a paltry conclusion to an adventurous life. Her doctor said it was not so serious, she had a bleeding ulcer and must watch her diet. The prognosis was, in fact, excellent. But Mildred, fifty-six and alone in California, found the doctor less comforting than most of the rest stops she had experienced.

III

California, right after the Second War, was hardly a civilized place for travelers. Millie, HJ, and Otis had a twelve-cylinder '47 Lincoln and snaked along five days between Sacramento and Los Angeles. "Comfort, comfort," said HJ as he surveyed the redwood forest and the bubbly surf while it slipped away from Otis, who had rolled his trousers to chase the ocean away during a stop near San Francisco. Howard Johnson was contemplative in California. They had never been in the West before. Their route, always slightly new, was yet bound by Canada, where a person couldn't get a tax break, and roughly by the Mississippi as a western frontier. Their journeys took them up the eastern seaboard and through New England to the early reaches of the Midwest, stopping at the plains of Wisconsin and the cool crisp edge of Chicago where two HJ lodges twinkled at the lake.

One day in 1947 while on the way from Chicago to Cairo, Illinois, HJ looked long at the green relief maps. While Millie kept busy with her filing, HJ loosened the tape and placed the map across his soft round knees. The map jiggled and sagged, the Mid- and Southwest hanging between his legs. When Mildred finally noticed that look, he had been staring at the map for perhaps fifteen minutes, brooding over it, and Millie knew something was in the air.

HJ looked at that map the way some people looked down from an airplane trying to pick out the familiar from the colorful mass receding beneath them. Howard Johnson's eye flew over the land—over the Tetons, over the Sierra Nevada, over the long thin gouge of the Canyon flew his gaze—charting his course by rest stops the way an antique mariner might have gazed at the stars.

"Millie," he said just north of Carbondale, "Millie . . ." He looked toward her, saw her fingers engaged and her thumbs circling each other in anticipation. He looked at Millie and saw that she saw what he saw. "Millie"—HJ raised his right arm and its shadow spread across the continent like a prophecy—"Millie, what if we turn right at Cairo and go that way?" California, already peeling on the green map, balanced on HJ's left knee like a happy child.

Twenty years later Mildred settled in her eighteenth-floor apartment in the building owned by Lawrence Welk. Howard was in New York, Otis and the car waited in Arizona. The pain did not return as powerfully as it had appeared that night in Albuquerque, but it hurt with dull regularity and an occasional streak of dark blood from her bowels kept her mind on it even on painless days.

Directly beneath her gaze were the organized activities of the golden-age groups, tiny figures playing bridge or shuffleboard or looking out at the water from their benches as she sat on her sofa and looked out at them and the fluffy ocean. Mildred did not regret family life. The HJ houses were her offspring. She had watched them blossom from the rough youngsters of the '40s with steam heat and even occasional kitchen-ettes into cool mature adults with king-sized beds, color TVs, and room service. Her late years were spent comfortably in the modern houses just as one might enjoy in age the benefits of a child's prosperity. She regretted only that it was probably over.

But she did not give up completely until she received a personal letter one day telling her that she was eligible for burial insurance until age eighty. A $1000 policy would gurantee a complete and dignified service. Millie crumpled the advertisement, but a few hours later called her Los Angeles lawyer. As she suspected, there were no plans, but as the executor of the estate he would assume full responsibility, sub-ject of course to her approval.

"I'll do it myself," Millie had said, but she could not bring herself to do it. The idea was too alien. In more than forty years Mildred had not gone a day without a shower and change of underclothing. Everything about her suggested order and precision. Her finger-nails were shaped so that the soft meat of the tips could stroke a typewriter without damaging the apex of a nail, her arch slid over a 6B shoe like an egg in a shell, and never in her adult life did Mildred recall having vomited. It did not seem right to suddenly let all this sink into the dark green earth of Forest Lawn because some organ or other developed a hole as big as a nickel. It was not right and she wouldn't do it. Her first idea was to stay in the apartment, to write it into the lease if necessary. She had the lawyer make an appointment for her with Mr. Welk's manage-ment firm, but canceled it the day before. "They will just think I'm crazy," she said aloud to herself, "and they'll bury me anyway."

She thought of cryonics while reading a biography of William Chesebrough, the man who invented petroleum jelly. Howard had known him and often mentioned that his own daily ritual of the scoop of vanilla was like old Chesebrough's two teaspoons of Vaseline every day. Chesebrough lived to be ninety. In the biography it said that after taking the daily dose of Vaseline, he drank three cups of green tea to melt everything down, rested for twelve minutes, and then felt fit as a young man, even in his late eighties. When he died they froze his body and Millie had her idea. The Vaseline people kept him in a secret laboratory somewhere near Cleveland and claimed he was in better condition than Lenin, whom the Russians kept hermetically sealed, but at room temperature.

In the phone book she found the Los Angeles Cryonic Society and asked it to send her information. It all seemed very clean. The cost was $200 a year for maintaining the cold. She sent the pamphlet to her lawyer to be sure that the society was legitimate. It wasn't much money, but, still, if they were charlatans, she didn't want them to take advantage of her even if she would never know about it. They were aboveboard, the lawyer said. "The interest on a tenthousand-dollar trust fund would pay about five hundred a year," the lawyer said, "and they only charge two hundred dollars. Still, who knows what the cost might be in say two hundred years?" To be extra safe, they put $25,000 in trust for eternal maintenance, to be eternally overseen by Longstreet, Williams, and their eternal heirs. When it was arranged, Mildred felt better than she had in weeks.

IV

Four months to the day after she had left Howard at the Los Angeles International Airport, he returned for Mildred without the slightest warning. She was in her housecoat and had not even washed the night cream from her cheeks when she saw through the viewing space in her door the familiar long pink jowls, even longer in the distorted glass.

"Howard," she gasped, fumbling with the door, and in an instant he was there picking her up as he might a child or an ice-cream cone while her tears fell like dandruff on his blue suit. While Millie sobbed into his soft padded shoulder, HJ told her the good news. "I'm chairman emeritus of the board now. That means no more New York responsibilities. They still have to listen to me because we hold the majority of the stock, but Howard Junior and Keyes will take care of the business. Our main job is new home-owned franchises. And, Millie, guess where we're going first?"

So overcome was Mildred that she could not hold back her sobs even to guess. Howard Johnson put her down, beaming pleasure through his old bright eyes. "Florida," HJ said, then slowly repeated it, "Flor-idda, and guess what we're going to do?"

"Howard," Millie said, swiping at her tears with the filmy lace cuffs of her dressing gown, "I'm so surprised I don't know what to say. You could tell me we're going to the moon and I'd believe you. Just seeing you again has brought back all my hope." They came out of the hallway and sat on the sofa that looked out over the Pacific. HJ, all pink, kept his hands on his knees like paperweights.

"Millie, you're almost right. I can't fool you about anything and never could. We're going down near where they launch the rockets from. I've heard . . ." HJ leaned toward the kitchen as if to check for spies. He looked at the stainless-steel-and-glass table, at the built-in avocado appliances, then leaned his large moist lips toward Mildred's ear. "Walt Disney is planning right this minute a new Disneyland down there. They're trying to keep it a secret, but his brother Roy bought options on thousands of acres. We're going down to buy as much as we can as close in as we can." Howard sparkled. "Millie, don't you see, it's a sure thing."

After her emotional outburst at seeing Howard again, a calmer Millie felt a slight twitch in her upper stomach and in the midst of her joy was reminded of another sure thing.

They would be a few weeks in Los Angeles anyway. Howard wanted to thoroughly scout out the existing Disneyland, so Millie had some time to think it out. She could go, as her heart directed her, with HJ to Florida and points beyond. She could take the future as it happened like a Disneyland ride or she could listen to the dismal eloquence of her ulcer and try to make the best arrangements she could. Howard and Otis would take care of her to the end, there were no doubts about that, and the end would be the end. But if she stayed in this apartment, sure of the arrangements for later, she would miss whatever might still be left before the end. Mildred wished there were some clergyman she could consult, but she had never attended a church and believed in no religious doctrine. Her father had been a firm atheist to the very moment of his office suicide, and she remained a passive nonbeliever. Her theology was the order of her own life. Millie had never deceived herself; in spite of her riches all she truly owned was her life, a pocket of habits in the burning universe. But the habits were careful and clean and they were best represented in the body that was she. Freezing her remains was the closest image she could conjure of eternal life. It might not be eternal and it surely would not be life, but that damp, musty feel, that odor she smelled on herself after the pain, that could be avoided, and who knew what else might be saved from the void for a small initial investment and $200 a year. And if you did not believe in a soul, was there not every reason to preserve a body?

Mrs. Albert of the Cryonic Society welcomed Mildred to a tour of the premises. "See it while you can," she cheerfully told the group (Millie, two men, and a boy with notebook and Polaroid camera). Mrs. Albert, a big woman perhaps in her mid-sixties, carried a face heavy in flesh. Perhaps once the skin had been tight around her long chin and pointed cheekbones, but having lost its spring, the skin merely hung at her neck like a patient animal waiting for the rest of her to join in the decline. From the way she took the concrete stairs down to the vault, it looked as if the wait would be long. "I'm not ready for the freezer yet. I tell every group I take down here, it's gonna be a long time until they get me." Millie believed her. "I may not be the world's smartest cookie"—Mrs. Albert looked directly at Millie—"but a bird in the hand is the only bird I know, huh? That's why when it does come . . . Mrs. A is going to be right here in this facility, and you better believe it. Now, Mr. King on your left"—she pointed to a capsule that looked like a large bullet to Millie— "Mr. King is the gentleman who took me on my first tour, cancer finally but had everything perfectly ready and I would say he was in prime cooling state within seconds and I believe that if they ever cure cancer, and you know they will the way they do most everything nowadays, old Mr. King may be back yet. If anyone got down to low-enough temperature immediately it would be Mr. King." Mildred saw the boy write "Return of the King" in his notebook. "Over here is Mr. and Mizz Winkleman, married sixty years, and went off within a month of each other, a lovely, lovely couple."

While Mrs. Albert continued her necrology and posed for a photo beside the Winklemans, Millie took careful note of the neon-lit room filled with bulletlike capsules. She watched the cool breaths of the group gather like flowers on the steel and vanish without dimming the bright surface. The capsules stood in straight lines with ample walking space between them. To Mrs. Albert they were friends, to Millie it seemed as if she were in a furniture store of the Scandinavian type where elegance is suggested by the absence of material, where straight lines of steel, wood, and glass indicate that relaxation too requires some taste and is not an indifferent sprawl across any soft object that happens to be nearby.

Cemeteries always bothered Millie, but here she felt none of the dread she had expected. She averted

her eyes from the cluttered graveyards they always
used to pass at the tips of cities in the early days.
Fortunately, the superhighways twisted traffic into
the city and away from those desolate marking places
where used-car lots and the names of famous hotels
inscribed on barns often neighbored the dead. Howard
had once commented that never in all his experience
did he have an intuition of a good location near a
cemetery. You could put a lot of things there, you
could put up a bowling alley, or maybe even a theater,
but never a motel, and Millie knew he was right. He
knew where to put his houses but it was Millie who
knew how. From that first orange roof angling toward
the east, the HJ design and the idea had been Millie's.
She had not invented the motel, she had changed it
from a place where you had to be to a place where
you wanted to be. Perhaps, she thought, the Cryonic
Society was trying to do the same for cemeteries.

When she and Howard had started their travels, the
old motel courts huddled like so many dark graves
around the stone marking of the highway. And what
traveler coming into one of those dingy cabins could
watch the watery rust dripping from his faucet without thinking of everything he was missing by being a
traveler . . . his two-stall garage, his wife small in the
half-empty bed, his children with hair the color of
that rust. Under the orange Howard Johnson roof all
this changed. For about the same price you were
redeemed from the road. Headlights did not dazzle
you on the foam mattress and percale sheets, your
sanitized glasses and toilet appliances sparkled like
the mirror behind them. The room was not just there,
it awaited you, courted your pleasure, sat like a young
bride outside the walls of the city wanting only to
please you, you only you on the smoothly pressed
sheets, your friend, your one-night destiny.

As if it were yesterday, Millie recalled right there
in the cryonic vault the moment when she had first
thought the thought that made Howard Johnson
Howard Johnson's. And when she told Howard her
decision that evening after cooking a cheese soufflé

and risking a taste of wine, it was that memory she invoked for both of them, the memory of a cool autumn day in the '30s when a break in their schedule found Millie with a free afternoon in New Hampshire, an afternoon she had spent at the farm of a man who had once been her teacher and remembered her after ten years. Otis drove her out to Robert Frost's farm, where the poet made for her a lunch of scrambled eggs and 7 Up. Millie and Robert Frost talked mostly about the farm, about the cold winter he was expecting and the autumn apples they picked from the trees. He was not so famous then, his hair was only streaked with gray as Howard's was, and she told the poet about what she and Howard were doing, about what she felt about being on the road in America, and Robert Frost said he hadn't been that much but she sounded like she knew and he believed she might be able to accomplish something. He did not remember the poem she wrote in his class but that didn't matter.

"Do you remember, Howard, how I introduced you to him? Mr. Frost, this is Mr. Johnson. I can still see the two of you shaking hands there beside the car. I've always been proud that I introduced you to one another." Howard Johnson nodded his head at the memory, seemed as nostalgic as Millie while he sat in her apartment learning why she would not go to Florida to help bring Howard Johnson's to the new Disneyland.

"And after we left his farm, Howard, remember? Otis took the car in for servicing and left us with some sandwiches on the top of a hill overlooking a town, I don't even remember which one, maybe we never knew the name of it. And we stayed on that hilltop while the sun began to set in New Hampshire. I felt so full of poetry and"—she looked at Howard—"of love, Howard, only about an hour's drive from Robert Frost's farmhouse. Maybe it was just the way we felt then, but I think the sun set differently that night, filtering through the clouds like a big paintbrush making the top of the town all orange. And suddenly I thought what if the tops of our houses were that kind

of orange, what a world it would be, Howard, and my
God, that orange stayed until the last drop of light was
left in it. I didn't feel the cold up there even though
it took Otis so long to get back to us. The feeling we
had about that orange, Howard, that was ours and
that's what I've tried to bring to every house, the way
we felt that night. Oh, it makes me sick to think of
Colonel Sanders, and Big Boy, and Holiday Inn, and
Best Western . . ."

"It's all right, Millie, it's all right." Howard patted
her heaving back. Now that he knew about her ulcer
and why she wanted to stay behind, the mind that had
conjured butterfly shrimp and twenty-eight flavors
set himself a new project. He contemplated Millie
sobbing in his lap the way he contemplated prime
acreage. There was so little of her, less than one
hundred pounds, yet without her Howard Johnson
felt himself no match for the wily Disneys gathering
near the moonport.

He left her in all her sad resignation that evening,
left her thinking she had to give up what remained
here to be sure of the proper freezing. But Howard
Johnson had other ideas. He did not cancel the advance
reservations made for Mildred Bryce along the route
to Florida, nor did he remove her filing cabinet from
the limousine. The man who hosted a nation and
already kept one freezer in his car merely ordered
another, this one designed according to cryonic speci-
fications and presented to Mildred housed in a twelve-
foot orange U-Haul trailer connected to the rear
bumper of the limousine.

"Everything's here," he told the astonished Millie,
who thought Howard had left the week before, "everything is here and you'll never have to be more than
seconds away from it. It's exactly like a refrigerated
truck." Howard Johnson opened the rear door of the
U-Haul as proudly as he had ever dedicated a motel.
Millie's steel capsule shone within, surrounded by an
array of chemicals stored on heavily padded rubber
shelves. The California sun was on her back, but her
cold breath hovered visibly within the U-Haul. No

tears came to Mildred now; she felt relief much as she had felt it that afternoon near ancient Jericho. On Santa Monica Boulevard, in front of Lawrence Welk's apartment building, Mildred Bryce confronted her immortality, a gift from the ice-cream king, another companion for the remainder of her travels. Howard Johnson had turned away, looking toward the ocean. To his blue back and patriarchal white hairs, Mildred said, "Howard, you can do anything," and closing the doors of the U-Haul, she joined the host of the highways, a man with two portable freezers, ready now for the challenge of Disney World.

Selling Out

When he was thirty, my father, a careful man, bought a "piece of the Rock," a twenty-thousand dollar chunk to be exact. At thirty-eight, in good health and during the Korean War, he doubled it. At forty-six with a slightly elevated BP (155/94) they let him buy fifteen thousand additional with a ten-percent premium hike. At fifty he beat the actuarial tables. We thought it was only an upset stomach. He dropped two Alka-Seltzers in a half glass of water and died before they melted. After funeral expenses I was left with $53,000, which the Prudential man wanted me to leave in on a million-dollar policy on myself.

"I'll take the fifty-three," I said.

My father's cousin, H.B., a broker, said, "For safety's sake let's put it in a fund. There you're protected. Who knows what can happen with an individual stock? And far be it from me to take upon myself the responsibility of a discretionary account for my orphaned cousin. However, if you'd like . . ."

"Buy the fund," I said.

The commissions came out to a little over three thousand: that left between forty-nine and fifty thousand. It was in 1965.

I put it all out of mind, worked in a bookstore, and went to community college at night. The fund reinvested the dividends and capital gains. In the hot market of early 1968 I had on one particular day, April 7, $187,000 in the fund. The next April 7 it was down to $81,000. I always check on April 7 because it's the day Dad died. Every Christmas when I get a calendar from H.B.'s office, right after I fold out its clever cardboard leg, I circle April 7 and try to buy the *Journal* for the eighth. I called H.B. in 1969 to tell him I was down $106,000 in one year.

"It's the goddamn war," he said. "It's killing the street. And the back-room mess is worse every day. Be glad you're in a fund. The Dow has been underwater for two years. I've got customers calling me saying, 'H.B., I'm dead, should I sell?' Another year like this and I'll be dead too. You can only take so many losses and that's it. Be glad you're in the fund . . . however if you'd like . . ."

"I'll stay in the fund," I said.

In October 1971 I was thirty, not in love, and remembered the fund. A doctor told me I had high blood pressure, ought to lose weight and get more exercise. I had "stroke potential," he said. I thought about it and decided to strike.

I quit the bookstore, shaved my beard, bought a blue gabardine suit, and started reading the *Journal* every day. I also read *Barron's* and the *Dow Theory Forecast.* I answered a Merrill Lynch ad and received a free Standard and Poor's list of all listed stocks in a little gray paperback that looked like a mouse next to my dictionary.

After a month and a half I realized it was futile for me to study the market and made my move anyway. I had planned to wait until April 7, but I was impatient.

In December, my shoes wet with slush, I slid into H.B.'s office wearing my blue suit.

"Please sell the fund," I said.

"What do you mean, sell the fund?"

"Sell it—write out a sell order. How long will the sale take?"

"A minute. It will take a minute, but why sell? Your fund beats the Dow every year. The market is weak."

"How's the back-room mess?"

"Better," he said. "If Nixon takes care of the inflation. You watch us move. Your fund is worth—Mary, add up these figures please." She came through the open door at his side from where I heard the noise of computers, adding machines, and girl talk. You could smell coffee. In seconds she was back with a slip of white paper for H.B. I noticed her ass when she bent to hand it to him. He looked only at the amount.

"About eighty-seven thousand dollars on today's market."

"Sell it," I said.

"Just like that?"

"Just like that. Are there any commissions?"

"No, you paid them all when you bought in."

"Do I have that money as credit with you right now?"

"As soon as the sale goes through, if you want it."

"Sell it."

"You're sure?"

"I'm sure."

"Mary, sell twelve thousand, four hundred and thirty and a fraction shares of Diversified Fund Ltd." He looked as if large numbers made him sad.

It was 9:07. At 9:11 Mary came back with a confirmation of sale, $87,211.18.

"You can bet one of the fund managers will call me about that sale. It's unusual for them to lose a big chunk all at once. Most people, you know, take it as monthly income. They have faith in the future of the economy."

"I'm going out in the lobby to watch the tape," I said, "and I'm going to start trading against that eighty-seven thousand."

"Trading what? Talk to me a little. How many cousins do I have? You could blow it in an afternoon, everything." Now there were tears in his eyes. I did not doubt his sincerity.

"I might," I said, walking into the lobby where the prices streamed under the ceiling in electric orange. He followed me from his office, and Mary, when I looked back, was peeking from out the back room, leaning way over on one leg.

I sat down in the front row on a padded theater chair. It was like watching a dull French movie. I had a pad and pencil and knew some of the ticker symbols from studying the Standard and Poor's booklet. The first one I recognized was Sony Superscope.

I have nothing against the Japs. The selling price at 9:15 was 18. I wanted to buy in round numbers but 5000 shares came to $90,000.

"Buy forty-five hundred Sony Superscope at eighteen."

On the seat next to me H.B. said, "He's lost his mind." He said it as if I wasn't there.

"Listen," I said, "if you don't want the commissions there are plenty of other brokers." I didn't even look at him but kept my eyes on the board. He added up the price of 4500 shares to be sure I had enough to cover, then he told Mary to buy. Then things were dull for maybe forty-five minutes. Sony was not a hot number at that hour. I watched my purchase go across. It took about a tenth of a second, about as long as it had taken my father's upset stomach to become cardiac arrest.

I smoked some filter-tip Kools that one of the other brokers gave me. H.B. went back to his office. I was almost sorry that I had put everything into the first buy. It made waiting dull. Watching for Sony, I practiced my recognition of the other symbols. I knew only about one in ten. I started checking some in the Standard and Poor's book, but I had only checked Kaiser Aluminum (KL) and US Industries (USI) before I saw Sony Superscope go across at 18¾. H.B. came out and slapped me on the back.

"You knew something, eh? So why couldn't you tell a cousin? Did I ever do anything that wasn't in your best interest?" He slapped me across the shoulders. At 11 Sony hit 19¾ and though I wanted to wait for even numbers, I was bored with SOS and sold. I recognized U.S. Steel and Pabst Brewing and bought a thousand of each. There was enough left to pick up 500 of an unlisted chicken-raising conglomerate that the man on the seat behind me had been watching all morning. At noon I was holding the steel, the beer, and the chickens.

"Mary," I said when I noticed her long thighs in a miniskirt under the flashing orange figures, "would you

run out and get me a strawberry malt and some french
fries from Mr. Quick?"

She hesitated. "We don't usually . . ." Then she must
have caught a high sign from someone in the office
behind me. "Glad to," she said as I gave her a dollar.
She smelled like an Easter egg.

At the noon break I noticed things in the office
surrounding me. The chairs were American Seating
(AmS), the desks Shaw Walker (ShW), the toilet
paper Scott (Sc). On H.B.'s desk was a Ronson pencil
sharpener (Rn), a Sheaffer pen (ShP), and, of course,
the back room was full of IBM (IBM) and Xerox (X).

I asked Mary if I could see the label at the back
of her blouse as she handed me the french fries. She
did not quite blush, waited for a sign, got none, bent
toward me as I rose to read Koret of California (KC)
above her second vertebra.

"Thank you," I said as she slinked toward the computers, glancing back to me the shared secret of size
eight.

I surmised that her underwear was nylon (DuPo).
Through the tinted safety glass (LOF) of H.B.'s outer
office I noticed two consecutive Mercury Montereys
(FM).

That afternoon I traded all of the above. A quarter
point I figured for commissions, a half point might
be a small profit, but I would have the pleasure of
watching the accrual of my father's life move across
the big board. Measured in tenths of a second, my
father and I controlled about two seconds of the
American economy. By 2 p.m. H.B. was constantly at
my side. One entire girl in the back room was assigned
solely to my transactions. She sweated through her
Ban Roll-On (BrM) 51½/62. My only loser was the
chicken conglomerate, down ¼. By 2:30 I had come
back to the $187,000 of April 7, 1968. I put it all into
Occidental Petroleum at 2:35 for two reasons: it was
volume leader of the day, and the President, Armand
Hammer (like the baking soda), was a friend of V. I.
Lenin during the revolution. I sold it at 2:58, making
an extra $41,000.

When the orange lights stopped circling the room, H.B. hugged me. "I'm crazy, not you," he said. "It will be a week before the back room can straighten out what you did today. You're a rich man now . . . you were before."

"That's capitalism," I said. "Mary," I called to the back room. She arose from her computer, stepped over a small hill of puts and calls. I held my arm out from my body at the elbow. She fit like destiny and moved in.

Vegetable Love

I

Ferguson was never crazy about chicken, but red meat he shoveled up between fork and thick bread and cleaned his mustache with the top of his tongue.

Annette Grim taught him otherwise. "I never make love to meat eaters," she said; "it adds the smell of the grave to post-coital depression."

They met at Safeway while he examined Jerusalem artichokes, wondering at the shape and aroma. She was on her way to the health-food island and Ferguson's cart blocked the best route. Just as he had decided to buy the artichokes, Annette pushed the cart aside and he turned to capture, full force, the loaded wire cart upon his groin.

"You poor man," Annette said when she heard his groan, and rushed to him as he leaned against the mushrooms. "You poor, poor, man. I once saw someone get poked in the nuts by an umbrella and they had to call an ambulance." They were alone in the vegetable aisle when she put her long fingers under his zipper, giving comfort as nonchalantly as if she were helping a blind man across the street.

"To me the body is a temple. Would you bring a steak to a temple?"

Later he reminded her that in the original temple they did slaughter animals, smoke the entrails, and did eat the flesh thereof.

"Paganism," said Annette Grim, but by then she had converted him almost beyond argument.

II

His pain blossomed into love. For him she cooked that day a stew of the Jerusalem artichokes, sweet potatoes, turnips, and carrots. Afterward they drank the broth blended with mint leaves, and Ferguson stayed with Annette, gratified by her flesh, but so hungry that at three a.m. he crept from bed and tried to find enough food to sustain him through the night. In her refrigerator she had only brewer's yeast, a coconut, and sprouted mung beans in a baggy thick with mold. In her cupboard were fresh spices from Oregon, a record player, dry mung beans, rolled oats, defatted wheat germ, two rows of empty glass bottles, and a color poster of a bowl of yogurt. Not even bread, he thought, as he slouched toward the bedroom, longing for a McDonald's.

In the first month of their relationship, Ferguson lost fourteen pounds. This was a blessing, since most of it was excess. His clothes, which had been tight, now fit him as they had in 1971 when he weighed one hundred eighty. A sign on her living-room wall reminded him, "The more flesh, the more worms." Yet, rarely from Annette herself did Ferguson hear any direct criticism of his eating habits or his one hundred eighty pounds née one hundred ninety-four. While he marveled at her, his own appetite shrank and his endurance increased. Annette could eat a cup of yogurt and a banana and manage the night in either innocent sleep or full passion without a hunger pain. She was five feet tall and weighed an unvarying one hundred and eight pounds. She was eighty percent protein and water. She used no deodorants, nor did she shave her legs or underarms or cut her hair. She brushed her teeth with baking soda and a one-thousand-sheet roll of toilet tissue could last her a month. She hadn't had a cold since the day after Nixon announced the bombing of Hanoi and Haiphong.

Next to her, Ferguson felt like an ineffective cancer. Full of dead meats, artificial flavors, and additives, he attached himself to her, but so whole was her purity that his soft and weak one hundred eighty pounds of pulsating tissue limped back to itself without touching what she called "t' e center of my consciousness." This she had worked out herself, a sort of Cartesian pineal gland that existed within her right rib cage. "This is its place, my body's soul lives here. This is not the spirit or soul that maybe doesn't exist. This is a real one. You can find it without God or Jesus or anybody else. It's just a spot in your body. Mine happens to be right here. When you find yours, let me know and I'll be glad for you."

III

Ferguson searched for his spot but found only heartburn and hunger pains. Still, in the first month of their love he did not knowingly cheat on Annette. Once, at lunch, he took a bite of a friend's hamburger, a small bite that was already swallowed before he even realized it was meat. "After all," he explained to his friend, "you don't live twenty-eight years taking meat for granted and then automatically think 'This is meat' every time you take a bite of a hamburger, do you?"

That night Annette shunned him, but powered perhaps by that single bite of ground beef, he forced her somewhat and with sad and open eyes she suffered the carnivore upon her.

When he could not sleep, he admitted the hamburger.

"You don't have to explain, Ferguson. I knew it. I can see meat in someone I love like an x-ray. It poisons the air."

"One lousy bite can't be that poisonous," he protested.

Annette closed her eyes, pulled the nylon comforter over her like a shawl, and slept soundly beside the guilty Ferguson.

IV

By the third month he was one hundred fifty-five and shrinking. He poked ragged new holes in his belt with a kitchen knife and the extra piece of leather at the front flapped against his empty stomach. Even his shoes were too wide. His friends at first told him to see a doctor, then they said a psychiatrist. Annette expressed no pride in him but she did not reject him either. They continued that bliss they had begun at the supermarket. Away from her he sometimes felt an overpowering hunger which he soothed with cold water and occasional peanuts. In her presence the hunger was no problem. Annette Grim had taken him one step further into the nature of life. The old Ferguson would not have quibbled with "You are what you eat." The new Ferguson would roll his eyes heavenward and in a low sweet voice, not really meaning to correct you, would say, "You are what you don't eat." *Feast Not, Want Not* she calligraphed in her own hand as a decoration for the wall of his office.

"Counting the time needed for consuming and properly digesting red meat, a person spends twenty percent of his day on this single occupation. Another ten percent, say, on the body-cleaning function needed by meat eaters in civilized society, and at least another ten percent sleeping time caused by too much amino acid combined with loss of oxygen, and you have a carnivore actually losing forty percent of his day to meat. Thus, so called convenience foods are an absolute necessity. They are to the modern meat eater what fire was to his apelike ancestors. You and I, Ferguson," she went on, "have forty percent more time; that's like adding twenty years to your life expectancy. What better thing to do for someone you love?"

Ferguson, who was a CPA and attended law classes at night, decided pragmatically that the only better thing was to marry her and spend the extra twenty years of life expectancy together in a vegetarian home of their own. When he proposed they were in her apartment on a soft couch with a broken spring which forced Ferguson to sit straighter that he wanted to and added to his nervousness. They were snacking on sunflower seeds after coming home from the movies.

When he asked, Annette closed her eyes and touched her spot. Ferguson, while he awaited her answer, imagined their first child, a girl thin as a moonbeam, lustrous of skin, jumping rope, almost popping the bands of gravity as she floated above the cracking white pavement crowded with grimy infants.

Annette, with fingertips pressed beneath her right breast, took the measure of an organ that sat within her, absolutely parallel to the heart and functioning to interpret the steady rhythms of her heart across the vastness of the chest and the many pitfalls of the digestive tract. She was solemn and her eyelids fluttered against the pressures of choice. When she opened her eyes, her voice was steady. Her spot spoke to her and it said, No—not yet, at least. "I have this strange feeling that even though I love you too, we aren't ready for each other: not yet, maybe someday. We can't push it." He knew her well enough to keep from protesting. "I don't think it can ever work out permanently until you have your spot too. It's an uncanny thing. I can't tell you what it is, but I know it's there and it only partly"—she looked sadder now than he had ever seen her—"it only partly has to do with what you eat or don't eat."

V

Something changed after the proposal. They were no longer the people who had met in the supermarket, who shared one another and a philosophy of diet. They were potential parents, potential owners of houses, cars, and major appliances. She lived in a furnished apartment, owned only a few garments, and refused to be proud of him for graduating, finally, from the South Texas College of Law after five and one half years of night-school study. He went alone to the graduation banquet, to celebrate with his class-mates, their spouses, and the dean of the college. Annette stayed in her apartment working on the rug which she had been making during the months of their romance.

"Enjoy yourself," she said as he left, wrinkling her tiny nose, smiling as if to tease him for going to a steakhouse to celebrate what she called "thousands of hours of studying dullness." According to Annette it was a fitting celebration. Ferguson and fifty-five fat, hard-working Texas night-school lawyers going out to munch upon the loins of cattle in a restaurant decorated like a covered wagon.

"I'll bring you back the bone," he said, feeling cruel and smug himself. This was their first real fight. She might not find anything worth praising in his past, but this one night with people who had shared his ambition in countless humid hours while night settled over Houston and the red neon sign of the beauty academy across the street peeped through the venetian blinds, this one night with his fellow law students she would not rob him of. It had nothing to do with food. He planned to eat fruitcake. It had been ordered for him by the banquet chairman weeks before.

Ferguson sat three chairs from the dean, shared in toasts to the college, to the dean, to the wives and families of these working men whose sacrifices had made daddy, against long odds, a lawyer. Ferguson felt especially cheated not having someone to clink his champagne glass with. Even the dean brought a wife. After they had toasted the Law itself, a cowgirl waitress placed in front of Ferguson "Sonny's Special," a ten-inch medium-rare filet, butterflied so that it spread open like a radish, exposing its sizzling innards. "I ordered fruitplate," he told her, but she was well along the table and his voice fell among the sound of plates and teeth meeting beef. Goddamn, Ferguson said to himself, and he sliced off a bite of the steak, hesitated, chewed, and when he saw that it was good, he ate with relish and a pinch of A-1 sauce the remainder of Sonny's Special, had an after-dinner liqueur and two cups of coffee. He thought he must look like a snake who had swallowed a whole piglet, but in the men's room mirror, his stomach did not bulge. On the contrary, his skin had a ruddy healthy glow he had not seen in some time. "If she can't celebrate one lousy night with me after my five and a half years, then the hell with her," he told his reflection.

He went home, not to her apartment and her x-ray senses. Not that Ferguson intended to hide the steak from her. He would admit it but without feeling guilty. He paid enough that night for his gluttony on a stomach accustomed for three months to vegetables.

In the morning she was gone, disappeared, evanesced as if she had never been there. The door was open, a yogurt carton scraped clean lay alone in the garbage bag. The cupboard empty, the refrigerator empty, open, unplugged, smelling baking-powder clean. The bare hangers in her closet looked to Ferguson like bright teeth in a corpse. He ran to the building supervisor, who told him, "Mizz Grim left real early in the morning in a taxicab. She gave her two weeks notice and cleaned the place up good."

At the Prudential Insurance building Ferguson learned the same. Annette Grim, who for more than a year typed policy amendments five days a week, had given a two-week advance notice and told the girl at the desk next to her that she was going to Dallas. For several hours Ferguson sat in the Prudential coffee shop trying to make himself get up from his small table and his cold cup of tea, but he could not leave until he knew where to go. "What about our camping trip?" he asked aloud. He put his head on the table and breathed deeply, hoping the oxygen would clear his head. His body was sluggish from the meat and wine of the banquet. He finally decided to go home and hope she would be there to tell him this was her joking way of saying, yes, she wanted to get married right this minute. She had quit her job so that they could start a family immediately, even before the camping trip.

But Ferguson's apartment was as empty as it had always been, and he, three months a lover and a vegetarian, four days a lawyer, and all his life a loner, sat down with a bowl of wheat germ and milk to contemplate the suddenly narrow vista of his future. Annette was, after all, not his. Only a handful of people even knew about them as a couple.

Thanks to his law degree, Shell Oil would move him on Monday from accounting to contracts. Without Annette the weekend looming before him seemed longer than the twenty added years of life expectancy which she had bequeathed to him as a free gift. He spent Saturday and Sunday in a total fast, re-examining his months with Annette, and found no clues to her sudden departure. The two weeks' notice to her landlord and to the Prudential suggested that Annette had well-laid plans, but this, Ferguson understood, was a guise. She did not fool him. He knew, in spite of the apparent facts, that had he not left her for that Thursday night banquet he would not be alone now. Had he gone to the banquet and at least not eaten the steak, that too might have been enough to sustain their love.

But he had gone and he had eaten, and the beef that passed through him came between them, perhaps forever. Ferguson arose from his two-day fast and prepared to seek within himself the spot that would solve the mystery of Annette and create the Ferguson she could live with.

VI

The lawyer waned. After the initial fast, he worked out his own penance. For thirty days he would do the brown-rice regimen. A diet that Annette said was okay but too austere and too low on fluids. For thirty days he would eat only the king of grains, brown rice with its perfect harmony of phosphorus and potassium. He prepared it in a pressure cooker so that it took only a few minutes to cook and lasted days. Finding no comfort in friends and in no mood for entertainment, Ferguson worked late on the Shell leases and lost weight. His plan was to use these thirty days of brown rice in two ways. First to cleanse his body from that meat orgy of the banquet, and second to hope that in some mysterious way his monkish diet would be communicated to Annette, who would forgive and return. When at the end of thirty days she had not returned, he put away the pressure cooker and resumed a more normal vegetarian diet. He was now down to one hundred forty-seven and had to buy some smaller-sized clothes.

His new boss, the head of Shell contracts, called him "the most dedicated young man I've ever seen," and took Ferguson to lunch in the executive dining room, where amid martini-drinking businessmen and special cuts of aged beef the dedicated young man ate, at company expense, a lettuce and avocado salad. "You're too thin," said the head of contracts; "have a roast-beef sandwich. It's Iowa beef." Ferguson smiled his thanks and rejected chicken salad as well.

He was beginning to realize that he might just have to get over her, that whatever diet or other penance he tried might not do it. After all, thirty-four days and not even a post card to a man who had virtually lived with you for three months, who had proposed and told you all his heart. Thirty-four days of silence when she knew how barren he was without her. This he did not deserve for one steak. She knew it, he knew it. It was something else.

VII

At one hundred forty-two pounds, Ferguson began to have mild hallucinations. Nothing colorful or spectacular, no dreamlike surreal dazzlers, only short episodic vignettes slightly more concrete than a daydream. It was as if, all at once, the characters in the daydream had a bright spotlight focused upon them. The light did not deter them. They went about their business, but it made Ferguson recognize the subtle difference between a daydream and a hallucination. There was nothing terrifying in these experiences, and he felt, in spite of his thinness, healthy and robust. The hallucinations were largely about oil and taxes. In the first episode that he recognized as a new phenomenon, the daydream was Ferguson as a Shell executive somewhere upon a Colorado slope looking over thousands of green acres beneath which there might be recoverable shale deposits. The scene was as standard as a poster. When it became a hallucination, the earth slowly opened, disturbing nothing on the surface, and droplets of oil shot up like slippery watermelon seeds. As far as the oilman could see, this happened, the droplets flying up rhythmically like coffee percolating. No results, only the image, and Ferguson was back reading the fine print in a Shell lease between Mr. Howard S. Sounders of Ardmore, Oklahoma, and the Company, regarding section 71 and adjoining properties of McClehlen's addition, Runyn County.

The episodes followed no pattern and happened at home as well as at the office. He considered seeing a doctor but he suspected the doctor would suggest psychotherapy, and Ferguson, though he might be in despair and loneliness, felt very certain of his sanity. Anyway, how explain to a doctor that you were hoping to find within yourself a hidden resource called a spot which had a true and absolute physical existence and yet might vary in location among peoples and had never been located in an autopsy. "Doctors look for causes of disease," Annette had once told him when they discussed her spot, "doctors look for causes of death; this is a cause of life." Although Ferguson disliked the mumbo jumbo of mysticism, he did not think the idea of a spot was so absurd. The analogy with nature was very clear to him. All sorts of land looked the same from the surface, only a good geologist could tell you exactly where to drill for oil. Life itself starting with one cell spread to many. Scientists were continually finding out the secret codes of genetic reproduction. A person's spot would one day also be labeled, perhaps called an I AM, a fingernail of an RNA itself a fingernail of a DNA, and all this history pummeling through you with so little commotion that, if you don't stop to look for it, it might lie undisturbed, like oil, for millions of years. Perhaps most people didn't need a spot, they were still in a spotless age, the way men for thousands of generations didn't need oil or uranium even though it was always there just waiting to be needed. Because of Annette Grim Ferguson needed his spot. She was the catalyst that had moved Ferguson, of necessity, beyond the frontiers of science. Doctors could not help, nor because of the personal and secular nature of the spot could theologians or friends or entertainment or art. Thus, Ferguson ate fruits, vegetables, grains, seeds, and lowfat milk products, did his work for Shell Oil, and hoped for a better life.

VIII

To help him find his spot, Ferguson tried, in order, yoga, transcendental meditation, dynamic tension, and aerobics. Nothing did it, but after some experimentation with these methods of body analysis and muscle control, he found certain combinations that offered, if not a spot, at least some release from his anxieties. He could combine the jogging with the dynamic tension by squeezing his hands together as he ran. The tension squirted from his palms down to his legs and was dissipated in a seven-minute mile. It surprised Ferguson that, even though he was losing all hope of ever regaining Annette, he had no desire to go back to his old eating habits. Meat had forever joined the ranks of certain other inedible materials, wood, steel, fabric, glass. For her he sought his spot, for himself he remained a vegetarian.

IX

When he reached one hundred thirty-four, Ferguson's entire aspect changed. He had apparently exhausted all the extra flesh that had remained in his cheeks, and suddenly his face looked as strong and bony as a fist. His forehead, his cheekbones, his nose, and his chin stood out like the knuckles in a clenched hand. Sixty pounds ago Ferguson had been round cheeked, almost teddy bearish in appearance. A few girls had like him because he was cute and cuddly. Now he had become an arrowhead.

Because he could concentrate with such perfect composure and for so long a time, Ferguson did the work of five men. In hours he read through the contracts

that took other lawyers days or weeks, and he rarely
made even the smallest of errors. In the office they
called him the computer, but as he continued to shrink
they changed his name to Pocket Calculator. His eyes
soared out of the bleak landscape of his face. They
sought Annette the way birds seek out a resting place
after long journeys. Because Ferguson's bird eyes found
no Annette they did not rest. He could awaken from
ten hours of perfect slumber with sleepless, raging
eyes. And these remembering eyes became the great
weight of his body. When they blinked long, he might
lose his balance and sway in the wind. He thought
of himself as a simplified diagram. There was a plumb
line extending directly from his eyes down to his
mouth, his belly, and his penis, and upward to his
brain. The line was taut and powerful. Yet something
was missing, a spot as intricate and important as any
other in the brain-to-penis complex.

At night after deep breathing exercises in the lotus
position and a three-minute shoulder stand, Ferguson
would lie completely still in his bed and examine the
front of his body as if the examining fingers belonged
to someone else. He would speak aloud to himself as
the finger doctors did their checking of the clean and
relaxed corpus under them. "Here," the digits would
pound at the solar plexus, "perhaps it is here, where
it hurts when I poke, here, in this little Mesopotamia
between the lungs." The fingers would pound at the
space between his ribs until he could barely catch his
breath, but no inkling of the spot. As far as the finger
doctors could reach, they touched and examined and
tried to root out the spot. And when all else failed, the
doctors became Annette. They found out his most
obvious weakness and pulled away at his solid flesh
until it melted and stained Ferguson with the realization of his loneliness.

X

Mr. Solomon, his boss in the contracts department, insisted that Ferguson take a two-week vacation.

"Longer if you like," he said, "and of course with full pay. You've done a year's work in a few months, go out and relax, have some fun." Solomon slapped him on the back in a broad gesture of camaraderie. But as he shook Ferguson's hand and pulled him closer the older lawyer said in a voice of honest concern, "Son, is there anything I can do to help you? Whatever it is, I know you won't talk about it, but I just want you to know that Harold Solomon cares. You're the best contracts man here, but I don't give a damn about that when I can see you suffering right in front of me. Do something about it on this vacation, son, and when you come back remember that Harold Solomon isn't just your boss, he's your friend."

Mr. Solomon's concern touched Ferguson but it also unnerved him. He realized for the first time how obvious his despair must be. It was five and one half months since the banquet. He weighed one hundred twenty-eight pounds now and domestic dress shirts ballooned around his chest. He switched to the modish homemade type, mostly Indian, which hung loosely over his shoulders and gave him the look of a very large and well-groomed Asian peasant. On the first day of his vacation, he took the Greyhound bus to Dallas, checked into the Holiday Inn under the name of William Glass, and rented a car. He could have driven his own car and registered under his own name. He did not understand why he acted so irrationally, but he decided to follow his whims and hope that they would lead him to Annette.

Ferguson did not roam the streets of Dallas looking for her, but he sought out the health-food shops and the vegetarian restaurants where he thought she might be. He had no photograph to pass around and her description—thin, fair, strong, beautiful, direct, knowledgeable, precise, self-assured—none of this really described her. Annette Grim was identifiable only by her spot, that roommate of her heart, which sat beneath her solemn nipple on the right-hand side of an otherwise biologically unspectacular chest. "I am probably in better condition than she is,"

Ferguson thought; "she probably doesn't run and do yoga." Perhaps he could even teach her something new.

In a restaurant called Pelops Arms, beneath a modern cartoon of Greek heroes wrestling with monsters, Ferguson sat eating an avocado, cheese, and mung-sprout sandwich. Dallas had even fewer health restaurants than Houston. In the midst of men who raised cattle for shipment to the dinner tables of America, there sat Ferguson eschewing red meats, disdaining poultry, laying off eggs, hardening and slenderizing a body that sought its own center, and while doing so rushed with all its pent-up energies toward unknown places, creating, like the universe itself, an area of empty space wherever it traveled. There sat Ferguson, just and thin and powerful, seeking his center like a dog after its own tail.

"Pardon me," the voice said, and Ferguson's raging eyes turned as always, looking for her, frightening by their intensity an innocent waitress delivering a bill for $1.79.

"Was everything all right?" she asked.

"Are you in a hurry?" Ferguson asked her in return.

She smiled at the empty restaurant. "You're the only customer," she said, and sat down opposite him. Starting from the day in the supermarket, Ferguson told her almost everything. This girl, Kathleen Simpson, a junior at SMU, herself not completely vegetarian, sat in awe as the story of Ferguson's search for a spot unfolded before her.

"I never heard of anything like it," she said, "but I believe in the soul so it is not so preposterous to me. I'm through here in an hour, I'll help you look. There's only a few places in Dallas where a girl like that might be and they're not far from here." Ferguson paid his $1.79 and sipped distilled water while he waited for Kathleen. She took him to the Garden of Eden, where long-haired men sold grain and seeds out of huge tin pails. She led him to the Cornucopia, which catered to SMU students and served only a modest vegetarian choice amid a wide meat menu. Caesar's Salad, a small downtown coffee shop that served luncheon greens to secretaries, was the only other place she could think of. Annette, of course, was in none of these restaurants, but since she had been a secretary, Ferguson thought this last one might be a good place for him to camp out and wait for her. Kathleen Simpson, brown eyed and friendly, wished him well.

The next day Ferguson haunted Caesar's Salad. It was very difficult to stay there for long. There was only a counter with eight stools and three small booths that at lunch and with squeezing could accommodate four each. Twenty customers maximum and two waitresses. By noon both of them knew Ferguson and suspected him. He explained but they asked him to do his waiting outside. Ferguson stood in the Dallas sun trying to shade himself beneath the awning of a nearby paint store. From the store window a cardboard peacock flashed many colors into the sunlight, dazzling him. He took a salt tablet and carried a paper cup of water with him, but the Dallas afternoon rose above one hundred and Ferguson felt weak and dizzy. He visited, on foot, the only Dallas landmark he knew, the place of the schoolbook depository and the grassy knoll. As he walked the route of the motorcade he tried to imagine the sound of the bullets, the scream of Jacqueline, Lyndon Johnson, fearful beneath a secret-service man. The book depository had been torn down, the grassy knoll was merely an overpass for a highway, and a small plaque marked the place where the President's head had been splintered.

For the first time Ferguson wondered about the spots of the great. Did someone like President Kennedy have a spot which he consulted when the Russians put missiles in Cuba? Had there been an inkling, a negative feeling, like Annette had about him, on that day in November when the young President put on his clean starched shirt, his cuff links and his garters, and shook his longish hair in front of the mirror to make certain that it would look fine in the hot Dallas wind? If important people had spots and listened to them, things would not go wrong in the world, Ferguson reasoned. Yet starting from himself and stretching right to the farthest astronaut hitting a golf ball on the moon, there was a line of chaos as direct as the plumb line that went through Ferguson. Who had absolutes? Even the Pope changed his mind. Only his Annette heard the hum of the rhythm of her body, while a tone-deaf world scrambled around her.

"I have tried," Ferguson said aloud in the shadow of the grassy knoll where hundreds had watched the motorcade speed up and curve toward Parkland Hospital; "I have fasted and meditated and relentlessly examined myself. I have known no stranger among women, nor have my lips touched the flesh of birds or animals." The desert heat struck him full force as he raised his face heavenward and saw for an instant the flaming sun, like a carbonated peacock bubbling in his eyes. He shielded himself with uplifted arms, and a Buick whisked by so closely that the string tie of his shirt thudded softly against the outside mirror of the automobile.

"Watch yourself, nut," the driver yelled back at him.

"I have been doing that," Ferguson answered, "I have been doing little else." To the grassy knoll and to the anonymous traffic Ferguson announced, "I know myself and have no spot. Kennedy had none, neither did Roosevelt, or Justice Frankfurter, or George Washington." Ferguson raced up the grassy knoll and proclaimed to the roaring highway, "You lost me too, Annette. Whoever you're huddled with now does not love you like I did. You were my spot and your spot didn't know it."

In the Dallas heat he ran along the side of the highway in his long-and-easy jogging stride. Along Dallas Avenue Ferguson ran, past post-office buildings and skyscrapers, through streets emptied by the hot sun. As he ran he clenched and unclenched his fists, letting the dynamic tension pulse through his arms as the crashing cement vibrated through his legs. Deeply he inhaled the city, its desert air and its poisonous oxides. As his ribcage stretched, Ferguson felt loose and lucid. He imagined that the plumb line was now stretched taut, that the final open space had been pulled out with a sudden jerk and had disappeared, leaving him unmarked down the middle. He raced past Caesar's Salad not even casting a glance. His second wind had come by the time Ferguson reached Pelops Arms. Entering at a gallop, he surprised Kathleen Simpson, who handed him distilled water.

"Did you find her?" she asked.

"Yes," Ferguson said, "will you run with me?"

"Where?"

"To Houston for dinner, and then through Mexico to the Pan American highway, along the banks of the Amazon, over the Chilean Andes right into Buenos Aires."

Kathleen hesitated, then she slipped off her short black apron, put down her green order pad, and in a long and fluent stride, side by side with Ferguson, headed south.

Inside
Norman Mailer

I

So what if I could kick the shit out of Truman Capote, and who really cares that once in a Newark bar, unknown to each other, I sprained the wrist of E. L. Doctorow in a harmless arm wrestle. For years I've kicked around in out-of-the-way places, sparred for a few bucks or just for kicks with the likes of Scrap Iron Johnson, Phil Rahv, Kenny Burke, and Chico Vejar. But, you know, I'm getting older too. When I feel the quick arthritic pains fly through my knuckles, I ask myself, Where are your poems and novels? Where are your long-limbed girls with cunts like tangerines? Yes, I've had a few successes. There are towns in America where people recognize me on the street and ask what I'm up to these days. "I'm thirty-three," I tell them, "in the top of my form. I'm up to the best. I'm up to Norman Mailer."

They think I'm kidding, but the history of our game is speckled with the unlikely. Look at Pete Rade-macher—not even a pro. Fresh from a three-round Olympic decision, he got a shot at Floyd Patterson, made the cover of *Sports Illustrated*, picked up an easy hundred grand. Now that is one fight that Mr. Mailer, the literary lion, chose not to discuss. The clash between pro and amateur didn't grab his imagination like two spades in Africa or the dark passion of Emile Griffith. Yes, you know how to pick your spots, Norman. I who have studied your moves think that your best instinct is judgment. It's your secret punch. You knew how to stake out Kennedy and Goldwater, but on the whole you kept arm's length from Nixon. Humphrey never earned you a dime.

Ali, the moon, scrappy broads, dirty walls, all meat

to you, Slugger. But even Norman Mailer has mis-
played a few. Remember the Chassidic tales? The
rabbit pose was one you couldn't quite pull off, but
you cut your losses fast, the mark of a real pro, and
I fully expect that you'll come back to that one yet to
cash in big on theology. Maybe at sixty you'll throw
a birthday party for yourself in the Jerusalem Hilton.
You'll roll up in an ancient scroll, grow earlocks, and
say, "This is the big one, the one I've been waiting
for." With Allen Ginsberg along on a leash you'll clank
through the holy 'ties living on nuts and distilled
water and sell you. ilms as a legitimate appendix to
the New Testament.

If I had the patience I'd wait for that religious
revival and be your Boswell, then I'd drive off that
whole crew of trainers and seconds who tag after you,
but by then I'll be almost fifty and maybe too slow to
do you justice. As the rabbis said: "Reputation is a
meal, energy a food stamp." It's *toches affen tisch*,
you understand that, big boy? I'm spotting you seventy
pounds, a dozen books, wives, children, memories,
millions in the bank. My weapons are desperation,
neglect, and bad form. I am the C student in a
mediocre college, the madman in the crowd, the quaint
gunman who rides into Dodge City because he's heard
they have good restaurants. We share only a mutual
desire to let it all take place in public, in the open.
This is the way Mailer has always played it, this I
learned from you. Why envy from afar when I can
pummel you in a lighted ring. Your reputation makes
it possible. You who are composed of genes and risks,
you appreciate the wildness of strangers. Anyway, you
think you'll nail me in one.

While I, for months, have been running fifteen miles
a day and eating natural food, you train by scratching
your nuts with a soft rubber eraser. You take walks in
the moonlight and turn the clichés inside out. For you
they make way. Sidewalks tilt, lovers quarrel. People
whisper your name to each other, give you wholesale
prices and numerous gifts. An "Okay" from Norman

Mailer makes a career. Power like this there has not been since Catullus in old Rome carried on his instep Caesar's daughter.

I'll give you this much: you have come by it honestly. Not by bribery and not by marriage, not by family ties and not by wealth, not by good luck alone or by the breaks of the game. You have plenty, Slugger, that I'll admit. But I do not come at you like a barbarian. The latest technology is in my corner. The Schick 1000-watt blow-dryer, trunks by Haspel, robe by Mr. Mann, Jovan cologne. Adidas kidskin shoes travel three quarters of my shin with laces of mandarin silk. From my flesh, coated with Vaseline and Desenex, the sweat breaks forth like pearls. My desperation grows muscular in the bright lights. I am the fatted calf.

You stand in your corner like Walt Whitman. No electric outlets, cheap cotton YMCA trunks, even your gloves look used. Your red robe just says "Norm." You wear sneakers and no socks. I should take you the Oriental way by working your feet up to blisters and then stepping on your toes, but I lack the Chinaman's patience. No, it will have to be head to head, although everyone has cautioned me about trading punches with you.

Last week a crowd of critics came out to my camp in a chartered bus. They carried canes and magnifying glasses. They told me to evaluate each punch from the shoulder. "Let your elbow be the judge," Robert Penn Warren said; "Sting like an irony," from Booth of Chicago. They told me that if I win I'll get an honorary degree from Kenyon and a job at one of the best gyms in the Midwest. Like a Greek chorus they stood beside my training ring and sang in unison, "Don't slug it out, move and think. Speed and reflexes beat out power. To the victor goes the victory."

"Scram," I yelled, spitting my between-the-rounds mouthwash. "Get lost you crummy bastards. You shit on my poems and laughed off my stories, now you want some of my body language. Go study the ambiguities of Harold Robbins." I was mad as hell but they stood firm taking notes on my weight and reach. Finally a group of kids carrying "Free Rubin Carter" signs ran them back to the bus.

The press is no help either. They are so tired of promoting Ali against a bunch of nobodies that to them I'm just another Joe Bugner. They rarely call me by name. "Mailer's latest victim to be" is their tag. The *Times* calls me a "man with little to recommend him. Slight, almost feline, with the gestures of a minor poet, this latest in a long series of Mailer baiters seems to have no more business in the ring with the master than Stan Ketchel had with Jack Johnson. No one is interested in this fight. The Astrodome will be bare, UHF refuses to televise, and Mailer has scheduled a reading for later that night at the University of Houston. Norman, why do you keep accepting every challenge from the peanut gallery? Let's stop this Christians versus Lions until there is a real contender. Now, if the Pynchon backers could come up with a site and a solid guarantee, that might be a real match."

You know what I say, I say, "Fuck the *Times*." They gave Clay no chance against Big Bad Sonny Liston, and four years later the "meanest, toughest" champ the *Times* ever saw dropped dead while tying his shoes and Muhammad built a Temple for Elijah M. So much for the sports writers.

But there are a few people who understand. Teddy White will be in my corner and Senator Proxmire at ringside. *The Realist* and the L.A. *Free Press* have picked me. The DAR sent a fruit basket. Outside the literary crowd I'm actually well liked. Cesar Chavez and the migrants from South Texas are coming up to cheer for me and my friend Ira from Minneapolis and the whole English department of my school. All the Democratic Presidential candidates sent telegrams; so did Bill Buckley, Mayor Beame, Gore Vidal, Irving Wallace, John Ehrlichman, and Herman Kahn. . . . All I can say is, when the time comes boys, I'll be ready, just watch.

II

Our first face-to-face meeting is at the weigh-in. He wanted to dispense with it and turn in a morning urine specimen instead. The boxing commission put the nix on that idea. Oh, he knew who I was before the weigh-in. We had traded photos, autographs, and once I had anthologized him. But face to face on either side of a big metal scale with our robes on and Teddy White rubbing my back while I stare bullets, that is something else again.

He nods, I look away. He can afford to be gracious. If I win, I'll make a handsome donation to UNICEF in his honor. For now, I button my lip. He chats with White about convention sites, claims that because of tonight he'll have an insider's edge if they do the '76 one in the Astrodome.

I come in at one hundred forty-four and three quarters, thirty-four-inch reach. He is two hundred fourteen and a thirty-inch reach. He spots me the reach and eighteen years. I give him seventy pounds and a ton of reputation. He has enough grace under pressure to teach at a ballet school, but the smile discloses bad teeth. I'll remember that. His body hairs are graying. I can see that he has not trained and could use sleep. My tongue lies at the bottom of my mouth. "Good luck, kid," he says, but I have removed my contact lenses and only learn later that it was the Great One in a magnanimous gesture whom I snubbed because I had to take a leak.

III

The Dome is a half-empty cave. At the last minute they lowered all tickets to a buck, and thousands popped in to see the King. To me the crowd means nothing. It is as anonymous as the whir of an air conditioner. I stare at the Everlast trademark on my gloves and practice keeping the mouthpiece in without gagging. "Stay loose," Teddy yells over the din, "stay loose as a goose and box like a fox."

I dance in my corner for three or four minutes before he appears. The crowd goes wild when that woolly head jogs up the ramp. He climbs through the ropes and goes to center ring. He throws kisses with both open gloves. He is wearing the same YMCA trunks and cheap sneakers, but his robe is a threadbare terrycloth without a name. It looks like something he picked up at Goodwill on the way over. The crowd loves his slovenliness.

"To each his own," I whisper to myself as I ask Teddy for a final hit with the blow-dryer. My curls are tight as iron; his hang like eggshells crowding around his ears. He throws a kiss to me; I try to return it with the finger but my glove makes it a hand.

The referee motions us to center ring. We both requested Ruby Goldstein but the old pro wouldn't come out of retirement for a match like this one. I then asked for the Brown Bomber and Mailer wanted Jersey Joe. Finally we compromised on Archie Moore, who has a goatee now and is wearing a yellow leisure suit as he calls us together for a review of the rules. I notice that he is wearing street shoes and think to protest, but I see that he needs the black patent pumps in order to make his trousers break at the step. A good sign, I think. Archie will be with me.

He goes over the mandatory eight count and the three-knockdown rule, but Mailer and I ignore the words. Our eyes meet and mine are ready for his. For countless hours I have trained before a mirror with his snapshot taped to the middle. I have had blown up to poster size that old *Esquire* pose of him in the ring, and I am ready for what I know will be the first real encounter. My eyes are steady on his. In the first few seconds I see boredom, I see sweet brown eyes that would open into yawning mouthlike cavities if they could. I see indifferent eyes and gay youthful glances. Checkbook eyes. Evelyn Wood eyes. Then suddenly he blinks and I have my first triumph. Fear pops out. Plain old unabashed fear. Not trembling, not panic, just a little fear. And I've found it in the eyes, exactly like the nineteenth-century writers used to before

Mailer switched it to the asshole. I smile and he knows that I know. Anger replaces the fear but the edge is mine, big boy. All the sportswriters and oddsmakers haven't lulled you. You know that every time you step into the ring it's like going to the doctor with a slight cough that with a little twist of the DNA turns out to be cancer. You, old cancermonger, you know this better than anyone. In my small frame, in my gleaming slightly feline gestures you have smelled the blood test, the chest x-ray, the specialists, the lies, the operations, the false hopes, the statistics. Yes, Norman, you looked at me or through me and in some distant future that maybe I carry in my hands like a telegram, there you glimpsed that old bugaboo and it went straight to your prostate, to your bladder, and to your heavy fingertips. In a second, Norm, you built me up. Oh, I have grown big on your fear. Giant killers have to so that they can reach up for the fatal stab to the heart.

No camera has recorded this. Nor has Archie Moore repeating his memorized monologue noted our exchange. Only you and I, Norm, understand. This is as it should be. You have given dignity to my challenge; like a sovereign government you have recognized my hopeless revolutionary state and turned me, in a blink, credible, at least to you, at least where it counts. I slap my fists together and at the bell I meet you for the first time as an equal.

IV

The problem now is as old as realism. You don't want all the grunts, the shortness of breath, the sound of leather on skin, and I don't want to tell you in great detail. But it's all there, the throwing of punches, the clinches, the head butting, the swelling of injured faces. If I forget to, then you put it in. For I am too busy taking the measure of my opponent to feel the slap of his glove against my flesh. The bell has moved us into a new field of force. We drop our pens. The spotlight is the glare of eternity, and what it has all come to is simply the matter of Truth. "Existentialist"

I call him, spitting out my mouthpiece, though in practice I have recited Peter Piper a dozen times and kept the mouthpiece in. "Dated existentialist. Insincere existentialist. Jewish existentialist . . ." I hit him with this smooth combination, but he continues to rush me bearlike, serene, full of skill and power.

"Campy lightweight," he yells, in full charge as I sidestep his rush and he tangles his upper body in the ropes.

I come up behind, and as well as I can with the gross movement of the glove I pull back his head and expose the blue gnarled cacophony of his neck.

"I am Abraham and you the ram caught in the thicket," I announce from behind. "I have been an outcast in many lands, I bear the covenant, and you full of power and goatish lust, you carry the false demon out of whose curved horn I will blow my own triumph and salvation."

"How unlike an Abraham thou art," he responds, gasping from his entanglement in the ropes. "Where is thy son then and where thy handmaiden Hagar, whom thou so ungenerously got with a child of false promise and then discarded into the wilderness? Thou art an assumer of historical identities, a chameleon of literary pretension."

I reach into the empty air for the sword of slaughter when Archie Moore separates us, rights Mailer, and warns me about hair pulling and exposing the jugular of my opponent.

Now we stalk one another at center ring. He, not having trained, not having rested, not having regarded my challenge as serious, he is ready almost at once to revert to instinctive behavior. He wants it all animal now and tries to bite off his glove so that he can come at me with ten fingers. But I am still in the airy realms of the mind. I see and discern his actions. How coarse appears the Mailer saliva upon his worn gloves, how disgusting his tongue and crooked teeth as they nibble at the strings. His mouth has become as a loom with the glove lace moving between his teeth on the slow, feeble power of his tongue.

"The Industrial Revolution," I yell across the ring, and his gloves drop, his mouth is open and agape. I land a hard right to his jaw and feel the ligaments stretch. At the bell he is dazed and hurt. He moves to his corner like an old man in an unemployment line.

I stand in the middle of the ring and watch the slow shuffle toward comfort of this man whom most enlightened folks thought I could not withstand for even three minutes. So carefully have I trained, so honest has been my fifteen miles of daily roadwork that the first round of exertion has scarcely left me breathless. While Norman is in his corner swishing his mouth, having his brow mopped, I am in mid-ring, stunned with my opening achievement. I have stayed a full round with him. I have seen the fear in his eyes and the beast in his soul. I have felt the heft of his sweating form in a heavy embrace. In the clinch, as our protective cups clicked against each other, there have I surmised his lust. For three metaphysical moments we two white men have embraced in violence while old black Archie pares his perfect fingernails in the midst of us.

"Don't forget the game plan," Teddy is yelling from my corner. He wants my help in pulling the blackboard through the ropes. I come out of my reverie to help him. Oh, I have been waiting for this moment, and now but for good old Teddy I might have forgotten. Like the most careful teacher printing large block letters for an eager second grade, I inscribe and turn to four sides so all can see, "The Naked and the Dead Is His Best Work."

When Norman reads my inscription, he is swishing Gatorade in his mouth while his second, Richard Poirier, applies with a Q-tip glycerine and rosewater to the Mailer lips. When my barb registers, he swallows the Gatorade and bites the Q-tip in half. Poirier and José Torres can barely keep him on his stool. They whisper frantically, each in an ear. Archie is across the ring getting a quick shine from a boy who manages, on tiptoe, to reach with his buffing cloth up to the apron of the elevated ring. Arch kneels to tip with an autograph.

When the bell tolls round two, I face a Mailer who has with herculean effort quickly calmed himself. He has sucked in his cheeks for control and looks, for the moment, like a tubercular housewife. I see immediately that he has beaten back the demiurge. We will stay in the realms of the intellect. His gloves are completely laced and his steps are tight and full of control. He dances over to the ropes and beckons me with an open glove to test his newness.

Who do you think I am, Norm? Didn't I travel half a world with no hope of writing a book about it to watch Ali lure George Foreman to the ropes? Not for me, Norm, is your coy ease along the top strand. I'll wait and take you in the open. You see, I learned more than you did in Africa. While you holed up in an air-conditioned hotel and resurrected those eight rounds for your half a million advance, I thumbed my way to what was once called Biafra. I went to the cemetery where Dick Tiger lies dead of causes unknown at age thirty-five in newly prosperous Nigeria. How did you miss Dick Tiger? You who were the first white negro, you the crown prince of nigger-lovers, you missed the ace of the jungle. Yes, he was the heart of the dark continent, the Aristotle of Africa. A middleweight and a revolutionary. While you clowned around with Torres and Ali and Emile Griffith, Tiger packed his gear and headed home to see what he could pick clean from the starvation and the slaughter. He went home to face bad times and bad people and was dead a week after his plane touched down. Where were you and the sportswriters, Norm, when Dick Tiger needed you? I at least made the trek to the resting place of the hero, and it was there in the holy calm of his forgotten tomb that I vowed to come back and make my move. No one offered me a penny for "The Dick Tiger Story" as told to me, so you won't get it now either. Come out to the middle, Norm. No, you're still coy, relaxed; well, two can play that one.

I sit down in the corner opposite him; I fan myself

with the mouthpiece. To the audience it looks as if we're kidding. He sloping against the ropes, I twenty-five feet away pretending I'm at a picnic in the English countryside. Real fight fans know what's up. There is only a certain amount of available energy. In the universe it's called entropy; in the ring it is known as "ppf," punches per flurry. Neither of us has the strength at this moment to muster the necessary ten to twelve ppf's to really damage the other. Fighters trained in the Golden Gloves or various homes for juvenile delinquents will go through the motions anyway. They will stalk and butt and sweat upon each other. But Mailer and I, knowing the score, wait out the round. Archie Moore leafs through the Texas Boxing Commission rules. Some fans boo, others take advantage of the lull to refresh themselves.

For me, every second is a victory. Round by round I wear the laurel and the bay. Who thought I could even last the first? Five will get me tenure, seven and I'll be a dean. Yes, I can wait, Norm, until you come to me in mid-ring with all that bulk and experience. Come to me with your strength, your wisdom, your compassion, and your insight. This time at the bell we are both giggling, aware each to each of the resined canvas upon which we paint our destinies.

I walk over to his corner where he sits on his stool, kingly again, not hurt as he was after round one. He offers me a drink from his green bottle. We spit into the same bucket. I know his seconds don't like me coming over there between rounds. Poirier turns away but Norman smiles, cuffs me playfully behind the neck. Together we walk out to await the bell.

For twice three minutes we have traveled the same turf. Ambition and gravity have held up in a dialectical encounter, but as round three begins, Mailer's old friend the irrational joins us. No matter that I actually see the pig-tailed form of my sister beckoning me between mouthfuls of popcorn to rush at you. Aeneas, Hector, Dick Tiger, they too saw the phantoms that promise the sunshine and delight after one quick lunge. My sister is nine years old. She wears a gingham dress.

She is right there beside you, close enough for Archie to stumble on.

"Watch out, kid," I say, "you shouldn't even be here."

"It's okay," Mailer says. "She has my permission."

She throws the empty popcorn box over the ropes. "Please take me home," she whimpers, and as she stands there the power enters me, the ppf quotient floods my own soul, and I rush, not in fear, not in anger, but in full sweet confidence, I rush with both fists to the middle of Norman Mailer.

First my left with all its quixotic force and then my sure and solid right lands in the valley of his solar plexus. Next my head in a raw, cruel butt joins the piston arms. Hands, arms, head, neck, back, legs. As a boy for the first time shakes the high dive in the presence of his parents, with such pride do I dive. And with the power of falling human weight knifing through the chlorine-dark pool do I catapult. As a surgeon lays open flesh, indifferently, thinking not of tumors but of the arc of his racquet in full backswing, with such professional ease am I engulfed.

I hear the wind leave his lungs. Like large soft earlobes, they shade me from the glare of his heart. The sound of his digestive juices is rhythmic and I resonate to the music of his inner organs. I hear the liver weakened from drink but on key still, the gentle reek of kidneys, the questioning solo of pancreas, the harmonica-like appendix, all here all around me, and the cautionary voice of my mother: "Be careful, little one, when you hit someone so hard in the stomach. That's how Houdini died."

Somewhere else Archie Moore is counting ten over a prone loser. Judges are packing up scorecards and handbags snap shut. I am comfortable in the damp prison of his rib cage. His blood explodes like little Hiroshimas every second.

"Concentrate," says Mailer, "so the experience will not be wasted on you."

"It's hard," I say, "amid the color and distraction."

"I know," says my gentle master, "but think about one big thing."

I concentrate on the new edition of the *Encyclopædia Britannica*. It works. My mind is less a palimpsest, more a blank page.

"You may be too young to remember," he says, "James Jones and James T. Farrell and James Gould Cozzens and dozens like them. I took them all on, absorbed all they had and went on my way, just like Shakespeare ate up *Tottel's Miscellany*."

"No lectures," I wasp, "only truths."

"I am the Twentieth Century," Mailer says. "Go forth from here toward the east and earn your bread by the sweat of your brow. Never write another line nor raise a fist to any man." His words and his music are like Christmas morning. I go forth, a seer.

The Yogurt of Vasirin Kefirovsky

Vasirin Kefirovsky stands six feet four and uses an extra-long rubber-tipped pointer. He is fond of spinning a globe with this pointer while his feet rest on the patio table. He dislikes gossip but revels in small talk. His wife, Emily, spends many of her mornings watching the yogurt incubate beneath blankets in her stainless-steel kitchen. Dr. Kefirovsky spins his globe and thinks from eight to eleven forty-five, then he drinks his yogurt and works all afternoon on *Earth Story*.

Today his morning schedule is interrupted by an interviewer from *Time* magazine, Robert Williams, assistant science editor.

Mrs. Kefirovsky sits with the two men at the patio table, keeping her eye on the weather. She sips a cocktail of Mogen David wine and club soda.

"I am what I am," says Professor Kefirovsky. "When I was a boy, I ate wide noodles brushed with cheeses. In middle age, no meat was too gamy. I ate your turtles, your rabbits, your unfit leghorns. I knew the earth before I knew my own belly."

"Your husband is a great man," the reporter tells Emily. "If the deep space probes bear out his ideas as well as Mariner II did, he'll be on the cover of *Time* someday. He'll be taught in the schools."

Kefirovsky puts down his pointer and uses a long forefinger for emphasis. "Eating has nothing to do with thinking," he tells the reporter. "I always thought clearly, but I thought too much about food. Now I think about nothing to eat. What is yogurt? It's milk and time and heat. What is the earth? It's rocks and time and bodies."

The reporter takes notes slowly. "But tell me this, Professor, have you resented being an outsider all these years? I mean, has the fact that the scientific community considers you something of a charlatan embittered your career?"

Kefirovsky spins the earth with his pointer. "Name me a big one who was not an outsider. Galileo, Copernicus, Paracelsus, Hans Fricht . . . Galen maybe was an insider, he gave back rubs to the Emperor. He was a chiropractor. If you're an insider you make Vicks cough drops or you work for the Ford Foundation."

"Well, Einstein, for one, was accepted by his contemporaries. He was not an outsider."

Kefirovsky stands and edges the pointer close to Williams' nose. "And Einstein made cough drops too. Only if you write this everyone will say how ungrateful Kefirovsky is. Now that people pay attention to him, he fills the magazines with dreck about Einstein. Not long ago I saw Einstein's brain. It's in Connecticut at a health institute. They take care of it like it's a member of the family in an iron lung. I knew Einstein and I knew his brother Victor, who sold Red Ball shoes in Brooklyn."

"Don't worry, Professor, *Time* isn't a gossip magazine. I won't write anything about Einstein."

"I don't worry and I don't think about eating food." Using his pointer as a walking stick, Kefirovsky strides into his garden bordered by petunias, roses, and white azaleas. The reporter follows.

"I came from Russia in a dressing gown. At Ellis Island I cut it below the pockets with a scissors, hemmed the bottom, and wore it for years as a satin smoking jacket. I had my teeth capped during World War II. I married in 1926 and have four sons all of whom served in the United States Army and were honorably discharged, except Gerald."

"And what does Gerald do now?"

"He makes cough drops."

Mrs. Kefirovsky returns to the kitchen with her

candy thermometer to check the yogurt's temperature. "I'll call you, Vasi, when it's a hundred and twelve."

Dr. Kefirovsky is neither tired nor angry. He suffers the reporter but his mind is elsewhere. His four sons are all organic chemists. They used to come together every year at Easter time and eat big meals of lake trout, poultry, beef, and Russian side dishes like stuffed cabbage, boiled potatoes, and fried smelt. Kefirovsky himself used to make two hundred gallons of wine a year. During the Christmas season neighbors and delivery men drank it from Pepsi-Cola quarts.

There are two ovens in his stainless-steel kitchen and a natural-gas pit-barbecue in his backyard. But Kefirovsky no longer cooks, barbecues, or makes wine. His sons and their families are refusing to come for another Easter. The mailman and the paperboy turn down the quarts of Christmas yogurt. The books he wrote thirty years ago about the collision of the planets are selling now, but his new thesis is scorned by people like Adelle Davis and Dr. Atkins. He has no publisher for *Earth Story*.

Williams asks, "When did you first begin to realize that cosmic accidents are recorded in human history?"

"I knew this as early as 1929."

"But what made you think of it?"

"I opened my eyes. I looked around. I talked to people. I read books. I wondered why a rinky-dinky town like Troy should be such a front-page story for a thousand years. I wondered why the Red Sea opened and how come the Chinamen knew about Noah's flood. I kept my eyes on the heavens. I read spectrograms. I made educated guesses. That's what science is.

"One day I came to Hans Fricht and I said, 'Hans, either I'm crazy or I know about history.' I showed him my data. 'You're not crazy,' he said. He called Einstein, who was then a nobody, a refugee in baggy trousers who thanked God when you talked to him in German and had hay fever in New Jersey.

"'*Er veiss vas er zagt?*' Einstein asked Fricht. He followed the mathematics but he missed the point. He didn't give a damn about history. Before he died he was a pen pal with Albert Schweitzer. I sent Schweitzer a copy of *Worlds in Confusion* but never heard from him. Fricht was going to write the introduction but he said Einstein needed the money, so Einstein wrote it in German and Hans translated it. Einstein had lots of bad grammar. Listen, I liked the man. I am not jealous of his success. He was right about many things. If he ate less, he would be alive today."

Emily Kefirovsky comes out the back door and down the two wooden steps to the patio. She approaches the flower garden carrying a blue cardigan over her forearm. "Vasi, the sun is behind the clouds. Here." She hands him the cardigan. "He's not a young man, Mr. Williams, although the cold never bothers him. During the winters in Berlin, even in Moscow, he never wore gloves. Here in Texas you can't tell from one minute to the next. The air conditioning makes him dizzy. I wish we could move."

Kefirovsky puts on the cardigan. "Go watch the yogurt," he tells her. "It will be ready to pour in a few minutes." He strokes the sweater to be certain it is just right. With his pointer he marks the spot where Emily stood. "My wife eats saturated fats. Look at yourself. Probably not forty and I'll bet your veins are closing up like artichokes."

"Maybe you're right, Professor Kefirovsky, but let's finish talking about you. I'm not important. I'm just an anonymous pencil at *Time*, but you're a famous man. Whether scientists like it or not your works are right up there in general sales, right up there with Dr. Spock and Dr. Rubin and Dr. Atkins."

"These are kids' stuff. Not just Spock, the other ones too. I've read all the diet books. Atkins is what they used to call a piss prophet. They ran them out of town in Germany. They would set up fairs and sell medicine like hucksters. They sent you to the toilet with litmus paper and when they read the colors they sold you their medicine. That's what Atkins is. And Rubin, he doesn't even know what Wilhelm Reich knew."

"Did you know Wilhelm Reich?"

"I knew him in the days before he made the boxes. He used to come over too, to talk to me like Eidler and Fricht and the others. He liked cold asparagus dipped in mayonnaise. He never drank beer. If they hadn't tortured him in California, I believe he would be alive today."

Kefirovsky leads the reporter, single file, through his garden along a circular path. Behind the flowers are green plants and shrubs, some in blossom. In the deep shade there are patches of soft dark moss. The professor points at various plants but does not describe them. "I am not a botanist. Pliny the Elder classified plants and Hippocrates' son-in-law classified people. There are many plants that can kill you but not a one that will eat you. I was an old man before I thought of this."

"Is that so significant?" The reporter has put away his ball point. His hands are clasped behind his back, the notebook sticks out of his pocket. He looks bored. From the kitchen Mrs. Kefirovsky calls out, "A hundred and eleven point eight." The Professor walks briskly toward the house. "After one hundred and ten we switch from the candy thermometer to the new digital types that give you an exact reading."

In the stainless-steel kitchen sink he washes his hands with green liquid soap and dries them carefully on a paper towel. The yogurt is in a three-quart glass jar immersed in water within a very deep electric frying pan. The digital thermometer lies in the yogurt just as snugly as if the mixture were a patient's milky tongue. Kefirovsky takes a plastic container from the refrigerator and spoons a sticky material into the yogurt. The aroma is strong and brisk, it smells almost like wintergreen.

"What's that?" Williams asks.

Mrs. Kefirovsky looks surprised. "He didn't tell you yet?"

"No, but I will," the Professor says. "Now we must wait for at least fifteen minutes while the entire mixture resonates at one hundred and twelve degrees

Fahrenheit. Then we pour it into pints, where it can stay for almost a week. The store yogurts are good for two months or more. Mine is not the same. This is good for six days only."

Mrs. Kefirovsky sits on a stool, her heavy legs dangling playfully. The reporter and the Professor are on chrome-and-vinyl kitchen chairs facing the yogurt. Kefirovsky has again taken up his pointer. "What I added to the yogurt is a sticky sweet extract of an Arabic plant called 'mahn,' spelled m-a-n. I imported it from Saudi Arabia, Egypt, and Morocco. The Moroccan one grows best here. I harvest it and freeze it. It's also good for the breath like chlorophyll gum.

"Fifteen years ago all you heard was chlorophyll. Then everyone got interested in outer space and transistors. I am the opposite. I started with space forty, fifty years ago, and now I'm back to chlorophyll. Science is like that. We are always breaking up substances to look for the soul of the material. My sons, the chemists, don't know this. They just do jobs for the oil companies."

"Not everyone is an original thinker like you, Vasi," Mrs. Kefirovsky states from her high position on the stool. "Mr. Williams, don't get the wrong impression about the boys. They're good chemists. But Vasi has no patience for people who learn to do something and then do it. He learns something and then he does something else."

"That's what science is," the Professor says.

"Twelve minutes, Vasi." Mrs. Kefirovsky watches the kitchen clock from her perch.

"I started thinking about this only a few years ago, after Hans Fricht died. He was the last of my colleagues. I noticed how all of us pallbearers could hardly carry him. I thought, We're just too old for such work. But that wasn't it. Hans Fricht, whom I loved like a brother, ate too much."

"He did," Emily adds. "He liked to eat small meals every hour while he worked."

"This started me thinking altogether about eating. Then I went to the old books, the way I did after I studied physics and astronomy. I thought to myself, if the heavens got into these books, why not the foods? So I read all the Greeks, mostly Homer, who is full of eating. I kept tables on who ate what, anybody I could find. Achilles lived on fifteen hundred calories a day and drank enough wine to die of cirrhosis by the time he was twenty-two. Priam had a hundred sons, yet Troy was only as big as a football field. Their food came in wagons from the east of the city because the Greeks never cut off their supplies. The Trojan horse is really a story about death from a full belly, but this is not the evidence I sought. I didn't want to interpret the books, I wanted the evidence right there in black and white for anyone to see."

"He didn't want people to say, 'Oh, there goes Kefirovsky again,'" says Emily. "He wanted it to be exact. Ten minutes, Vasi."

"So I kept reading the myths, the Upanishads, the Book of the Dead, the I Ching, until I found it right before my eyes."

"Where?" Williams asks, although he makes no attempt to take notes.

"Exodus. Right there in Exodus. This served me right for not checking earlier. But outside of the Flood I had never found very much decent natural history there. Anyway, that's where it was, Exodus 16:13. Have you heard of manna, 'manna from heaven'?"

"Do you mean what the Israelites ate in the desert?"

"Don't call them 'Israelites,' you make them sound like flashlights. They were no kind of 'ites.' The Egyptians called them Abirus. And they weren't in the desert. The best evidence is that the Sinai peninsula was in partial bloom at the time, enough to sustain nomads if they went, now and then, into Canaan or Egypt for grain."

"Well, forgive me, Professor, I'm only a layman."

"You make that sound like 'amen.'" Kefirovsky laughs. "The flashlights said 'amen' in the desert." He stands and walks over to the yogurt surrounded by simmering water.

"Still eight minutes," Emily calls out.

The Professor jabs his pointer at Williams' white patent shoe and looks the reporter in the eye. "I know what the flashlights ate."

"Yogurt?"

Kefirovsky goes to the window and grins out at his rose garden.

"In Exodus they call it 'a fine flakelike thing like hoarfrost on the ground.' They say it tasted like wafers made with honey."

"Vasi lets me put a little honey in his, it's the only sweet he uses and it's because of that passage that he lets me do it. Six minutes."

"Do you know what they call yogurt now in the Middle East, where it is a staple?"

Williams says he does not know.

"They call it *Leben*. This means 'life' in German. And that Moroccan plant whose sweet milk is thick as motor oil, the Arabs call that one *man*. Do you see what hangs on in language? Man and life. Plain as the nose on your face. Once you know it, it's all over the Bible. 'Man does not live by bread alone' is only half a sentence."

"Wait a minute, Professor, I'm not sure I follow this. The linguistic hints are one thing, but how could yogurt appear in the desert?"

"You ask questions just like Herman Eidler asked. Right away to the first cause. Well, I don't know how yogurt appeared to the Abirus. That's for the theologians. I am a scientist. Science is two things, a problem and a guess. The earth is rocks and organisms decaying together at a fixed rate and under uniform pressure. In Exodus it says that this flakelike stuff melted when the sun grew hot. I don't know. I don't sell cough drops. But I can tell you this, the recipe has been before our eyes for a few thousand years and nobody has read it. They all say, look what the flashlights gave us, ethics, morals, ten commandments. But everybody else gave us the commandments too. Every priest in Egypt, every Hindu, every Parsee, every Chaldean, every Hammurabi, even the African cannibals roasting children had do's and do nots. We read the Bible but we missed the recipes."

"Four minutes, Vasi." Mrs. Kefirovsky slides off the stool. Beyond the stainless-steel kitchen she disappears amid the dark wood furnishings of other rooms. "I'll be back in time," she says as her voice trails away.

Kefirovsky stares at his yogurt. The digital thermometer reads a constant one hundred and twelve degrees. "Pretty soon we'll pour and when it cools you can have some. If I'd been making this thirty years ago, my friends might still be here. We used to meet on most Sundays just to joke about things. Herman Eidler would come and Hans Fricht, of course, and Jerome Van Strung. Sometimes Einstein came over from Princeton. You would call us a think tank. They were just a bunch of krauts smacking their lips over wurst and sauerbraten. We worried about the war. Eidler lost his whole family and his wife's family. Van Strung had letters from Walter Benjamin that nobody else ever saw. They all liked to play croquet on my lawn. Sometimes I read sections from *Worlds in Confusion* out loud while they swung their mallets. Fricht was a beekeeper and clean as a Band-Aid. Einstein and Van Strung could walk barefoot over the dogshit.

"And after croquet it was food and beer. All the time, Einstein knew about the bomb and ate heavy meals. He never talked about his work. I naturally did and Fricht talked about his bees and Van Strung talked literature. When the war was over, Eidler brought us, one Sunday, three dozen Nathan's hot dogs straight from Coney Island in an ice chest. He came in a government car with a chauffeur. He brought them with buns and everything, but the ice melted onto the bread. Emily rewarmed the hot dogs and we ate them plain. That was the way we celebrated VE day. We ate and we talked.

"There is a former football player in California who writes to me. He eats only on the weekends and has done this since he retired as a defensive player four years ago. He knows many people in California who survive on nuts and figs. We are doing metabolism and blood tests on him and keeping data. In the summer he runs a camp for overweight boys. Parents bring their sons there just to watch a man not eat and be cheerful and busy all week."

"Vasi, it's fifteen minutes." Emily reappears with a large funnel and a photo album. Dr. Kefirovsky removes the thermometer, puts on two stove mittens, and lifting the big glass container out of the boiling water, pours his yogurt into the funnel above the small glass containers which will house the mixture.

"It's not ready yet," Emily says, "still lumpy." Kefirovsky pours the pint of liquid back into the three-quart jar. "We'll have to wait a few minutes more for the *man* to melt. It happens sometimes because it doesn't freeze uniformly. It doesn't hurt anything."

"We would do this once a week if it was just for Vasi," Emily says. "But we make it most days to give to others. All the neighbors get some and we mail throughout the area in winter when the spoilage rate is low."

"You mail it in glass containers?" the reporter asks.

"No, we mail it in plastic with tight lids. It can go about three days without refrigeration when it's fresh. Most of them probably don't even taste it. In '72 we mailed one to Nixon and one to McGovern special delivery. Not even a thank you from either one. A few people have heard about it and come to ask for some."

"Have you ever tried to sell it?"

"He talks like Gerald," Kefirovsky says, and walks back out to the garden still wearing his oven mittens.

"I didn't mean to offend him," the reporter says to Emily.

"It's all right. He's sensitive because Gerald, actually all of the boys, stand up to him." She opens the photo album to what seems to be recent Polaroid snapshots of healthy middle-aged men and women surrounded by children. "We have wonderful sons and grandchildren. They respect their father too, and they wouldn't try to stop him from doing whatever he wants to do. But they won't allow me to be on the yogurt diet. Don't get me wrong, I like it and believe Vasi is discovering scientific truths, but I eat it and I'm still hungry. Gerald ships me cornfed beef from Iowa. I have to send a photograph every month to prove to him that I'm not losing weight like their father. Vasi used to weigh over two twenty, now, you can see for yourself he's a string bean. The doctors say he's healthy, but he should take vitamins. Since he's been growing *man* down here, he's eaten nothing but the yogurt and *man*. We moved here from New Jersey when he realized Texas was the right climate for the *man*. We tried Florida and California first, and he ate other food there because he admits that yogurt without *man* isn't enough. The boys told him to sell the recipe, but he wants to get the book out first, *Earth Story*, to explain all about it. Otherwise it would just be another food product.

"I hope you understand that with Vasi there is no halfway. He is his own laboratory. The boys know this. Gerald says, 'One laboratory is enough for him. Let him starve himself, but if I catch him forcing you to live on that stuff, I'll break his bony back.' That's why he won't speak to Gerald. But Gerald loves him. All the boys do and the grandchildren too. You can't just make a whole family, twelve grandchildren and all, stop eating everything but yogurt and *man*.

"It's one thing to have a theory about history. The boys backed him one hundred percent on that. And it wasn't easy. Here they were studying to be scientists and all the famous scientists saying their father was a fraud. Gerald quit one chemistry class because of something the teacher said about Vasi. The boys think he might be right about the yogurt too, but they don't want him to starve me and to starve their families. That's not wrong, is it? Did Pasteur give his kids TB or Salk carry around polio?"

"It's not the same." Dr. Kefirovsky is back in the kitchen carrying a fresh sprig of the *man* plant. "I wear these mittens because the plant is full of stickers. I'm just showing you a sprig. Outside, we milk it like the maple trees in Vermont."

"Is it a lot like maple syrup?" the reporter asks.

"Much thicker in texture. It freezes slowly and looks like peanut brittle when I put it in the yogurt."

Williams feels his pocket to make sure the notebook is there. He uncrosses his legs and seems ready to leave.

"I'm afraid, Dr. Kefirovsky, that I really don't follow all of this. Don't get me wrong, I appreciate your showing me exactly how you make this yogurt even though I'm here to talk about your earlier work. What I don't see is the jump from your discovery that yogurt is Old Testament manna, to the point of excluding all other food. I mean the . . . flashlights ate other food too, didn't they?"

"Not for forty years. For forty years they lived on this and then, only then, were they ready to pick up the business of destiny. This was a time out in history, just like during a football game. This is built into the organism. In sleep, in a nervous breakdown, in menopause, the body is always saying 'time out.' Social organizations too. Governments. There is the New Deal and then an Eisenhower. The Revolution and then Stalin. Going out of Egypt, then forty years in the desert. That was the only time they did it right.

"Imagine if in 1922 we Russians had sat down on the steppes, sat down in our cities, sat down by the Black Sea, in the Urals, in Siberia, all over, Russians sitting down saying to each other, 'Time out. Congratulations on the revolution, now let's have a time out for forty years to eat *man* and yogurt.' Would there have been Stalinism? Would the people swill vodka and be fat as pigs? There are two things to learn from Exodus. Take time out and eat the right thing."

"So you think everyone in the world should at least temporarily go on this diet?"

"First they should have their teeth pulled."

Emily laughs, showing hers. "The boys never even took you seriously on that, Vasi." Kefirovsky opens his mouth and with his forefinger goes in a circle pushing his upper lip and then his lower lip away from his empty gums.

"I hadn't noticed," the reporter says.

"Exactly, it doesn't matter. I happen to have lost mine nine years ago from pyorrhea. When I learned what I now know, I gave away the false ones. Teeth are an evolutionary accident. There is no doubt that we're losing them faster than chest hair. We needed them only until the domestication of animals. For six or seven thousand years teeth have been an anachronism."

"To whom did you give your false teeth? I find that pretty unusual."

"To the Illinois College of Optometry. They have all the manuscripts. I went there in 1927."

"That's news to me. I don't recall that in your biographical profile."

"I didn't stay for a degree. At the time Hans Fricht was a professor of optics there. I knew little English. A Russian astronomer was not needed anywhere. Hans said to me, 'Become an eye doctor, there is nothing to it.' He got me a scholarship. It was the first place in this country where we lived. Later I went to New Jersey. The optometry trustees asked for my notebooks and my old eyeglasses. In 1965 they made a Kefirovsky room. In 1973 I sent my teeth also."

Kefirovsky checks the mixture. "Five minutes more should do it. The only thing I'm not sure of is the forty years. I don't know if the time out has to be that long or if it can be shortened. Do you think you could eat this for forty years?"

"Exclusively?"

"Exclusively."

"I don't think so, Professor, at least I wouldn't want to try."

"I am seventy-seven years old. In order for me to try it forty years I would have to live to be one hundred and sixteen. This is possible, but unlikely. There will perhaps be no other scientist to follow in my footsteps. Science will produce more Corfam and SST engines. The keys to natural history lay shrouded for thousands of years, now we refuse to see the one true gift of the gods. Easy, abundant, tasty, and wrapped in a time out. If the clergymen would wake

up, they would see it. What is the promised land?
Milk and honey and time. What is yogurt? Milk and
bacteria and time. Why did the people who lived on
manna for forty years want a land of milk and honey?
Why not a land of pomegranates? Why not a land of
barley and sesame seed and olive oil? Why not wine
and cheese? Where else do you read about milk
and honey? Nowhere. I've looked. And what sort of
honey would you find in a semiarid climate where
the annual rainfall could hardly support a large bee
population. If Hans Fricht was alive, he would be an
immense help now. He knew bees from A to Z. He
would have seen immediately. He used to say, 'Where
the bee sucks, there suck I,' and Eidler and Van
Strung would laugh at him saying that while he hit
the croquet ball and jumped up and down when he
had a clean blocking shot. He knew the bee signal
language before anybody wrote about it. Hans could
have understood birds too if he would have tried. We
all worshiped that man. Einstein brought him page
after page of dull formulas by the thousands until one
day Hans said to him, 'This is it, you *glücklich* kraut.
You've finally got something worthwhile here.' And
that's the only time he ever praised Einstein. But it's
once more than he praised me. He used to say to me,
'Vasi, lay off, they're not ready for you. Try a hobby.'
When I left optometry college, he thought I should
be a pharmacist. But I was lucky, I got a job at the
Institute. Hans himself was unemployed for twenty-
two years. They made him leave the optometry faculty
when they found out he was not an optometrist. After
that he was a sponge, a hanger-on, a misfit. Imagine
such a misfit. He wouldn't take a penny from anyone.
He was an expert sewer and knitter. One of the
great minds of the twentieth century making his own
suits and sweaters. He raised his own vegetables. The
man lived on a few hundred dollars a year. His friends
made sure he had plenty to eat and that was our mistake. We tried to be generous and our butterball
turkeys, our triscuits, our dark beer, and our wurst,
all this killed him."

Kefirovsky is almost breathless. He leans on his pointer and his body shakes with sobs.

"Vasi loved Hans Fricht," Emily says. "You would have too. There was a scientist and a human being. Godfather to all the boys."

"It's a shame that he had such a hard life," the reporter says. "I've actually never heard of him."

"That is science," says Kefirovsky.

"If Hans was alive," Emily adds, "he wouldn't let you starve yourself like this. That's why you're so weak that you can hardly talk for a few minutes. You're the thinker, let someone else starve to prove you're right. Thousands of college students are looking for jobs like this. They swallow goldfish and squeeze into telephone booths and now they kiss for two weeks at a time. These people could prove you're right, and you could live to see it. Ask the reporter."

"She has a point, Professor. Lots of students do paid experiments. But I don't want to get into the midst of a family squabble about this."

"Look at him," Emily screams, "look at him. How can you say you don't want to mix in? You've listened to a brilliant scientist talk, don't you want to save his life?"

Kefirovsky remains calm. He smiles at the reporter and raising his pointer directs the rubber tip at his wife. "She means well, but in spite of my many explanations Emily does not see that it is the yogurt that keeps me alive and well. At my age the average man has been dead for seven years."

"From two hundred and ten pounds to one-forty-five, that's how it's keeping you alive." She addresses the reporter. "Write this in *Time* magazine, that he can't walk stairs, that I have to tie his shoes. He's dizzy from air conditioning, and he chokes on the heat. He sits at his desk and starves himself. For two years I've watched. Enough is enough."

Still smiling, Kefirovsky says, "The revolution that is coming will make you forget Marx. Eating three meals will be like having three wives. Ordinary people by the millions will have their teeth pulled and drink happily ever after. Science and scarcity change the world. The yogurt will end scarcity, another time out is coming. You'll see. Marx and Malthus will be as forgotten as Paracelsus and Agrippa. Do you know what they worried about? Thousands of years ago Heraclitus, a smart man, thought the earth was packed tight as a suitcase. Everyone is wrong. Someday I'll be wrong too. That is science. In the meantime, it's time out. The Babylonians were a thin people but the Philistines gorged themselves. Huns were thinner than Romans. It's the law of history. Look at the Ethiopians. Look at the black Africans who weigh eighty pounds and can chase a giraffe for three days without food or water."

"It's terrible to watch." From her seat on the kitchen stool, Emily sobs and watches the kitchen clock. "The five minutes are up, Vasi." Emily wipes her eyes and once more raises the funnel. The Professor takes up his mittens and approaches the calm yogurt in the midst of bubbling waters. "This time it's good and ready." He holds the heavy glass jar steadily, the blue veins in his forearms stretch and tremble with the exercise, but Kefirovsky's pouring hand is still and even. Expertly, Emily moves the funnel from one pint bottle to the next, spilling only droplets on the stainless-steel counter. As coordinated as a ballet, their hands move the thick milky liquid over and into its bottles in a silent rhythmical pattern. As the big jar becomes lighter, the Professor does not quicken the pace of his pouring nor does Emily speed the funnel. The yogurt drops like long thick tongues into the bottles and it stops at the very tip of each one without overflowing. It bubbles for a second and then expires. With thick corks Emily seals ten bottles while Kefirovsky and the reporter watch her strong fingers. She leaves two unsealed. Kefirovsky pours his yogurt into a yellow glass decorated with the figures of parrots. "Do you want to drink yours or eat it with a spoon?" he asks the reporter.

"I'll drink," Williams says. "Isn't Mrs. Kefirovsky having any?"

"No," she says, "I have a steak in the broiler. I usually drink one at night while Vasi is reading."

The Professor raises his glass. A slight steam rises from the yogurt. With the gesture of a toast he extends his glass toward Emily, who stands in front of the ten corked bottles. Her eyes are vaguely red, and in the silent kitchen the noise of a broiling steak begins to be heard. Emily nods and smiles at Kefirovsky, who then makes the same gesture to the reporter. "To science," Emily says as the two men slowly raise to their lips the white flakelike liquid, thick as dew and fine as the hoarfrost on the ground.

Understanding
Alvarado

I

Castro thought it was no accident that Achilles "Archie" Alvarado held the world record for being hit in the head by a pitched ball.

"Because he was a hero even then," Fidel said, "because he stood like a hero with his neck proudly over the plate."

When people asked Mrs. Alvarado what she thought of her husband's career, she said, "Chisox okay, the rest of the league stinks. Archie, he liked to play every day, bench him and his knees ached, his fingers swelled, his tongue forgot English. He would say, 'Estelle, let's split, let's scram, *vámonos a* Cuba. What we owe to Chisox?'

"I'd calm him down. 'Arch,' I'd say, 'Arch, Chisox have been plenty good to us. Paid five gees more than Tribe, first-class hotels, white roomies on the road, good press.'

" 'Estelle,' he would say, 'I can't take it no more. They got me down to clubbing in the pinch and only against southpaws. They cut Chico Carasquel and Sammy Esposito and Cactus Bob Kuzava. What we owe to Chisox?'

"When it got like that, I would say, 'Talk to Zloto,' and Zloto would say, 'Man, you Latinos sure are hotheads. I once got nine hits in a row for the Birds, was Rookie of the Year for the Bosox. I have the largest hands in either league and what do you think I do? I sit on the bench and spit-shine my street shoes. Look there, you can see your greasy black mug in 'em.' Zloto always knew how to handle Alvarado."

Zloto came to Havana, showed Fidel his hands, talked about the '50s. Fidel said, "They took our good men and put them in Yankee uniforms, in Bosox, Chisox, Dodgers, Birds. They took our manhood, Zloto. They took our Achilles and called him Archie. Hector Gonzalez they called Ramrod, Jesús Ortiz they made a Jayo. They treated Cuban manhood like a bowl of chicos and ricos. Yes, we have no bananas but we got vine-ripened Latinos who play good ball all year, stick their heads over the plate, and wait for the Revolution. Fidel Castro gave it to them. It was three and two on me in Camagüey around November 1958. There were less than two dozen of us. Batista had all roads blocked and there was hardly enough ammunition left to kill some rabbits. He could have starved us out but he got greedy, he wanted the quick inning. When I saw that he was coming in with his best stuff with his dark one out over the middle, I said to Che and to Francisco Muñiz, 'Habana for Christmas,' and I lined his fascist pitch up his capitalist ass."

"I'm not impressed," Zloto said. "When I heard about the Bay of Pigs I said to myself, 'Let's wipe those oinks right off the face of the earth.' You took Cuba, our best farm property, and went Commie with it. You took our best arms, Castro, our speed- and our curve-ball artists. You dried up our Cuban diamonds."

"Zloto, Zloto," Fidel said. "Look at this picture of your buddy, 'Archie' Alvarado. Don't you like him better as 'Achilles'? Look at his uniform, look at his AK 47 rifle."

"I liked him better when he was number twenty-three and used a thirty-six-inch Hillerich and Bradsby Louisville Slugger to pound out line drives in Comiskey Park."

"There's no more Comiskey Park," Fidel said. "No more Grace, no more Chuck Comiskey to come down after a tough extra-inning loss and buy a drink for the whole clubhouse. No more free Bulova watches. The Chisox are run by an insurance company now. You punch a time clock before batting practice and they charge for overtime in the whirlpool bath."

"That's goddamn pinko propaganda," Zloto said.

"You've been outta the game, big Victor," Fidel said. "You've been sitting too long out in Arizona being a dental assistant. You haven't been on the old diamonds, now AstroTurfed, closed to the sun, and air-conditioned. You have not seen the bleachers go to two-fifty. While you've been an Arizona the world changed, Zloto. Look at our Achilles, four fractured skulls, thirteen years in the big time. Played all over the outfield, played first and played third. A lifetime mark of two ninety-nine and RBIs in the thousands. He never got an Achilles day from Chisox, Bosox, Tribe, or Birds. When he came home Fidel made him a day, made him a reservist colonel. I did this because Achilles Alvarado is not chickenshit. You, Zloto, know this better than anyone.

"Achilles said to me the first time we met, 'Fidel, the big time is over for Archie Alvarado, but send me to the cane fields, give me a machete, and I'll prove that Alvarado has enough arm left to do something for Cuba.' A hero, this Achilles 'Archie' Alvarado, but they sent him back to us a broken-down, used-up pinch hitter with no eye, no arm, and no speed.

"'Achilles, Archie,' I said, 'the Revolution was not made for Chisox, Bosox, Bengals, and Birds. We didn't take Habana for chicos and ricos. Cuba Libre doesn't give a flying fuck for RBIs. The clutch hit is every minute here, baby brother. Cuba loves you for your Cuban heart. I'll make you a colonel, a starter in the only game that counts. Your batting average will be counted in lives saved, in people educated, fed, and protected from capitalist exploitation.'"

"Cut the shit, Fidel," Zloto said. "I'm here because Archie will be eligible for his pension in September. He'll pull in a thousand a month for the rest of his days. That'll buy a lot of bananas down here, won't it?

"You may think that you understand Alvarado, Fidel, but I knew the man for eight years, roomed with him on the Chisox and the Bosox. I've seen him high, seen him in slumps you wouldn't believe. I've seen him in the dugout after being picked off first in a crucial situation. You wouldn't know what that's like, Castro.

I'm talking about a man who has just met a fast ball and stroked it over the infield. He has made the wide turn at first and watched the resin of his footprint settle around the bag. He has thrown off the batting helmet and pulled the soft, long-billed cap from his hip pocket. The coach has slapped his ass and twenty, thirty, maybe forty thousand Chisox fans start stomping their feet while the organ plays 'Charge,' and then he is picked off in a flash, caught scratching his crotch a foot from the bag. And it's all over. You hear eighty thousand feet stop stomping. The first baseman snickers behind his glove; even the ump smiles. I've seen Alvarado at times like that cry like a baby. He'd throw a towel over his head and say, 'Zloto, I'm a no-good dummy. Good hit and no head. We coulda won it all here in the top of the ninth. That Yankee pitcher is good for shit. My dumb-ass move ruined the Chisox chances.' He would sit in front of his locker taking it real hard until the GM or even Chuck Comiskey himself would come down and say, 'Archie, it's just one game that you blew with a dumb move. We're still in it, still in the thick of the race. You'll help these Sox plenty during the rest of the year. Now take your shower and get your ass over to a Mexican restaurant.' The Alvarado that I knew, Castro, that Alvarado could come back the next afternoon, sometimes the next inning, and change the complexion of a game."

Fidel laughed and lit a cigar. "Zloto, you've been away too long. The Archie you knew, this man went out of style with saddle shoes and hula hoops. Since the days you're talking about when Alvarado cried over a pick-off play, since then Che and Muñiz are dead and two Kennedys assassinated. There have been wars in the Far East and Middle East and in Bangladesh. There have been campus shootings, a revolution of the Red Guard, an ouster of Khrushchev, a fascist massacre in Indonesia, two revolutions in Uruguay, fourteen additions to the U.N. There has been détente and Watergate and a Washington-Peking understanding and where have you been, Zloto? You've been in

Tucson, Arizona, reading the newspaper on Sunday and cleaning teeth. Even dental techniques have changed. Look at your fluorides and your gum brushing method."

"All right, boys," Mrs. Alvarado said, "enough is enough. What are we going to prove anyway by reminiscing about the good old days? Zloto means well. He came here as a friend. Twelve grand a year for life is not small potatoes to Archie and me. In the Windy City or in Beantown we could live in a nice integrated neighborhood on that kind of money and pick up a little extra by giving autographs at Chevy dealerships. Fidel, you know that Archie always wanted to stay in the game. In one interview he told Bill Fuller of the *Sun-Times* that he wanted to manage the Chisox someday. They didn't want any black Cuban managers in the American League, not then. But, like you say, Fidel, a lot of water has gone under the bridge since those last days when Archie was catching slivers for the Bosox, Chisox, and Birds. These days, there might even be some kind of front-office job to round off that pension. Who knows; it might be more than he made twenty years ago when he led the league in RBIs."

Castro said, "Estelle, apart from all ideological arguments, you are just dreaming. Achilles was never a U.S. citizen. After a dozen years as one of Castro's colonels, do you really think Uncle Sam is going to say, 'C'mon up here, Archie, take a front-office job and rake in the cash'? Do you really think America works that way, Estelle? I know Zloto thinks that, but you've been down here all this time, don't you understand capitalist exploitation by now?"

Estelle said, "Fidel, I'm not saying that we are going to give up the ideals of the Revolution and I'm not deluded by the easy capitalist life. I am thinking about only getting what's coming to us. Alvarado put in the time, he should get the pension."

"That's the whole reason I took a week off to come down here," Zloto said. "The commissioner called me

up—he heard we were buddies—and said, 'Zloto,
you might be in a position to do your old friend
Alvarado some good, that is if you're willing to travel.'
The commissioner absolutely guaranteed that Archie
would get his pension if he came back up and established residence. The commissioner of baseball is not
about to start mailing monthly checks through the
Swiss embassy, and I don't blame him. The commissioner is not even saying you have to stay permanently
in the U.S. He is just saying, 'Come up, get an apartment, make a few guest appearances, an interview or
two, and then do whatever the hell you want.'"

Fidel said, "Yes, go up to America and tell them how
mean Fidel is, how bad the sugar crop was, and how
poor and hungry we Cubans are. Tell them what they
want to hear and they'll pension you off. The Achilles
I know would swallow poison before he'd kowtow to
the memory of John Foster Dulles that way. They sent
an Archie back home, but Cuba Libre reminded him
he was really an Achilles."

"Fidel, let's not get sentimental," Mrs. Alvarado
said. "Let's talk turkey. We want the twelve grand a
year, right?"

"Right, but only because it is the fruit of Achilles'
own labor."

"Okay, in order to get the money back we have to go
back."

"I could take it up in the United Nations, I could
put the pressure on. Kissinger is very shaky in Latin
America. He knows we all know that he doesn't give
a fuck about any country except Venezuela. I could
do it through Waldheim, and nobody would have to
know. Then we could threaten to go public if they
hold out on what's coming to him."

Zloto said, "America doesn't hold out on anybody,
Castro. Ask Joe Stalin's daughter if you don't believe
me. You guys are batting your heads against the wall
by hating us. There's nothing to hate. We want a
square deal for everyone. In this case too. As for
Kissinger, he might carry some weight with the Arabs,

but the commissioner of baseball cannot be pressured. That damned fool Alvarado should have become a citizen while he was playing in the States. I didn't know he wasn't a citizen. It was just crazy not to become one. Every other Latin does."

"But our Achilles, he was always different," Castro said. "He always knew that the Chisox, Bosox, Birds, and Braves didn't own the real thing. The real Achilles Alvarado was in Camagüey with me, in Bolivia with Che, with Mao on the Long March."

"The real Achilles was just too lazy to do things right," Mrs. Alvarado said. "He didn't want to fill out complicated papers, so he stayed an alien. As long as he had a job, it didn't matter."

"Zloto," Fidel said, "you one-time Rookie of the Year, now a fat, tooth-cleaning capitalist, you want to settle this the way Achilles would settle this? I mean why should we bring in Kissinger and Waldheim and everyone else? I say if a man believes in the Revolution, what's a pension to him? You think I couldn't have been a Wall Street lawyer? And what about our Doctor Che? You don't think he would have made a big pension in the AMA? I say our Achilles has recovered his Cuban manhood. He won't want to go back. Estelle does not speak for him."

"Fidel is right," she said. "I do not speak for Archie Alvarado, I only write his English for him."

"If Estelle wants to go back and be exploited, let her go. Do you want those television announcers calling you Mrs. Archie again as if you had stepped from the squares of a comic strip? Does the wife of a colonel in the Cuban Army sound like a comic-strip girl to you, Zloto?"

"Fidel," Estelle said, "don't forget the issue is not so large. Only a trip to the Windy City or Beantown, maybe less than two weeks in all."

"You are forgetting," Fidel said, "what happened to Kid Gavilan when he went back to see an eye surgeon in New York. They put his picture in *Sepia* and in the *National Enquirer*, the news services showed him with his bulging eye being hugged by a smooth-faced Sugar Ray Robinson. They wanted it to seem like this: here are two retired Negro fighters. One is a tap dancer in Las Vegas, the other has for ten years been working in the cane fields of Castro's Cuba. Look at how healthy the American Negro is. His teeth are white as ever, his step lithe in Stetson shoes, while our Kid Gavilan, once of the bolo punch that decked all welterweights, our Kid stumbles through the clinics of New York in worker's boots and his eye bulges from the excesses of the Revolution. They degraded the Kid and the Revolution and they sent him home with a red, white, and blue eye patch. That's how they treated Kid Gavilan, and they'll do the same to Achilles Alvarado."

"Well, goddamn," Zloto said, "I've had enough talk. I want to see Alvarado; whether he wants to do it is up to him."

"That," Castro said, "is typical bourgeois thinking. You would alienate the man from his fellows, let him think that his decision is personal and lonely, that it represents only the whims of an Alvarado and does not speak for the larger aspirations of all Cubans, and all exploited peoples. The wants of an Alvarado are the wants of the people. He is not a Richard Nixon to hide out in Camp David surrounded by bodyguards while generals all over the world are ready to press the buttons of annihilation."

"No more bullshit, I want to see Alvarado."

Estelle said, "He is in Oriente Province on maneuvers with the army. He will be gone for . . . for how long, Fidel?"

"Achilles Alvarado's unit is scheduled for six months in Oriente. I could bring him back to see you, Zloto, but we don't operate that way. A man's duty to his country comes before all else."

"Then I'm going up to see him and deliver the commissioner's letter. I don't trust anybody else around here to do it for me."

"We'll all go," Fidel said. "In Cuba Libre, no man goes it alone."

II
On Maneuvers in Oriente Province

The Ninth Infantry Unit of the Cuban Army is on spring maneuvers. Oriente is lush and hilly. There are villages every few miles in which happy farmers drink dark beer brewed with local hops. The Ninth Army bivouacs all over the province and assembles each morning at six a.m. to the sound of the bugle. The soldiers eat a leisurely breakfast and plan the next day's march. By two p.m., they are set up somewhere and ready for an afternoon of recreation. Colonel Alvarado is the only member of the Ninth Infantry with major-league experience, but there are a few older men who have played professional baseball in the minor leagues. Because there is not adequate protective equipment, army regulations prohibit hardball, but the Ninth Infantry plays fast-pitch softball, which is almost as grueling.

When Fidel, Zloto, and Estelle drive up to the Ninth Army's makeshift diamond, it is the seventh inning of a four–four game between the Reds and Whites. A former pitcher from Iowa City in the Three I League is on the mound for the Reds. Colonel Alvarado, without face guard or chest protector, is the umpire behind the plate. His head, as in the old days, seems extremely vulnerable as it bobs behind the waving bat just inches from the arc of a powerful swing. He counts on luck and fast reflexes to save him from foul tips that could crush his Adam's apple.

When the jeep pulls up, Reds and Whites come to immediate attention, then raise their caps in an "Olé" for Fidel.

"These are liberated men, Zloto. The army does not own their lives. When their duties are completed they can do as they wish. We have no bedchecks, no passes, nobody is AWOL. If a man has a reason to leave, he tells his officer and he leaves. With us, it is an honor to be a soldier."

When Zloto spots Alvarado behind the plate he runs toward him and hugs his old friend. He rubs Alvarado's woolly black head with his oversize hands. Estelle is next to embrace her husband, a short businesslike kiss, and then Fidel embraces the umpire as enthusiastically as Zloto did. An army photographer catches the look of the umpire surprised by embraces from an old friend, a wife, and a Prime Minister in the seventh inning of a close game.

"Men of the Revolution." Fidel has advanced to the pitcher's mound, the highest ground. The congregated Reds and Whites gather around the makeshift infield. "Men of the Revolution, we are gathered here to test the resolve of your umpire, Colonel Alvarado. The Revolution is tested in many ways. This time it is the usual thing, the capitalist lure of money. Yet it is no simple issue. It is money that rightfully belongs to Colonel Alvarado, but they would degrade him by forcing him to claim it. To come there so that the capitalist press can say, 'Look what the Revolution has done to one of the stars of the fifties. Look at his stooped, arthritic back, his gnarled hands, from years in the cane fields.' They never cared about his inadequate English when they used him, but now they will laugh at his accent and his paltry vocabulary. When they ask him about Cuba, he will stumble and they will deride us all with the smiles of their golden teeth.

"The commissioner of baseball has sent us this behemoth, the Polish-American veteran of eleven campaigns in the American League, Victor Zloto, who some of you may remember as Rookie of the Year in 1945. This Zloto is not an evil man, he is only a capitalist tool. They use his friendship for the colonel as a bait. Zloto speaks for free enterprise. He has two cars, a boat, and his own home. His province is represented by their hero of the right, Barry Goldwater, who wanted to bomb Hanoi to pieces. Zloto wants the colonel to come back, to go through the necessary charade to claim his rightful pension, and then return to us if he wishes. Mrs. Alvarado shares this view. I say no Cuban man should become a pawn for even one hour."

"What does the colonel say?" someone yells from the infield. "Does the colonel want to go back?"

The umpire is standing behind Castro. He is holding his wife's hand while Zloto's long arm encircles both of them. Castro turns to his colonel. "What do you say, Achilles Alvarado?"

Zloto says, "It's twelve grand a year, Archie, and all you have to do is show up just once. If you want to stay, you can. I know you don't like being a two-bit umpire and colonel down here. I know you don't give a shit about revolutions and things like that."

Castro says, "The colonel is thinking about his long career with the Chisox, Bosox, Tribe, and Birds. He is thinking about his four fractured skulls. He justifiably wants that pension. And I, his Prime Minister and his friend, I want him to have that pension, too. Believe me, soldiers, I want this long-suffering victim of exploitation to recover a small part of what they owe to him and to all victims of racism and oppression."

Colonel Alvarado grips tightly his wife's small hand. He looks down and kicks up clouds of dust with his army boots. He is silent. Zloto says, "It's not fair to do this, Castro. You damn well know it. You get him up here in front of the army and make a speech so it will look like he's a traitor if he puts in his pension claim. You staged all this because you are afraid that in a fair choice Archie would listen to reason just like Estelle did. You can bet that I'm going to tell the commissioner how you put Archie on the spot out here. I'm going to tell him that Archie is a softball umpire. This is worse than Joe Louis being a wrestling referee."

"Think fast, Yankee," one of the ballplayers yells as he lobs a softball at Zloto's perspiring face. The big first baseman's hand closes over the ball as if it were a large mushroom. He tosses it to Castro. "I wish we could play it out, Fidel, just you and I, like a world series or a one-on-one basketball game. I wish all political stuff could work out like baseball, with everybody where they belong at the end of the season and only one champion of the world."

"Of course, you would like that, Zloto, so long as you Yankee capitalists were the champions."

"The best team would win. If you have the material and the management, you win; it's that simple."

"Not as simple as you are, Zloto. But why should we stand here and argue political philosophy? We are interrupting a game, no? You have accused Fidel of not giving Alvarado a fair opportunity. I will do this with you, Zloto, if Achilles agrees, I will do this. Fidel will pitch to you. If you get a clean hit, you can take Alvarado back on the first plane. If not, Alvarado stays. It will be more than fair. This gives you a great advantage. A former big leaguer against an out-of-shape Prime Minister. My best pitch should be cake for you. You can go back and tell the commissioner that you got a hit off Castro. Barry Goldwater will kiss your fingertips for that."

Zloto smiles. "You're on, Castro, if it's okay with Archie and Estelle." Colonel Alvarado still eyes the soft dirt; he shrugs his shoulders. Castro says, "Do you think this is a just experience for you, Achilles Alvarado? This is like a medieval tournament, with you as the prize. This smacks of capitalism. But this once, Fidel will do it if you agree that your fate shall be so decided."

"What's all this about fate and justice," Estelle says. She takes the ball from Castro. "Archie had eleven brothers and sisters and hardly a good meal until he came up to the Chisox. He cracked his wrist in an all-star game and that cost him maybe four or five years in the big leagues because the bones didn't heal right. It's a mean, impersonal world with everything always up for grabs. Alvarado knows it, and he accepts it. He is a religious man." She throws the ball to her Prime Minister. "Get it over with."

The teams take their places, with Castro replacing the Three I League pitcher. Zloto removes his jacket, shirt, and necktie. He is six five and weighs over 250. His chest hairs are gray, but he swings three bats smoothly in a windmill motion as he loosens his muscles. Castro warms up with the catcher. The Prime Minister has a surprisingly good motion, more sidearm than underhand. The ball comes in and sinks to a right-handed batter like Zloto. Colonel Alvarado takes his place behind home plate, which is a large army canteen.

"Achilles Alvarado," says Castro, "you wish to be the umpire in this contest?"

"Why not?" Zloto says. "It's his pension, let him call the balls and strikes. If it's a walk or an error, we'll take it over. Otherwise, a hit I win, an out you win."

"Play ball!" the umpire says. Castro winds up twice, and his first pitch is so far outside that the catcher diving across the plate cannot even lay his glove on the ball. Fidel stamps his foot.

"Ball one," says the umpire.

The infield is alive with chatter: "The old dark one, Fidel," they are yelling. "Relax, pitcher, this ox is an easy out, he can't see your stuff, there's eight of us behind you, Fidel, let him hit."

Zloto grins at the Prime Minister. "Put it down the middle, Mr. Pink, I dare you."

Fidel winds and delivers. Zloto's big hands swing the bat so fast that the catcher doesn't have a chance to blink. He has connected and the ball soars a hundred feet over the head of the left fielder who watches with astonishment the descending arc of the power-driven ball.

"Foul ball," says the umpire, eyeing the stretched clothesline which ended far short of where Zloto's fly ball dropped.

The power hitter grins again. "When I straighten one out, Castro, I'm gonna hit it clear out of Cuba. I never played in a little country before."

Castro removes his green army cap and runs his stubby fingers through his hair. He turns his back to the batter and looks toward his outfield. With a tired motion he orders his center fielder to move toward left center, then he signals all three outfielders to move deeper. Estelle Alvarado stands in foul territory down the first-base line, almost in the spot of her complimentary box seat at the Chisox home games.

Zloto is measuring the outside corner of the canteen with a calm, deliberate swing. He does not take his eyes off the pitcher. Castro winds and delivers another wild one, high and inside. Zloto leans away but the ball nicks his bat and dribbles into foul territory, where Estelle picks it up and throws it back to Castro.

"One ball, two strikes," says the umpire.

"Lucky again, Castro," the batter calls out, "but it only takes one, that's all I need from you."

The Prime Minister and the aging Rookie of the Year eye one another across the sixty feet from mound to plate. Castro rubs the imagined gloss from the ball and pulls at his army socks. With the tip of a thin Cuban softball bat, Zloto knocks the dirt from the soles of his Florsheim shoes. The infielders have grown silent. Castro looks again at his outfield and behind it at the green and gentle hills of Oriente Province. He winds and delivers a low, fast ball.

"Strike three," says the umpire. Zloto keeps his bat cocked. Estelle Alvarado rushes to her husband. She is crying hysterically. Fidel runs in at top speed to embrace both Alvarados at home plate. Zloto drops the bat. "It was a fair call, Archie," he says to the umpire. "I got caught looking."

"Like Uncle Sam," Castro says as the soldiers stream in yelling, "Fidel, Fidel, the strike-out artist." Castro waves his arms for silence.

"Not Fidel, men, but Achilles Alvarado, a hero of the Cuban people. A light for the Third World."

"Third World for Alvarado. Third strike for Zloto," an infielder shouts as the Ninth Army raises Fidel, Achilles, and Estelle to their shoulders in a joyful march down the first-base line. The Prime Minister, the umpire, and the lady gleam in the sun like captured weapons.

Zloto has put on his shirt and tie. He looks now like a businessman, tired after a long day at a convention. Fidel is jubilant among his men. The umpire tips his cap to the army and calms his wife, still tearful atop the bobbing shoulders of the Cuban Ninth.

"Alvarado," Estelle says, "you honest ump, you Latin patriot, you veteran of many a clutch situation. Are you happy, you fractured skull?"

"Actually," Alvarado whispers in her ear, "the pitch was a little inside. But what the hell, it's only a game."

Gas Stations

Chances are you've been here too. World's largest, eighty-three pumps, forty-one urinals, advertised on road signs as far east as Iowa. Oasis, Wyoming, U.S. 40, hard to miss as you whiz on by. Even Jack Kerouac on an overnight cross-country spin used to stop here for soft ice cream. In the golden days they had their own tables, all those fifties beats, way in the back by the truckers' shower room. They lumbered in with the long haulers, left their motors running just like the diesel men, wore leather too and drank half cups of coffee. The truckers said "shit" more. Busboys, in retrospect, could tell them apart by the poems on the napkins.

The counter is fifteen yards long and there must be two hundred tables. The waitresses wear roller skates except when carrying expensive meals. Everyone chews gum. The girls are all named Ellie. At their waists, just above the apron, they make change like busdrivers out of metal slots. Quarters fly onto tables, dimes trickle down their legs.

I order hashbrowns and eggs, whole-wheat toast, and coffee. My Chevy is being gassed out front, pump number forty-eight. The place mat tells the incredible story of the man who made all this possible. He dreamed a dream fifty years ago on a cold hillside. He was a Wyoming shepherd boy nuzzled against members of his flock in the biting wind. He dreamed that all his bleating herds became Cashmere goats at five times the price, that Wyoming shriveled up and dove into Texas. He awoke with frostbitten ears, fingers iced into the wool he clutched. While that man awaited the slow-rising sun to warm his limbs and awaken his herds, he vowed a vow.

105

"This won't be a barren wasteland," he vowed; "men will know that here I froze one night so that after this men shall freeze here no more." He slapped his herd with a long crook. His collies awoke as if it were spring and stretched on their forepaws. The man spit into the icy wind. He named the spot Oasis.

I look up from this saga on the place mat to recall, in the midst of travel, the tiny oasis of my youth, Ted Johnson's Standard. On our own block flew the Texaco star and the Mobil horse, but you couldn't pay us not to fill our Pontiac at Ted Johnson's Standard. He was the magician of the fan belt. With an old rag and one tough weathered hand, he took on radiators foaming and in flame. Where other men displayed girlie calendars, Ted Johnson hung the green cross of safety.

Although he looked like Smokey the Bear, it was engine neglect and rowdy driving that he cautioned against. Whenever a kid short-cut onto Bridge Street across his pumps, Old Ted raised the finger of warning. "Stay to the right, Sonny," he would yell, shaking his gray head over the lapse in safety. He had spotless pumps, his rest rooms glowed in the dark, he bleached the windshield sponges, but it was safety that drew us all to Ted. He wouldn't take your money until he had checked your spare. And it must have worked. He never lost a regular customer to a traffic fatality. He kept the number of deathless days posted above his cash register. At night, after he counted his receipts, Ted read the obituaries and added another safety day. I remember at least 7300. Twenty years of Ted's customers rolling down the road with their spare tires at the ready. They didn't need their suction-cup saints, Ted passed out his own stick-on mottos for the dashboard.

> Don't switch lanes
> Always signal first
> Use the rear view mirror

Yes, Ted Johnson's Standard, here in the middle of the world's biggest rest area, I long for you. They don't clean my windshield and my hood is tinkered with less than a fat girl's skirt. At night, Ted, they won't even make change and in the best of times you have to beg for the rest-room key.

You treated our cars, Ted, like princes from afar. The way Abraham must have washed the feet of angels, so you sponged windshields fore and aft. And those glass-headed pumps of yours looked like the Statue of Liberty lowering her torch to us, cozying up to our rear end.

My waitress rolls up. Her name is Ellie. "We're out of eggs," she says, "how about oatmeal? Twice the protein and none of that troublesome cholesterol. A man your age can't be too careful."

"I'm only thirty," I tell her.

"Not so young. In Korea, in the middle of veins, they found cholesterol at nineteen. The oatmeal's on special today. Think about it." I think about oatmeal while I continue the place-mat saga of Oasis, Wyoming. In 1930 there wasn't a road within a hundred miles. The shepherd boy was twenty-eight then and rode the freight to Grand Forks, South Dakota. With his stick and his collie and his dream, he rode east and almost succumbed, once in Kansas City and again in Chicago, to a fortune in the stockyards. By 1940 he had made a million in suet and owned a mansion on Lake Shore Drive. Big stock men from all over came by to sample his roast beef and pork chops and talk business. Swift and Armour sent him Christmas gifts. The dog was his only memento of Wyoming.

Still, the millionaire was restless. His vow came back to trouble him. The autumn of 1941 was the worst freeze Chicago ever knew. By October the leaves in all their splendor froze upon the limbs. Thanksgiving was twenty-two below zero, the average for November. People coughed chilled blood into the streets. The stockyards closed. On December 7 the Japanese attacked Pearl Harbor and the millionaire suet man knew who the Jonah was. "I hustled ass back to Wyoming," he said, "before the enemy could make it his own."

First he leveled the land and built towers of fluorescent lamps. There was still no road within fifty miles, but now the man thought of nothing but his vow. "The road will come," he said, and he invested his million in a pinball arcade, a small wax museum, and the earliest version of the restaurant. The gas pumps were an afterthought.

Ellie brings me oatmeal.

"No charge if you don't like it," she says. "They've got twenty pounds of it in the kitchen. It'll be lumpy by noon anyway." She looks over my shoulder while I taste. Her long hair touches the milk in the spoon, the steam rises to both our nostrils.

"It's good," I say.

"It has to be," Ellie answers; "the big boss eats it himself." She nods toward a bald man about twelve tables east of me. He wears a baggy thin-lapeled suit and is daydreaming through his smoky windows. When I finish breakfast I walk over to shake the hand of the man whose history has filled my place mat. He attempts to smile for me but can't quite do it.

"Troubles," I ask, "when you have eighty-three pumps and are a place-mat legend?" He collapses over the table. He buries his head in his hands.

"Personal problems?" I ask. "Health? marital? emotional?"

He picks up his head. "Psychiatrist?" he inquires.

"Only a traveler," I respond, "heading west." He sits up and looks around to make sure that nobody is listening to us. He pulls me close to his shrunken lips. "Arabs," he moans into my ear. "When they couldn't buy the Alamo they started putting the pressure on Oasis. They want Coney Island too and Disneyland. Our government is worrying about U.S. Steel and Armour beef, they don't know the desires of desert folks. I do. My people come from Lebanon, also a land of milk and honey."

To cheer the man I tell him about Ted Johnson's Standard, the example that has strengthened me through breakfast. "A white tile building," I tell him, "round as a mosque. Inside, it was like a solarium. Cut flowers bloomed from the carcasses of dried-out batteries. The Lions Club glass and the March of Dimes cup twinkled in their fullness. Only one grade of motor oil there, the very best, and six-ply treads, mufflers with welded reinforcements, belts and hoses of the finest Indian rubber . . ."

"Enough," says the Oasis man, "you're just a piss-call romantic mooning over the good old days of Rockefeller. Wake up. Ted's Standard belongs to OPEC now. It flies the sign of the Crescent. Turbaned attendants laugh at the idea of a comfort station. They mix foreign coinage in your change."

"What about your help?" I motion toward my Chevy, where a swarthy man peeks beneath the hood. He wipes the oil stick clean with his lips and spits into the radiator.

"Just Mormons in make-up," the Oasis man says. "You can't find a real Arab out here, but I do my best. I want to get the country ready for what's coming. I give out free headdresses all through the holy month of Ramadan. For a nickel I'll sell you an 'Allah Lives' bumper sticker. We closed down on the day Faisal was assassinated. You can't buck the future."

"And what about the Ted Johnsons," I ask, "the men in uniform who made our stations great?"

"Underground," he says, "with the hat blockers and egg candlers, praying for the resurrection of the downtown."

"I don't believe it's so bleak," I say.

"Bleak for you and me," the Oasis man answers, "not so bleak along the Nile and the Euphrates. Every thousand years or so Mesopotamia gets a shot in the arm. It's just history. You can't buck it. You go along."

"I don't see it that way, Mr. Big, no sir, I don't."

Ellie rolls up with another ladle of oatmeal for the boss. "Beware," he says, "watch out for price fixing in radial tires and don't believe what the company tells you about STP." He rouses himself for a moment from his melancholy. "We serve three thousand meals a day here. Where are you headed, California?"

"Righto," I say, not even surprised that he has guessed it.

"Your own station or a dealer owned?"

"Franchise direct from J. Paul Getty, option to buy in five years." The Oasis man can tell that I'm proud of myself.

"Dummy," he says, "in five years you'll be a slave in Tunis." Ellie pulls up a chair and joins us.

"No," I say, "in five years I'll be like Ted Johnson. I'll be fixing flats and tuning engines in the happy hills outside San Francisco. I'll have an '81 Chevy, loaded, and watch the Golden Gate Bridge hanging in the fog."

"More oatmeal for you two?" Ellie asks. "It'll all be lumps by noon." Her perfect legs in their black hose roll toward the kitchen. Sparks fly from her wheels.

"Young man," he tells me, looking away now through the window at what is visible from this angle of his eighty-three pumps, "take it from the King of Octane, there's not a fart's chance for you out there. Go back to school. Learn dentistry. The Third World will need attention to its teeth."

Ellie is back with oatmeal and hot coffee. She sits with us, makes a thin bridge out of her fingers, rests her chin on it as she stares at my oatmeal.

"You've had your day, Mr. Oasis," I tell him. "If the place mat is to be trusted, you've been hot and cold, rich and poor. Now you can sit at your window and watch the cash roll in. Ted Johnson never looked up except when he had a car on the rack. He called his place a service station. Your name was your credit over there."

The millionaire's mouth finally makes it into a huge smile. "How many pumps will you have?" he asks.

"Three," I tell him loudly. "One each, regular, premium, and no lead and no locks on the rest room." He breaks into giggles. People at other tables are looking but I don't care.

"That's right," I continue, "and rubber machines

and ten-cent cokes if I can get them." He is almost
rolling in the aisle now. Tears of happiness leak from
the corners of his eyes. "Firecrackers and recaps," I
continue, "wheels balanced by hand, and even
mufflers and pipes."

"Stop," he yelps amid his giggles. "I can't take any
more." But I want to go on. "I'll lend out tools too and
give a dollar's worth to anyone who's broke."

Ellie looks into my heart. "Take me with you,"
she says. "I'll check crankcase oil and clean windshields. I don't want to be a harem girl." Her look is
as grim as mine. We leave him howling at the table.
I pay my bill and buy her a pair of magnetic dogs.
Beside my Chevy, Ellie removes her roller skates. Her
black hose hooked around my antenna rise in the
wind. Through the rearview mirror I see in pursuit
the disguised Mormons. Awkwardly they mount their
camels and raise curved swords to the east. My electric
starter drowns their desert shrieks. Three hundred and
forty cubic inches rumble. I buckle up, Ellie moves
close. Careful on the curves, amid kisses and hopes
I give her the gas.

My Real Estate

I

I have always believed in property. Though a tenant now, I have prospects. In fact, Joanne Williams, my realtor, thinks I have the greatest prospects in the world. She has always dropped in on me now and then, but these days she comes up almost every time she leaves her seat for popcorn or a coke. She brings her refreshment with her and she refreshes me. She has done so right from the start, ever since I first realized that I really wanted to own my own home.

She picked me up outside my apartment house. She gave me her card. We shook hands. She looked me over.

"You want a bungalow," she said, "two bedrooms, one and a half baths, central air, hardwood floors. You don't need the headache of a lawn."

In her big Oldsmobile we cruised the expressways. Short skirts were the style then. Joanne drove in bursts of speed. She was learning conversational Spanish from a Berlitz eight-track recording that played as we headed toward the fringes of the inner city, where she said there were "buys."

"Hágame usted el favor de . . ." said the tape.

"There are a lot of Spanish speakers entering the market," said Joanne. A small card on her dashboard, the type that usually says "Clergy," proclaimed, *Se Habla Español.* "Once you show someone a house," she said, "it's a moral obligation. You take them in your car, buy them lunch, introduce them to some homes in their price range. It's as if you've been naked together." She had long thin legs, all shin until they disappeared only a few inches below where her panty hose turned darker. When the tape ended, she asked if I was a wounded veteran and then if I had ever been in the army at all. She was sorry.

"With a VA loan you could float into a house. Conventional will be tougher. Still, you've got thirty years to cushion one or two percent." She shrugged her small shoulders, asked me about how much I earned.

I declined to say. Her skirt edged higher. I never knew what a VA loan meant. When I saw the VA signs around the housing developments, I thought that the whole thing was exclusively for veterans, that there were lots of crutches and wheelchair ramps and VFW halls in there. She laughed when I told her this.

"There is a lot to know in real estate." She was twenty-eight, she said, and divorced from a man who had liked furnished apartments. My efficiency in the beams is also furnished, but with great luxury. Simmons' Hide-A-Bed, chrome-and-glass coffee table, Baker easy chair, Drexel maple bed and dresser. There is a hunting tapestry on my living-room wall. My bathroom fixtures are gold leaf and the tub has a tiny whirlpool. When she wants nothing else, Joanne sometimes comes up just to soak her toes in the hot bubbles.

When she was the salesperson and I the client, she told me I was her first bachelor. "I know your type," she said. "When I went to singles' bars, you were all I ever met. You thing apartments are where you'll meet people, you believe the managers who show you game rooms and swimming pools. Listen to how people talk. In apartments they don't have 'neighbors'; they say, 'He lives in my complex.' If you want to meet people, you buy a house."

Joanne refused to believe that I wanted a house for reasons other than neighbors and schools. "So what if you have no wife and children," she said, "why not be near kids that are well educated, less likely to soap your windows on Halloween and put sugar in your gas tank."

I told her the simple truth. "I want a house because my people have owned land and houses in Texas for four generations. We lived here with the Mexicans and the Indians. I'm the first Spenser who hasn't owned a tiny piece of Texas."

"You still can live with Mexicans and Indians," she told me, "in the Fifth Ward. But if you go there, you'll go without me."

She drove extravagantly and used no seat belts. I slid toward her on all the turns. She used the horn but not while listening to the tape. "In the suburbs," Joanne said, " I can put you into a two bedroom plus den and patio for eighteen five. I can get you all electric kitchens and even sprinkler systems for a lot less than you'll pay for an old frame bungalow close in." But no matter what she said, she couldn't convince me to look at Sharpstown and Green Acres and Cascade Shores. They sounded like Hong Kong and Katmandu. I grew up in Houston and never knew about these far-away places until I started noticing some of the addresses printed on the checks we took in at the store. Sometimes it was a long distance call to trace down a local bad check.

"My great-grandfather fought at the Alamo," I told her. "He was one of those who left when Santa Anna gave them a last chance. My grandad owned a farm near where the Astrodome is now." This was the first time the Dome entered our conversation. Joanne was unimpressed and it didn't seem very important to me either. The Dome was just another big building, the colonel who owned it, just another big businessman, and my grandad just another old memory, dead fifteen years.

In my case she was wrong about the suburbs, but Joanne did have an instinct for a client's needs. She was flexible. The one thing she could not do was pretend to like a house. If she didn't like the place, she got out fast, sometimes without leaving her card. She held her nose all the way to the car and refused to answer questions about the place. "Go back without me," she said, "go alone or take a lawyer or an interior decorator." Even when she liked a house, she made the home owners open their drapes. "I want to see everything in the bright light," she said. She came into a

house like an actress to center stage. Buyers and
sellers moved close to the walls. She sized places up as
she walked through in long strides. She noticed in-
accuracies in thermostats and recommended plasterers
and electricians as she passed needed repairs. Whenever there was a child, she chased him down to pat
his head. On our first day we spent three hours together. At four thirty, she told me there was a Mexican
couple, thus the tape. At seven there was an Open
House in Sharpstown. I should call her in the morning.

The next day, Sunday, she was at my door at
eight a.m. She had a tennis dress so white that it
literally blinded me as the sun reflected from it into
my dark apartment.

"Sorry to wake you," she said, "but I was in the
neighborhood and I need to use a phone, please."
While I showered she made what seemed like dozens
of calls. She had played tennis from six to eight.
"Sunday is my big day. I have three listings in Mont-
rose and one in Bel Air. With good weather we'll close
something today." She joined me for what was her
second breakfast. I knew that as she ate she was item-
izing my establishment and judging my taste. She
was doing even more than I thought. We finished
breakfast at eight forty-five. "I don't have to be in Bel
Air until ten fifteen," she said, and took off her tennis
dress.

Joanne's style was intact, flawless, efficient. She was
done in time to have a quick shower herself and give
me a brief rundown on mortgage rates.

Later in the week, as she led me from house to
house, I learned more personal information, facts from
the life of Joanne Williams. She rattled them off as
briskly as the square footage of a room. Born in
Chicago, moved to Houston at fourteen, married high-
school sweetheart; at twenty-five, childless, living in
a furnished apartment where Chuck still resided only
a few complexes east of me; left Chuck and job as
legal secretary; became cocktail waitress. There amid
"tips that would make your head swim," she met
Vince, her sales manager. "What the hell," Vince asked

her, "is a girl with your personality doing as a waitress? You should be out on the street." He opened his Multiple Listings book and started to show her some pictures. "There's a five-bedroom rancher that can bring you a four-thousand-dollar commission." Vince told her to think of herself as an obstetrician. A house on the market was like a pregnant woman. She had to go, she would burst if nobody helped. You wanted to make it fast, painless, smooth.

She worked days for Vince, nights as a waitress. "At the end of the month I sold that five-bedroom rancher that Vince had randomly picked out of the book." "It was no accident," he said, "it was your career. I showed you the picture of it." She sold close to a million dollars in each of her first two years. This year she wanted to go over.

"The kind of house you want is chickenfeed," she told me, "but I've got the time for it. And who knows, you might one day have a rich friend who'll use me to buy a mansion in Green Meadows."

Because I was in the eighteen-to-twenty-two-thousand range with conventional mortgage, mediocre credit, and less than ten percent down, Joanne could not give me her best hours. I drew dinner times and late nights usually, but this made it convenient for us to eat and occasionally sleep together. She did not have to mix business and pleasure, any more than she had to hurry. Speed and pleasure and business all combined in her like the price and sales tax. The only noise she made was a small grinding of the teeth like a nervous signature on a deed. We rarely kissed and used only the most explicit embraces.

And Joanne did not pressure me to buy a house. As I wavered and mused upon closing costs and repair bills and termites and cockroaches, she just paid less and less attention to me. Finally, in spite of mutual fondness, we never saw each other at all. I kept up with her though by her signs around the city. She married Vince, but because his Italian name was so long they both used hers. Williams and Williams signs, bright orange with a green border sprang up throughout various better neighborhoods. Whenever I saw the sign, I knew that there Joanne had once opened drapes and frightened owners. She and Vince made a good team. He ran the office and took care of all the paperwork. This left her free to sell. Judging by the frequency of her signs, I guessed she now sold many millions in a year and had forgotten me as a truly bad investment of her time.

I underestimated her loyalty and her memory. Months after our last encounter I met her in the express lane at Krogers. It was around supper time and she was buying three Hershey bars.

"With all the money you must earn now," I asked, "can't you take time out for a regular dinner?"

"Sweetheart," Joanne told me, "you never did understand real estate." She bought me a Hershey bar too. I left my less-than-purchases in the cart and followed her to a long white Cadillar. "Deductible," she said, "might as well." She made a U-turn and parked across the street among a group of vans belonging to plumbers who had gone home for the evening. She checked the clock on the panel. "I should be in River Oaks in thirty minutes to show five bedrooms, but they'll wait a few minutes if they have to."

They didn't have to. In the back seat of the Cadillac Joanne was her old self. I looked up and saw wrenches and plungers hanging from the ceilings of the plumbers' vans. "I haven't forgotten you, Jack," she said. "Every time I see a two bedroom one bath in the medical-center area I mean to give you a call."

"Congratulations," I said, "on your marriage [I had read about it in the financial pages, they took out a quarter-page ad] and your own business."

"Yes," she said, "it's wonderful. If interest stays down we might even go into our own development."

II

When I next saw her, it was at my own apartment complex. I was on the balcony looking out at the tennis courts below me. Joanne saw me, halted her doubles match, and invited me to bring them all some cokes after the set.

Vince was as tall as Joanne but so thickset that she seemed to tower above him. He played the net and she took the long ones that he couldn't reach. She wore a tennis dress exactly like the one I remembered. Joanne introduced me to my landlords, Ben and Vera Bloom.

"I'm glad to have a tenant like you," Ben Bloom said. "You know the kind of people that usually rent these, twenty-two year olds that like to drink beer and screw and write on the walls. They never dump their garbage, but every time they see a roach they run to call the manager. You can't satisfy people like them. No matter what you do they move out. They break leases. Who's going to take a traveling salesman to court?"

Vince treated me like an old friend, claimed that he recognized my name as a former client of their old company. When he and Joanne went into the business for themselves, most of the old company came along with them. "We closed the deal for the land you're standing on," Vince said, "so you might say we did a little bit to help you find a place." He seemed to feel guilty that their company had not matched me with a house. "It's his own fault," Joanne said, "he had chances; by the time he decides someone else has put in a bid."

"Oh, one of those," Vince said. Still he invited me to join them that night at the ball game. The Astros were playing the Cubs. "I've never been to the Dome," I admitted.

"It's a separate world," Ben Bloom said. He wiped the perspiration from his eyes and took off his tennis glove. "People like me put up these developments and tract houses and zoned subdivisions, but not the Colonel. The Colonel left us to fuck around with the small stuff. He went for the pie in the sky."

"And he made it," Vera said; "he put us on the map more than the moon did. Nobody even remembers the moon any more, but just mention Houston at a convention and they all ask about the Dome."

They were going to a party celebrating the fifth anniversary of the stadium. Joanne asked me to meet them at the Colonel's penthouse.

That night, watched by ushers and security guards, I entered the penthouse in the beams. I felt underdressed in my corduroy trousers and sports shirt. Joanne, I noticed, was wearing a black dress with a cut-out back, but Vince was as casually dressed as I. They made me feel very comfortable in the Colonel's living room. The Blooms were there and many other couples. The tuxedoed ushers carried trays full of martinis and Tom Collinses.

"It's a nickel-beer night in the grandstand," Vince said. "No matter how much you drink you won't be able to keep up with the slobs down there. You couldn't get me to nickel-beer night. They piss down all the corridors leading to the men's rooms."

Joanne took me by the elbow and introduced me to some guests. She was relaxed and elegant. I had never seen her in company before, only in business and in bed. She was not even wearing a watch.

"What can I do," she told me when I asked, "I'm here for the evening just like the baseball players. When there's nothing to do, I play ball. That's something else you don't know about real estate."

If I could have looked out from this Dome toward the east, I would have seen my grandfather's former seventy-five acres only a city block away. There are gas stations and motels on the property now and the roller coaster of an amusement park. My grandfather died broke in the Christian Brothers Home for the Aged. He sold his land right before World War II to buy a liquor store. My dad ran the store.

While I was thinking what might have been if Grandad had held onto the land instead of going into the liquor business, the Colonel rolled in, a big gray-bearded man in an expensive-looking wheelchair. An Astros blanket lay across his knees. A nurse in white and an usher in her gown stood on each side of the chair. Ben Bloom proposed a toast. "To the head of the Dome," he said, "to the man who made it all possible." We clinked our glasses. The Colonel could neither drink nor hold the glass.

"A bad stroke," Joanne whispered to me, "during the first football season. He's never even felt the Astro-Turf, poor man." She smiled and went over to pat the Colonel on the shoulder. He seemed to understand everything but could barely speak.

As the nurse wheeled him through the guests, it came my turn to meet the great man. The room seemed more crowded, Joanne was nowhere in sight.

"Jack Spenser, sir," I said, not really knowing how to explain my presence, "my grandfather once owned seventy-five acres on Old Spanish Trail. I'd like to buy myself a house in this area."

I could not be sure if he had even heard me. The nurse pushed with some effort his polished chair over the thick carpeting. The room was quite full now, of people with drinks and loud voices. Nobody was watching the TV or cared about the game itself hundreds of feet below.

"Lyndon Johnson used to stay in this suite," I heard someone say, "and get drunk on his ass for the whole weekend. He'd send the Secret Service out to the ranch so everyone would think he was there worrying about Vietnam. It would have taken a pretty shrewd assassin to look for him way up at the top of the Dome."

The splendor of the Astrodome was not the baseball I knew. My dad and I used to go to Texas league games at Haynes Stadium for Saturday-night double-headers. We packed a lunch and a lot of mosquito repellent and sat out in the bleachers for twenty-five cents each. My hero was a black first baseman named Eleazer Brown who never made it to the big leagues. He was six foot eight and for a while did play with the Globetrotters. When my dad closed the liquor store after the eighth robbery and his second bullet wound, the police brought him to a line-up to identify one of the hold-up men. It was a cinch. Dad knew the big torso of Eleazer Brown even when Eleazer was slouched over and in dark glasses. "It was a sad day for me," Dad said, "fingering that coon who could hit the ball five hundred feet. That's him, I told the cops, and you know, in spite of everything, I almost went up and asked that black bastard for his autograph." At least Brown hadn't shot at Dad; it was has friend who did that, an average-sized numbers runner from Dallas.

The roof of the Dome was so high, I had read, that you could put the Shamrock Hotel into it. I tried to imagine the biggest thing I could, the Goodyear blimp, dwarfed against the ceiling. As a store manager I was entitled to one ride a year in the blimp. When I first met Joanne, I had taken her as my guest. She pointed out landmarks to the children of other managers. When we landed, she ran toward her car. "It made me nervous," she said, "it reminded me of a mobile home."

"I've been looking for you," Joanne said. "The Colonel wants to see you. He never asks for anybody."

"Why does he want me?"

"Who knows," Joanne said, "but it's a great honor. Vince and Ben thought you went down to the game. Go ahead, he's in the other room with his nurse." I knocked at the door.

The Colonel and his nurse awaited me in a smaller sitting room. I was surprised that he smoked a pipe. The nurse held it for him between puffs. As I waited for the Colonel to begin, the nurse played with the pipe stem. With a small knife she shaved the dark tobacco and repacked the bowl. She caressed the stem. It took the Colonel a long time to say anything. He had to get his mouth in the right position. I could see how difficult it was for him. When he did begin, the words came out loud and uneven, like a child writing on a blackboard.

"Your grandpa," he got out, "was a dumbass son of a bitch." He puffed on the pipe and then the nurse repacked it. I waited for the second sentence.

"He could have had a piece of the world . . . wanted a liquor store instead." As the Colonel, between puffs and silences, got out his story I learned that he had bought most of the Dome land from Grandad and had offered my ancestor a part of what, at that time, was going to be a housing development. Just as I hesitated with Joanne over my would-be bungalow, so Gramps had hemmed and hawed with the Colonel and finally taken his money instead for the liquor-store enterprise.

"We grew up together on the Buffalo Bayou," the Colonel said. "He sold booze during prohibition and never forgot that he made easy money then. Before he kicked off, I told him about the Dome and he laughed in my face. Now," the Colonel went on even more slowly, "now the laugh is on me. I put the top on baseball. I made my own horizon. I shut out the sky. But I've got no arms and no legs and no sons and no daughters." He took a long, long pause and rejected the pipe. The noise from the party in the outer rooms surrounded our silence. It made the Colonel's slowness even more dramatic.

"I never liked Old Jack Spenser [I was named for Grandad], and I jewed him out of his land. Fifty bucks an acre was a steal even in those days. He had liquor on his mind all the time."

While the Colonel kept pausing, I tried to remember what I actually had heard about the land on the Old Spanish Trail. I knew it had been Gramps' land, but when he went senile I was just a boy. All I remember is his crazy laugh in the Christian home. We used to have to bring him dolls when we came as if he were a baby. He died in '56, and Dad only made it two years beyond that. The liquor store was busted. Mom moved to Colorado with my sister.

"For a liquor store, he gave up this." With difficulty the Colonel made a neck gesture that suggested arms wide open. "I can't stand all these outsiders that keep coming down here. I'd like the Dome to be just for us Texans. That real-estate girl told me you wanted your own house. You're smarter that your grandad." Then the Colonel made me an offer. I thought about it overnight, asked Joanne's advice the next day. "I only think of single dwellings," she said, "the family is the unit I work with. Ask someone who knows big spaces." But without further advice I did it on my own. What was there to lose?

III

That was almost three years ago. Now, I don't work for Goodyear any more. I don't have to. The Colonel pays me two hundred a week plus room. He only leaves the Dome to go to the doctor's office in Plaza Del Oro across the street. I have my own apartment next to his and my only real job is getting up to turn the Colonel at three each morning so he won't get bedsores. The night watchman lets me in. The Colonel is asleep on his right side. He snores quietly into his beard. Since I'm pretty tired too, it's all a blur. I pull the special pad from beneath his hips and put it on the other side of him. I grab his arms as if they're ropes and give a good hard pull, then I go back to the other side of the bed and roll his hips over. He never wakes up.

Lately Joanne has been saying that I'll inherit the Dome someday because he's got no heirs. "He picked you because you're a Texan, because he knew your grandpa. He doesn't need other reasons. What else is he going to do with it?" When she tells me how rich I'm going to be, she snuggles up close and spends an extra few minutes. The high interest rates since '73 have really hurt her business and her marriage. She doesn't talk about it too much, but things are not working out between her and Vince. "He wants to go commercial," she says; "I can't work beyond the family. He wants to use leverage. He talks about a real-estate trust. I look at houses as walls and roofs. Vince calls them instruments and units." They have filed for divorce.

This year, for the first time, Joanne bought an Astros season ticket. Sometimes I go down to watch an inning or two, and when I come back, there she is in my whirlpool. She is as fast and smooth as ever. Interest rates and marriage have not changed her. She doesn't look around for Jack Spenser's perfect house any longer. "You'll own the Dome soon," she says; "you'll call all the shots."

I don't think the Colonel is likely to make me his heir but there is no doubt that it's possible. He calls for me every few weeks just to talk. He's getting weaker but he still likes to tell me what a dumbass Grandpa was. I agree and have taken over the nurse's job with the pipe. So far it's been no real problem. If the Colonel wants to call Grandad a dumbass all the time, that's his privilege.

In most ways my life is pretty much the same, but living in the Dome has killed my interest in baseball. When I do watch an inning or two, it's only to look at the scoreboard or the mix of colors in the crowd or to listen to the sound of the bat meeting the ball. What I like to do most is walk behind the grandstand and watch the people buying refreshments. There are one hundred twenty-six places in the Dome where you can buy beer. People line up at every one of them. There are eight restaurants and six of them have liquor licenses. While Astros and Dodgers and Cubs and Giants are running the bases and hitting the balls, the Colonel is making a fortune on beer and liquor. My Grandpa, I think, wasn't such a dumbass. He just had the wrong location.

Joanne has lots of plans for later. She wants to marry me. She says that we could keep the name of her business and use all the signs she has left over from her years with Vince.

"We won't need the money," I tell her, "we'll take a vacation around the world."

"No," she says, "first we'll evict the baseball team and the conventions. We can make a big profit on these auditorium seats. Then we'll put up modern bungalows, just the kind you wanted. They'll be close to downtown and have every convenience. There's room here for dozens. Even the outdoors will be air-conditioned. We'll put good private schools in the clubhouses and lease all the corridor space for shops and supermarkets. A few condominiums down the foul lines," she says, "and a hospital in center field. The scoreboard will be the world's biggest drive-in movie."

I go along with her. She gets more passionate when she talks this way, more involved with me. She's been saying these things for quite a while now and keeping track of the Colonel's health. He is so slow these days that he falls asleep between words. I don't think he can last much longer. Joanne gets very excited when she sees his pale face being wheeled past my door. "We'll move into his place," she says, "and use this as my office." I'm sad when I think of the Colonel becoming something like my Grandpa playing with dolls, but I didnt take Joanne too seriously until a few days ago when after some drinks and a whirlpool bath she put on a long hostess gown and went back to her box behind third base. I followed because I was suspicious of the gown. She walked right over the railing onto the field. She took the third-base umpire by the arm and led him to the mound. "Let's get some sunlight in here," she yelled to the top of the Dome, "let's see what it would be like with new tenants. It's a good neighborhood. There's a lots of shade and well-kept lawns, and the neighbors"—she looked at Walt Alston in the visitors' dugout—"the neighbors seem friendly and sincere." She left the umpire at the pitcher's mound and started taking her long strides toward the outfield.

"Rates can't go much higher," she told the Dodger infield, "but if they do you'll be extra glad you bought now. A house isn't like other investments. Stocks and bonds don't give you the direct benefits of housing. There is nothing else like it on God's earth. Yearly deductions, shelter, comfort, and all of it at capital-gains rates."

"Do you have children?" she asked the second baseman, who looked on in bewilderment. "If you do you'll appreciate the lack of traffic. You can send three-year-olds to the store without any worries." By center field her stride was almost a gallop. "Don't worry," she called to the Dodgers' black left fielder, "you'll be able to live here too. It will take a few years, but the whole world is changing."

A squadron of park policemen caught up with her on the way to the bullpen. They led her back to the third-base box, where I waited alongside the manager, who knew me and told the police to let her go in my custody. The policemen were gentle with her and the crowd cheered as she put those long smooth legs easily over the high railing. She threw kisses in all directions. The scoreboard spelled out "charge" and the organist played "Funny Girl." I led her up the ramp toward the escalator. "The place will sell, Jack. Everybody loves it. That AstroTurf will save a bundle on gardening too. We can do it, Jack, I know we can. When the Colonel leaves it to you, can we go ahead with it?"

She was all motion in my apartment. I could hardly restrain her from going into the Colonel's penthouse and strangling him with a pillow. "I'm only kidding about that," she said. "We're at the top now, we can wait."

As she ran the water for another whirlpool bath to relax her I thought of my great-grandfather saying good-bye to Davy Crockett and walking out of history, his son selling out to the Colonel, and my own dad bankrupt by liquor. Far below us someone was stealing a base. Next door the Colonel was struggling for a word. Cartoons blinked from the scoreboard. I took off my clothes. "It must run in the family," I said, thinking of Gramps laughing in the empty hallway of the Christian Brothers Home. I laughed out loud too. "If I get the Dome, do anything you want with it," I said. "Just save me room for the world's largest liquor store." In the midst of bubbles, I joined her. We sparkled like champagne.

Noon

Think of me as two hundred and sixty-three lines of broken light per second scattered through twenty-one years. Prick me and I short. In a sense, it explains everything, in a sense . . .

It does not. Television is television and murder is murder. The Senate subcommittee hearings on violence and TV reached no final conclusions, nor did the Eisenhower (Milton) committee or the Kerner commission. I'm sorry to sound so factual, so lawyerish, but we agreed to be honest with each other. Remember?

Okay, but my parents were married on *Bride and Groom* in 1952 just when TV started to explode, when the cities grew antennas like baseball gloves. I have the kinescope of Mom and Dad and Bud Collyer. A happy organ leads into Bud's solemn, "Kenneth Cook of Cleveland, Ohio, and Edith White of Elmira, New York . . ." You see a cameo close-up of Edith, then of Ken. They're locked arm in arm, but, you know, when I used to watch it as a kid I thought she was in New York and he was in Cleveland. I thought they only looked together the way Walter Cronkite and Eric Sevareid do no matter where they are. I thought that Edith and Ken only got together after that Ivory Soap commercial when Bud said, "And now the nation is waiting to hear a tale of love and heroism, another chapter in America's matrimonial pastime, *Bride and Groom.*" Bud was really something. He could wring a story out in fifteen minutes without getting maudlin like Jack Bailey. But Edith, she was a decade too early. In color and on something like *The Price Is Right* she would have been a killer. A slip of the tongue. What I mean is she had a long horsy face, but zip, fire, a personality. It explains a part of me. *Bride and Groom* was not her vehicle. All she could do on that show was look solemn as if a fuck would do her in. She tapped her eyes with a white lace hanky while Bud ran down Dad's medals. He had "courage to spare," Bud said. That explains another part of me. Bud read a letter from General Ridgway saying that Kenneth Cook was a credit to the U.S. Army. Ken Cook belched in Bud's face and that cagey pro said, *"Gesuntheit."* I've run it back dozens of times. It's a genuine drunken, stinking belch from way down deep. It would have knocked you or me back into the camera, but Bud never blinked. That's a pro for you. Also a credit to the nation.

I'm willing to listen if you really think this is important to the case.

It is the case. No *Bride and Groom*, no me. My beginning and my end is television. It's too bad they abolished the death penalty. Now there's nothing theatrical in criminal law. A man's life is not at stake, only a certain kind of boredom. The defendant is hereby ordered bored to death in prison rather than in Elmira or Cincinnati. It's a shame I couldn't have done this in the good old days. I'd make them forget Caryl Chessman in a hurry. You lawyers have it made all right, you come out golden. Not even a ghost to haunt you when you blow one. Fifty bucks an hour and a clean conscience.

I earn nothing from your case, I am court appointed. You seem to forget that wealth is not one of your qualities. You're not Lee Harvey Oswald and I'm not Perry Mason. Let's go on.

I won't plead insanity.

You wouldn't have a chance, you planned too carefully. But with luck and a sympathetic jury you might come off with second degree or maybe even manslaughter.

My childhood should count for second degree. Manslaughter is a misnomer. I killed one of the seven deadly sins, the electric version of Horatio Alger. I have no guilt, no remorse. I felt worse when I stepped on ants in the second grade. As I was saying, their wedding film is the major memory of my childhood. We had no black-box Kodaks, no snaps of me month by month, no marks along the wall to measure junior's growth. Suddenly, there I was fourteen with acne and hard-ons. The only thing I know about my father is the way he looked in that fifteen-minute segment of *Bride and Groom*. He wore his army uniform full of ribbons and medals. She said the producers told him to because that's what they wanted him to talk about, that he'd been a war hero. He also did not own a suit. She was already pregnant. If they'd known, probably the producers wouldn't have let her on the show. Things were very wholesome in those days. Bud Collyer and God Bless You at the end of the wedding. It wouldn't surprise me if every girl on *The Dating Game* takes the pill and I don't believe they send any chaperones on those pre-honeymoon trips either. Don't look so impatient counselor, I told you that television was the subject so I'm not just making sand castles. This is part of my defense. Because my mother was pregnant, I too am a member of the *Bride and Groom* cast. That fifteen-minute filmstrip and the Bell and Howell projector that brings it to life are my inheritance and my history. The ragtag Kroehler North Carolina sofa that I now use as porch furniture was one of the gifts to the newlyweds, so is the Sunbeam toaster popping to this day. Mother died in the wreck of a '54 de Soto downpaymented with the three hundred in cash from the show.

If not for *Bride and Groom*, they would never have married. She was only two weeks pregnant and he had probably kicked in a few bellies with his pointed-toe Stetsons. He had been drunk since before the war ended. I don't think he ever knew exactly who she was and she only wanted the prizes. The producer made up a little history of how they met. She was working in a drugstore in Elmira and noticed his medals when he came in for a bottle of cough medicine. A nice twist, the girl noticing his chest.

She was demure in a black cotton servant's outfit set
off with a gingham apron. Miss Soda Fountain amid
the pharmacists, coy as doctors, opening brown
Latinate bottles in the back room. Her chipped and
polished fingernails moved a damp rag across the
counter where his heroic elbows were soon to rest.
"Got any cough syrup?" he asks, not even coughing
to seem authentic. Not a cringe, not a blink from
either. Eyes meet. She clutches the rag like it's money
in the wind. His Purple Heart tinkles like a nickel
against the counter. She inhales. Awed by the spectacle
of his chest, her own bosom grows toward his asym-
metrical eyes. "What kindja want?" She points to
expectorants, but his eye stays on her tit like it's a
rifle sight and he's about to machine-gun the row of
glasses and the angular mirrors making pieces out of
them behind her. "Is it love at first sight?" asks Bud.
"Yes," they coo on national television, holding sweaty
palms, their cheeks berouged, the camera grinding
out for their son this moment and no other. But in
the drugstore it is different. She leans farther, her black
outfit exhaling starch to his nostrils still soaked in the
Orient. He has smelled war women, blood and dirt
hopping on his cock like seals jumping for sardines.
"G.I. fuckee wuckee." No sir. This American snatch
comes down on him cool as the eucalyptus in his cough
syrup, a cross between her tits. Jesus really did die
here, drowned by the trickling sweat of hours on her
feet peddling cokes to crew cuts who say "Gee whiz"
and wait like saints for the next three-dimensional
comic book.

"And that love at first sight brought this inspirational
story to us. We thank you Ken and Edith for sharing
it with America." First she shared herself in the basement of the drugstore at lunch hour, lounging over the
cases of Budweiser empties. Even then he is almost
too drunk to unhook his army belt, but she is gentle as
Florence Nightingale. And there I come, a phoenix
from the empties, while she claws his khaki shirt and
bites in half a distinguished-service medal. You should
have settled for the cough syrup, Ken. For your ail-

ment she offered only what you had rent too often with
soft-nosed bullets. She told me none of it was true,
but I believe it all; the story as told on *Bride and
Groom* is my cosmogony. I would sooner give up
Adam and Eve, Abraham, Noah. . . .

Please, let's get on to 1973. You could spend hours
on 1952.

I will when I take the stand. You'll see. If you're in
a hurry don't show up for the trial. It will be my
Harvard and my Yale, my novel and my family. I am
going to filibuster the legal system. They'll have to gag
me like Bobby Seale. I want to be remembered as the
most eloquent murderer in American history. Maybe
they'll do a TV series based on my life. I could be a
consultant and have a fat salary in prison. By the way,
are you taping this? Good. Maybe we can just play the
tape and I won't have to repeat it all in court. We
can put the little Sony on the Bible, I'll preread the
"I solemnly swear" part, then we can cut right to the
soundtrack from *Bride and Groom*. "Do you, Edith
White, take this man, Kenneth Cook? . . ." It would
make all the connections without my having to explain
again. With good editing the tape could even antici-
pate some questions from the state.

Please.

All right. We agree that no murder is simple, although the act is as easy as brushing your teeth.
You've gone to law school—I've read *Crime and
Punishment*. Neither of us probably believes most of
what we've learned. I find zero similarity between
myself and Raskolnikov. I am closer to those unknown
anarchists who threw bombs at czars just like cheer-
leaders being flowered in confetti.

Please.

All right. I grew up doing two things at once.
Watching television and whatever else was at hand.
Usually homework or dishwashing. My high-school
job was in the very drugstore where they met, changed
only by the addition of a TV blaring all the time.
Most recently I was a security man at National Department Store. My entire job was watching people

move around the store, on a seven-inch closed-circuit screen. I could switch channels from say lingerie to sporting goods to the main door, but mostly they wanted me to keep my eyes on girls' sportswear and the record department.

A voyeur's dream that job was. I sat alone in an office created by combining three dressing rooms. The door was marked SECURITY—KEEP OUT. On my little screen were girls pulling dresses off the racks, standing in front of full-length mirrors gazing at what they might be with a few yards of new cotton or rayon. I didn't see them naked, of course, that would have been crude as well as illegal. I saw them in the mirror as they stood fully clothed, holding the new thing in front of them with the plastic hanger at their neck looking like a forked goiter. They had to decide which ones to try on. "Three dress limit in the dressing room," the sign said. They had to be careful, these little Cinderellas. Careful not to take their clothes off or squander a whole lunch hour on any old dress. I watched their eyes for the decision-making process. With the right camera angle I could always tell a thief. A customer loves that dress or record she is about to buy. She thinks of what her friend will say about her in the new hiphuggers. In a thief's eyes there is no lust. Even when she truly desires the object, she has only a job to do. The pleasure must come later when she is alone with her reward.

I think psychologists and other security men might disagree with that.

They would be wrong.

Please, let's get on with your account of that day.

I can't tell it any faster. Don't they teach legal etiquette. Just because I'm sane doesn't mean I have to expedite the case, does it? Anytime you want out, just say so Mr. Court Appointee. If they talk to me, I could probably get F. Lee or Percy Foreman or Melvin Belli . . . I don't know the names of any other lawyers.

Okay, I'm sorry for rushing you, you're my last interview this afternoon and I'm not hungry.

A pity. I was going to invite you to stay for dinner. The prison food is better than I'm accustomed to, living alone as I have for three years—make note of this for my defense—living alone for three years eating pork and beans, Dinty Moore stews, Chef Boyardee spaghetti. I use nothing uncanned. For some reason I am suspicious of both the frozen and the fresh. The fresh I suppose because it is all too easily and quickly subject to decay, the frozen because it is cold against my breast as I walk the three blocks from the supermarket.

The cans are heavier than frozen foods, aren't they?

A good point, counselor; obviously my major interest is in conserving heat.

Let's not get cute.

You started it—but again the point is made. I came to California for the heat, not to get Larry Love. I never even watched *Trade or Betrayed* my first few months here. I came for the year-round sun and it has cleared my skin.

When did you first see Larry Love?

I saw him in a drugstore in Beverly Hills.

And you recognized him?

I did.

Did you speak to him?

I tried. My hate was immediate and sincere. He was buying a hairbrush. The salesclerk fawned over him. I was eating an ice-cream cone, my uncanned luxury. He was tall and strong looking, much handsomer than he seemed on my fourteen-inch black-and-white Admiral. "Larry," I said to him.

"I haven't got time now, friend, watch the show and I'll think of you." He was gone to a waiting Cadillac illegally parked. He should have stayed for the end of my sentence, it was really his sentence. "Larry, I'm going to kill you." He missed the crucial part. Larry Love and Pontius Pilate left too soon for answers.

But why did you decide to kill him, why not other emcees, other stars?

Have you ever watched *Trade or Betrayed*?

Only in the last week, since I've taken your case.

I can see that Larry must have been the show, it's not much without him.

Of course not, would Hell be the same without Satan?

Let's be legal, not theological. I would like a simple statement of why on April 7, 1973, you, in full view of millions, shot and killed Larry Love.

To you my answers probably sound like most other murder cases. The old love-hate combine again.

Go on.

Even if it's a cliché?

Even so.

Okay, I love *Trade or Betrayed.* I think it's the greatest entertainment of the twentieth century.

Go on.

I won't say more now, at least not about the aesthetics of the show—but in the sheer brilliance of concept it rivals the subtlety and simplicity of science. Think of its elements. Tina Rodriguez, the first important character since Harpo Marx who does not speak on screen. She has no horn, only silky thighs and a magic hand that points to a box wherein lies some housewife's dream. Tiny herself has the shiny beauty of a major appliance. A night with her would clean your clothes, freeze and cook your meals, compact your trash. She is the end of all process, the statue of property in front of those big stars-and-stripes boxes. Meanwhile Larry is out in the audience forming the equation to which she is the answer.

I've seen the show. I know how it works. People dress up and make fools of themselves.

That's what I used to think. I used to think it was their own fault. People have always been making fools of themselves. Think of *Beat the Clock* or *Stop the Music.* And what about *Truth or Consequences?* Bob Barker has grown into an eccentric millionaire getting ladies' clubs from Burbank to eat crow for a twenty-five-dollar gift certificate from the Spiegel catalogue. I've never made an attempt on his life. Dennis James, Bill Cullen, Allen Ludden, I have no animosities for other daytime TV people. They're okay with me, a relief from the soap operas. But with Larry it was different. Sure the prizes are the stars, while the people dressed up as club sandwiches and cartoon characters hopping and popping at the chance to win something —the people are subhuman. Okay, so far I've said only what every reasonable person probably thinks when he first watches the show. I said it to people too. I thought it was camp that I liked *Trade or Betrayed.* I was wrong. After several years of watching, I realized that Larry is not kidding. He appears daily like the sun to remind you what the world is. Larry is the culmination of television. He teases you like Art Linkletter (who is another one I'd get if CBS hadn't cut him), but Larry is oh so sweet when he wants to be, giving comfort like the late Hal March consoling a $32,000 loser into a Cadillac. Ted Mack was the purest of the bunch. Every ragtag piece of talent wanted thirty seconds of playing a musical comb or twirling a baton while the wheel of fortune spun like Ted Mack's tongue spooning down the Geritol. What they did mattered not. The show came on at four p.m. on Sunday. But Larry slips in at the meridian promising electric comforts if you exploit your greed. He heats you for an afternoon of shopping. I found his statistics once in *TV Guide* and sent them under my name to an astrologer in Minneapolis. Do you know who Larry resembles most on the list of the five hundred most famous men in history?

I haven't any idea.

Abe Lincoln. And the match is identical. How's that for irony. Honest Abe and Slippery Larry, the two faces of a coin. The implications are immense. It affirmed my faith in astrology.

But what about your reasons for the murder?

Isn't the slightest bit of it becoming clear?

I'm sorry, but I don't follow you.

Get thee behind me, Satan. . . .

Please try to be less cryptic.

Did you get that on the tape?

Yes, it's a sixty-minute tape, you'll hear it end, so don't worry.

I hadn't stopped, counselor, I only paused for dramatic effect. When I recognized that Larry was Satan, I decided to kill him. The act was a straight-forward moral choice. I had a clear and distinct knowledge of his evil and I decided to do something about it.

And you expect to present that as your defense? A jury won't even have time for coffee before they put you away for life.

Are all lawyers like this, or am I cursed with a bottom-of-the-class special?

Mr. Cook, I told you that I can resign at any time. I don't have to take any abuse from you, and if you don't speed up your statement I'm going to leave, abuse or no abuse.

Okay, Mr. Law and Order, I can see that you really don't want the whole story, only the blood and guts. How it happened and then good-bye and good luck. You're the Joe Friday type, only the facts, ma'am, stiff-lipped anal personality. Okay, I'll give it to you like it was. I'll save the best stuff for the court, where you'll sit with hands in your pockets because you had no patience with me before the trial. You won't have a thing to say to the newsmen crowded around the door of the courtroom. They'll think its only legal aplomb. You won't be unique. A lot of stupidity passes for style. Not Larry, though, that was one smart son of a bitch. I'll never take that away from him.

How did you get into the audience?

Like everyone else. I waited a year for tickets, dressed up, and stood in line on La Cienega Boulevard.

How were you dressed?

You know that's one thing I don't like to talk about.

If I were a psychiatrist I might ask why, but as a lawyer I only want to know if your costume had any-thing at all to do with the murder.

Only in the sense that my own folly enraged me and I had a headache from the fruit. All right, I'll tell you —it's not that important. I came dressed as a basket of fruit. All over myself I hung plums, apricots, bing cherries. I wore grapes as ankle bracelets and a necklace of pumpkin seeds and artichoke leaves. On all parts of my chest, the berries hung from me at the end of strips of surgical tape. Hollowed out cantaloupes were my kneepads. On my head was a wide-brimmed straw hat with about two pounds of apples and pears glued on. I carried a vinyl inner-tube cushion, the kind hemorrhoid patients use, so I wouldn't squash the fruit against my legs. I went to all this trouble because I wanted to be sure he would notice me. Snug in my pocket lay a Browning automatic for which I paid three times the price of the Italian rifle that got John Kennedy.

Larry was good that day. He and Mike Fields did the audience warm-up themselves, telling salesman jokes and teasing Tina Rodriguez, who stayed spectral on the stage, moving like Tinkerbell between the stoves and refrigerators that stagehands were sliding behind Japanese screens. I had an aisle seat in the third row. I knew there was better than a fifty-fifty chance that he'd pick me. My sign said "Cornucopia." I knew that he wouldn't be able to resist making a joke about "corny" and "cornucopia," then he would ask me why I didn't have any corn. It happened precisely as I had anticipated it, and this too reinforced my belief that I was acting a destined role, that all my judgments were correct.

But the wait, the wait was unbearable. The murder was a breather compared to that. I am tall as you can see, and wearing that high hat and sitting on the vinyl inner tube made me even more conspicuous. The woman on my left was one of those screaming nymphomaniacs Larry always culls out. She was dressed as a safety match. "I'd like to strike up a trade," her sign coyly stated. From neck to knees she read "Ohio Blue Tip." "I really am from Columbus," she said. She kept threatening to eat my fruit. "I didn't have any breakfast or lunch. I couldnt keep a thing down, I was so nervous about all this. Now I just want to eat your hat." She also deserved killing, but my eyes stayed on his sharkskin suit gliding up and down the stairs, while he searched his pockets for the right envelopes. "Now, we're going to use Larry's money machine, right, Fred? For the second gimmick, okay. Then Mike will come down with the box. Be sure you flash a card on that so I won't forget."

He pretended not to notice me during the warm-up while he teased a pair of twins from Mississippi who came as a fire hydrant and a dog. Their mother sat in the nonparticipants section and broke out in broad southern, "Give it to 'em, sisters, give it to 'em." She thought they were already on the air and urged her daughters, "The box, the box." Mike calmed her down. The audience loved it, but I could see Larry decide on the spot not to use them. Little did he know what lay quietly hidden in my cornucopia. The match pounced up and down whenever he faced us, but Larry was slick, playing to the sides, to the people who have no real chance of getting on the show. He used them to break the ice while those of us in the middle sat sweating in the studio lights. I watched Tina and desired her from afar. About ten minutes before air time he left us with Mike and an assistant director who wanted to make sure we all watched the applause sign.

"If Larry picks you, just do what he tells you. And remember, this is a half-hour show. If you stall too long on your choices, Larry can disqualify you. It's happened before. All winners come backstage afterwards to fill out IRS and delivery forms. We want you to have fun. Hold up your signs when Mike says, 'And here's America's number-one trader, Larry Love,' and then put them on the floor unless Larry asks for yours."

He was a wretched man the assistant director. Pale as an onion, he looked as if Larry kept him in a shaded cage except for this brief daily performance.

The red lights flashed all around. My sign was in the air. Larry strutted down the aisle in the light blue suit and the witch next to me pulled a German prune off my chest. "I can't wait, I'll faint." She ate noisily and I hoped she would choke on the pit.

Larry had everything, style, wit, charm, generosity, and hundreds of dollars in his pocket. For his opening

bit he pretended to light a corncob pipe that he took
from an old man at the back of the room.

"I haven't got a match, let's see, should I use this?"
He pulled a five hundred dollar bill from his pocket.
"No," we moaned in unison. Hands clutched toward
the aisle as if they were saving a drowning child.

"Okay then, I won't smoke. I'll give this money to
Irene Henderson, right here." Larry played her like
an instrument. She was a buxom negress from Pennsylvania dressed as an angel. She was two rows behind
me, but when she flapped her big arms to show Larry
how angels fly, she splattered me with a combination
of sweat and fluffy goose down coming loose from her
wings. Larry got her to try to fly, then he allowed her
time to tug at her big afro while she tried to decide
whether to keep the five hundred or go for the box,
a big American flag guarded by Tina Rodriguez in
pale green shorts and a halter. Tina's soft hand opened
to the box as if she were introducing a foreign
dignitary. The black woman moaned and tried to
locate her husband somewhere deep in the audience.

"I'll keep the money," she screamed. Tina waved
her magic hand, the flag-box slid away revealing a
Speed Queen washer-dryer, a six-hundred-dollar
number. "But still a very good deal for Irene Henderson, who has herself five hundred dollars, right, little
angel?" Larry leaves her squeezing bills. He monkeys
around with three people and a purse, then he has
newlyweds guess the prices of a series of items: popcorn, olives, shaving cream, and an electric saw. The
couple misses everything by a mile, ruining his chance
to give away a car. Larry gives them fifty dollars to
go to a supermarket and learn something about prices.
You can see the anger in his eyes; the newlyweds have
cost him the highlight of the show, the suspense over
a car. America needs a big number now. I am facing
forward, stony, ice in my veins, but I know he comes
by the match popping up and down beside me. "Me,"
she is saying with private sincerity, "please, God, let
him pick me." Over and over her prayer in my ear as
Larry pauses at our row, checking the match, a pound

cake, a bottle of champagne, and then me, his destiny in the sweet garb of nature. I tower over him as he reads my name tag. My head is pounding from the weight of the hat. He tells me to take it off so he can see my face. He looks into my eyes the way Ken and Edith must have gazed at one another in that Rexall store in Elmira. I have the momentary impression that he is clairvoyant, that he knows me and fears me not. He puts his arm around me and offers a choice, the box Tina is standing in front of on the stage or the one Mike is bringing down the aisle toward us. Tina has changed into a red velvet gown that brushes against the box, ten feet tall and covered in aluminum foil. The lights glare off it and off the pale skin of Tina. "The big box," says the match, "the big box," in her prayerful tone. Larry has made the predicted joke about corn and cornucopia. I pretend to fidget with my belt while I bring out that gleaming beauty, my Browning automatic.

"Larry," I say, "there is no choice and we both know it." The moment has come. Without a gasp the audience disappears into silence. Mike crawls under his box, which contains, I suppose, a tea service from the Michael C. Fina Company. The assistant director starts up the aisle but stops and then retreats when I put the Browning squarely at Larry's Brylcreemed temple. Larry is preternaturally calm, as if there is only a washing machine at stake. "Go ahead if you must," he says, "in this business time is money." The last impulse I have toward him is one of admiration, the kind of admiration you have for something so wholly conceived that its essential nature is untouched by experience. Larry is encased like a zoological specimen. In that last instant I see that he is more eternal than my desire to destroy him. My finger twitches at the Browning, my resolution wavers. From the stage, for the first time in her silent decade, comes the voice of Tina, more passionate than her velvet gown. "Shoot," she calls out as I caress the trigger until Larry's head seems but an extension of my arm. A second time comes her voice clear as a cathedral organ,

"Shoot." From under the box where he had sought refuge, Mike Fields implores me no less richly than Tina, "Shoot quickly." The silent audience picks up the cadence. They yell for me to shoot just the way they called out "the money" or "the box" earlier. Larry flashes his white teeth. On a steady palm he blows a soft kiss in the direction of Tina. To me he forms "shoot" with his lips as if he's cheating at charades, and holding him tight as a lover, I do. I hear the Browning hit the floor before Larry does. He falls first to his knees, his head against my arm so that I feel his teeth scrape my life line. I move back and he goes down hard, his last sound the magnified scratching of his starched shirt against the microphone.

I must have gone into shock immediately after it happened because I don't remember anything until I was outside on La Cienega Boulevard pulling the fruit off my body. The surgical tape stung and the sun almost knocked me over. It felt like that gaudy noon heat just sat on me. For shade I crouched under the awning of a bookstore. There were no customers, only paperbacks being watched by a security camera. My breath fogged the window. I tried to go in for the air conditioning but the door was locked. I must have been outside only a few minutes, but I felt like I was locked into one of those portable steam cabinets where your head sticks out like a vegetable and the rest of you shrinks away in the hiss. I choked against the window but nobody noticed me. A tourist bus coming into the ABC lot almost knocked me over. The driver's horn was still in my ear as I returned to the *Trade or Betrayed* set. Yes, I came back, just like the saying. It took Raskolnikov hundreds of pages to return, I did it in less than a block. As soon as I opened the heavy studio door I felt much better. A studio policeman shoved me against the back wall. "No talking," he said, "we're still on the air."

Mike Fields, holding Larry's microphone, stood between Irene Henderson and the Ohio Blue Tip, who were competing for the big trade of the day. The black angel pecked kisses at Mike as if she were drilling his teeth. On stage, Tina waved her thighs at two hundred dollars' worth of Masland carpeting. Larry himself lay compact in the aisle, a small bundle near my vacated seat. His patent shoes gleamed. The din of competition did not affect me as I concentrated on Larry's Lincolnesque silhouette shaded in dark ooze like the trickle from beneath a refrigerator. The organ picked up the *Trade or Betrayed* theme and we faded, he and I now completed, into one p.m. and *The Newlywed Game*.

Patty-Cake, Patty-Cake ... A Memoir

I

When he took walks, G.R. hummed "Cruising down the River." Now and then he munched on red pistachio nuts and spit the shells over the curb. I had to trot to keep up with his long steps. Once we got to the bakery, he'd go donut wild. Cream puffs, eclairs, even the cherryfilled Danish were nothing to him. He headed for the plain brown donuts, what my father called fry cakes. He ate each one in two bites, coming down exactly in the middle of the hole everytime. Daddy would give him a couple dozen like nothing. Everybody on Franklin Street gave things to G.R. There wasn't a housewife who didn't feel proud to fry him a few donuts herself. And why the hell not? He raked their leaves, carried groceries, opened doors, and smiled at the old folks. He was an Eagle Scout. I was just his nigger sidekick but people liked me for being that. Much later I got good jobs, loans, even my own business because of being his sidekick. But when we started, it was G.R. that needed me. He used to think my old man gave him the donuts because he was my buddy. He didn't know for a long time how much people liked him.

"Christ," I used to tell him, "Daddy would give you fry cakes even if you stomped me once a week. He likes you, G.R. You're his neighbor."

In fact we were sort of double neighbors. Our houses were on the same block and his father's paint store was just down the street from the American Bakery, where my dad was the donut and cake man.

G.R. and I hung around the Bridge Street branch of the public library. He read the sports books and I did the science fiction. Then we'd go to the bakery and he'd start to wolf down the fry cakes. He ate all he could, then stuffed his pockets. My old man just used to laugh and throw in a few more. A dozen was a light snack to him. After football games, he always had his twelve fresh ones waiting in the locker room. He never shared, although he was generous with everything else. He ate them with his cleats and helmet still on and sometimes mud all over his face.

When my father died, G.R. and I were in college. He came over to the Alpha Kappa Psi House, hugged me, and said, "Sonny, you know how he did it, you've got to take over." And like a dumb ass, I did. I made them at night in the big Alpha Kappa Psi deep fryer. But G.R. always paid for the ingredients.

You've got to remember that this was 1937 and he was the social chairman of the DU's, the best of the white houses, and a big football player, and I was still his nigger sidekick from home to everyone except the brothers of Alpha Kappa Psi, where I was the house treasurer.

It only took about an hour once a week or so, and he liked them so much that I just couldn't stop. It would have been like weaning a baby. I didn't want to put up with all his moping. G.R. wasn't unhappy much, but when he was, the whole DU house could burn up and he wouldn't leave his room. I was the only one he let in. He'd sit and stare at a 12 × 5 of his father and mother in front of the paint store. He'd say things like, "Sonny, they did a lot for me and no goddamn girl is going to ruin it." Or if it wasn't a girl, it was a goddamn professor or sometimes a goddamn coach.

After a mope he'd be good for two dozen and a half gallon of milk. The brothers used to call me his mammy. "The big old ballplayer needs mammy's short'nin' bread," they used to say when they'd see me starting up the deep fryer after an emergency call from someone at DU. That's why half the house called me mammy, even though my actual nickname was Sonny. In the Michigan Ensign for 1938, there I am in the group picture of the only black frat house in

Ann Arbor. "Sonny 'Mammy' Williams," it says, "Treasurer." G.R. is all over the book with the DU's, the football team, the Audubon Society, the Student Union, the Intrafraternity Honor Council. I counted him eight times and who knows how many I missed.

I think the only reason I ever went to Ann Arbor instead of JC like my sisters was that he was going and he got me a piece of his scholarship somehow. But when he went to law school, I said, "No dice, ace, I'm not hauling my ass up to Harvard." And I got a job back in Grand Rapids working for Rasberry Heating. Law School was the first time he got by without the fry cakes and he said he was a grump all three years.

"I lost seventeen pounds and almost married a girl I didn't love," he told me when he came back. "I lost a lot of my judgment and some of my quickness. Harvard and Yale may have class, Sonny, but when you come down to it, there's no place like home." He came back from Harvard as patriotic as the soldiers shipping back from Guam a few years later. I met him at the Market Street station with a sign that said, "Welcome back, Counselor," and a dozen hot fry cakes. His Ma and Dad were there too and his brother Phil. He hugged us all, ate the donuts, and said, "If you seek a beautiful peninsula, look around you." Then he said it in Latin and we thought it was lawyer's talk and we looked the train station over real good. Then he told us it was the motto of the state of Michigan, which was founded in 1837 and was the first state west of Pennsylvania to have its own printing press. He said he wasn't leaving Michigan for a good long time, and if it wasn't for the war a few months later, I don't believe he would have.

The war started in December and he came back from Harvard in the June before that. The first thing he did was make me take my two weeks from Rasberry and head up to the Upper Peninsula with him. "To the thumb, Sonny, to the tip of Michigan where three great lakes sparkle and iron and copper dot the landscape."

I still couldn't say no to the guy so I went along even though I knew the Upper Peninsula was for Indians and not for Negroes.

We drove two days in my '35 Chevy, up through Cadillac, Reed City, Petoskey, Cheboygan. The roads were bad. When we had a flat near the Iron River, it took an hour for another car to come by so we could borrow a jack. I wished all the time that we were on our way to Chicago or Cleveland or Indianapolis or someplace where you could do something when you got there. But old G.R. was on a nature kick then. I believe Harvard and no fry cakes had about driven him nuts. While I flagged down the jack, he stood beside the car and did deep knee bends and Marine push-ups. He took off his shirt and beat his chest. "Smell the air, Sonny, that's Michigan for you," he said. People were suspicious enough about stopping for a nigger trying to flag them down without this bouncing Tarzan to scare 'em worse.

When we finally got the ferryboat to take us to Mackinac Island, I knew it was a mistake. The only Negroes beside me were the shoeshine boys on the boat, and here I was in a linen suit and big straw hat alongside Mr. Michigan, who was taking in the Lake Superior spray and still beating his chest now and then and telling everyone what a treat it was to live in the Thumb state. Everybody thought I was his valet, so when I caught some real bad staring I just went over and brushed his jacket or something and the folks smiled at me very nicely. I didn't want trouble then and I don't now. I've been a Negro all my life and no matter how hard I try I can't call myself a black.

Another thing I tell people and they can hardly believe is that I don't think G.R. ever once said anything about my color. I don't believe he ever noticed it or thought about it or considered that it made a bit of difference. I guess that's another reason why I didn't mind baking his donuts.

But Mackinac Island was a mistake for both of us. I was bored stiff by talking about how good the food was in the hotel and taking little rides in horse-drawn carriages. G.R. seemed to like it, so I didn't say much.

One morning he says, "Sonny, let's get clipped," and I go with him to the hotel barbershop without giving it a thought. After being there a week, I must have lost my sense, too, to just go along like that. He sits down in one vacant chair and motions me to the other. There are a couple of thin barbers who look like their scissors. I'm just getting my socks adjusted and looking down at "Theo A. Kochs" written on the bottom of the barber chair when my thin man says almost in a whisper, "I'm sorry, sir, but we don't do Negro hair." G.R. hasn't heard this because his barber has snapped the striped sheet loudly around him and is already combing those straight blond strands.

I step out of the chair. "No hard feelings," he says.

"None," I say, "I didn't need a haircut anyway. I'll just wait for my friend here."

"Fine," he says, and sits down in his chair to have a smoke while he waits for another customer.

When G.R. gets turned around and sees this little barber lighting up, he says, "Sonny, c'mon, I thought we're both getting clipped this morning."

"I'll wait, G.R.," I say, hoping he'll let it go.

"No waiting," he says. "It's sharp country up here, we've got to look sharp for it, right, boys?" He looks at my little barber who blows some smoke and says, "I'm sorry, but we don't cut colored hair here. In fact, I don't think there's a spot on the island that does. We just don't get that much in colored trade."

"What do you mean you don't cut colored hair?" G.R. says.

"Just what I said." The barber is a little nervous. He stands up and starts to wash some combs, but G.R. is out of his chair now and facing him against a row of mirrors.

"What do you mean by colored?" he asks the barber.

My barber looks at his partner. I am getting pissed at G.R. for making something out of this. I should have known better. At home I wouldn't just walk into the Pantlind or the Rowe Hotel and expect to get a haircut.

"It's okay, G.R.," I say. "Sit down and let's get going. We've got lots to see yet, Indian villages and copper mines and remnants of old beaver trappers' lodges."

"I want to know what this man means by colored," he says, crowding the little barber against a display of Wildroot Cream Oil. The other barber, G.R.'s, says, "Look, mister, why don't the both of you just take your business someplace else." G.R. is a very big man and both barbers together don't weigh two fifty. He says it again. "I want to know what this man means by colored." He is trailing them in the white cover sheet with black stripes and a little paper dickey around his neck. He looks like Lou Gehrig in a Yankee nightshirt. My barber is afraid to say anything but the other one says, "Well, look at your friend's teeth real white, see, and the palms of his hands are brownish pink, and his hair is real woolly. I couldn't pull that comb I just used on you through that woolly hair now, could I?" G.R. looks surprised.

"And when you've got white teeth and pinky brown palms and woolly hair and your skin is either black or brown, then most people call you colored. You understand now?"

"But what's that got to do with haircuts?" G.R. asks. Nobody knows what to say now. The barbers don't understand him, so I step up and say, "They need special instruments to cut my hair, G.R. It's like he says, those puny little combs don't go through this, see. I got to go to my own kind of barber so he'll know how to handle me."

G.R. was edgy all through his haircut and he didn't leave a tip, but once we left the barbershop I believe he forgot the whole thing.

But the way he was with those barbers, that's how he operated with girls too. What I mean is, he didn't understand what they were getting at. And this was a shame because he really attracted the ladies. They didn't all come at him like ducks to popcorn, but if he stayed at a school dance for an hour or so, the prettiest girl there would be over talking to him and joking and maybe even dancing with him. He never did anything but talk and joke them. He'd walk home with me. I'd say, "G.R., that Peggy Blanton was giving you the eye. Why'd you pass up something like that?"

"Training," he'd say, or "Hell, Sonny, I came to the dance with you and I'm leaving with you." If there'd ever been a good-looking colored girl there I sure wouldn't have left with him. Don't get me wrong, G.R. was a regular man, nothing the matter with his glands; he just wasn't as interested in girls as most of us were. One weekend in college he drove to Chicago with me and some of the brothers of Alpha Kappa Psi. The brothers wanted some of that good jazz from down around Jackson Avenue and G.R. wanted to see the White Sox play baseball. He took a bus to Comiskey Park for a doubleheader and met us about eight at the Blue Box, where those great colored jazz groups used to be in those days. G.R. stood out like a light bulb. We'd been there all afternoon just mellow and strung out on the music. G.R. came in and wanted to talk baseball. Don't forget that in those days the White Sox really were white and the brothers could have cared less what a group of whites were doing that afternoon up on Lake Shore Drive.

"You should have seen Luke Appling," he was saying; "there's not a man in either league who can play that kind of shortstop." Nobody paid any attention to G.R. He didn't drink and the music was just noise to him. He had taken a book along and was trying to read in the candlelight at the Blue Box. You had to feel sorry for him. It was so dark in there you couldn't see your fingers at arm's length. The atmosphere was heavy with music, liquor, women. I mean the place was cool, relaxed, nobody doing more than tapping a glass, and he sits there squinting over a big blue book, underlining things and scratching his head like he's in the library. He was alone at a table so he could concentrate, but I kept my eye on him just in case anything came up. Pretty soon two really smooth numbers come over to his table. Now you'd call them "Foxes." They were in evening gowns and very loose, maybe even

drunk. He was the only white man in the place and
they kind of giggled at him and sat down. I couldn't
hear a word they said but I watched every move. I
could see because they'd started using a spotlight for
the small stage and G.R. was a little to one side of it.

One of the girls starts rubbing the spine of the
blue book. The other one takes his finger and puts
it on the page. She uses his hand like a big pointer.
Maybe she's asking him what some of those big words
mean. They're both real close. I start to get a little
jealous. I've been there all day with nothing like that
kind of action. But, it's like I said, he had a way with
the girls. They seem to be talking a lot. The girls are
real dreamy on him, one under each arm. It looks like
he's reading out loud to them because one of them is
holding the book up for him to read from. Whatever
he's reading is really breaking the girls up. One of
them is kind of tickling his belly with a fingernail between the buttons of his shirt. Sam Conquest and his
combo were doing a set then that really had us going.
I mean, as much as I was keeping an eye out for G.R.,
I was into the music too and couldn't really be sure
about what my buddy was getting himself into. All I
know is that I slipped into the music for just a couple
of minutes and when I looked back he was gone. So
were the girls and his book. What the hell, I thought,
anyone else would, why not G.R. too?

It wasn't until we got back to Ann Arbor and were
alone together in his room that G.R. told me what
really happened with those two girls.

"I was robbed," he said. "They got about four
dollars, but it was all I had. I think Shirlene did it."
He showed me his finger with a Band-Aid on it. "I
cut myself on the sequins of her dress. She was giving
me kind of a chest rub and my arm was around her.
I thought she really liked me, Sonny. I cut my finger
real deep on one of those sequins. Doris went to the
drugstore for a Band-Aid. While she was gone, I think
Shirlene got her hand into my trousers and took the
four bucks. I was telling them about World War I.
They were interested in Woodrow Wilson and the

League of Nations. I don't know why they robbed me. If she would have asked me, I'd have given her the four dollars, you know I would have, don't you, Sonny?"

"G.R.," I said, smiling but real sad about him, "you good-looking DU social chairman, you football captain and White Sox fan, what the hell is ever going to happen to you in the real world? You can't tell robbery from love, you don't have the ear for music or the eye for color. You can eat donuts and tackle people, you're a good citizen. Get tough, get mean, drink whiskey, swear, slap some chicks around, fuck a few, stop saying yes ma'am, turn in your homework late, cut football practice, cheat on exams, wear dirty socks . . . I mean, Jesus Christ, be like everybody else." I broke down then. I liked him so much the way he was that it killed me to say these things, but I did it for his sake. Somebody had to warn him.

He put his arm around me while I sobbed. "Sonny," he said, "I'll try."

II

When he ran for Congress he laid off the fry cakes. By then, with his help in getting me a loan, guess who owned the American Bakery? He was making good money as a lawyer. I thought he was crazy to run for the Congress. When I heard it on the radio, I brought a dozen fry cakes fresh from the oven right up to his office in the Federal Square Building. He had a little refrigerator where he kept his milk and his lunch. I hadn't even taken off my white baker's outfit. Some court photographer happened to be in the building and snapped a picture of me in whites carrying the donuts and looking mad as hell. Right after he became the President, *The New York Times* printed that picture and I started getting flooded with requests from TV. That's when the President's baker thing got started. I sold the American Bakery in '58 and have hardly dipped a fry cake since then, but once a story gets on TV you're stuck with it. Never mind that I'm in auto leasing and sporting goods now; the "President's baker" is what I'm destined to remain.

But the day of that picture was an important one: it was the last day of our real friendship. I slipped past a secretary and gave him the dozen. His desk was full of papers. "Later," he said. "Right now," I told him, and I stood there waiting. He was always more sensible after donuts and milk. I went right to his refrigerator and brought out the bottle of Sealtest. I stood there until he was done. "G.R.," I said, "why the hell are you doing this? Aren't you the man who told me you'd never leave Michigan? You've got your friends here and your family, what's all this about going to Washington, D.C.? If you want politics, what about being mayor?"

"Sonny, there's a big country out there and most of it is full of Democrats. And there's untold Communists around the world just waiting to get their fingers on your bakery and my law office and everything else we've been working for."

"G.R.," I said, "if you leave this town you're making the mistake of your life."

He looked up at me from his desk. "Sonny, if you're not for me you're against me."

"Get your fry cakes in D.C.," I told him, "and your friends too." I walked out. I voted against him that time and in every other election, and as far as I know he never again tasted one of my donuts. He moved to D.C. that January. Every year I get a Christmas card and a district newsletter, but until he became President that was it. Not even a phone call when he was in town. What the hell, I thought to myself, he turned his back on his old friends but I guess it's what he really wanted. He spent twenty-five years in D.C. without me and without those donuts and he didn't seem to miss Michigan all that much either. I, who was his nigger sidekick and his college "mammy," never saw his wife or his kids. When his dad died I went to the funeral, but the crowd was so big I didn't even get into the chapel. At the cemetery it was private. I thought I saw G.R. in one of the limousines while they were loading the casket in, but you can't run up and talk to a man at a time like that. Yessir, G.R. and I were through, cold turkey, until that night last August when Nixon resigned.

To tell you the truth, until the minute it happened none of us believed Nixon would ever be out of there until '76. When they interrupted the Tigers game with the news, you could have knocked me over with a feather. People all over town started walking around the streets like they were drunk. The JCCs painted a big Home of the President poster and had it up at the northern city limits within an hour. My mother, who's in a home now, called up to remind me that she taught the President how to tie his shoes. He was fast, Mama remembered, and double knotted every time. And the truth is, although I had resented him being a Congressman all those years, I spent a few minutes just saying out loud, "G.R., Mr. President." I said it over and over. I was still saying it when I got a phone-in telegram from his press secretary. "Sonny— Emergency. Air Force One will pick you up midnight Grand Rapids airport." It was signed G.R. A White House operator read it to me at ten o'clock while I was watching the newsmen do a wrap-up on Nixon. He wasn't officially President until the next day but already he could send Air Force One out to do his errands.

I knew what this meant. I packed a blue suit and my own deep fryer, and it's a good thing I did. With all the stuff in that White House kitchen, there isn't a single deep fryer. I heard one of the cooks grumbling that Jackie Kennedy had it thrown away and Johnson used to eat all his fries on the ranch. Nixon only cared for pan-fried. The cooks were mighty suspicious. Here was the new President who they didn't even know sending over his own old boy with a personal deep fryer.

I was met at the airport by a nice young fellow. He took my grocery order. The Presidential limousine waited outside the all-night Safeway while we shopped. I overbought, made twelve dozen because for all I knew he wanted to treat the whole cabinet. By seven on the morning of the day he was to become the President, G.R. had his fry cakes, crisp on the outside, soft on the inside. I was a little nervous in case I'd lost my touch but this was one sweet batch. An FBI man delivered all twelve dozen. The White House cooks treated me very uppity. They were all tears about Nixon, wondering whether he could stomach bacon and eggs for his last breakfast, and here I was whipping out twelve dozen donuts for the new boy. They didn't know if they could keep up with an appetite like that.

I hung around the kitchen because I didn't know where else to go. You wouldn't believe the chaos. Nixon sent back the coffee, bacon, and eggs. He was going to be on TV at ten. They sent up cream of wheat, rye toast, coffee, and vegetable juice. It came back too. The juice glass was empty but there were lipstick stains on it.

"The poor man hasn't moved his bowels yet," the cook said when he saw Nixon giving his last speech. "Without morning coffee, he is cement. He hasn't slept either. Oh God, what's going to happen to all of us?" He looked at me and then spit into the sink. We were crowded together watching a twelve-inch Sony color set.

I had a late breakfast with the kitchen staff and hung around the TV for G.R.'s swearing-in and his speech. I played some gin rummy with a few maids. Limousines kept pulling up outside but the whole place was quiet as a white funeral parlor. Just before noon that same young man who met my plane came into the kitchen and gave me an envelope. There was a regular Central Air Lines ticket in it, but for first class, a hundred dollar bill, and a note. The note said, "Just like old times. Thanks, G.R."

I watched him on TV with Nixon's kitchen help. They were all zombies by noon. One of them said he dreamed that Nixon changed his mind in the air and was going to phone in at eleven fifty-nine to say hold off that swearing-in. I was the only one blindly excited and proud. And I don't have to tell you that my man was cool as a cucumber and straight as an arrow. There were some snickers in the kitchen when the camera showed General Haig brushing some crumbs off the new President's lapel. I saw them in color, the yellow crumbs I knew. "Here fellas," I said, tossing the hundred in the air, "have a drink on your new boss."

I was home by nightfall and haven't heard from him since. I guess that he's trying to make a go of it with that bunch of cooks he inherited. Still, who knows G.R. like I do? When it gets really tough in that oval office he'll start to smell the fry cakes. When that happens, watch out Kissinger and the Joint Chiefs. Mr. Donut and Dixie Cream won't be enough. His lips will start to twitch and his teeth will bite the air. He'll remember the glorious peninsula and the three Great Lakes of the Thumb. His mouth will water for the real thing. And when that happens, in the pinch, the President knows old Sonny won't let him down.

ABOUT THE AUTHOR

MAX APPLE is a writer in his early thirties. He was born and raised in Grand Rapids and was educated at the University of Michigan, from which he received a Ph.D. He currently teaches at Rice University in Houston, Texas. His stories have appeared in *American Review, Esquire, The Georgia Review, New and Experimental Literature*, and the *Ohio Review. The Oranging of America* was selected as the best book of fiction of 1976 by the Texas Institute of Letters.

READ TOMORROW'S LITERATURE—TODAY

The best of today's writing bound for tomorrow's classics.

☐	2600	**RAGTIME** E. L. Doctorow	—$2.25
☐	2640	**THE SUMMER BEFORE THE DARK** Doris Lessing	—$1.95
☐	11712	**ONE DAY IN THE LIFE OF IVAN DENISOVICH** Alexander Solzhenitsyn	—$1.95
☐	11197	**THE END OF THE ROAD** John Barth	—$1.95
☐	2997	**AUGUST 1914** Alexander Solzhenitsyn	—$2.50
☐	10425	**THE GOLDEN NOTEBOOK** Doris Lessing	—$2.25
☐	7925	**AMERICAN REVIEW #25** Theodore Solotaroff, ed.	—$2.45
☐	7926	**AMERICAN REVIEW #26** Ted Solotaroff, ed.	—$2.95
☐	10271	**GRAVITY'S RAINBOW** Thomas Pynchon	—$2.95
☐	10471	**THE SOT-WEED FACTOR** John Barth	—$2.50
☐	10625	**BEING THERE** Jerzy Kosinski	—$1.75
☐	10689	**V.** Thomas Pynchon	—$2.50
☐	11407	**THE PAINTED BIRD** Jerzy Kosinski	—$1.95

Buy them at your local bookstore or use this handy coupon for ordering:

Bantam Books, Inc., Dept. EDO, 414 East Golf Road, Des Plaines, Ill. 60016

Please send me the books I have checked above. I am enclosing $_____
(please add 50¢ to cover postage and handling). Send check or money order
—no cash or C.O.D.'s please.

Mr/Mrs/Miss_____

Address_____

City_____State/Zip_____

EDO—1/78

Please allow four weeks for delivery. This offer expires 7/78.

WOLFE
WOLFE
TOM WOLFE

THE NAMES THAT SPELL GREAT LITERATURE

Choose from today's most renowned world authors—every one an important addition to your personal library.

Hermann Hesse

☐	2906	KNULP	—$1.95
☐	2645	MAGISTER LUDI	—$1.75
☐	2944	DEMIAN	—$1.75
☐	10060	GERTRUDE	—$1.95
☐	10136	THE JOURNEY TO THE EAST	—$1.75
☐	10266	SIDDHARTHA	—$1.75
☐	10352	BENEATH THE WHEEL	—$1.95
☐	10466	NARCISSUS AND GOLDMUND	—$1.95
☐	11289	STEPPENWOLF	—$1.95
☐	11510	ROSSHALDE	—$1.95

Alexander Solzhenitsyn

☐	11712	ONE DAY IN THE LIFE OF IVAN DENISOVICH	—$1.95
☐	2997	AUGUST 1914	—$2.50
☐	7409	STORIES AND PROSE POEMS	—$1.50
☐	10246	THE LOVE-GIRL AND THE INNOCENT	—$1.50
☐	11300	CANCER WARD	—$2.50

Jerzy Kosinski

☐	10625	BEING THERE	—$1.75
☐	11100	STEPS	—$1.75
☐	11407	THE PAINTED BIRD	—$1.95
☐	2613	COCKPIT	—$2.25

Doris Lessing

☐	2640	THE SUMMER BEFORE THE DARK	—$1.95
☐	10425	THE GOLDEN NOTEBOOK	—$2.25
☐	7937	THE FOUR-GATED CITY	—$1.95
☐	11717	BRIEFING FOR A DESCENT INTO HELL	—$2.25

André Schwarz-Bart

☐	10469	THE LAST OF THE JUST	—$1.95

Buy them at your local bookstore or use this handy coupon for ordering:

Bantam Books, Inc., Dept. EDG, 414 East Golf Road, Des Plaines, Ill. 60016

Please send me the books I have checked above. I am enclosing $_____ (please add 50¢ to cover postage and handling). Send check or money order —no cash or C.O.D.'s please.

Mr/Mrs/Miss_____

Address_____

City_____State/Zip_____

EDG—1/78

Please allow four weeks for delivery. This offer expires 7/78.

Bantam Book Catalog

Here's your up-to-the-minute listing of every book currently available from Bantam.

This easy-to-use catalog is divided into categories and contains over 1400 titles by your favorite authors.

So don't delay—take advantage of this special opportunity to increase your reading pleasure.

Just send us your name and address and 25¢ (to help defray postage and handling costs).